'In its scope, style and substance, *The Emperor's Children* is an attempt to return the novel to its golden age; it is engaged in a conversation with George Eliot, Henry James, Dostoevsky. Its psychological realism is perfect, its characters . . . thrillingly real, alive and utterly convincing in their subtleties of thought and the ticking of their minds.

Messud's prose is a timely and intensely pleasurable reminder of the possibilities of the English language. To use the word clarity about her style – dense, chaste, luminously intelligent – is to return the word to its origins; this is style as illumination, shining a searching yet sympathetic light on the minds and inner worlds of her characters, and as a radiant mode of moral inquiry' *The Times*

'Intelligent and unsparing . . . [Ms Messud] excels at depicting the neurotic uncertainties of people who know they are privi-leged but feel sorry for themselves anyway. But it is the finesse with which she satirises these people but still leaves you caring what happens to them that is the book's great achievement. *The Emperor's Children* is likely to be one of the most talked-about novels of the autumn, and not just by New York thirty-somethings in the media. Buy two copies; give one to a friend' *The Economist*

'Messud has captured a moment, and she has captured it bril-liantly . . . Messud has written a big book about the gleaming surfaces of life, and what they conceal. Her ambition – positively nineteenth century, I think – is outweighed only by her talent' *Evening Standard*

'Elegantly written . . . Pellucid prose and clear-eyed but compassionate observations . . . Messud beautifully captures the uncertainties, kindnesses and betrayals acted out in this playground of the privileged, using the lightest of touches to change what appears to be black and white into subtle shades of grey . . . Messud masterfully reveals a bigger picture behind the intimate portraits' *Irish Independent*

'Of all the works that have pored over the terrible events of [9/11], one novel is currently standing out from the crowd: Claire Messud's *The Emperor's Children* . . . In the best tradition of James and Wharton, Messud shows us a world where competing versions of the way to live one's life fight it out to the bitter end' *Scotsman*

'From the moment the book opens, one senses a writer of confidence and maturity, expansive, sure of her ground and savouring her own sonorous prose . . . Messud has proved in her previous novels that she is an intelligent and ambitious writer whose fiction is concerned with matters well beyond the personal and domestic . . . There is much to enjoy here, not least Messud's delicate yet devastating use of irony, her nuanced portrayal of character and motive and her vivid descriptions' *Sunday Telegraph*

'A splendid American novel, contemporary yet historical, with an avalanche of characters flowing across the world from Australia to Manhattan to small-town America and to Florida . . . This is an ambitious, confident, most readable book by a first-rate storyteller with the youth and vitality to spread a huge canvas and enjoy filling it' *Spectator*

'In creating portraits of her characters that are both incisive and gentle, Messud successfully straddles satire and compassion. . . . This novel brilliantly captures its characters' vulnerabilities and every facet of their rawness and discomfort, taking us on an unlikely but fascinating tour of their lives in the Big Apple' *Scotland on Sunday*

'Claire Messud is a novelist of unnerving talent . . . *The Emperor's Children* is a masterly comedy of manners – an astute and poignant evocation of hobnobbing glitterati in the months before and immediately following September 11 . . . [It] is, on its surface, a stingingly observant novel about the facades of the chattering class – with its loves, ambitions and petty betrayals – but it is also, more profoundly, about a wholesale collision of values . . . *The Emperor's Children* is full of satirical chiding, but it's one of the most delightful – even delicious – forms of such chiding I've encountered . . . Among its many pleasures, this novel indisputably reminds us of one truth that cannot be declared fungible: the obdurate reality of the human imagination. *The Emperor's Children* is a penetrating testament to its power'
New York Times Book Review

'Deftly switching between six points of view, Messud crafts a gripping story of clashing ambitions, compromised loyalties, and the love/hate relationship between the powerless and the powerful. As the characters hurl toward that terrible September day, the narrative goes beyond mere social satire, deepening into a hypnotic, moving read' *Village Voice*

'Known for her acuity in examining life's profound issues through intellectually probing and nuanced prose, Messud now evinces a higher level of sophistication in this darkly symbolic and overtly satiric examination of the culturally enclosed world of today's East Coast media cognoscenti. Tangy dialogue, provocative asides, glittering imagery, and nimble postulations build towards an electrifying and edifying conclusion' *Booklist*

'[*The Emperor's Children*] demonstrates Ms. Messud's growing range as a writer, her ability to shift gears effortlessly between the comic and the tragic, the satiric and the humane . . . Ms. Messud delineates this Manhattan world with quick, sure, painterly strokes, relying less on Tom Wolfeian status details and obviously satiric vignettes than on her psychological radar for how people talk and behave . . . Ms. Messud does a nimble, quicksilver job of portraying her central characters from within and without – showing us their pretensions, frailties and self-delusions, even as she delineates their secret yearnings and fears. At the same time, she uses their stories to explore many of the same questions she explicated so masterfully in *The Last Life* – questions about how an individual hammers out an identity of his or her own under the umbrella of a powerful family, questions about the ways in which people mythologize their own lives and the lives of those they love' *New York Times*

'Ambitious, glamorous, and gutsy . . . A marvel of bold momentum and kinetic imagination. The story propels the tangled lives of a set of thirtyish Manhattanites right toward the historic fissure that ushered in twenty-first-century America' *Elle*

THE EMPEROR'S CHILDREN

Claire Messud was educated at Yale and Cambridge. Her first novel, *When the World Was Steady*, and her book of novellas, *The Hunters*, were finalists for the PEN/Faulkner Award; her second novel, *The Last Life*, was a *Publishers' Weekly* Best Book of the Year; all three books were *New York Times* Notable Books of the Year. She is the recipient of a Guggenheim Fellowship, a Radcliffe Fellowship and the Strauss Living Award from the American Academy of Arts and Letters. She lives in Somerville, Massachusetts with her husband and children.

THE EMPEROR'S CHILDREN

CLAIRE MESSUD

PICADOR

First published 2006 as a Borzoi Book by Alfred A. Knopf, New York

First published in Great Britain 2006 by Picador

First published in paperback 2006 by Picador

This edition first published in Great Britain 2007 by Picador
an imprint of Pan Macmillan, a division of Macmillan Publishers Limited
Pan Macmillan, 20 New Wharf Road, London N1 9RR
Basingstoke and Oxford
Associated companies throughout the world
www.panmacmillan.com

ISBN 978-0-330-44448-4

The author gratefully acknowledges the invaluable support of the
Guggenheim Foundation, the Radcliffe Institute, and the Strauss
Living Award of the American Academy of Arts & Letters.

This is a work of fiction. Names, characters, places, and incidents either are
the product of the author's imagination or are used fictitiously. Any resemblance
to actual persons, living or dead, events, or locales is entirely coincidental.

Visit **www.picador.com** to read more about all our books
and to buy them. You will also find features, author interviews and
news of any author events, and you can sign up for e-newsletters
so that you're always first to hear about our new releases.

For Livia and Lucian, who changed everything;
And, as ever, for J.W.

The General, speaking one felt with authority, always insisted that, if you bring off adequate preservation of your personal myth, nothing much else in life matters. It is not what happens to people that is significant, but what they think happens to them.

– Anthony Powell, *Books Do Furnish a Room*

MARCH

CHAPTER ONE

Our Chef Is Very Famous in London

"Darlings! Welcome! And you must be Danielle?" Sleek and small, her wide eyes rendered enormous by kohl, Lucy Leverett, in spite of her resemblance to a baby seal, rasped impressively. Her dangling fan earrings clanked at her neck as she leaned in to kiss each of them, Danielle too, and although she held her cigarette, in its mother-of-pearl holder, at arm's length, its smoke wafted between them and brought tears to Danielle's eyes.

Danielle didn't wipe them, for fear of disturbing her make-up. Having spent half an hour putting on her face in front of the grainy mirror of Moira and John's bathroom, ogling her imperfections and applying vigorous remedial spackle—beneath which her weary, olive-shaped eyes were pouched by bluish bags, the curves of her nostrils oddly red, and her high forehead peeling—she had no intention of revealing to strangers the disintegration beneath her paint.

"Come in, darlings, come in." Lucy moved behind them and herded the trio toward the party. The Leveretts' living room was painted a deep purple—aubergine, in local parlance—and its windows were draped with velvet. From the ceiling hung a brutal wrought iron chandelier, like something salvaged from

3

a medieval castle. Three men loitered by the bay window, talking to one another while staring out at the street, their glasses
of red wine luminous in the reflected evening light. A long,
plump, pillowed sofa stretched the length of one wall, and
upon it four women were disposed like odalisques in a harem.
Two occupied opposite ends of the divan, their legs tucked
under, their extended arms caressing the cushions, while
between them one rested her head upon another's lap, and smiling, eyes closed, whispered to the ceiling while her friend
stroked her abundant hair. The whole effect was, for Danielle,
faintly cloudy, as if she had walked into someone else's dream.
She kept feeling this, in Sydney, so far from home: she couldn't
quite say it wasn't real, but it certainly wasn't her reality.

"Rog? Rog, more wine!" Lucy called to the innards of the
house, then turned again to her guests, a proprietorial arm on
Danielle's bicep. "Red or white? He's probably even got pink,
if you're after it. Can't bear it myself—so California." She
grinned, and from her crows' feet, Danielle knew she was forty,
or almost.

Two men bearing bottles emerged from the candlelit gloom
of the dining room, both slender, both at first glance slightly
fey. Danielle took the imposing one in front, in a pressed
lavender shirt and with, above hooded eyes, a high, smooth
Nabokovian brow, to be her host. She extended a hand. "I'm
Danielle." His fingers were elegant, and his palm, when it
pressed hers, was cool.

"Are you now?" he said.

The other man, at least a decade older, slightly snaggle-
toothed and goateed, spoke from behind his shoulder. "I'm

Roger," he said. "Good to see you. Don't mind Ludo, he's playing hard to get."

"Ludovic Seeley," Lucy offered. "Danielle—"

"Minkoff."

"Moira and John's friend. From New York."

"New York," Ludovic Seeley repeated. "I'm moving there
next month."

"Red or white?" asked Roger, whose open shirt revealed
a tanned breast dotted with sparse gray hairs and divided by a
narrow gold chain.

"Red, please."

"Good choice," said Seeley, almost in a whisper. He was—
she could feel it rather than see it, because his hooded eyes did
not so much as flicker—looking her up and down. She hoped
that her makeup was properly mixed in, that no clump of
powder had gathered dustily upon her chin or cheek.

The moment of recognition was, for Danielle, instantan-
eous. Here, of all places, in this peculiar and irrelevant enclave,
she had spotted a familiar. She wondered if he, too, experienced
it: the knowledge that this mattered. Ludovic Seeley: she did
not know who he was, and yet she felt she knew him, or had
been waiting for him. It was not merely his physical presence,
the long, feline slope of him, a quality at once loose and controlled, as if he played with the illusion of looseness. Nor was
it the timbre of his voice, deep and yet not particularly reso-
nant, its Australian inflection so slight as to be almost British.
It was, she decided, something in his face: he knew. Although
what he knew she could not have said. There were the eyes, a
surprising deep and gold-flecked gray, their lines slightly down-
turned in an expression both mournful and amused, and the

particular small furrow that cut into his right cheek when he smiled even slightly. His ears, pinned close to his head, lent him a tidy aspect; his dark hair, so closely shaven as to allow the blue of his scalp to shine through, emphasized both his irony and his restraint. His skin was pale, almost as pale as Danielle's own, and his nose a fine, sharp stretch of cartilage. His face, so distinctive, struck her as that of a nineteenth-century portrait, a Sargent perhaps, an embodiment of sardonic wisdom and society, of aristocratic refinement. And yet in the fall of his shirt, the line of his torso, the graceful but not unmanly movement of his slender fingers (and yes, discreetly, but definitely there, he had hair on the backs of his hands—she held to it, as a point of attraction: men ought not to be hairless), he was distinctly of the present. What he knew, perhaps, was what he wanted.

"Come on, darling." Lucy took her by the elbow. "Let's introduce you to the rest of the gang."

This, dinner at the Leveretts', was Danielle's last evening in Sydney before heading home. In the morning, she would board the plane and sleep, sleep her way back to yesterday, or by tomorrow, to today, in New York. She'd been away a week, researching a possible television program, with the help of her friend Moira. It wouldn't be filmed for months, if it were filmed at all, a program about the relationship between the Aborigines and their government, the formal apologies and amends of recent years. The idea was to explore the possibility of reparations to African Americans—a high-profile professor was publishing a book about it—through the Australian prism. It wasn't clear even to Danielle whether this could fly. Could an American audience care less about the Aborigines? Were the situations even comparable? The week had been filled with meetings and bluster, the zealous singing exchanges of her business, the pretense of certainty where in fact there was none at all. Moira firmly believed it could be done, that it *should* be done; but Danielle was not convinced.

Sydney was a long way from home. For a week, in her pleasant waft of alienation, Danielle had indulged the fantasy of another possible life—Moira, after all, had left New York for Sydney only two years before—and with it, another future. She rarely considered a life elsewhere; the way, she supposed, with faint incredulity, most people never considered a life in New York. From her bedroom in her friends' lacy tin-roofed row house at the end of a shady street in Balmain, Danielle could see the water. Not the great sweep of the harbor, with its arcing bridge, nor the ruffled seagull's wings of the opera house, but a placid stretch of blue beyond the park below, rippled by the wake of occasional ferries and winking in the early evening sunlight.

Early autumn in Sydney, it was still bitter at home. Small, brightly colored birds clustered in the jacaranda trees, trilling their joyous disharmonies. In earliest morning, she had glimpsed, against a dawn-dappled shrub in the backyard, an enormous dew-soaked spiderweb, its intricacies sparkling, and poised, at its edge, an enormous furry spider. Nature was in the city, here. It was another world. She had imagined watching her 747 soar away without her, a new life beginning.

But not really. She was a New Yorker. There was, for Danielle Minkoff, only New York. Her work was there, her

friends were there—even her remote acquaintances from college at Brown ten years ago were there—and she had made her
home in the cacophonous, cozy comfort of the Village. From
her studio in its bleached-brick high-rise at Sixth Avenue and
Twelfth Street, she surveyed lower Manhattan like a captain at
the prow of her ship. Beleaguered and poor though she sometimes felt, or craving an interruption in the sea of asphalt and
iron, a silence in the tide of chatter, she couldn't imagine giving
it up. Sometimes she joked to her mother—raised, as she herself had been, in Columbus, Ohio, and now a resident of
Florida—that they'd have to carry her out feet first. There was
no place like New York. And Australia, in comparison, was,
well, Oz.

This last supper in Sydney was a purely social event. Where
the Leveretts lived seemed like an area in which one or two
ungentrified Aboriginal people might still linger, gray-haired
and bleary, outside the pub at the end of the road: people who,
pint in hand, hadn't accepted the government's apology and
moved on. Or perhaps not, perhaps Danielle was merely imagining the area, its residents, as they had once been: for a second
glance at the BMWs and Audis lining the curb suggested that
the new Sydney (like the new New York) had already, and
eagerly, edged its way in.

Moira was friendly with Lucy Leverett, who owned a small
but influential gallery down at The Rocks that specialized in
Aboriginal art. Her husband, Roger, was a novelist. As John
parked the car outside the Leveretts' large Victorian row house,
Moira had explained, "Lucy's great. She's done a lot on the art
scene here. And if you want to meet Aboriginal artists, to talk
to them for the film, she's your woman."

"And he?"

"Well"—John had pulled a rueful moue—"his novels are no bloody good—"

"But we like him," Moira finished firmly.

"I'll give him this much, he's got great taste in wine."

"Roger's lovely," Moira insisted. "And it's true about his books, but he's very powerful here in Sydney. He could really help you, if you needed him."

"Roger Leverett?" Danielle thought a moment. "I've never heard of him."

"Not surprised."

"As in 'our chef is very famous in London.'"

"Come again?"

"There's a nasty-looking little Chinese restaurant in the East Village with a handwritten sign in the window—a dirty window, too—that says 'our chef is very famous in London.' But not in New York, or anywhere else outside of London."

"And probably not in London either, eh?" John had said, as they approached the Leveretts' front door.

"Roger Leverett *is* very famous in Sydney, sweetheart, whatever you say."

At supper—prawns and quails' eggs with squid-ink noodles, followed by emu, which closely resembled steak and which she had to force herself to eat—Danielle sat between Roger and a beautiful Asian boy—Ito? Iko?—who was the boyfriend of an older architect named Gary at the other end of the table. Ludovic Seeley sat next to Moira, his arm languidly and familiarly draped over the back of her chair, and he leaned in to speak to her as though confiding secrets. Danielle glanced over every so often, unable to stop herself, but did not once, until the passion fruit sorbet was before them, find him looking her way. When he did, his spectacular eyes seemed again amused, and they did not waver. It was she who lowered her gaze, shifting in her chair and feigning sudden interest in Ito/Iko's recent trip to Tahiti.

The evening now seemed to her an elaborate theater, the sole purpose of which was meeting Ludovic Seeley. That anyone could care for Lucy or Roger or Gary or Ito/Iko in the way Danielle cared for her friends in New York seemed almost implausible: these people, to her, were actors. Only Ludovic was, in his intimate whisperings and unbroken glances, very real. Whatever that meant. Reality, or rather, facing it, was Danielle's great credo; although if she were wholly honest, here and now, she believed a little in magic, too.

Roger, beside her, was jovial and solicitous. Mostly, Danielle felt her host was a narcissist, delighted by the sound of his own voice and the humor of his own jokes, and by the pipe he fiddled with and sucked upon between courses. He was generous with the red wine, more so to her and himself than to those farther afield, and he grew more positively loquacious with each glass.

"Been to McLaren Vale? Not this time? When do you leave? Ah, well then. Next time, promise me you'll get to South Australia, do the wine route. And there's great scuba diving off the coast. Been scuba diving? No, well, I can see you might be intimidated. I used to do a lot of diving in my day, but you can get yourself in some very nasty situations, very nasty indeed. About twenty years ago—I wasn't much older than you are now—how old are you? Thirty? Well, you don't look it, my girl. Such fine skin. It must be those fine Jewish genes—you are Jewish, aren't you? Yes, well, anyway, the Reef. I was up diving with some mates, this is before Lucy, she'd never let me do it now. I was living up near Brisbane, finishing my second novel—*Revelation Road*, you probably don't know it? No, well, I'm not vain about these things. It was a great success at the time. And anyway, this trip out to the Reef was the reward, you know, for a job well done, the editor was jumping up and down in Sydney he was so mad about the manuscript, but I said, screw it, George, I'm entitled to celebrate before I come back, because once you're in this world you're in it, aren't you? So where was I? The Reef, yes. It was my first time out there, by helicopter, of course—first time in a copter, if you can believe it—and we were four blokes . . ."

Roger's blithe torrent grew murkier to Danielle with each sip of claret, and she pasted her smile—quite genuine; she was enjoying herself, and lord knew it wasn't effortful—in permanence upon her face. She smiled while slurping the inky noodles, while dissecting the antennaed prawns. She felt as though she smiled even while chewing the rather tough emu fillet, plucking the dense slices from their bed of bloodied polenta. She smiled while glancing at Ludovic Seeley, who did not glance back, and smiled at Moira, at Lucy, at John in turn. When Roger went to fetch the dessert—"I do the wine, my dear, and the clearing up. The fetching and carrying. And I make the meanest risotto you'll ever taste, but not tonight, not tonight"—Danielle turned to Ito/Iko and learned that he was twenty-two, an apprentice in a fashion house, that he'd known Gary eight months, and that they'd recently had the most fabulous holiday in Tahiti, "very Gauguin, and so sexy. I mean, the people on that island are *so* sexy, it's to die."

"Is that where Captain Cook got killed, in the end?" Danielle asked, feeling very culturally *au fait* to be dropping the founder's name.

"Oh no, doll, that was Hawaii. Very different vibe altogether. Totally different." Ito/Iko flashed a broad smile and fluffed at his hair, which was, she decided, slightly tinted with blue, and glistening in the candlelight. "You haven't been here very long, have you? Because *everyone* knows it was Hawaii. I mean, I know it was Hawaii, and I dropped out of school at sixteen."

After the meal, the party resettled in the living room, where Ito/Iko curled under Gary's arm like a chick beneath a hen's wing. Danielle gratefully abandoned her wineglass at the table, and sat sipping water as movement and general conversation buzzed around her in a pleasant fog. She felt a thrill of alarm— of life—when Ludovic Seeley took the armchair to her right.

"What takes you to New York?" she asked.

He leaned in, as she'd seen him do with Moira: intimacy, or the impression of it, was clearly his mode. But he did not touch her. His shirt cuff glowed against the plum velvet of the chair arm. "Revolution," he said.

"I'm sorry?"

"I'm going to foment revolution."

She blinked, sipped, attempted silently to invite elucidation. She didn't want to seem to him unsubtle, unironic, American.

"Seriously? Seriously, I'm going to edit a magazine."

"What magazine is that?"

"The Monitor."

She shook her head.

"Of course you haven't heard of it—I haven't got there yet. It doesn't exist yet."

"That's a challenge."

"I've got Merton behind me. I like a challenge." Danielle took this in. Augustus Merton, the Australian mogul. Busy buying up Europe, Asia, North America. Everything in English and all to the right. The enemy.

Lucy, bearing coffee, appeared suddenly, tinily, before them. "He's done it before, Danielle. He's a man to be afraid of, our Ludo. He's got all the politicians and the journos on the run in this town. *The True Voice*—have you seen it?"

"Oh. Moira told me about it. I mean, she told me about you."

"We don't see eye to eye on pretty much anything," Lucy said with a conciliatory smile at Seeley, touching her delicate hand with its black nail polish to his lavender shoulder. "But my God, this bloke makes me laugh."

He bowed his head slightly. "A true compliment. And the first step on the road to revolution."

"And now you're going to take on New York?"

Danielle's skepticism evidently made him bristle. "Yes," he said clearly, his gray eyes, their hoods fully retracted, now firmly and unamusedly upon her. "Yes, I am."

Danielle rode home in the backseat with her eyes shut for most of the way. She opened them periodically to glimpse flashes of the city, the sulfurous lights on the asphalt and the marine sky. "Roger certainly loves to talk," she said.

"Did he tell you about his novels? Bore you senseless with unwieldy plots?" Moira asked.

"No, scuba diving. And the wine route. Better than that Asian guy."

"Gary's new boyfriend? He seemed sweet."

"Sweet?" John scoffed. "Sweet?"

"He was sweet. No, he really was. But not very interesting."

There was a silence, during which Danielle longed to ask about Seeley but did not want to seem to care. Of the evening's underwater blur, Seeley was all that stuck out.

"Did you talk to Ludo at the end?" asked Moira.

"Ludo, is it now?" John said. "My dear, aren't we grand?"

"Is he really a big deal?" Danielle hoped her voice was neutral. "He seemed a little creepy, or something."

"He's moving to New York, you know," said Moira. "He's been hired in to launch a mag—they sacked the first guy, you may have read about it. Merton thought his vision was wrong—Billings, was it? Billington? Buxton, I think. Big scandal. Makes Seeley the chosen boy, plucked from halfway across the world. He's going sometime very soon."

"Next month," Danielle said. "I gave him my e-mail. Not that he'll need it, but in case he's at a loose end. Trying to be neighborly."

"That's a good one," John said. "Seeley at a loose end. That I'd like to see."

"Think he'll succeed?" Danielle asked.

"*He* thinks so," said Moira. "In fact, he knows so. But he doesn't give much away, so it's hard to know what he's really plotting. And it's hard to know whether he's running to something or running away. He's made such a splash here in the past, what is it, five years—Christ, he's only what? Thirty-three? Thirty-five? A baby!—and he's got a lot of friends—"

"And a lot of enemies," said John.

"And I just don't think there's any challenge for him here anymore, that's all. But a ton of hassle. With this kind of backing—jeez, Merton's choice!—he probably reckons he'll conquer New York, and then the world."

"Like Kim Jong Il, eh? Or Saddam Hussein?" said John.

"Well, it might not be as easy as he expects," said Danielle, thinking herself surprisingly witty in spite of the quantities of red wine. "It may just be a case of 'our chef is very famous in London.' "

"That it may," John said, obviously satisfied at the thought. "That it may."

CHAPTER TWO

Bootie, the Professor

"Bootie?" Judy Tubb yelled, in her housecoat at the bottom of the stairs, washed in the dull, pearly light of the reflected snow outside. "Bootie, are you going to come down and help dig us out, or what?"

Met by silence, she set a foot upon the creaking step, her hand on the polished wooden ball at the banister's base, and started, as loudly as she could, to climb. "I said, Bootie? Did you hear me?"

A door opened and her son ambled into view on the gloomy landing, pushing his glasses up his nose and squinting. His old-fashioned brown flannel pajamas were rumpled around his soft bulk, and his first preoccupation seemed to be that his mother not catch sight of his pale and generous belly: he clutched at his pajama strings and hoisted up the bottoms, revealing instead his oddly slender ankles and his long, hairy toes.

"Have you been sleeping all this time, since breakfast?" Judy spoke sharply but felt a burst of tenderness for her befuddled boy, as he wavered before her, almost six feet tall. "Bootie? Frederick? Are you still asleep?"

"Reading, Ma. I was reading in bed."

"But there's two feet of snow in the drive, and it's still coming down."

"I know."

"We've got to get out, don't we."

"School's cancelled. You don't have to go anywhere."

"Just because I don't have to teach doesn't mean I don't need to go anywhere. And what about you?"

Frederick pushed a fist behind his glasses and rubbed his left eye.

"You're supposed to be looking for a job, aren't you? You're not going to find one lying around in bed."

"There's a snowstorm on. Everything is cancelled, not just school. There's nowhere to go today, and no jobs to get today." He seemed suddenly solid, even stolid, in his bulk. "Besides, my reading isn't nothing. It's work, too. Just because it's not paid doesn't mean it's not work."

"Please, don't start."

"Ask Uncle Murray. Don't you think he spends his days reading?"

"I don't know what your uncle does with his time, Bootie, but I'd remind you that he's well paid for it. Very well paid. And I know that when he was your age, he was in college and he had a job. Maybe two jobs, even. Because Pawpaw and Nana couldn't afford—"

"I know, Ma. I know. I'm going to finish my chapter. And then if it's stopped snowing, I'll shovel the drive."

"Even if it's *still* snowing, Bootie. They've plowed the road twice since seven."

"Don't call me Bootie," he said as he retreated back into his bedroom. "It's not my name."

*

Judy Tubb and her son lived in a spacious but crumbling Victorian house on the eastern side of Watertown, off the road to Lowville, in a neighborhood of other similarly sprawling, similarly decrepit buildings. Some had been broken up into apartments, and one, at the end of the street, had been abandoned, its elegant windows boarded over and its porch all but caved in; but that was simply the way of Watertown. It was still a good address, a fine house on a fine square lot at the good end of town, as respectable as it had been twenty years before when Bert and Judy had moved in with their little daughter, Sarah, and Bootie not even on the way.

Born a mile from this house, Judy had lived her whole life in town, except for college and a few years teaching in Syracuse. Watertown was to her as invisible as her skin, and she no longer saw (if she ever had) the derelict storefronts and sagging porches. The grand downtown, once known as Garland City, its stone buildings and central plaza constructed on an imperial scale, impressed her only rarely as forlorn: mostly it seemed, as she drove through it to the high school or to the Price Chopper, of a blind and consoling familiarity. So, too, with their neighborhood, their house: she cleaved to them lovingly, simply because they were hers.

The house itself had steep steps at its front, and a small cement patio with a little balcony overhanging, which opened off the upstairs hallway. The Tubbs had had aluminum siding put on in the early eighties—white, simple—but it had grown grubby and mottled with moss and mud, and was in places dented by fallen gutter pipes or bowed by the work of zealous squirrels or birds who had made their nests between the siding and the exterior wall. The remaining wood trim was painted green, but it had been worn bald in spots and was everywhere cracked and peeling. The snow covered the worst of the building's indignities (including a rotting patch of brick in the foundation), and softened its outlines, so that the peaked roof—once of slate, now of poorly stapled asphalt sheeting—seemed to rise with a solid confidence into the clouded sky.

Inside, the Tubbs' home was still elegant—except, perhaps, Bootie's room, a territory to which Judy laid no claim. Little had been done to the rooms in years—she had not had the courage for even a coat of paint since Bert's death from pancreatic cancer four years before—and they had about them, perhaps in consequence, a heavy, darkened aspect; but she kept the house clean, its wood polished, its linoleum waxed, even its windows (at least in summer, when the storms were taken down) washed. There was little to be done about the stubborn dottings of mold on the basement wall (she blamed the aluminum siding, after all these years, which kept the house from breathing) or in a patch on the blue bathroom lino behind the toilet. But by and large, Judy considered that all was in fine repair, the old cabinets and wide-planked floors, even the small red-and-blue-lozenged stained-glass window over the front door, which she knew—Bert had discovered it; he loved researching such things—had been ordered from a Sears catalogue all the way back at the turn of the last century.

She loved her house, largely though not only for the history that it held, and she was most partial to the upstairs—the grand, bright bedroom overlooking the street that she had shared with her dear husband, and where, were it not for the hospital, he would have died; the broad hall with its balcony and gleaming banisters; even the faded pink flowered carpet

along the floor, with its faint smell of dust, which she knew so
intimately that she could locate, in her mind, its gnawed edges,
its threadbare patches and its irremovable stains. As she moved
from that hallway into her beloved bedroom, worrying about
her sullen son (it was the age, she kept telling herself, his and
the culture's), she felt she walked into the light: the two large
windows cast a shadowless opalescence onto the sprigged wall-
paper, the family photos on top of the bureau. Even her
discarded stockings, still carrying from yesterday the shape of
her solid limbs, appeared outlined in light, luminous. Her
hands and her hair, a grayed cloud, had carried up from the
kitchen the smell of coffee, and the vents at her ankles pushed
a warm wind around the floor. In spite of Bootie, in spite, in
spite, in this moment at least, she felt happy: she was not too
old to love even the snow.

Judy Tubb made her bed—tidily, smoothing the bottom
sheet and removing the stray gray curls from her pillow, then
squaring and tucking the top sheet, the mustard wool blanket.
She fussed over the bedspread, its evenness on both sides, the
plumpness of the pillows beneath its folds. She had no truck
with duvets, flimsy and foreign: she liked the weight of a bed
made with blankets, and the work of it. She showered, dried,
and dressed in the bathroom in the hall—the house was Victorian, and had only the one bathroom in spite of four
bedrooms—and emerged in her favorite blush turtleneck
beneath the avocado angora cardigan she had knitted last
winter. In truth, she had knitted it for her niece, Marina—God
only knew why, because they weren't close; except that she
loved to knit and had already made a dozen sweaters for her
daughter and her grandkids. But it wasn't quite finished in time

for Christmas, and somehow she had known, when she opened the gift Marina had sent—a crimson velvet scarf with cutaway flowers in it and silk tasseled fringe, like the shawl of a Victorian madam—she had just known that the sweater wasn't right. She'd sent a Borders gift card instead, and kept the sweater for herself. As for the scarf, there was nowhere in Watertown, New York, that she could wear it—certainly not to teach Geography to the sophomores and juniors at the high school—so she had wrapped it up in tissue and put it in the back of her dresser drawer. The funny thing was, she loved the cardigan as if it had been a precious gift, and she somehow thought of it as a gift *from Marina,* which made her think more warmly of the girl after all, and which, in a roundabout way, it was.

As she bundled herself into her parka, her Bean boots, her pink woolly toque (also her own handiwork, a pretty lace pattern with a bobble on top), and took, in her mittened hands, the aluminum shovel from the porch, she worried about Bootie, upstairs in his pajamas like a boy. She wouldn't ask him again to help with the shoveling—he could perfectly well hear the rhythmic scrape and shuffle of her movements from his window overhead—but she hoped against hope that he might come down of his own accord. Of course if he did come, it would mean another day he hadn't bathed. She didn't like to nag him about it (who wanted to be that kind of mother, always picking and finding fault?), but she couldn't remember hearing the tub run once in the past week. He took only baths, not showers, and those rarely; but when he did he lingered an hour in the cooling water, reading one of his infernal books.

Judy Tubb tackled the snow in the driveway first and, in spite of the delicious cold of the shovel through her mittens, in

spite of the cold sting pinkening her cheeks, in spite of the satisfying soreness she felt, almost immediately, in her lower back,
she felt her good humor evaporating as she thought again about
her boy. Her darling and only. Her prize. What was it now?
March, it was March now, and almost Easter. And Bootie had
graduated almost a year ago, at the top of his class. She'd never
imagined he would still be here, or would be back here; and
when, in September, he'd gone off to Oswego, she'd thought
that it was the beginning of his life in the wider world. No
telling what he could accomplish. And if Bert were still alive,
he'd see that his youngest had fulfilled the promise, that all the
saving (Bert had been an accountant, and wisely parsimonious)
had been for *something*. For Bootie to shine. It was Sarah who'd
given them trouble, pregnant at nineteen and married at
twenty, but now she had a good job at the savings and loan and
three tow-headed, boisterous kids, and her Tom had proven
a good husband and settled into his work running Thousand
Islands boat tours out of Alexandria Bay in the summer and
plowing on a state contract in the winter. Heck, Tom would
probably drive down from the bay and shovel out her drive
before her own boy stirred himself to help her. He was a good
son-in-law, even if she'd hoped, once, for better.

But Bootie: he was going to be a politician, he'd said, or a
journalist like his uncle, or maybe a university professor. That's
what the kids had called him at the high school: the professor. He'd been a chubby boy, and bespectacled, but always
respected, even admired, in a funny way. He'd been valedictor-
ian. And then home at Christmas with twenty or thirty extra
pounds on him and a fistful of incompletes, saying that college
was bullshit, or at least Oswego was bullshit, that his teachers

were morons and he wouldn't go back. She suspected a girl, some girl had broken his heart or embarrassed him—he wasn't easy with girls, not confident—or else his roommates, two tight lunk-headed athletes with beer on the brain; but Bootie wasn't telling, or not telling her. And since Christmas he'd spent all his time in his room, reading and doing God knew what on the computer (was it pornography? That would be okay, she could understand it in a young boy, but as a distraction, not an obsession; and if only she knew), or in the grand pillared library downtown, where the heat was always too high and the air smelled funny and where, to be honest, he had to order books from out of town to get anything more serious than Harlequin romances or the Encyclopedia Britannica. Had he looked for a job? Not once until last month, when she gave him an ultimatum, told him he'd have to pay rent one way or another, if he wouldn't go back to school; so that now he made a big show at breakfast with the classifieds, circling factory jobs and short-order cook positions and suggesting—it was the only time he laughed these days—that he could sell used cars at Loudoun's Ford & Truck, or wait tables at Annie's off the interstate.

And now here he was on the porch, no gloves, no hat, ski jacket over his pajamas, wielding the second rusty and old shovel, like a weapon, with the steam of his breath fogging his glasses.

"Cut it out, Ma," he called. "That's enough, now. You've made your point. I'll do the rest." And with uncommon vigor, he set to throwing the loads of snow so that they sent up a fine spray, a second snowstorm across the drive, and she stood awhile staring at this unlikely apparition, pajama bottoms caked in snow, dark curls awry and glistening with flakes, and—forgive her, she couldn't help it—imagining the neighbors, too, through their curtains, staring, wondering what had gone wrong with that brainy Tubb boy that he'd fallen so fast from phenomenon to freak; and without a word, she handed him her new, fine shovel and took back the decrepit one, and stomped back onto the porch, knocking snow from her boots and, cheeks burning from the cold and the shame, but surely he couldn't, he mustn't, see, she went back inside and heard the stiff-springed screen door snap bitterly behind her.

CHAPTER THREE

Reflexology

Julius had been getting on Marina's nerves, so she asked him to press her feet. The massage of her arches in particular—they were fraught with agonizing, knobbly bumps that an Indian acquaintance had informed her pertained to the spine; or was it the intestines?—seemed designed to cool her irritation. Not that Julius would stop speaking—he was saying something, as he flexed her foot this way and that, about *War and Peace,* about how he never knew in life whether to be Pierre or Natasha, the solitary, brooding loner or the vivacious social butterfly; or else that he never knew whether he *was* Pierre or Natasha, which in Julius's case made as much sense—but that she would not, in the same way, have to hear him, being inundated instead by immediate sensations that reverberated upward from her extremities and filled the foreground of her mind.

She had only herself to blame: after two weeks alone in her parents' house outside Stockbridge, up every night till the small hours gaping out into the oddly restless dark, before retreating to her parents' bed with a paring knife beneath her pillow and, on evenings when the deer, or bears, or who knew what, had snapped branches in the woods behind the house, with a chair propped, probably ineffectually, against the bedroom door, Marina had decided she needed company.

The house, fifteen minutes' drive from the village with its pillared inn, chintzy shops, and year-round tourists, lay at the end of a winding gravel drive, in a clearing among the trees. Largely evergreens, they loomed dark and furry against one side of the house, while leaving an uneven circle of lawn elsewhere, a lawn around which Marina's mother, Annabel, had dug borders and planted bulbs and perennials, tasty snacks for the local fauna tired of foraging through the winter. At the bottom of the garden was a folly, a trellised, domed, screened enclosure in which, in summertime, Marina liked to loll with a book; but which, in winter, dark, bleak, and abandoned or, today, its screens smattered with snow and its trellises bare, looked more like a hunter's blind or sniper's lair, with alarmingly good sights upon the house.

The house itself was a pseudo-colonial, a modern construction that aimed, insofar as was possible, to mimic the antique. Blockish, two-storied, glinting a researched barn-red, it presented to the gravel drive, which circled before it, a center porch and four leaded windows—neatly shuttered and hung with lace curtains—up and down, on either side. At the back, however, the house abandoned all historical pretense and, to Marina's solitary dismay, offered French doors and long, tall, uncovered windows—a rash of terrifying permeability—to the sniper's cupola and the blackened woods. When she fried an egg or watched television, when she squinted at herself in the bathroom mirror after dark, Marina was painfully aware that she was, if not watched, then watchable. Hence her parents' bedroom: it faced the drive.

With time, she discovered, she grew more rather than less anxious, as she deemed that her imaginary stalker had the opportunity—she knew he was imaginary, but still—to memorize her routines, to learn even where she slept (although, of course, she devised elaborate feints, turned and left on lights in unused rooms; changed the bathroom that she used; and sometimes performed ablutions or poured juice or cereal in the dark, so as to baffle and confuse). And one morning waking near noon after another pointless, exhausting vigil till almost dawn, Marina decided, with a certainty that was not panicked but was also not negotiable, that she could not possibly be alone any longer. Or rather, that she could hold out only for the length of time it would take someone to reach her, like a hiker in the desert who, with the certain promise of relief, can endure, extraordinarily, one more waterless day.

And so she had summoned Julius. Danielle was off on the other side of the world and most of her other friends had jobs that prevented them from renting a car and driving to Massachusetts at a moment's notice. Julius, of course, was prevented from renting a car by the fact that he did not drive, but he was freelance and could bring his work with him, and Marina had offered (rashly, she felt now, on the third day of his visit) to drive to the train station in Albany, more than an hour away, to pick him up. This meant, of course, that his departure was at once wholly in her hands and yet not in her control at all: she would have to take him, when the time came, but this very power ensured that she could not ask him to go, could not even suggest it without the risk of offense (he was nothing if not sensitive, her Julius); and now she was no longer certain which she dreaded more, the house's hollow silence when she drifted through it alone like some pale ghost, or the echo of Julius's chatter, which seemed constantly to fill even the vacant rooms and to linger there like some electronic hum so that still, upon waking, in the darkness of dawn, she could feel that she was not alone. And now it had snowed: overnight and all morning the flakes had fallen, muffling the landscape and muting the light. She would have felt safe, snowbound alone (because what mad intruder could plot an assault when evidence, the inevitable footprints, would lead directly to his capture?), but what to do? So she had put Ella Fitzgerald on the stereo and asked Julius if he would mind, terribly, exercising his reflexology skills.

As she peered at him, curled cross-legged at the other end of the sofa in shadow, her foot in his lap and the white snow light like a halo behind his head, Marina felt sorry for Julius. The Pierre/Natasha riff was born of another disappointment in love, another boy who had at first appeared to relish Julius's flittering intensity, had called his frog-face beautiful (even in the gloom his dark, googly eyes were shimmering), and yet who had, with humiliating speed, turned from him, against him, deriding him as hopeless and his affection as stifling. Julius, baby-faced, scrubbed, wore a pink cashmere pullover and a silk cravat, even here, even in Stockbridge, and had gelled his black bird-fluff hair. His ears stuck out as if in outrage at this most recent betrayal and his tongue slid out periodically to lick his lips in a tic as consistent as it was unconscious.

"I've told you before, you need an older guy," Marina broke in, a little unsure of where her friend had rambled in his monologue. "A much older guy. Someone settled."

"But that's my point." Julius flicked his tongue. "Eric *was* older. I mean, not a ton, but thirty-eight, old enough to know what he wanted. And he didn't want me."

"Maybe you pushed things too fast?"

He made a spitting sound. "Puh-lease. It's not like I tried to move in with him or something."

"But how long had it been? A month? Less?"

"Three weeks."

"When I'd been seeing Al for three weeks, we were barely dating. I mean, he was seeing other women, still, and I was at least pretending to see other guys."

"But you were twenty-four then."

"But just because we're thirty—I mean, you're a guy, sweetie. There's no biological imperative for you."

"Besides, look where it left you, in the end."

Marina withdrew her foot and sat up straight. "We did go out for five years," she said. "We *lived* together. We made it work."

"Until it didn't anymore."

"Until then, yes." Marina sniffed. "But it wasn't—it doesn't mean—"

"I know. But I don't think that right now you're in a position to tell me how to play it."

Marina stood and proceeded to turn on the large beaten-copper lamps around the living room, revealing suddenly a bath of color, of pinks and oranges and terracotta, the burnt umber of the sofa—all her mother's creation, supposedly Mediterranean in atmosphere, it did seem to make the room warmer, and the garden beyond correspondingly unwelcoming. She could glimpse, in its leached gray gloom, the shadow of the snow-covered folly, its contours now—on account of Julius, she had to admit—forlorn rather than menacing.

"I don't mean that," Julius conceded. "I don't know. The situations aren't really comparable."

"No, they're not." Until last August, Marina had been living with Al—Fat Al, her friends called him, because he had a belly on him, of which she had claimed to be fond—but they had finally called it quits, officially because she needed to be on her own in order to "get her life together," but actually because Al was tired of supporting her financially (or else, as Danielle had suggested to Marina, Marina had made him tired by her constant vocal neurosis about this fact), and also, and more gravely, because he'd been to bed, and possibly more than once, with a colleague of his at Morgan Stanley. It wasn't, Marina had protested to Danielle (and pointedly *not* to Julius, who, if he knew, did so secretly and did not let on), because he'd screwed somebody else, but because the woman he had chosen was so demeaningly dull. And if he could do that, Marina had said, it meant she'd been wrong about him all along, and all her friends, who had for so long tactfully refrained from saying so, had been right.

This rupture, both unexpected and, in some more profound way, preordained, had greatly altered Marina's outline in the world. She sometimes felt as though she were a changeling, as though someone completely new had taken on the identity of Marina Thwaite—or rather, as if someone who was seen from the outside to be completely new had done so, while beneath the surface she remained unchanged. Not unlike that process of kitchen cabinet refinishing, in fact, whereby you simply glued a new sheet of plastic or plywood onto your old cupboards without even needing to remove the canisters of flour or sugar or the box of soggy Cheerios.

In truth: after splitting up with Fat Al (who didn't, most painfully, even *try* to keep her), Marina had struggled powerfully, and continued to do so. From being the most settled among her friends—none of them, at twenty-five, had been close to marriage, whereas she and Al had already bought a queen-size bed—she suddenly became the least rooted. She had no apartment of her own, no money with which to procure one, and so, not long before her thirtieth birthday in November last, after wearing out her welcome on sofabeds around the city, she had moved back to her childhood room in her parents' Upper West Side apartment. As if that weren't humiliation enough, she'd had to accept an allowance from them, merely in order to live.

For all she had no visible job, Marina wasn't idle. She was merely inefficient, or so her father, the famous Murray Thwaite, master of efficiency, assured her. At about the same time as she'd started seeing Fat Al, a time now so distant as to seem mythological, Marina had taken on a book project. She'd been a young intern at *Vogue* at the time, and as a celebrated native beauty (surely this wasn't of no account? She would vehemently have denied it; and yet, as Danielle had more than once complained to Julius, Marina had no idea of what it would be like to be anything less than beautiful: "Sometimes I just want to say to her, what if you walked into a room, Marina, and nobody stopped talking, and nobody turned around? What if nobody offered to cut your hair for free or to carry your luggage? What then?") and as her celebrated father's adored daughter, a hot commodity, she had been invited to lunch by a powerful editor, a man of her father's age and a sometime family friend, who was pleased to be seen in San Domenico with such a babe—Brown University graduate, mind you, not all good looks and no substance—and who urged her to submit a proposal to his firm. After casting about for a month or more, which seemed, at the time, like forever, a time during which she'd been always afraid he might retract his invitation, Marina had come up with an idea for a book about children's fashions and—for this was the spin—about how complex and profound cultural truths—our *mores* entire—could be derived from a society's decision to put little Lulu in a smocked frock or tiny Stacey in sequined hotpants. At the time, the proposal had had more heft than this, of course; but that was years ago and Marina now, at least in part, a different (or "refinished") person, was no longer particularly interested in her book, nor impressed by its thesis, nor could she remember ever having been, and she labored on largely because she had long ago spent all the advance money received, and she would not see the rest until a suitable manuscript was delivered.

For some, this might, of course, have speeded the process; but Marina would not put her name—on her *first* book, and she her father's daughter—on something of which she was not proud, even as she had come to doubt that pride in this effort was possible. The breakup had slowed her considerably, as had her subsequent itinerant state, and, if she were honest, her installation at home. Her editor—the third in charge of the book, as the years rolled by; a round-cheeked, freckled boy whom she was certain was younger than she, with an upturned nose and the puppyish name of Scott—had in recent months begun to pursue her, and had uttered ominous pronouncements about final deadlines. Marina now was worried that if she did not turn in the manuscript they would ask for their money back (such things certainly did happen, had happened to people she knew), a not insubstantial sum now dispersed to the ether. At her mother's suggestion, then (her father being someone for whom work was inseparable from society, to whom the isolation of Stockbridge without children or house-guests was anathema), Marina had retreated to the quiet of the country for what had been dubbed—not by her; she knew it wasn't so—"the last push" on the book.

It was now mid-March, and she had committed to stay until May, but if anyone had actually asked she would have conceded that she did not think she would last that long. Like with Fat Al: if anyone had ever asked her if this was the man for the rest of her life, she would at once have said he wasn't enough. So, too, this work in the house in Stockbridge was but a pretense of work—all the odder, of course, for the fact that there had been, until recently, nobody to witness that pretense. Now, with Julius, Marina was embroiled in a pretense, almost convincing to herself, of not being able to work any longer because her oh-so-productive solitude had been broken. She both wanted Julius to leave and, for fear of the quiet, of course, but also of the work undone, the work undoable, she wanted him to stay. Besides which, he was a very good cook.

"On account of the snow," he said now, in the alarmingly cheerfully lit living room, by way of making amends for his earlier comments, trailing his long fingers along the rusty chenille of the sofa's back, "on account of this super-dreary weather, I think we should have comfort food for supper, don't you?"

"Like baked beans on toast?" She was still annoyed.

"I thought a cheese soufflé, actually, m'dear. With sautéed potatoes and a little steamed spinach on the side, just so there's something good for us. And if you're still peckish, I'll whip up a sabayon, if you promise to talk to me while I stir."

"It's a lot of egg, Jules." Her reluctance was feigned: sabayon was her favorite dessert.

"We're not that old yet," said Julius. "We can count cholesterol next year."

CHAPTER FOUR

As for Julius Clarke

As for Julius Clarke, he was not what you might expect him to be. He was not from New York, and he was not from California, or Washington—state or district—or even Oregon. Nor was he, in spite of his unplaceable Anglo accent, from the British Isles nor from any point in the transatlantic. He hailed from Danville, Michigan, a small town an hour from Detroit. His friends knew this only if they had known him since his first year in college, when, in the freshman face book, a provenance, a home address, was ignominiously posted next to each photograph. He'd worked hard to erase the traces of his past—viz the paisley cravat, the pink cashmere (albeit worn through at the elbows), the fluting voice—and yet somehow, at some moment or another, everyone, it seemed, had met his father, Franklin Clarke, to whom it seemed impossible that Julius should have any connection and who was his past incarnate.

A big, physically awkward man with a square head and jowls, Frank Clarke had been a Green Beret in Vietnam, which was where he had met Thu, Julius's mother, after whom the boy took. After the war, Frank and Thu had settled back in Danville, where Frank taught history at the high school and coached basketball, while Thu, whose English was charming but never proficient, worked from home as a seamstress and dressmaker. Julius was the second of three and the only boy, all of them dark and wide-eyed and frail like their mother, so that Frank, with his loud voice and hulking back, came into his home like Gulliver into Lilliput. In spite of local expectations—Julius had been a fruit from the beginning, and was teased as a sissy in grade school—tough Frank doted as much upon his boy as upon his more conventionally successful daughters, and now came as often as his schedule and his agoraphobic wife permitted, to visit Julius in New York. When he did, the incongruities were rife, and delightful: the sight of Frank, sitting in the armchair in Julius's cramped and dark studio, poring over his son's reviews, his thick thighs in their chinos like extra pieces of furniture protruding into the room; or father and son at the East Village diner Julius frequented, earnest Frank in his navy windbreaker, baseball cap on the banquette beside him, looking for all the world—Julius knew it even if his father did not—like his son's suburban john, a married sugar daddy getting a bit of boy on the side. If it occurred to Frank that the patrons on Avenue A might interpret the scene in this way, then it didn't bother him: he was affectionate with his son and fussed with the boy's clothes and tousled his hair, his pride in Julius's accomplishments seemingly endless, his delight that his son was a New Yorker evident for all to see—although for himself, make no mistake, Danville was home and just fine. (Needless to say, nobody had met Thu except a friend who had driven across the country after college and had swung through Michigan on purpose. But he had stayed on the West Coast, and the only reliable report he'd filed was that Thu was a great cook of both Vietnamese and Western food, a fact Julius's friends might have inferred from her son's talents.)

What, then, were Julius's accomplishments, those of which his father was so proud? The anxiety, surely, was that they were few, and fading. Known in college for his vicious wit, Julius had sashayed into New York—or, more precisely, into the offices of the *Village Voice*—with a youthful certainty that attitude could carry him. And for a long time, it had: everyone in the down-town literary set knew who Julius was, and pointed him out to newcomers at parties. His devastating but elegant book reviews were often cited; his less devastating but no less elegant film and television reviews rather less so; but still: throughout his twenties, he lived a life of Wildean excess and insouciance that seemed an accomplishment in itself, the contemporary exam-ple of the enfant terrible. The insouciance, of course, masked endless and wearisome neuroses, to which Marina and Danielle were privy. He was a failure at intimacy, if not at sex (he had no shortage of partners; but they were only shortly upon the scene). He was always broke (hence the threadbare cashmere), but it was vital, or so he maintained, that the secret of his penury not get about: "This is New York, guys. And people without money aren't noble, they're beggars." He apparently did not suspect that everyone already knew. He was aware that at thirty he stretched the limits of the charming wastrel, that some actual sustained endeavor might be in order were he not to fade, wisplike, away: from charming wastrel to needy, boring failure was but a few, too few, short steps.

His friends had suggested that he take on a job—editing something, or even a regular column, to stabilize his income—but Julius was loath to do so, claiming that regularity was bourgeois. Danielle and Marina had often discussed his life behind his back—between themselves, when they sometimes referred to Julius not by name but as La Grenouille, on account of his protruberant eyes and his flat, rather mushy nose, a nickname they had tried upon him years before and immediately retired because it so upset him. They couldn't figure out what claimed so much of their friend's time: he didn't have cable television, and he had no cash to spend. They surmised, from apparently unwitting hints he dropped, that pornography and dirty talk over the Internet took up hours of each day; then again, further hours vanished in trysts arranged with his virtual correspondents. He had enough sex for all of them put together, Marina joked—indeed, she wondered whether in coming to Stockbridge he felt like a drunk in a dry county—and very occasionally, as with this fickle Eric over whom he was so undone, Julius attempted to push further, to forge some sort of relationship. All three friends had the impression that over the years, inadvertently, Julius was having sex—safely, mind you; that is, if Marina and Danielle believed his assurances—with his entire gay generation in New York, like pulling the string of a bag, little by little, so that eventually he would know everyone, would have a stronger professional network and better connections than anyone else. Danielle had even suggested—laughingly, of course—that perhaps this would be his sustained endeavor, his accomplishment.

This, like so many other things, was not a joking matter for Julius, who preferred to instigate and to control his comedies. More than his friends, Julius was interested in power. It wasn't a focused preoccupation: there wasn't a *type* of power that he sought, just the absolute, brute fact of it. Political, social, financial—everything except perhaps moral power, so precious to Marina, which didn't interest him in the least. He would as soon have had dinner with Donald Trump or Gwyneth Paltrow or Donatella Versace as with Marina's father, Murray Thwaite, for example; and he was interested in Murray Thwaite only on account of his ability to shape public opinion, not because of any intrinsic value in the opinions themselves. He was good at seduction, itself a seductive power: he had it, he used it, it worked. He wanted his whole life to be that way. An inchoate ball of ambition, Julius knew that he had soon, soon, to find something to be ambitious for; otherwise he risked terminal resentment, from which there was no return.

In his conscious mind, ever generous, he had come to Stockbridge, to this isolated house among deer and who knew what other wildlife (he'd seen plenty of wildlife in his Michigan childhood and, being thoroughly metropolitan, had no desire to see any more, just as he had no desire to be cold or to get his feet wet), to support his dear friend in need. He prided himself on making the extra effort—it was a quality Danielle and Marina had always commented on. And in this case, he knew that Marina was struggling with her manuscript, that she required bolstering and diversion, and he felt his journey (that interminable train ride, in a carriage that had smelled, faintly but inescapably, of urine) to be an altruistic duty. But then again: he'd been gravely hurt, this past week, by Eric's rejection, and relished the chance to lick his wounds. And he would be fed at Marina's house, he knew, and well, if he cooked, while in his own home he had only a frozen loaf of sliced bread, a jar of olives, and no money for even the farmers' market. Marina, so naïve, or so oblivious (sometimes he wasn't sure which),

Marina, who thought she was impoverished when living off the
fat of her parents—Marina got on his nerves as much as he got
on hers. She didn't seem to be aware of this, of the fact that he
had to bite his tongue (as if her experience with Fat Al gave her
any authority to advise him in matters of the heart!), of the
effort it cost him to make nice. It all came down to entitlement, and one's sense of it. Marina, feeling entitled, never really
asked herself if she was good enough. Whereas he, Julius, asked
himself repeatedly, answered always in the affirmative, and
marveled at the wider world's apparent inability to see the light.
He would have to show them—of this he was ever more
decided, with a flamelike conviction. But he was already thirty,
and the question was *how?*

CHAPTER FIVE

Poetry Makes Nothing Happen

As the seminar drew to a close, Murray Thwaite felt the tickle in his throat that was a demand for both a cigarette and a drink. Darkness had fallen outside the classroom windows and the students, in spite of the rebuke of the fluorescent light, slouched and slumped, undignified, in their plastic chairs. They'd lasted pretty well, for students, and had shown animation, even enthusiasm, for his firsthand account of the late sixties and early seventies antiwar movement—in fact, they'd seemed at once incredulous and thrilled to imagine the quad of their own dear institution, right outside these very windows, teeming with renegades, Murray, long-haired, among them— but after three hours they were drained, avid for their cafeteria suppers, the slovenly warmth of their dorm rooms, and the mindless chatter (what did these kids talk about?) of their peers.

Thwaite's friend and host, Eli Triplett, noting the clock upon the wall and the drooping lids of his flock—even, perhaps, hearing the urgency in Thwaite's throat-clearing— graciously brought the discussion to a close. "And, my ducks," he concluded, in his Manchester bass, "you've no idea how lucky you are to have had this opportunity. A heartfelt thanks to Murray Thwaite for taking the time to come up here." There was a smattering of applause, heartfelt, Thwaite thought, and he delicately bowed his large, silvered head. "Remember we're meeting in the AV center next week at seven, for the film."

"What is it again?" asked a surly boy in overalls, who had fiddled endlessly with his goatee throughout the class, and had seemed to munch upon his facial hair with his upper teeth, giving new meaning, Thwaite thought, to the "goat" in "goatee."

"Costa-Gavras. *Missing*. We're on to our government's South American involvements next, Adam. A whole new set of horrors."

"*Our* government, Eli?" Thwaite murmured as the students wrapped themselves in their swishing outerwear. "You surprise me. Have you sworn an allegiance I'm unaware of?"

Triplett laughed. "They take it amiss, you know, the Bolshie ones, if I suggest I'm not implicated. It's one thing to criticize your own family, as you well know, and quite another to criticize someone else's."

"So you're lying to them, essentially?" Thwaite, still seated, raised an admonitory eyebrow.

A girl lurking by the corner of the table tittered audibly.

"Roanne. Murray Thwaite, Roanne Levine. One of the department's best."

Murray Thwaite stood, a full six foot three, and extended a hand to the young woman, who was as small as a girl, her face shadowed by voluminous black curls. "Thank you for your question about Lowell," he said. "It's a relief to find a young person who knows that once upon a time, poetry *did* make things happen."

Roanne giggled again and tucked her hair behind one ear,

revealing a round, smooth face and a wide mouth. "Auden, right? I'm a double major, English and History."

"They overlap more than you think." Thwaite turned to Eli, aware out of the corner of his eye that the girl lingered. She was quite pretty, and she had remained alert to the last. "Where's your watering hole, then?"

"Just a couple of blocks down. Not far, not far."

"Professor—I mean, Mr. Thwaite?"

Cigarette already in hand, though unlit (he was by now familiar with the infuriating regulations of institutional buildings, enforced with the same draconian rigor as those in airplane bathrooms), Thwaite started for the door, with a swift glance over his shoulder to encourage Ms. Levine.

"I just wondered—I have a few questions—for the school paper—a profile?" She was at once pushy and timid in a way that appealed to him.

"A budding journalist as well?"

Roanne Levine laughed again. The laughter might, in time, grate; but Thwaite was, by his own admission, ever curious. And she was pretty. "Why don't you join us for a drink?"

Eli cleared his throat.

"I don't know—Professor Triplett? I don't want to— Well, just quickly, maybe, if you don't mind? Or another time, if that would be better?"

Vaguely irritated by Eli—was this, too, a rule, like the smoking? But he didn't even teach here; what could he care?— Thwaite said, "No, now is good. We have eternity for sleeping."

The bar was Irish, and old-fashioned, with sticky wooden tables and chairs and a sticky concrete floor. Ill lit, it relied for much illumination upon the neon sign in the window. There was an ashtray on every table, and beer mats with shamrocks on them. Thwaite and Eli ordered scotch and water, while Roanne, after some hesitation, asked for a White Russian.

"More a food than a drink, my dear girl," Thwaite observed.

"I know, I know, but they make the best ones here. It's what I always have."

"Quite right, then, that you should have it now. Be true to yourself, I always say."

There was a slightly awkward silence. Thwaite could tell that Eli was struggling not to fill it, that he hoped the discomfort might hurry the girl on her way. Undeterred, she took a notebook from her backpack and flipped through it with artificial busyness. "I wrote out some questions," she said. "I hope you don't mind?"

The questions, it transpired, were largely personal, and hence had the effect, perhaps desired, of making Thwaite look more closely at the girl and listen less to what she asked, let alone to his answers. He loved to talk—as he'd told Triplett before coming to the class, he loved to *teach*—but talking about himself did not interest him. He noticed that she had a habit of pulling her sweater cuff down over the wrist of her left hand and clutching at it while she scribbled. Her legs, in long black boots, were not merely crossed but fully entwined beneath the table. And she looked up at him from behind the curtain of her hair like a doe or a rabbit. She seemed younger and more charmingly ignorant with each question, but earnest, which he found winning. And he could tell—surely by now he could tell—that she found him attractive, and not just in an avuncular way. They all had a second round, and were nearing the ticklish question of a third, when Eli, who had grown increasingly restless, felt the professional need plumply to intervene.

"I bet you've got enough now for a full biography, Roanne," he said, pushing back from the table. "I'm just going to settle this tab, and maybe you could finish, here. Mr. Thwaite doesn't have all night, and I'm sure you have other things to do, too."

"Don't worry about him," said Thwaite when Eli had stepped away. "He's just looking out for you."

"Well, I did have some more questions, just a few, but—"

"Tell you what," he interrupted her. "Why don't you give me your number, and I'll give you a call later." He watched for her reaction, but there was none. "Or tomorrow, and we can finish up then."

She wrote her details in a spiky hand and pulled the sheet from her pad. "Thank you so much," she said breathily. "This has been amazing."

He wouldn't call her, of course, and she wouldn't really mind. But this way, she would feel that a genuine connection had been made, that she had impressed herself upon him, which was surely her desire. He stuffed the paper into the pocket of his coat, already bulging with taxi receipts, matchbooks, and slips such as this one. Who knew? Maybe he would call, some other time if not tonight. It was important to leave open the possibility.

Roanne Levine, with a wave at her professor, slipped out into the mucky night—the little bit of snow had melted and the sidewalks glistened wet—and Thwaite agreed to follow Eli—and perhaps some others? Eli had his cell phone—to a bistro down in their neighborhood, on Amsterdam.

When he got home, well past one, Annabel had left on only

the table lamp in the hall. Unable, briefly, to remember whether his daughter was in residence or not, and certain that his wife, whom he had not telephoned, would be annoyed if wakened, Thwaite did his best to tiptoe along the Oriental. Whether on account of his gait or the gloom or, indeed, the sloshing quantities of scotch and burgundy he had consumed he could not later have said, but he simply did not see the mound of vomit until it had surrendered moistly and noisily beneath his right shoe.

"Fuck," he hissed. "Fuck, fuck, fuck." It was, he knew, the cat again: the Pope, their seventeen-year-old bony Abyssinian, ever haughty and standoffish and now, frankly, decrepit and repellent. She had been a gift to Marina, then an adolescent yearning for a pony or a dog, and Thwaite still considered the creature his daughter's responsibility. Never mind that she was—now he remembered—up in Stockbridge for the month. It still was not, nor could it ever be, his role to clean up cat sick. He kicked off his right shoe with the help of his left, then bent gingerly to remove his left with his hand. As he resumed his stealthy progress down the hall, the sullied brogues remained side by side, startled, as if their wearer had spontaneously combusted.

CHAPTER SIX

The Pope Is Sick

When Danielle had been back a week, long enough to emerge from the fog of jet lag and long enough to discover—she had known it all along—that her Australian project wouldn't fly in spite of all the work she'd put into it, she called the Thwaites to get Marina's phone number in the country. She'd thought to reach Annabel, perhaps (a nonprofit family lawyer and usually out during the week, but sometimes, mysteriously, at home), or more likely Aurora, the housekeeper. Murray Thwaite, by whom she was still, after all these years, intimidated, had his own line in his study and didn't pick up the house phone. But it was Marina herself who answered, her soft, rather tentative voice apparently webbed by sleep.

"Did I wake you up? It's after eleven."

"Mmm."

"What are you doing back here, anyway?"

Marina explained about Julius's visit, the big snowstorm, how they had both felt freaked and claustrophobic in the house, and how she had offered to drive him home to town. "I thought I'd go right back up there," she said, "but it just seemed as though there was a bunch of stuff to take care of here, you know?"

"Like what?"

"You know—messages, e-mails—"

"But you had your computer up there, didn't you?"

"Yeah, but—I don't know. My dad needed a hand with some research, and then he was going to a big dinner, you know, the other night, and he asked if I'd be his date, so I stayed for that . . ." Marina frequently escorted her father to public events. Annabel almost never went, and sometimes people who were unaware of the bond between Murray and Marina mistook her for his trophy wife.

Danielle didn't approve of her friend's uncritical devotion to her father, but there was no point saying anything. Marina would just grow surly. It was one of few topics that could elicit frank cattiness: once she'd even said, "If your father wasn't a builder in Columbus with no clue about your life, I might think you had something to offer, here." After which they hadn't spoken for almost a month, until Marina called to apologize. Danielle's father was a contractor, not a manual laborer, anyway. And just because he was more interested in practical matters than in the type of navel-gazing in which all New Yorkers (including Danielle herself) indulged, did not make him a figure of fun. Danielle's father wasn't easy, sure, but he wasn't a joke. Her irritation lay in her voice when she asked, "How's the book coming along?"

Marina sighed. "Fine. You know. I mean, fine. How was Australia?"

"Great. Tiring. And pointless." Danielle told Marina about Moira and John—Marina didn't much care for Moira, which Danielle suspected had to do with the fact that Danielle looked up to her—and their pretty house by the water. She talked about the meetings she'd had with Aboriginal leaders, with the multicultural affairs minister, about what she'd learned of the appalling history of race relations in Australia. And she told her friend about the meeting with her boss, Nicky, upon her return in which he'd told her that they'd changed their minds and decided to go instead with a program Alex had proposed about what had become of welfare mothers taken off the rolls. "He didn't think the story was 'timely' enough."

"That sucks, Danny. I'm sorry."

"It's timely enough over there, for God's sake. And Jones's book is coming out here in a few months—you know, the guy I told you about that puts the case for reparations here."

"Any chance he'll change his mind again?"

"Minimal. It's all about funding. I think that's the real reason—the cost of sending a crew all the way over there and putting everyone up. But that wasn't the reason he gave."

"So now?"

"Back to the drawing board. I've got an idea for something about the current wave of satirical press and its role in shaping opinion. You know, about the blurring of left and right politics in pure contrarianism. People who aren't *for* anything, just against everything."

"Is there a wave of it?"

"Well, *The Onion* moved here, and there's the *New York Observer,* and *McSweeney's,* and there's a new paper starting up later this year, with this Australian guy I met over there."

"If you say so."

"My idea is that it's kind of like Russia a hundred years ago, the nihilists, right? Like in Dostoyevsky and Turgenev."

"That'll really fly with your bosses."

"I'm serious. Everybody thought they were just disgruntled misfits, and then there was a revolution."

"I don't see it. Revolution in America?"

"I didn't mean that. It's not like I think there's going to be a Marxist regime in twenty years. But it'd be interesting to find out what they think they're doing, what they think they're doing it for."

"For laughs, no?"

"Maybe. It's just an idea, right now."

"Do you want to come over, go out for coffee?"

"I'm at the office." Danielle's office was on Lafayette near Bleecker, far downtown. Marina always seemed to forget that Danielle was employed, that she had to be seen, by people who paid her, to be working.

"Okay, dinner then?"

"Where?"

"I'm broke. I spent my money on a new pair of boots—I really needed them, but I can't afford to go out. We could eat here, though."

"With your parents?"

"I don't even know if they're around tonight. It might just be you, me, and the Pope."

"Is she okay these days?"

"Not really, actually. There've been some unfortunate vomiting incidents. But she won't throw up on your lap or anything. How about seven?"

The Thwaites lived on Central Park West in the upper Eighties, in a building that, while manifestly grand, particularly to someone from Ohio, was by no means the most elegant among its neighbors. Its lobby, for one thing, was little more than a wide corridor, with two drably upholstered wing chairs propped against a wall and, between them, a glass table upon which rested an elaborate but unaesthetic arrangement of silk flowers. The light in the corridor was greenish, dim and lavatorial, barely illuminating the shallowly carved figures that marched, in pseudo-Egyptian fashion, along the pink stone tiles as far as the elevator. The floor, incongruously, was of a black and white parquet, upon which all but the softest slippers echoed ominously. And the elevator itself—paneled, with brass fixtures and a single tiny red velvet stool, presumably for its operator's comfort—seemed again of a different, though no less ancient, era.

And yet, after the inauspicious public space—it was, perhaps, a New Yorker's rare attempt at understatement?—the Thwaites' apartment, which Danielle had now known for more than a decade, was a delicious and resplendent haven. The elevator opened directly into its front hall, a luxury that still struck Danielle as grand, and from the foyer elegant rooms were visible on all sides. To the right, through a generous archway, lay the long, broad swath of the living room, its silk-curtained row of windows giving onto the park, its floor covered by a single immense Oriental rug. There was space enough for the gleaming black lacquer Steinway that nobody seemed to play (Marina had rebelled and refused lessons after the age of eleven), and for a plump and inviting array of sofas and armchairs all covered in ivory and gold, brightened by jewel-colored pillows. On the walls hung modern pictures, which Danielle had been led to understand were largely gifts from artist friends of Marina's parents, although among them was, unexpectedly, a pastel portrait, on brown butcher paper, of Marina as a girl of eight or nine, her black hair pinned up with a ribboned barrette and her puff-sleeved blue dress tightly smocked across her chest: this, surely, was a commission, and one that Danielle could not fully place, as it seemed, in style and tone, to date from the forties or fifties, a moment of frank conservatism in this officially liberal house.

Off the corridor to the left, through a swinging door that remained largely closed, lay the kitchen, and next to it, again through an archway, the dining room, a tribute to Roche Bobois or some other seventies designer. The armless chairs were of sleek black leather, as unembellished as office chairs; the table, unembellished too, was of a burnished wood inlaid with jet trim; and the lighting, which made the sisal rug glow as if gilded, emanated from demi-lunar frosted sconces set about the walls like sentinels. Above the slender sideboard—which, miraculously, was suspended or cantilevered in such a way that it had no legs—hung a substantial canvas, a wavering sea of golds and browns, which was Danielle's favorite picture in the apartment.

From these known public rooms, the Thwaites' world stretched back along the broad hallway—bedrooms, Marina's first, a library, bathrooms, endlessly, till at the very last lay, she knew, Murray Thwaite's inner sanctum, the study in which he worked (overlooking, like the drawing room, the vast inspiration of the park) and which, after all these years, she had never penetrated.

When Danielle arrived at the Thwaites', however, and was shown up by the doorman—a fat-shouldered Serb with a flamboyant mustache and a mournful physiognomy, who seemed to have been squeezed into a uniform two sizes too small—she was greeted not by Marina but by Murray Thwaite himself. He stood in the foyer in his shirtsleeves, his feet in crimson leather slippers, tumbler in hand.

"Mr. Thwaite," Danielle began, in some surprise.

"Murray, my dear. How many times do I have to tell you? Murray, please. You'll make a man feel old." He bent and kissed her cool cheek, pressing his bristled jaw to her smooth one. He smelled of tobacco and a cologne that mimicked gin and tonic (was it Eau Sauvage?), not powerfully but pleasantly. He took her coat and hung it lopsidedly on a hanger.

"Would you like me to take my shoes off? Because it's wet out, and I know some people—"

"Only if you care to reveal your pretty feet." He grinned at her, his square, familiar, and forbidding face in its frame of silver hair suddenly softer, even cute. He had what was called in old novels a twinkle in his eye. He had also, she could see, the drinker's creeping blood vessels across his cheeks. "Actually, I'd keep them on if I were you. There's some nasty stuff around on our floors, lying in wait."

"The cat?"

"Marina told you? I was ambushed myself the other night. But come in, sit down, let me get you a drink."

"Is Marina here? I don't know if she mentioned, but she invited me for dinner."

"She didn't mention, but it doesn't matter. Welcome. She's run out at the last minute—something about a haircut."

"François?"

"That's it." François was a fashionable stylist who had cut

Marina's hair for free since she was seventeen. In return, she let him take occasional publicity pictures of her coiffure, and once, years ago, she had participated in a fashion show. The only inconvenience was that he did her hair only when he had a spare moment—a cancellation, or after hours. Clearly an opening had suddenly presented itself. "She's already been gone almost an hour. She should be back soon."

"And Annabel?"

"Held up at the office. Some kid beaten black and blue she has to keep from being sent home tonight. Filthy job."

Danielle was plumped in the center of the large white sofa. Feeling small and embarrassed, she smoothed her skirt and smoothed the white cushions around her, and smoothed, unnecessarily, the tights upon her calves before accepting a glass of wine—white, at her request—from Murray Thwaite, who remained standing.

"Please," she said, "don't let me keep you from whatever you were doing—I'm sure you're busy—I can just wait here till she comes."

"Don't be silly. I can't think of a nicer interruption. I was just getting fed up with the state of the union one more time. It can wait till later. So tell me what you've been up to, since last we spoke?"

Danielle wondered when they had last spoken, or spoken for longer than it took to exchange the most trivial of politenesses. She could not know, of course, that she resembled Roanne Levine, but with a slightly smaller mouth, better breasts, and without the aggravating laugh. She could not know that Marina's father was seeing her as if for the first time.

"I've been to Australia," she said brightly, grateful to have something of at least possible interest to her host. "To research a program I was working on—but which seems to be doomed."

Murray Thwaite then asked about the program, and the reasons for its fate. He said he knew Jones, the author of the book Danielle had read, and that he was interesting but a hothead and a lover of the limelight. "I'm not sure he wrote it so as to get whites actually to *do* anything. More a question of getting famous, and getting his ass in an endowed chair out at—where is it he teaches again?"

They did, in fact, have a conversation, one in which Danielle forgot, in time, to be nervous, and lost the urge to fidget. Murray Thwaite perched first on the arm of a chair, then on the piano stool, his long, restless body folding over toward her so that it seemed, if he leaned any farther, that his chin might meet his knees. He was distracted only by the Pope, to whose plaintive and apparently unmotivated yowl he growled, "Scat. Scat, you damned creature, scat."

Annabel came home before Marina did, bearing a bag of groceries and with her trenchcoat flapping. "Christ," she called to Murray from the hallway, before she knew that Danielle was there, "what a god-awful disaster of a day." When she rounded the corner to the living room and spied her daughter's friend upon the sofa—or rather, by then standing, as Danielle had risen, almost guiltily, at the first sound of Annabel's arrival— her face unfurrowed and the rasp in her voice melted away: "Danielle, sweetheart, it's been ages! Let me drop my coat and then I want a proper *hug* . . ."

Danielle then endured a further twenty awkward minutes in the Thwaites' kitchen while Annabel—her graying blond hair slipping slightly from its bun, but her oyster-colored pantsuit

(Armani, Danielle thought) impeccable in spite of the god-awful disastrous day—dithered amiably, but with what Danielle identified as covert irritation, over whether the pork chops she'd brought back could be stretched to feed four; until she decided, at Murray's urging, that they ought simply to order Chinese and be done with it.

As this minor domestic drama was played out, Danielle had the peculiar sensation of having usurped her friend's role in the Thwaite family, and more than that, of having usurped it at some moment in the distant past, a decade or more ago: she felt like a teenager, as she used to feel in the kitchen of her parents' house in Columbus (before the divorce, of course), and she was suddenly, powerfully aware of the profound oddity of Marina's present life, a life arrested at, or at least returned to, childhood. Danielle couldn't imagine eating nightly with her parents, not only because they now lived in different states and didn't speak to each other, but because she was entering the fourth decade of her life and hadn't been through the wearying rigamarole of family life for anything more than a few almost supportable days since she was seventeen and had gone off to college.

By the time Marina appeared on the scene—with a perfect but sensuously rumpled bob that only her black not-quite-straight hair could successfully have carried—Danielle had decided that her friend needed to be rescued. Her own life—a studio on West Twelfth Street in which the foot of her bed ended only four feet from her so-called kitchen—seemed to her Spartan enough, in an era in which so many of their peers had sprouted paper fortunes and idled in giant lofts, or even brownstones, pretending to develop dot-coms of inexplicable function. The idea that at thirty Marina couldn't point even to a futon or a folding chair and claim it as her own was perhaps, in some vanished ethos, admirable; but it was also faintly pathetic.

Yet Marina, in her parents' kitchen, did not appear pathetic; the thought didn't seem to have crossed her mind. She twirled to show off what she—or rather, François—called "the bounce" of her haircut, and then propped herself against the counter within reach of an open bag of potato chips, occasionally dipping in a dainty hand and plucking a lone chip upon which to nibble. (Danielle noticed this because her own tendency was to grab a handful at a time and methodically crunch her way through them; as a result of which she forebore from taking any Thwaite potato chips at all.) Marina related amusingly what she had seen in François's salon, a spat she'd witnessed between two colorists over the highlights in a blond woman's hair. "She had half her hair in foil, half not, and she was watching these two guys behind her in the mirror like a tennis match. You should've seen the expression on her face," Marina said, waving a chip. "It was priceless."

While Marina spoke, Annabel took out the placemats and cutlery, the plates and glasses. The only interruption she offered was a generalized "Chopsticks?," which was met with approval; so she took four sets of chopsticks from the cutlery drawer as well. Danielle helped her to set the dining room table, so that Marina was really speaking only to her father. He uttered benign appreciative sounds and even laughed, but was simultaneously reading an article in *The New York Review of Books* that had arrived in the mail and been brought up by Annabel. Marina, unfazed by this divided attention, spoke on.

Was Annabel annoyed? Danielle wondered, as she folded a napkin (cloth—Aurora even ironed them) at each place. Neither her husband nor her daughter did anything to help, and yet Annabel was the only one among them who had put in a day at an office—well, Annabel and she herself, the unexpected guest, now diligently lending a hand. Annabel didn't *look* annoyed; she looked distracted. Danielle remembered the beaten child Murray had referred to.

"Did you have a long day?"

"Sorry?" Annabel almost started. "Long day? Yep. Tough case. The kid's really a problem. He wants to go home, and his parents—his mother and stepfather, that is—want him home and no foster family will touch him because of his record—he pushed a foster mother down the stairs and she broke both legs—and you'd think the obvious answer would be just to send him home, make everyone happy. But he's had a dislocated shoulder, a broken wrist, and two black eyes in the past six months. That's what being at home is like. He wants to be there to protect his mother."

"What's your job in all this?"

"I represent the kid. That's what my agency does." Annabel had founded the organization, when Marina was just a little girl, a nonprofit that worked with social services. "Somebody's got to look out for him."

"The kid? Wow. How old is he?"

"Fourteen. And big. Not so much tall—big. But the stepfather's a lot bigger, in every way that matters." She paused in her work, put her hands on her hips, surveyed the dining table. Next door, in the kitchen, they could hear Murray talking now, something about his recent book tour. Marina was silent.

"He loves to knit—can you imagine it?" Annabel began again. At first, Danielle didn't know what she was talking about. "Somewhere in all the sadness and violence, there's this gentle kid. His grandmother taught him how, and he does it in the waiting room—a big stripy scarf, or a hat with purple snowflakes on it. He's bent over those needles, waiting, his tongue sticking out while he works away. So earnest. His grandma's in a home now. Alzheimer's. And I feel like all he wants is to crawl into her lap, or my lap, or anybody's lap, who could please, for once, just take care of him. This big, scary kid, capable of all kinds of mayhem, and he loves to knit." Annabel sighed. "It's awful—he could be tried as an adult, these days, if he did any real damage. And I frankly think that's his aim. Not the trial, of course. The damage. He hates his stepfather—who wouldn't, after all? The guy's an abusive brute and a drunk. And I think he wants to kill him."

"I bet that happens a lot."

"No, I mean, I think he really, literally, wants to kill him. And he's just dumb enough, poor boy, and just smart enough. So Danny, you can imagine, I had to make sure he wasn't going home tonight."

"What did you tell the judge?" Danielle assumed there was a judge involved somewhere in this case.

"Not that. As you might imagine."

"Poor kid? He sounds like a nightmare."

Annabel looked directly at Danielle. "He *is* a nightmare. But it's complicated."

"Poor you, then."

Annabel gave a brisk smile. "Doesn't do anyone any good to

think that way. 'Buck up, duckie' was my college roommate's motto. And quite right, too."

However frequently Annabel repeated this disturbingly Waspy mantra (where had she gone to college? Vassar? Bryn Mawr?), Danielle didn't think it had had much impact on Marina, who was, at that moment, paying the Chinese food delivery man in the foyer with her father's credit card. Or maybe that wasn't quite right: maybe Marina was so busy bucking herself up that she had forgotten, or never noticed, that she was standing on nothing, poised in the void. The way, earlier, she had been talking so vividly, so amusingly, to no one at all.

After supper—Danielle found the Chinese food tasty, particularly the moo shoo pork, but it was also lukewarm and very swiftly glutinous on their plates—Murray Thwaite pushed back his chair and revealed, yet again, his impressive height. "Ladies," he said, running a hand through his silver hair. "If you'll excuse me?" Then, "Marina darling, did you print out those dates for me?"

"It was printing when I left for François, Daddy. I'll just get it for you."

"And Marina darling," he called after her, "your hair looks divine." He turned back to the table. "Maybe half an inch too short? But it'll grow. Good to see you, Danielle. You're looking quite beautiful yourself, you know." He kissed her; she blushed and muttered. "And darling"—to his wife—"will you tell me when it's eleven? That idiot is on Charlie's show tonight."

"If I'm still up I will. If not, I'll get the girls to do it."

Annabel and Danielle cleared the plates, and Marina resurfaced just as her mother finished putting them in the dish-washer.

"I think Popey's done it again, Mom. There's a stink in the living room, but I can't find it."

Annabel sighed. "Off you go, you two. I'll take care of it."

The only thing about Chinese is that the whole place smells of it afterward," said Marina, as she shut the door to her bedroom behind them and moved to light the scented candle on her dresser. "Lavender of Provence okay?"

"I don't smell a thing."

"Moo shoo pork? You don't still smell it? Ugh." Marina gave an exaggerated shudder. "How about a little Chopin?"

"Whatever."

Marina's room was disorganized, in as charming a way as its owner. The chair at her desk was draped with discarded clothes, her dresser cluttered with lipsticks, pens, and an uncapped bottle of perfume, its amber liquid illuminated by the candle's flickering flame. The bed was messily made up, imprinted with the ghost of Marina's supine form, and scattered with a few books and a splayed sweater. The lamps shone low, their light eggy, and through the half-open closet door, Danielle could see competing bursts and tufts of clothing and a jumbled pile of shoes.

"Your mother must be exhausted," Danielle said as she moved the laptop to the floor, its little green light glowing, and settled into an oyster-colored armchair, lifting her feet onto the ottoman. Marina, busy choosing a CD from the shelf by her stereo, didn't reply. "I feel guilty," Danielle went on, "making extra work and then not helping." What she meant was that she felt guilty about how little Marina had helped.

"Don't be ridiculous, Danny. She's not doing anything she wouldn't do if you weren't here." Marina flopped onto her bed, which was richly pillowed and covered with a terra-cotta duvet dotted with smiling suns. Like everything else in Marina's evening, it reminded Danielle of adolescence.

"M," she said, "is this really going okay?"

"What?"

Danielle gestured broadly. "This. Everything. The book. Living at home, for God's sake. It can't be easy."

Marina put her hands behind her head and closed her eyes. "No. Of course not, if you really want to know. How could it be okay?" She opened her eyes—they were a beautiful deep blue, almost purple, bright and clear, the color her father's eyes must once have been, before they became popped and bloodshot. "But what else am I supposed to do? I'm completely broke, and my parents have been really nice about it, but you see what it's like. It's driving me crazy." There was a silence. "I just don't know what I can do," she said again.

"You could get a job, sweetie."

"A job?" Marina snorted. "And how would I get this book finished then?"

"Well, I don't know. But people *do,* you know. They work at night, or early in the morning, on their own stuff. Even a part-time job. It just seems to me you really need your own space."

"I wouldn't know how to get a job, by now. I really need to finish the book, that's all. That's the first thing."

"But—" Danielle paused. "Just tell me true, *are* you going to finish it? When are you going to finish it?"

"It's due in August."

"Wasn't it due last August? And the Christmas before that?"

Marina sat up. "So I'm slow. So it's late. What's your point, exactly?"

"I don't have a point. I think you're stuck, is all. And if things aren't getting better, then they're getting worse, you know what I mean?"

"Did Julius tell you about his latest love disaster?"

"Okay. I'll leave it alone. But think about it. We can all help you find a job. I can ask around. *You* could ask around. Hell, your dad could ask around."

"Fine." Marina crossed her legs in the lotus position, pausing to pull back the flesh of her buttocks. She sat up very straight and took a deep breath. "I don't want to go into this again, because I know it just bugs you and you'll tell me to get over it, but you don't have any idea what it's like to be Murray Thwaite's daughter. I don't want some job just because he got it for me, and I can't see just taking any dumb thing because it's somehow 'good for me' to have a job. I've got to believe, I mean, I *know* that I'm more serious than that."

"You mean, you're better than that."

"Whatever. I want to—it sounds so trite, but I want to make a difference. By writing. Doing something important. And I don't mean, I don't know, covering Staten Island PTA meetings for the *New York Times*"—a college friend of theirs had recently, enthusiastically, taken such a position—"which we both know I couldn't get even if I wanted to."

"Everybody starts somewhere."

"What is this? Cliché night? I'm starting with my book. It's just taking a while, a bit longer than I expected."

Danielle made the same sweeping movement with her hands that she had made before. "Whatever," she said. "It doesn't matter. So, what about Julius's latest broken heart?"

CHAPTER SEVEN

"Introducing Murray Thwaite"
by Roanne Levine (newspaper staff)

Few contemporary journalists are as versatile, as erudite, and as controversial as Murray Thwaite. Now sixty, Thwaite is best known for his monthly articles in *The Action,* and his frequent essays in *The New Yorker* and *The New York Review of Books.* He has also written or edited twelve books, including *Rage in the System* and *Underground Warfare in Latin America.* His most recent book is a collection of his essays about late capitalism, called *Waiting for the Fat Lady to Sing.* Thwaite appeared on campus recently to address Professor Triplett's History 395 seminar, "Resistance in Postwar America," where he spoke about the work he did in his youth in the anti–Vietnam War movement. A tall, handsome man with thick silver hair, a square jaw, and piercing blue eyes, his tweed jacket is elegant and a little old-fashioned. He waved his hands a lot when he spoke. He is a dynamic speaker, and unafraid of the most challenging questions. One student asked whether he really thought his antiwar activism had made any difference, and Mr. Thwaite literally pounded the table when he answered, "Absolutely. It may not have done as much or worked as fast as we hoped—not fast enough to save thousands of young lives on both sides of the conflict—but you'd better believe it made a difference. If there's any purpose to a democracy," he went on, "it's to ensure that the voice of the people is heard, and that the will of the people is abided by. That's not idealism, that's a fact. And a responsibility. Every one of you in this room has a responsibility to be educated, to form your own opinions based on facts, and to educate others."

Mr. Thwaite, a longtime New Yorker, was born upstate in Watertown, near the Canadian border, in 1940. The son of a schoolteacher and a homemaker, he was the elder of two children. He earned a scholarship to Harvard in the late 1950s, where he studied History and graduated in 1961 at the age of twenty. After spending a year in Paris on a Fulbright scholarship studying the French Resistance Movement during World War II, he traveled around Europe for another year before coming back home and settling in New York. He started his journalism career while he was overseas: "I wrote to a man at the *Boston Globe,* the father of one of my classmates at Harvard, and asked if he'd be willing to look at my work if I sent it. He said yes, and the first piece I sent him was a feature about how Berliners were feeling about the [Berlin] Wall, which was brand new then. After that, I went to England and interviewed striking miners. He published both pieces, and told me to keep 'em coming. Franco's Spain, democracy in Turkey, I just got going. I went to Sicily and wrote about a Mafia town. It was a great year."

I asked Mr. Thwaite if he'd considered staying in Europe and becoming a foreign correspondent: "I suppose I did, for a while," he answered. "But I thought there was a lot to come home for. There was a lot going on. Once Kennedy was assassinated—that clinched it for me. I came back in time to travel the South and speak to people about the Civil Rights Act. That's also when I first got involved in the death penalty issue, which is still something I care a lot about today. And of course there was already escalation in South Asia, the war was already in full swing, so there was that, too."

Mr. Thwaite, a heavy smoker, kindly agreed to be interviewed after class, and we had our conversation over drinks at Mulligan's, where he seemed to feel right at home. If he'd been wearing a tie, he would've loosened it. At one point, he asked me when I was born, and when I said "1981," he laughed. "Do you know where I was in 'Eighty-one?" he said. "I was in El Salvador and Guatemala, reporting on what the U.S. government was doing—covertly, of course—down there. I bet you can't even imagine it."

Mr. Thwaite, who married Annabel Chase, a children's rights lawyer, in 1968 ("I wore velvet pants," he says, "and she had flowers in her hair"), has one daughter, Marina, who was born in 1970. She graduated from Brown in '93 and is working on her first book. "I never told my daughter to become a writer," he said. "Quite the opposite. I figure, if you can do something else, do. Because it's a stimulating life, but an uncertain one. I did bring her up though to understand that integrity is everything, it's all you've got. And that if you have a voice, a gift, you're morally bound to exploit it."

Mr. Thwaite has most recently used his voice to criticize dishonesty in the Clinton administration. "I don't care what a guy does with his pecker," Mr. Thwaite says of Clinton, "but he lied to the American people as though they were his wife, and he lied to her, too. Not to mention his policies. If that's what liberalism has come to, we're in trouble. Invading or bombing overseas to distract us, whenever the heat is on at home. What about Sudan, remember that?" He goes on, "The liberals in this country deserve better. Christ, Jimmy Carter was better. This guy has set us back twenty years." He doesn't have much patience for George W. Bush, either, whom he calls "our puppet dictator by decree." The new president "wasn't even elected" and "has fewer brains than my Abyssinian cat. An exceptionally gifted feline, by the way."

Always funny, Mr. Thwaite is also deadly serious: "None of this is a game," he says of politics and journalism. "It may look like it, it may look like a circus sometimes, but that's only from the luxurious vantage point of the United States in 2001. Ask people anywhere else—Bosnia, Rwanda, the Middle East, sure, but also China, Algeria, Russia, even Western Europe, and they'll remind you of what you ought to know: this is life and death stuff. There's nothing more important than this."

Mr. Thwaite, who has taught in the past at NYU and at the journalism school here, may be coming to teach again at Columbia sometime soon. "I'd love to," he says, flashing a broad grin and lighting another cigarette. "I love to teach."

CHAPTER EIGHT

An American Scholar

Frederick Tubb lay in the bath, carefully holding his book above the water with both hands. Borrowed from the library, it was encased in plastic and so better protected from his inevitably damp fingers than had been many other books similarly handled, but it was a heavy volume and he had already imagined letting it fall wholesale into the tub, where it would swiftly encounter the floating white bulk of his torso, though not before being soaked and ruined. The book was a novel: *Infinite Jest* by David Foster Wallace. He was about a hundred pages in, and he couldn't tell what he thought about it. Bits of it made him laugh, but he couldn't seem to keep track of the broader premise, or plot (was there a premise, or plot?). He often found this, in one way or another, with novels, but with this one more than with many. He didn't much like reading novels—he preferred history or philosophy—or poetry, although he could read only a little poetry at a time, because when a poem "spoke to him" it was as if a brilliant, agonizing light had been turned upon some tiny, private cell of his soul. Larkin had this effect—but he had heard a lot about this one, first from kids at Oswego whom he didn't particularly respect, but then from people on the Net, and in particular from this book discussion group that he'd sort of joined. They weren't reading *Infinite Jest* now; they'd read it last fall while he was wasting his time in microeconomics along with two hundred other duped freshmen, or trying to stay awake in Professor Holden's composition class full of jabbering fools. But a few members of the online discussion kept referring to it, like it was the Bible or something. A definition of the zeitgeist, one person had written, a particularly lively female correspondent on whom Bootie had a virtual crush. So he was reading it to catch up. He was reading it to be educated, which was, along with self-reliance, his current great aim. To be able to comment knowledgeably on one of the voices of his time.

The bathroom around him was steamy in the early afternoon sun. Its fixtures, mustard yellow, were oddly small for the space: a pedestal sink and a low toilet and the bathtub in which he lay, barely covered by water, his knees bent up so he might keep his toes submerged. The blue linoleum, flecked with iridescence, was largely covered by a fringed blue rug, and another, U-shaped, decorated the toilet's base like a Christmas-tree skirt. His mother had made the frilled blue curtains at the window, and the now-balding towels—also sky blue—had been chosen, long ago, to match the color scheme. It was the bathroom he had always known, with its knocking pipes and frosted glass, its white tiles laid, not quite straight, by his father before he was born. Bootie looked around him, sighed, feeling at once safe and oppressed in his bath, wanting to stay there all afternoon and wanting to escape forever at the same time.

If only it weren't quite so long, he thought as the water around him cooled. He lifted the plug chain with his toe and let some run out, even as he flicked on the hot tap with his right hand to rebalance the temperature. His left wrist wavered under the full burden of the book, but he did not drop it. Maybe he could read just half of it? Would that be enough? Because he had a stack of several other novels he'd assigned himself to get through by June, and they were long, too: *Moby-Dick, Gravity's Rainbow, War and Peace.* The very thought of them made him sleepy.

His mother was mercifully out at school this afternoon, explaining to her students about the rice crop in China or the still shifting borders of the former Soviet countries, information they weren't listening to and had forgotten before the day was out. Bootie himself had sat in her classroom, not so many years before, and once the class was done with, he'd asked his sister, Sarah, also a graduate of Mom's Geography, a few years before Bootie, what had stayed with her over time. She'd said, "Jeez, Bootie, I don't know. I remember that we did South America and the countries were totally confusing to me. Doesn't some place down there speak Portuguese instead of Spanish? But mostly I remember being embarrassed for Mom, when somebody like that Jody guy—remember him?—would act out and Mom would turn really red and seem like she might cry. Or like in winter, when we had class first period, and her nose would always run, and I didn't know which was worse, seeing that glistening drop hanging off her nostril, or the really geeky way she had of rubbing it with a Kleenex all the time. That's what I mostly remember, Bootie, is being embarrassed."

At least Judy Tubb didn't know that her kids had been embarrassed by her. It was but one of the many facts she didn't know about her children. Like the fact that he was angry, too: angry with her for expecting so little of him, for holding him so close. For being someone who couldn't see the wider world, the world beyond Watertown, in which anything might be possible. She thought her brother, the extraordinary Murray Thwaite, was a man of little consequence, while she revered the memory of Bootie's father, a man Bootie, too, had loved— a gentle, mild man, good with his hands, the man who as a schoolboy had been universally liked and infrequently remembered. But he had known, even on the cusp of adolescence, before his father grew sick, and gentler, and quieter, and above all sadder (so that sad and sick were horribly what most remained, for Bootie, at least), that Bert Tubb was not a man who could fathom his son. A subscriber to *Time* and *National Geographic,* he had been a reader of neither, a man who lived for his family, for the football thrown in the yard of a Saturday, and the reassuring ritual of six o'clock supper in the paneled dining room (meat loaf with gravy on Sundays, always), and who eyed his plump, fumbling, bibliophilic boy with loving alarm. He wanted Bootie to be good enough at everything, just good *enough,* to get out and play, and even near his death had expressed the strange (to Bootie) worry that without a father, Bootie would be stuck all the time in his books. You couldn't disagree with his mother's love for such a man—he'd been a very good man—but Bootie couldn't understand, quite, in what scheme of things Bert Tubb was elevated above Murray Thwaite, his mother's own brother, alive, for one thing, and, in every admirable way, extraordinary.

Moreover, Judy Tubb so doted upon Bootie that it pained him—she didn't know how much. Sometimes it actually choked him, like a collar, a thick, ungiving collar at his throat. Or like Bootie's life now: she didn't understand it in the least, seemed to think that he'd left Oswego because of some broken romance, or because he hadn't the athletic prowess of the roommates he'd dubbed Lurk and Jerk. But it wasn't anything so primitive as that: it had been a revelation, one Tuesday morning at nine, two weeks before Thanksgiving, when he'd been making his way across the frost-tipped lawn listening to Ellen, a girl from his high school who lived two floors below him and who even at that sleepy hour was chirruping like a monkey and cracking gum between her teeth. They were on their way to microeconomics ("I can't get no, marginal utility . . ."), to the raked concrete auditorium in which they huddled twice a week, and Ellen, no fool at least by Watertown standards, said, "I heard from Amy, you know, that sophomore? That Watson has this whole code for recycling exams? So, like, if we get the finals from the past eight years, they're all in the library, right? So if we, like, sit down with them and figure out the code, or maybe Amy's roommate has it in her notes from last year, right? Then we'll know, like, exactly what's on the exam. Cool, eh?"

She had looked up at him in the powdery morning light, her breath a cloudy puff emerging from her mouth, her hair plastered, wet, doglike, to her scalp, her piggy, upturned nose red not just at its broad end but across its shallow bridge as well, and he'd looked at her and she had said, "Bootie? Are you even listening?," and it was as if the morning sun had just crossed the horizon, although it was already fully day. He had a revelation. What he said was "Or else, Ellen, we could just study for the exam. Which might be as effective as Amy's stupid scheme." But what he thought, which didn't come to him so much in words as with a visceral force, was "This is a farce. I am living, we are all living, a complete farce."

Over the course of that day and the days that followed, this
initial realization opened, like a flower, and refined itself. In
some muted way, its seeds had been with him for a long time,
and certainly since the previous March, when he'd learned that
Harvard had indeed given him a place (he could still feel the
elation, if he allowed himself to; that, too, had been visceral;
and so fleeting), but that they weren't offering him a proper
scholarship, just a load of complicated forms to fill out and the
promise of a mountain of debt. He'd read these documents
repeatedly and had even called the college admissions office
from school for clarification, and when what he thought he'd
understood proved indeed to be true, he resolved never to tell
his mother that he'd been accepted to Harvard, simply to pretend it had never happened. He knew that she would try to
make the numbers work, would frown over the papers and talk
about second mortgages and selling her mother's diamond ring
(after all, Uncle Murray went to Harvard, didn't he? he could
hear her jaunty voice saying), and even then, he could see it
ahead of time, she would end up with her head in her hands at
the kitchen table because it simply couldn't be managed. He
told Mr. Duncan, the college counselor, that he really wanted
to go to Oswego because it was close by, and he didn't want
some stupid, snooty private college, that he'd only applied to
prove to himself he could get in, and please not to mention to
his mom about Harvard because she'd be after him to go there,
and Duncan was, of course, dumb enough to buy it and
clapped Bootie on the back with some guff about how wise
he was and the greatness of the Oswego football team. "They
aren't great," Bootie thought. "They're just local, and they're all
you know."

Not that there was anything wrong with Mr. Duncan's enthusiasm. But the realization that had germinated in Bootie's brain was that what might be good enough for Mr. Duncan, or for Ellen Kovacs, was not going to be good enough for Frederick Tubb. The Land of Lies in which most people were apparently content to live—in which you paid money to an institution and went out nightly to get drunk instead of reading the books and then tried to calculate some half-assed scheme by which you could cheat on your exams, and then, at the end of the day, presumably simply on account of the financial transaction between you, or more likely your parents, and said institution, you declared yourself *educated*—was not sufficient for Bootie. And no matter what his mother or his sister said (believing, of course, that he hadn't gotten a place in the Ivy League), or Mr. Duncan (believing it to be Bootie's heartfelt choice), it wasn't just the same to go to Oswego as it would be to go to Harvard. The two weren't remotely comparable. He knew that at Harvard there were probably some people caught in the Land of Lies, but he knew, too, that there would be— or rather, as it didn't matter now, that there *would have been*—other people, serious people, like himself.

So Bootie had called an end to the farce. He didn't care about diplomas or exams or institutional endorsements (although, more than once since returning to his mother's home and to his old bed, he had dreamed that he was at Harvard, long, full, sun-filled dreams in which he seemed, oddly, to wear a suit); he cared about learning. And so, with the application that had distinguished him throughout high school, that had transformed him into a figure of at least grudging respect, he was going to teach himself. But of course all his mother saw—all the world saw—was idleness and unemployment. She'd even asked him last week in an anxious whisper whether he spent all that time on the computer looking at pornography. She was clearly going to make his education difficult. All of Watertown was. Perhaps the entire world would, too. But it was obvious that Frederick Tubb needed to strike out on his own, to find a way and a place to pursue his autodidactic course unimpeded. He would shuck this life, a snake shedding its skin, and with it the great, fingering neediness of his mother. Let Sarah deal with that: Sarah who wanted nothing better than two kids and two cars and maybe *Oprah* in the afternoon. He would go somewhere where nobody would ever call him "Bootie," and where he could have conversations about Kierkegaard and Nietzsche, about Camus and Kurt Vonnegut. He was thinking, as he lay in the bath with David Foster Wallace, turning the pages and pretending to absorb their contents, of going to New York. It seemed silly, even absurd, an unattainable aspiration. But part of him still unacknowledgeably rued his decision to turn down Harvard, to cleave to the attainable. And he didn't want to be someone who thwarted himself, his own worst enemy.

Maybe it would take a little time to sort out the details. He didn't know many people in New York, beyond Uncle Murray and Aunt Annabel. He wanted them, to be close to them, to be granted access to their mysterious world. His uncle was, without question, a great man; and Bootie would try to be worthy of him. He had to try. He didn't have any money to speak of. But he did still have his car, a red '89 Civic with muffler problems and a curling trail of rust along its underbelly, the inevitable and almost endearing result of an automotive life spent in the snow belt, like smoker's cough or a miner's black lung. The car wasn't worth much, and he would be loath to sell it, but it was something, a way out in the first instance.

CHAPTER NINE

Rumpelstiltskin

Julius wore his one Agnès B. suit, a charcoal wool with fine, almost imperceptible pin stripes and narrow lapels that revealed, to the trained eye, its not inconsiderable age, and yet which he liked to think, in its slight unstylishness, showed him to be careless rather than modish, *above fashion.* At parties, he referred to it as his "signature suit," hoping thereby to imply that there were others, perhaps a whole rack of them, to which he was not quite so partial. But of course in this context he did not refer to it at all: in this context, with a frayed but expertly ironed dress shirt (he was not his mother's son for nothing) and a slender but amusing paisley tie picked up at a thrift shop, the suit was merely a uniform.

Herded out of the subway and into the harried stream of suited men and women that flowed along the early morning canyons of the business district, Julius held himself upright and strove to maneuver with his usual grace. It was all about acting, merely playing a role, and nobody who knew him needed ever to know. He slid into the office block on Water Street and presented himself to the receptionist at Blake, Zellman and Weaver on the thirty-eighth floor. She, a trim black woman with one blue eye and one brown one, scrutinized the suit and, he feared, the shirt's peeling collar, before showing him to his desk.

Rather than gawp at the office around him, at the spread of desks and low partitions that so resembled a human parking lot, he focused instead, as they proceeded, upon her high, full behind, clad in black silk, which rose and fell with each step, and on the rustling of her stockings as her thighs met beneath the cloth. It occurred to him that many men would find this sexy, would find sexy her brazen and uneven stare, and the close, high cap of her hair. She was probably flirted with, he thought, even harassed. Her life was lived in what was, to him, a foreign language.

She, too, seemed to know this, as she turned to survey him once again, indicating the broad, fake-wood desk with its humming computer and said, "Here. Mr. Cohen will be in within the half hour." She crossed her arms. "I don't know if Rosalie left any instructions. I guess you'd better just wait. Or ask Esther." She pointed at the desk next to his, or rather next to Rosalie's, as if it were animate. "If you need me, dial one-nine-three," she said, and swished away.

Julius installed himself in the plump upholstered chair, fiddling with the plastic pump beneath its seat to adjust the height—Rosalie was clearly short—and resting his hands on the plastic armrests while he rolled the chair back and forth. Beneath the desk waited a pair of tiny black pumps with high heels—yes, she was short—and next to the computer stood a framed posed photograph of a man, woman, and small girl, this last in a pink tulle party dress with a broad sash. The mother was presumably Rosalie: next to the photo was a mug, clean (he checked), which said "#1 MOM" on the side. She had very white teeth, and dark curls like her daughter, and matte, olive skin. He imagined that she and her family were on vacation in Mexico or Cuba or El Salvador, taking the little one to see her grandparents. Although perhaps she was just at home in Brooklyn—no, Queens, perhaps even the Bronx—tending the girl in illness, or awaiting the delivery of a new fridge. No, they'd told him a week. They wanted him all week. So it was planned, a vacation, even if she was at home. Maybe they were moving house. Maybe Esther would know, when she arrived.

Julius needed money this badly. He was temping. He'd sworn he wouldn't do it again—he hated the condescending glares of women like the receptionist, the peremptory demands of his temporary bosses, the stale office air and the tedium of the hours—but now that he was forced to, he'd sworn to himself that nobody he knew would ever know. It would be only for a few weeks. It was too shaming: he couldn't expose this vulnerability, this rank need for cash, even to his dearest friends. He knew it was a strangeness in him—as if Danielle, say, would criticize! But there was always Marina, and he didn't know which was worse, her contempt or her compassion. No: let them think he was at the gym all day, or trawling the Web for trysts. Let them think he was sleeping, for all he cared, or taking drugs, as long as they didn't picture this. Twenty dollars an hour. He could type fast, and he needed it.

Esther, when she arrived, proved not to be the buxom, forty-something Jamaican woman he had imagined, but rather an earnest white girl of about his own age, dressed in an oddly Victorian blouse with ruffled cuffs and a sort of pinafore. Shy, but amiable, with a soft, high voice, she showed him the men's room, the coffee machine, the Xerox room. She introduced him to the guys in the mailroom, two sharply dressed black youths who looked—or so he thought—admiringly at the Agnès B., and to Shelley and Marie who, along with himself and Esther, shared the dividing walls of their enclave. He wanted to ask her what, exactly, the offices of Blake, Zellman and Weaver were *for,* what Mr. Cohen himself did all day; but before he was able to, Mr. Cohen arrived.

Again, Julius's expectations were confounded: Cohen— "David, *please*"—was not a fifty-year-old with a paunch, a wedding ring embedded in his puffy fourth finger, and the whiff of Metro North on his clothes, but rather a slender, famil- iar-looking young man with trendy glasses and a bespoke suit who met Julius's gaze with a quizzical expression. Above all, Julius was aware of two discomfiting facts: Cohen—David— was younger than he, Julius; and he was gay.

Did Julius find David attractive because he was—with wiry dark hair and pale skin, a strong nose and jaw, deep-set dark eyes—or merely because of the thrill of potential, the unlikeli- hood of being coupled to such a person in the teeming, heterosexist corporate culture? Perhaps the frisson was born of the taboo, amid all that fluorescence, the acres of discreet carpet, of the sense that Julius might have to *convince* David of his own worth in this setup, which cast him as dogsbody rather than an enviable and ethereal man-about-town? Perhaps, he knew Danielle would have said, it was Pavlovian, merely an obsessive introduction of desire into an environment in which it had no place, Julius as ever seeing the world in terms of Eros, a particular power play in a world of other, more concrete powers? Or maybe he felt the infinitesimal lingering of David's gaze upon him, a look not merely of recognition but almost (could he have imagined it?) of appreciation . . . and yet, in no time, David was piling tasks upon his desk, pink slips with notes scrawled upon them and fat legal documents with emendations that required Julius to find the original files in the orderly but mysterious morass of Rosalie's computer.

The company, it seemed, engaged in middle man activity, the procuring of rights—of abstractions—that permitted, elsewhere, the actual trading of information (also abstract) for huge sums of money. Which was, of course, itself abstract. It was as though the entire office were generating and moving, acquiring and passing on, hypotheticals, a trade in ideas, or hopes, to which value somehow accrued. Why was it, Julius wondered as his long fingers chattered at the keyboard, and Rosalie and her family grinned at him in the corner of his eye, that no value seemed to accrue to his own ideas, his own hopes? Were they simply not abstract *enough*? But that wasn't entirely true: some value did adhere to him—people who read his pieces knew his name; indeed, he couldn't be entirely sure that David didn't know his name, which would be half relief and half humiliation—but it wasn't a monetary value. He couldn't ever, on the strength of his opinions, have ordered a bespoke suit like David's; and yet David, procuring and negotiating rights for what amounted to someone else's intellectual property, probably would have been shocked to realize that his secretary was, in some public way, more powerful than he. Julius could stop thousands of people from buying a book or seeing a film. He did it all the time.

Julius was not someone who still believed, the way Marina and even, to some degree, Danielle did, in a moral or intellectual value inherent in something that society did not want. He knew too well—he'd had to know it, ever since the days of Danville, Michigan—that if nobody wanted it, a thing—even genius, a word he had used unsparingly about himself in youth—was useless. But he couldn't seem to gauge the connection between desire and reward. He knew how to create desire in others—desire for himself, that is—and in darker moments, of which there were plenty, he exploited that knowledge, because it made him feel better, and because he could. But he couldn't figure out where desire (other people's) turned to riches (for him).

If nothing else, David, all of twenty-eight at the most, must have some understanding of how to turn air—or straw, for that matter—into gold. He determined to attach himself to David, to exploit the delicate current of electricity that ran between them, and in the course of his week at Baker, Zellman and Weaver, to learn from his boss. He might even be able to pull a brief but sparkling affair from the escapade (the frame, beneath the suit, looked compact and enticing; then again, it was a very good suit). Julius decided to charm David, to stifle his own stirrings of embarrassment at his minion's role, and to strut out on Mr. Cohen's arm before Friday night. Let the receptionist see it, too.

CHAPTER TEN

Talking to a Grown Child

Because his desk faced the window, Murray Thwaite did not at first realize that his daughter had opened the door to his study, directly behind his back, had entered, and had sat, cross-legged, upon the divan against the wall. To have accomplished this silently was no mean feat, because the divan, untouched by Aurora in accordance with his instructions, was piled end to end with manuscripts and file folders, with stacks of hardcover volumes riffled by Post-it notes, with yellowing newspapers, clipped and unclipped. In order for Marina to have sat—and to have sat in her yogic position—she had to have moved at least two piles onto the floor.

Although he wouldn't show it (not over such a trifle), he was irritated by the intrusion. It was a household rule that nobody entered Murray's office without first knocking; and that unless the door was already ajar—which he was fairly certain it hadn't been—one did not knock at all, except in dire emergency. Nobody touched his papers, nobody moved his piles, nobody entered the inner sanctum unbidden: as he had explained more than once, in this room his brain was laid out, in all its idio-syncrasy. To be in this room was to be in his head; and he relied

upon his household to behave accordingly. Which, almost
unfailingly, they did.

On this evening, past midnight, Murray Thwaite had been
so certain of his privacy that he had taken the file from his
locked desk drawer, the book file he thought of as his life's
work, the project that, when it was completed, if it was ever
completed (but what, then, would he do, if it were completed,
if it was indeed his life's work?), would at last and indisputably
elevate his name from the ranks of competent, even courageous
journalists and thoughtful columnists to the rare air of the
immortals. It was a work—he hesitated even to form the word
in his mind, and yet his sense of self, of what this was all *for*,
depended upon that formulation—of philosophy. Partly aphor-
istic, partly essayistic, it was to be the distillation, crystalline,
of all he had learned, and knew, and had come to live by. In his
mind, although not on paper—he was not yet ready, even after
all these years, to commit such intimacies to paper, let alone
to the too readily accessible, alarmingly traceable computer—
the book had a title: *How to Live.* Simple, pithy—and yet, he
feared, grandiose, too grandiose for what was yet only an
uneven pile of handwritten pages, blotched with coffee rings,
dog-eared, marked-up, read a thousand unsatisfied times by
one, and only one, pair of eyes. Annabel knew of this manuscript, the way a child knows about Narnia, with a mixture of
hope and incredulity; and since returning home, Marina
seemed to have surmised that some vital, unscheduled enterprise was secretly afoot (never mind that it had been begun
almost a decade before, when she was away at Brown), something she referred to with an ironic obliquity as "Dad's Thing."
Aside from these two, nobody at all knew, as far as Murray was

aware, of this text. (How could he know, and why would he imagine, that Marina had in fact told Danielle and Julius and possibly others that her father's next big project was a top-secret manuscript that not even *she* had yet seen; so that among her acquaintances there circulated rumors about "Murray Thwaite's Thing," rumors that suggested an exposé of the CIA or the Communist Party or, from one particularly silly corner, cookery—*Brunch Recipes from Murray Thwaite's Kitchen*—but did not, of course, could not, come close to the truth.)

The manuscript made him nervous: he didn't know how to proceed with it. He'd never written anything like it before. The number of its pages grew or shrank depending only on his humor, as he could read the same passage twenty times, finding it splendid, illuminating, the first nineteen, and daft or banal, the twentieth. And even then, he would determine purely on a whim whether to discard the offending sheet or whether, indulgently, to put the page aside in hopes that a twenty-first reading, in a sunnier frame, would restore its luster to the offending prose. Because the manuscript made him nervous, he frequently avoided it, often for months at a time; a tic that, given his prolificity and the constant public demands upon him, was not difficult to justify. Only when he felt himself to be genuinely settled, not merely unmolested but, in some profound sense, unmolestable, did he take out this infinitely precious file.

As he had felt, this evening, until his daughter—he loved her, adored her, of course he did; but he did ask himself, as he noted her faded pajamas, her curled bare toes, why this woman, no longer in her first youth, was living still, or again, in his house—had intruded.

"Daddy," she said, picking without looking at a small scab on her ankle. "Are you busy?"

"Am I busy, pet?" He peered above his glasses with what he hoped was a loving sternness. "What does it look like?"

"I know the door was shut—but I thought—I really need to talk to you—"

"We could have talked at supper, my beauty."

"It's, well, it's not that it's private, although it sort of is; it's mostly that you'll understand, and Mom . . . I wanted to talk to you on your own."

Murray removed his glasses, allowed them to dangle professorially while he chewed upon a stem. He did not say anything.

"But if you've got a deadline?" Her anxiety rang false. He knew that she didn't care whether he had a deadline; she cared only about the conversation she wanted to have with him. In this sense, in her single-mindedness, he might even have said her bloody-mindedness, she was her father's daughter. Only sometimes, such as now, did the trait annoy him. But he knew that she would have been, on approaching his inner sanctum, as apprehensive as she was determined; he could feel from afar the clamminess of her palms, the palpitations of her heart, and, with a sigh, the sigh of parental responsibility, he resigned himself. He shuffled his papers, slid them into their folder, turned it facedown, all with a nonchalance that suggested they were of no possible importance, and shifted himself in his chair, so that he could look properly at his daughter and, as she required of him, converse.

"So," he said, and held out his flat hands.

Marina gave half a laugh. "You make me feel silly now,

Daddy. It's suddenly all formal, like there's a script, and I don't know—"

He cut her off. "Do you want to ask me something, or do you want to tell me something?"

Marina thought a moment. "Neither. Both. What kind of a question is that?"

"Marina dear, you've got to think clearly. You've got to learn to articulate your thoughts clearly. Clarity is the key."

"You make it sound so simple."

"But it is. That, at least, is simple."

"You make everything sound simple. And it's *not*. You're always so *certain* of everything."

He sighed. "Don't whine, Marina. It doesn't become you. And don't speak nonsense. There are those things about which I have sufficient information to be certain. And then there is a great deal, of course, that is a muddle."

Marina nodded, played with her toes, would not look at him. He was, in so many ways, extremely proud of her—not least of her beauty, which was, to him, each time a surprise, as though unwittingly he had thrown a perfect pot, or cultivated a perfect bonsai—but she could be, she was being, trying. They heard a siren approach on the avenue below, heard its rising shriek, and then the fall as it passed them, continued away. As if she had been waiting politely for it to finish, Marina began, "I just wanted to ask for your advice. About—you know. Things."

"Which ones? The book?" He was tiring of the pretense of her book; not least because it made him wonder whether *his* book—not *The Fat Lady*, which was doing very nicely, thank

you, but *the* book, this book beneath his elbow—was as farci-
cal a sham as his daughter's.

"No." She peered up at him through her hair, which she had
coquettishly encouraged across half of her face. "Or not just
that." She paused. "It's the whole setup. I mean, I'm thirty now,
aren't I?"

"You are."

"And when you were thirty you were already famous."

"Famous?" He shrugged modestly, a shrug as artificial as his
daughter's earlier anxiety. He could see her seeing the falsehood; they knew each other well. And then he said, and meant,
"It was a very different time. It was a different world."

"Yes, but you were doing important things from the start.
You had convictions."

"World events—there was an opportunity—I believed in a
lot of things, some of which hold true today, and a lot of which,
well . . . as we were saying, very little is certain."

"But Daddy, what am I going to do?"

Murray Thwaite blinked. She was so lovely, and so charming, but she'd been these things for a long time, all her life; and
he thought he had instilled in her the importance of being
more than they. He did not want to suspect that she was not
bright; he knew her, he knew she was bright. Not as bright,
perhaps, as her friend Danielle, but intelligent enough for there
to be no excuse, no possible excuse for this behavior. He manifested his displeasure by breathing, dragonlike, through his
nose. He could feel his nostrils flaring. To give her time, he lit
a cigarette, emptied the dirty ashtray into the wastepaper basket
at his feet. Aurora lined the baskets with plastic shopping bags

to facilitate her cleaning, and the butts and ashes rustled against the plastic like leaves in a breeze.

"Danielle thinks I should get a job," Marina said at last.

"What kind of job did you have in mind?"

"That's the thing. First off, should I even have one when I'm trying to finish the book—and then, you know, a *real* job would be so demanding, after all, that's what an interesting job is supposed to be; and an easy job, a dumb job, well, at that point, who am I kidding?"

Murray Thwaite had little patience for this. He suddenly saw his daughter as a monster he and Annabel had created—they and a society of excess. He was about to begin "When I was your age . . ."; but suddenly could hear his own father's voice in his head, intoning these words that he had sworn to himself—he remembered it, his irritation—he would never speak to his own children. He said instead, "You know you're welcome here as long as you like. A bed, a roof, your dinner, you've got, and a little cash too, as long as your mother and I can manage it."

Marina nodded, as if chastened by his generosity, waiting for what might follow.

What, he wondered, should follow? "But the question is, what do you want to do with your life?"

"I want—you know, what I've always wanted, Daddy. To do something important."

Could she not hear herself? Even that student at Columbia—what was her name? Anne? Maryanne? Roanne, that was it—even she had surely not been so naïve, and ten years younger, too. "Meaning?" he pressed.

"With writing. I'd like to write something—articles, a book—that mattered."

"But on what subject? What do you believe in?"

"Not children's clothes, that's for sure," she snorted, ruefully. "I don't know. There are so many things. You, of all people, know what it's like—"

"Different issues are important to different people, my girl, as you are well aware. It's not just a matter of picking something off a list, of following someone else's ideas. If I've taught you anything, surely I've taught you that? You've got to find your subject. Or a first subject, something to start with."

"But how?"

"Maybe in the first instance your friend has a point. Maybe you should get a job of some kind."

"In journalism?"

"In anything that interests you. Teach school. Work for an aid agency. Work for an *ad* agency, for God's sake. Just a job."

"I suppose what I worry is"—Marina gave her father a self-deprecating smile, to his mind one of her most bewitching expressions—"I worry that that will make me ordinary, like everybody else."

"My beauty"—he stood to give her a hug, pointedly cutting short the interview, and she, too, unfurled from the divan, stepping as daintily as a dancer over the piles she had relocated to the floor—"nothing under the sun could make you ordinary. Nothing, ever. Now, I need to work. Because, you see, I do have a job. It concentrates the mind."

He let her get as far as the door before he spoke again: "Will you finish this book, then, after all the work you've done on it?"

She had her hand upon the doorknob. He could tell from the way that she held it that she was feeling its cool brass, and the shape of her palm, her fingers, around its surface. He felt that he knew her—the line of her spine, the curve of her eyes— and that he did not really need her to answer his question.

"I don't know yet," she said. "I'm still trying to figure it out."

He nodded. She was in the hallway, the door not quite shut when he called, a final time, her name: "Marina?"

"Yes, Daddy?"

"Do you know your friend Danielle's e-mail, offhand? I said I'd forward some stuff to her about that Jones fellow, you know, the one she wants to make a flick about."

"That's so sweet." Marina smiled, showing only her head around the door. "It'll mean a lot to her."

Once Marina had gone, Murray Thwaite sat again before his open folder. He took a clean sheet of paper and wrote at the top: "Chapter Ten: Counseling an Adult Daughter." He crossed this out, wrote "Conversations with an Adult Daughter"; and then, "A Grown Child Ponders How to Live." At the last, he settled upon "Talking to a Grown Child," which words sat in the middle of the page in black ink, in his long, narrow capital letters. He smoked several cigarettes while looking at this phrase, and emptied the tumbler of scotch that rested on his blotter, its sweat sunk into the green paper in a solemn little ring. Eventually, he put this sheet of paper on top of the manuscript pile and returned them all to the folder, and to the drawer, which he locked carefully. She had—this was, of course, what one's children did—ruined his stride, spoiled his momentum.

MAY

CHAPTER ELEVEN

A Mother Knows Best

Whenever Randy Minkoff came to town, there were three things she always wanted to "do": a Broadway show; a walk—and once, even, with much giggling and protestation, but ultimately much delight, a carriage ride—in Central Park; and, most important, the Metropolitan. She tried to visit other museums as well, different ones each time, and on this visit she proposed the Frick and the Pierpont Morgan, or perhaps the Public Library; but it was to the Met that she returned, as awed each time she climbed the marble steps as she had been, she always told her daughter, when first she came to New York City, a girl of eighteen in her freshman year at Ohio State, traveling with a group of girlfriends over spring break, to her own parents' noisy displeasure.

"The charm never wears off," she would announce gaily, in her throaty, unfiltered voice. "I wish sex was as reliable." And she would laugh, heartily and from her chest, roundly amused at her own daring.

Not that Danielle's mother was having much sex, as far as Danielle could tell. After the divorce, she'd moved to St. Petersburg at the urging of her old friend Irene Weinrip, also a divorcée and comfortably installed in a condo by the water.

Randy Minkoff hadn't worked anywhere but for her husband's company for years, but as she told Irene, or Irene told her, it was never very clear in the recounting, one thing Randy knew was property. You weren't married to a developer for all those years without knowing property. So she had taken her real estate exam, had launched into the bright world of St. Petersburg housing, and had found new joy in her life. Small, dark, and beaky, like her daughter, she had thickened with age and carried her significant breasts before her, but she didn't let what some might have seen as the infelicities of her physique deter her fashion sense.

"Men *like* something to hold on to, and as long as you've got a good corset, you can look great in anything," she informed Danielle. She favored wide-legged pantsuits, herself, with clingy tops—occasionally patterned after the pelts of endangered species—and high heels. She liked gold jewelry, or even jewelry that looked like gold—she was not snobbish in her tastes, and had more than once picked up an item she adored from QVC—and she chose garments that would flatter her naturally lovely skin and the artificial golden copper wave of her hair. She was ebullient, even overbearing, with a voice that seemed to contain within it a lifetime of heavy smoking (although she had quit when Danielle was eight) and a certain adipose resonance. As a real estate agent, particularly for retirees, silver-haired snowbirds from Canada and the northern Midwest, she was popular, frankly successful; as a girl among middle-aged girls, dynamic and a joker; but when it came to men, Danielle knew that her mother talked about dates but did not go on them, that she referred jauntily to sex but could not, since the divorce—it hadn't been her idea, after all—look without wari-

ness upon any of the opposite sex but her son. And perhaps
even he was suspect.

Danielle liked to believe that in matters of the heart she was
different from her mother, even though they shared so many
other traits. But Danielle's intimate life, while more peopled
than Randy's, was not more evidently fulfilled. Nor, of late—
since an intermittent long-term beau named Tim had left
her in order, swiftly, to marry a nineteen-year-old college
dropout—any more promising than Julius's. Danielle rather
pitied her mother, stout and plucky and "done," beetling
toward sixty as though she enjoyed it, as though she'd never felt
more fully herself; and yet Danielle worried, when Randy
Minkoff landed in New York and installed herself at the Days
Inn on Eighth at Forty-seventh in a room that, she brashly
insisted, was no smaller than her daughter's studio ("It fits *two*
queen-size beds, Danny. Two of 'em!"), that her mother pitied
her. Certainly, Randy worried about Danielle ("When I was
your age, sweetie, you and Jeff were running around the house
buck naked, screaming, if you can believe it. Such delicious
tushes . . ."), and projected—so Danielle believed—all her
unacknowledged lack of fulfillment onto her child. She didn't
seem to be as impressed as many, as even Danielle was sometimes, by her position as a documentary producer for a
prestigious series. Randy Minkoff thought this unreliable work,
because one was dependent for its success upon so many
uncontrollable factors. This contradicted one of her kooky self-
help beliefs, adopted in the new, the reborn, post-divorce
Floridian era; and so Danielle had not told her mother that the
Australian project was dead (Randy *had* been impressed by the
voyage to the Antipodes, by the paid business-class ticket), but

had instead suggested that it was on hold, temporarily. She spoke breezily about her current idea, with an indifference she didn't feel, to try to imply that this was a mere trifle, a notion batted about until the financing for two months in New South Wales was fixed.

Danielle spoke this way in line for lunch with her mother at the Metropolitan's swankier restaurant, pitching her voice low against the cathedral echo of the other patrons and the ambling hordes. They were waiting, too, for Marina to join them—Randy loved Marina, little suspecting that Danielle's dear friend told her own mother that Randy was "really sweet, but, you know, vulgar in that Miami way"—and after the meal they would stroll through the park to the children's zoo, which, like so many other celebrated landmarks in New York that hold such resonance for so many it is a wonder they don't ring like bells, was very special to her: "Don't you remember? Our first family visit to New York, and little Jeffy fell off the Alice in Wonderland toadstool and got a giant purple bump on his forehead, and you, you, Danny, saw a chimp, was it, peeing in its cage and you went straight ahead and wet your pants, do you remember? You stood there gaping at the monkey and then all of a sudden we realized that your little white tights were sopping wet, and even your shoes . . ." Danny claimed not to recall this early humiliation, but had had the vivid picture drawn for her so many times that she could not be sure: it was emblazoned now in her memory. Today, and not for the first time, Marina, too, would be party to the recounting of this myth; but not yet, not till after lunch.

Already, Randy and Danielle had spent the morning in the museum, a sun-filled Wednesday morning in May, when

Danielle had taken the day off work especially (her mother was visiting midweek because the rates and fares were cheaper: she knew property, and she knew travel, and above all she knew a bargain), only to find herself wandering the penumbral catacombs of the Met's fashion galleries, ogling the dimly lit cases of evening gowns and brocaded slippers, of embroidered skirts and feathered hats, all elegantly posed upon faceless, hairless mannequins in what was, to Danielle, a titillating but disturbing travesty; and to her mother, unabashedly the museum's greatest attraction. Randy liked the jewelry second-best, the Roman earrings and bracelets that she could then find reproduced in the museum shop; but Danielle drew the line at these, which were, for her, like the corridors of antique china, a matter of complete indifference.

Museum pace, the idling drag of it, had tired and frayed them both, although particularly Randy, whose three-inch heels ("A small woman, Danny, should never wear less," she often said, casting a glance of mock reproval at her daughter's flats) had made the soles of her feet hurt and pinched her bunioned toes. They had therefore retreated earlier than anticipated to the restaurant, only to find the crowd far greater than they'd expected, and so they had joined the line.

Danielle had finished explaining the outline of her "revolution" program, and was listening, half-heartedly, to her mother's enthusiastic prattle about their cousin Melvin's infatuation, in the sixties, with the libertarian party in Illinois—before, of course, he got interested in organics and bought his farm in northern California, twenty years ahead of the curve (what was the link here, Danielle wondered, amazed as ever at her mother's capacity for wildly lateral thinking and endless shaggy dog stories, barely aware that these, like so many others, were gifts she had inherited), when she glimpsed, or thought she did, the high, clear forehead of Ludovic Seeley. He stood ahead of them in line, almost near the front, his long and slender frame bending forward with the gesture of intimacy she had remarked upon their first meeting. It was by this angle that she first knew him. She craned her neck to see who he was talking to, and found his interlocutor was young, female, and attractive, Eurasian perhaps, with big dark eyes, tiny hands, and—Danielle stepped frankly out of line, and looked down— doll's ankles, which wavered above shoes whose heels made Randy's look modest. Their conversation was animated, almost heated. You could tell that Seeley was trying to persuade the woman of something, and that although she was polite, maybe interested, even, she didn't agree. Danielle decided that they didn't know each other well; and in spite of her automatic suspicions, she decided they weren't an item. Or not yet; maybe that was the reason for his focused suasion.

"Which is why I think Karen has her weight problem, don't you?" Randy touched her daughter's arm with her manicured copper-colored nails.

"Mom?"

"Mel's oldest, Karen. The one who wanted to be an actress."

"Oh, yeah."

"But she's gotten obese. I mean, not just plump, obese. And I think it's the organics, don't you?"

Danielle watched the maître d' escort Seeley and his date to a secluded table for two. She couldn't see either of them once they had sat down, which she thought wistfully would make it difficult to seem by chance to run into him. Danielle had known that Seeley had arrived—she'd been told by someone, technically a rival of his, at Condé Nast, that he'd rented an apartment on Gramercy Park within three days of landing, in early April—but she hadn't contacted him. She'd been meaning to: he was, or would be, an essential part of her revolution program, if and when she got the green light. She was fairly certain that he'd agree, as the publicity for his paper could be tremendous; but the series director wanted to wait till September, when *The Monitor* was to be launched, before making a final decision. Still, it wouldn't be inappropriate, under these circumstances, for her to pop over, so briefly, to his table, simply to reintroduce herself. Not with her mother, though—she didn't want Randy involved in this encounter. Nor Marina either, if she thought about it. Perhaps it would be better to e-mail him—she'd already obtained that address; indeed, she knew it by heart—than to allow all the variables there present free range.

"That's how *I* feel about refined sugars myself," Randy Minkoff was saying. "And I think it's quite common."

"Yeah, maybe."

"Are you even listening to me, Danielle Minkoff?"

"Of course I am, Mom."

"So how heavy is your father these days?" Randy liked to hear that her ex was losing the battle of the bulge.

"I haven't seen him for ages, Mom. But he's on Atkins, and he says he's lost twenty pounds."

"Hmm." Randy drew herself up and adjusted her suit jacket over her leopard-spotted bosom. "That I'd like to see." She seemed to be muttering to herself. "Twenty pounds? Twenty pounds."

Danielle rolled her eyes, albeit discreetly. She had long been the go-between, and knew her mother's behavior for deliberate theater. Even when they were married, Randy had pestered her husband about his weight: he was a big man, who snacked in his office on bologna slices, straight from the packet, or on string cheese, the kind for little kids. His embrace had winded Danielle when she was small—"You don't know your own strength," Randy used to scold him, with Danielle in tears. The sort of man, not blubbery but thick, solid, hairy, like a bull, on whom twenty pounds either way wouldn't make much difference.

"Marina's here, Mom. Here she comes." And Marina breezed toward them, carrying on her fresh cheek the springtime air and the impression, if not the scent, of blossom. She swung before her a tiny bright box of a purse—clearly an extravagance, or a gift—and waved it aloft like a censer as she approached.

"Mrs. Minkoff," she breathed, with what sounded to Danielle, impossibly, like muted jubilation, her arms wide, "it's so great to *see* you!" And Randy, charmed, a little daunted, as ever, by the Thwaite aura and sophistication, by a warmth that nevertheless carried about it an untraceable but distinct tinge of superiority, opened her mouth in an "O" and looked coyly through her lashes.

Hunched forward over the table against the cavernous cacophony of the restaurant, the three women were playing the dessert game—each trying to hide her sentiments about the course while simultaneously attempting to gauge those of her companions; a routine in which the younger two rightly surmised that Randy was more hopeful for a sweet than they were anxious to avoid one, so that they ordered, eventually, a single chocolate pot de crème and three spoons—when a shadow, the lean shadow of Ludovic Seeley, blocked their table's light. He seemed, strangely, to bring a silence with him; or at least, a silence seemed to fall.

"Isn't it Danielle? Danielle Minkoff?"

Danielle made as if to stand.

"Please, don't move—I'm sorry to interrupt; but I saw you— here, of all places!—and did want to say hello."

"Hello." Danielle smiled, prettily, she hoped. "How long have you been here?"

"Almost a month, already. I wanted to e-mail you, but I lost the address."

"I totally understand," Danielle said, thinking to herself that if she'd been able to procure his address, he could have found hers if he'd wanted to. She didn't know quite what to say next. He hovered, smiling politely at the table. "I'm sorry," she said, "how rude of me. My mother, Randy Minkoff; and Marina Thwaite."

He bowed his head as he shook their hands. She wouldn't have been surprised to hear him click his heels. Danielle couldn't see anywhere behind him the Eurasian beauty.

"Are you here with friends?" she asked.

"A colleague—or rather, someone I hope to take on as a colleague. At the moment she's with the competition."

"Are your offices near here, then?"

"No." Seeley gave a clipped laugh. "This isn't our, how to put it? Demographic. This isn't our demographic."

They all smiled—inanely, Danielle felt. The silence hung.

"Let me give you my details," she said at last. As she told Marina afterward, "I couldn't figure out why he was just *standing* there." She rummaged in her bag for paper, a pen. "And I'd love to have yours. I've been wanting to be in touch anyway about a project I'm working on—so this is actually very . . ." She trailed off, trying to make the pen write.

"Serendipitous," finished Marina, showing her teeth, looking straight at Seeley. "I think that's the word."

Later, after the walk in the park, after the umpteenth recounting of the tale of young Danielle's wet pants, after Marina had gone home and Danielle and her mother had returned, following a coffee break (sleeved cups with domed tops full of whipped cream and plastic packet of chocolate-covered graham crackers in hand), to Randy's room, where Danielle sat on the edge of one of the queen-size beds and swung her feet petulantly back and forth while her mother, propped against the headboard of the other bed, shoes off and feet up, surfed channels with the mute on—at this late point in the day her mother said, "I liked him, sweetie."

"Who?"

"That guy, at lunch. The one with the sexy accent."

"I hardly know him."

"Whatever you say, sweetie."

"Mom, look: he's a guy I met at a dinner party in Australia who just moved here for work. That's all."

"He seemed very"—Randy wriggled her shoulders as if beset by a frisson—"intimate."

"Oh, please. He's that way with everybody."

"Do you think so?" Randy let the television rest on the Cartoon Network. Shaggy and Scooby were alone in a basement when the lights went off, leaving only four blinking eyes on the darkened screen. "A mother sometimes knows best, Danny. I'm just mentioning, for the record, that I liked him."

CHAPTER TWELVE

Danielle's List

When she got home near midnight, Danielle found a message from Marina on her answering machine, to which she listened as she put on her electric kettle (a British-inspired luxury learned from Moira, who was never without one) for a cup of mint tea.

"Great to see your mom, Danny. She's so funny! And the way she adores you is so, you know, touching. If it's not too late, call me when you get in? I'm dying to know more about that Australian guy—he's your revolutionary, right? Call me, okay?"

Danielle took off her shoes. She put them tidily away in the cupboard, in their space on the shoe rack. The only way to live sanely in her tiny space was to live pristinely. Her mother teased that her studio hardly looked inhabited; but Danielle loved it. She felt, in her aching legs (how many miles had they walked that afternoon?) a trembling of relief simply to be there. It was small, but not depressing. She lived on the fifteenth floor of a white-brick 1960s building, the tallest of its kind for some blocks in all directions. It had a clean, inviting lobby and a doorman, and when she opened her front door—one in a long row of identical doors along a brightly lit, blue-carpeted hallway that somehow successfully absorbed the odors and sounds of communal living, at least for the most part—she entered a rectangular oasis, framed at one end by a large, south-facing picture window, waist high, unembellished, that in the day-time, even in winter's darkest weeks, filled the room with light, and at night opened, like a complex painting, onto a vista of twinkling lights and changing sky, of silhouetted buildings and their jumbled rooftops. Just as her neighbors' lives were muffled from her consciousness by the solidity of the building's con-struction, so, too, the window's double glazing shut out all but the most enraged sirens, so that her room felt deliciously her-metic, still new, still clean.

In order to have her sitting area by the window, so that she might read and write and think bathed in light and the sparkling illusion of the city, she had chosen to set her bed near the kitchen and the door. She knew that to most people this decision would seem unaesthetic, peculiar (and even she worried, sometimes, about the proximity of food to her bedclothes), but she only rarely allowed visitors, and those that she did knew her well enough not to comment upon her choice. The apartment was entirely, was only, for her: a wall of books, both read and unread, all of them dear to her not only in themselves, their tender spines, but in the moments or peri-ods they evoked. She had kept some books since college that she had acquired for courses and never read—Fredric Jameson, for example, and Kant's *Critique of Judgment*—but which sug-gested to her that she was, or might be, a person of seriousness, a thinker in some seeping, ubiquitous way; and she had kept, too, a handful of children's books taken from her now-dis-mantled girlhood room, like *Charlotte's Web* and the *Harriet the*

Spy novels, that conjured for her an earlier, passionately earnest self, the sober child who read constantly in the back of her parents' Buick, oblivious to her brother punching her knee, oblivious to her parents' squabbling, oblivious to the traffic and landscapes pressing upon her from outside the window.

She had, in addition to her books, a modest shelf of tapes and CDs that served a similar, though narrower, function: not like Julius, fanatical about music, nor particularly educated, she was aware that her collection was comprised largely of mainstream choices that reflected—whether popular or classical—not so much an individual spirit as the generic tastes of her times: Madonna, the Eurythmics, Tracy Chapman from her adolescence; Cecilia Bartoli, Anne-Sophie Mutter, Mitsuko Uchida; more recently Moby and the posthumously celebrated folk-singing woman from Washington, D.C., who had died of a melanoma in her early thirties, and whose tragic tale attracted Danielle more than her soft covers of familiar songs.

Her self, then, was represented in her books; her times in her records; and the rest of the room she thought of as a pure, blank slate: her fine white sheets and puffed pillows (she had a weakness for linens, and had even bought a set from Frette, an extravagance for which she punished herself by using them only on special occasions, such as her birthday); her olive loveseat, big enough for her to lie in, with her knees tucked up; her broad desk, a sheet of polished wood on trestles, which faced the window and held upon it all the elements of her "home office." She had splurged on the office chair, an ergonomic marvel that her mother had encouraged her to buy and had helped her to pay for ("Believe me, sweetie, nothing is more important than a healthy back. Nothing! Remember that trip to St. Thomas over spring break when you were twelve, and your father threw his back out? He slept on the floor for two months after that, baby. Two months! And I don't think his back's ever been the same since. Not that I'd know now, of course. Let's buy the chair"). She did not display photographs or mementoes of any kind. She abhorred tchotchkes. On the walls, she had hung four Rothko reproductions, large, discreetly framed posters that reminded her of the Rothko chapel in Houston, which she had once visited with her family when it was still a family. The bleeding washes of color—green, gray, blue, lavender, purple—still invited her to contemplation, still soothed her, each time she sat before them. She still felt—or could, if she kept the overhead light off and the posterish flatness of her pictures remained unrevealed, the way an aging woman's wrinkles are melted in the shadows—that she might lose herself in the verdigris palette, a slightly different hue for each mood.

This evening, with her mint tea, she crawled onto the olive sofa and gazed at the purplest panel, the moment before dawn or the evening celebration, as she alternately thought of it. Perhaps she ought rather to have been moving into olives and grays, toward sleep; but just as her legs hurt, so too did her brain, which felt jangled and frazzled by the day as if by a constant humming. She felt the need to sort through her competing anxieties, to find a hierarchy and a rhythm for them, to make an internal list: sunrise, sunset, sunrise, sunset. Breathe in, breathe out.

1. It was after eleven. She did not want to call Marina. She did not want to call her mother, either, knowing her tucked beneath her acrylic fleece blanket at the Days Inn uptown, but

had promised that she would ("I just need to know my baby's home safe. You understand?") and so did, a hasty murmured good night couched, on both sides, in rote protestations of love.

2. She not only did not want to telephone Marina, she found herself irritated at the very prospect. Was it because of Marina's use of the word "touching," perhaps? Or was it not at least partly also because she did not want to talk to Marina about Ludovic Seeley? Oh, of course she had already talked a fair bit to Marina, to everyone, about Seeley-the-idea, but not about Seeley-the-person; and there was, had been, at the very sight of him, at the front of the line at the restaurant, a pull that Danielle felt to be inevitable, personal, even spiritual—a magnetic attraction. Her mother, she knew, believed in such things; believed in such a thing in this very instance—and which she vividly recalled having felt, and felt keenly, even in Sydney; had, if she were honest, allowed so strongly to hold sway that the very idea for her revolution program had been, was—it was true, and too embarrassing ever to acknowledge—simply a pretext to contact him again, and more than that, actually to spend time with him, to force herself (though not literally, of course) upon him. And having made this decision, instinctive and barely conscious, already over two months ago, Danielle had allowed the *idea* of her connection to Seeley to flourish, in the privacy of her imagination, in the privacy of this delicious studio; and now, most problematically, inevitably, and perhaps thrillingly, he was again real, flesh, blood, and hooded eyes, with those long, cool fingers and the pressing, withholding glance. He was real, and in New York to stay. That was enough, surely, to have to contend with without throwing into the

dilemma the fatuous wheedling and prying of Marina-on-the-prowl. Because surely Marina had seen, as Danielle's mother had seen, Danielle's discomfort; she had surely felt the voltage in the air of their mundane exchange? Or worse, perhaps Marina hadn't seen or sensed it, perhaps, then, this current was pure figment, a one-sided attraction so entranced by its own force that it could not gauge—that Danielle could not gauge—the indifference with which it was met? (After all, he did lean in, lean over, every woman: it was by his angle that she had known him first, and only then by the brow, by the aristocratic profile.) Either way, whatever way, Danielle did not want to talk to Marina tonight. She did not want to talk to her about Ludovic Seeley. She would have to, perhaps even tomorrow; but not now.

3. Besides which, she felt awkward with Marina in one other, albeit small, respect. It had to do with Marina's father. Since her supper at the Thwaites' back in March, Danielle seemed to have struck up an e-mail correspondence with her host. He had sent her, in the first instance and vaguely surprisingly, some data about Professor Jones, although she thought she'd explained that her "reparations" program had been axed. But she'd been flattered—how not to be?—by the thoughtfulness of one so important and so busy, and she had thanked him, wittily, she'd considered at the time, although she couldn't now recall what she had said; and in order not to seem impolite, or self-absorbed (these were again, as ever, early lessons of her mother's, regarding, in this case, the manners of correspondence, which replayed an endless loop in her head, along with—and why, she still wondered?—the maternal injunction, so difficult to follow, not to begin a letter with the word "I"),

she'd asked him about his current projects, about whether he was teaching and what article he was working on; never expecting, of course—it was mere politesse on both sides—that he would reply to her, would jokingly ask her opinion of whether he should teach the following spring at Columbia or perhaps even Sarah Lawrence; that he would mention that he had been rereading William James for a chapter on which he was working and ask her opinion of *The Varieties of Religious Experience;* that she would go so far as to order the book from Amazon— there it was, behind her left shoulder, tucked among her other volumes as though it had always been there—and to read the section to which he referred in order properly to respond to his comments. Their exchanges felt to her innocent—he didn't flirt with her, as she understood the word; if anything, his tone was professorial, avuncular. But there was something not quite right about it all, some touch of titillating betrayal in their pithy messages, whether the slightest flutter of the sexual or merely an inappropriate ascription of the father-daughter bond, Danielle could not have said. One thing was certain: not only had she, Danielle, felt no urge to mention the correspondence to Marina, not beyond the first exchange about which they had laughed together ("That's *so* my dad!" Marina had said, not hearing what he had written, clapping her hands together with delight), but she was almost certain that Murray Thwaite had remained similarly mum. Marina was not guileful, and Danielle knew that if her father had spoken of their e-mails, Marina, in hurt surprise, would have said to Danielle, "How come you never said?," to which Danielle would reply— she'd planned it, imagined it many times, the breeziness of her tone—"Didn't I? I'm sorry. I thought we'd talked about it."

And surely, surely, there was something a little strange in even that imagined conversation, even though she couldn't put her finger on it? It certainly sometimes made her pause when she was with Marina and they were confiding in each other, or even merely chatting, and feel a tingle of discomfort, of excitement, in her spine.

4. Then there was the question of Randy Minkoff's Thursday. She wanted to take her daughter to a nail salon on Madison Avenue about which she'd read in *Vogue,* and she had revealed, this evening, that she had secretly, unilaterally, procured appointments for them both at two-thirty. This although Danielle, having taken all Wednesday, had proposed to see her mother only in the morning on Thursday and had agreed to attend the regular series meeting at three. How to disappoint Randy ("You've no idea how stylish this place is—I booked it as a treat already a month ago, all the way from St. Petersburg. And if it wasn't for Irene's friend Malva, who's a regular, we would *never* have got in!")? How, without revealing a professionally deleterious lack of commitment, to miss the scheduled meeting? How could her mother have put her in this situation? Or was it—she had to wonder—that she somehow *allowed* herself thus to be manipulated? Her mother wouldn't do this to Jeff, who had a banking job in Dallas; she wouldn't even try. They could both imagine the way Jeff would puff out his already full cheeks, purse his mouth like a blowfish, and say, "Sorry, Mom," with a little shrug. "Fuggedaboudit. Not going to happen." And although he was only five foot six and looked funny in suits, with his thick neck and short arms, although he was almost two years younger than Danielle, he would have about him an authority—was it just masculinity, however

compromised?—that would make Randy Minkoff fold at once, barely regretfully, with a piercing brightness that suggested that she'd known all along he would have more important things to do. Why was that? Because if Danielle tried to put her foot down—and tonight, upon hearing about the appointment, she had blanched, even cringed, but had said only "Wow, Mom. I've got this meeting at work. But I'll see what I can do"—she knew (how did she know? But she did) that Randy Minkoff would crumple and cry. Than which there was no more prolonged and exhausting scene in the Minkoff family repertoire, and which was hence to be avoided at all costs.

5. And finally, not pressing but niggling, there was the matter of Julius. Of what might have happened to Julius, exactly. She missed him. Since forever he had been, in his funny, intermittent way, a gold strand in the dull fabric of her days. He made her laugh; he made life glitter. And so suddenly, he'd vanished. Not that she thought he'd been brained by a pineapple finial and left to bleed to death on his studio floor; nor that he'd been sold into the white slave trade, nor taken hostage by radicals—no, she'd received sufficient signs of life to know that he was well, even, perhaps, better than he'd ever been. Or so he had claimed, in a postcard from a fancy hotel in Miami, the Delano, where he'd gone for the weekend with his new boyfriend, this mysterious David, who'd been on the scene for what? Two months now? Was it longer? But whom nobody, or nobody among their friends, had yet been privileged to meet. Danielle and Marina had joked that perhaps David didn't exist, that perhaps he was yet another of Julius's impressive illusions, like the imaginary appointments that had kept him so hard to catch for years. It would, after all, be a good ruse, and not entirely at

odds with the fantasist in Julius, the imp whose more extravagant whims had grown less and less common as they'd all grown older (back in college, he was always lying grandly, outrageously, about where he'd been and who he'd been with; just as he would adopt everyone's best anecdotes and brazenly tell them back to their former owners as his own, only somehow embellished, improved, somehow better; but he didn't do this anymore); but Danielle had seen the Miami postmark on the card, which itself was hotel stationery, and she knew that in order for Julius even to be there, David had to be real. Had they met on the Internet? Or in a nightclub? Julius wasn't telling, when she could reach him, which had her believing that their first encounter had been sordid. (Sometimes, Danielle thought that the antics she imagined for her friend were more outlandish and unlikely than anything anyone would really *do;* and yet, whenever Julius did provide her with graphic details, rarely now, they made her feel a complete innocent, made her feel like her mother.) Danielle knew that she ought, foremost, to feel a vicarious thrill, an excitement that Julius seemed to be enjoying better luck in love than ever he had before; but she felt instead anxious and suspicious, all the more so because this David—how old was he? What did he do? Where did his money come from?—did not, so it would seem, deign to meet her, or Marina, or anyone else for that matter. Julius, when she did speak to him, said elusive and exclusive things like "We're going to 'our' restaurant tonight. A sort of mini-anniversary dinner"—as if in two short months a lifetime's history had been grafted between them, and had summarily erased all Julius's years in New York with his friends. How could they have "a restaurant" already? Did they also (most probably) have a song?

A time of day? An avenue? But Danielle wasn't a fool, even in
her irritation. Above all what she wanted was to retrieve Julius,
whose sharp tongue could cut to the comic quick of any situation, who could mimic anyone (he did a great Murray
Thwaite), who would come over at two in the morning if you
called him, and who always made her feel the glums were sur-
mountable. And her mother had always told her that you didn't
catch flies with vinegar. To get Julius back, this David must be
won over, and soon; and she and Marina would have to devise
the Trojan horse with which to do it. If only she could glean
useful facts about him, beyond the last name Cohen and the
fact that he, like Julius, despised facial hair. If David were con-
quered, then Julius would stop hiding. That was the logic. And
on her mind because that morning, before leaving to meet her
mother, she'd had an e-mail from Julius containing another
rebuff: he would have loved to see her mother on Friday night,
Randy's last in the city—he called her "the inimitable Randy
Minkoff," and he loved to tease Danielle about how her mother
could train drag queens—but that he and David were going
out to the Hamptons for the weekend to see some friends of
David's. Julius, in the Hamptons? Julius at a barbecue, or walking, even fully clad, along a beach? "What about the *sand*?"
she'd said to Marina at lunch, when her mother was in the bathroom. "He's far too fastidious for sand!" But the long and the
short of it was that by now her pride was wounded, on behalf
of her mother as well as herself; and she was, she could admit
it to the Rothkos at least, vaguely indignant that Julius, of all
people, who had always seemed to her far shakier a romantic
prospect than anyone else she knew, had finally, apparently,
withdrawn so firmly from the running. She couldn't let on to

anyone that she was annoyed—she didn't want to be the sort of person who was—but the fact remained that irritation was in her, incontrovertible as a crumb in her throat.

Unable to think of a sixth thing, Danielle moved from sofa to bed, but not without hanging up her skirt and rolling her blouse in a small ball for the laundry; not before flossing (she didn't want to; but felt virtuous when she had) and brushing and coating her skin in a costly cream flogged to her by her dermatologist who, in coming out with a sales pitch at all, had stunned her into surprised submission. Thus purified, bland as a lamb, Danielle lay naked between her fine sheets, bodily weighted and, she hoped, cleared in spirit; and still, for a good hour, in the semi-darkness, she thought she could detect her worries darting like wisps in the corners of her blameless room.

CHAPTER THIRTEEN

Great Geniuses

By the second week of May, Bootie Tubb had been away from home for three weeks. He had finally left at the time the crocuses and snowdrops, late that year but still ahead of the grape hyacinths of which his mother was most fond, were unfolding their hesitant bright colors in the flowerbed along the front of the house. Spring was so late coming that ridges of mud-blackened ice still lingered at the edges of the lawns and curbs as he'd pulled out of town, a rimed lacing of the landscape that, in its persistent ugliness, made him glad to go.

He hadn't extricated himself as frankly as he would have hoped, but he hadn't had to sell his car, either. Instead, he'd spent a month, the last of that endless winter, working hourly shifts for his brother-in-law, Tom, who, in addition to state plowing contracts, had a sideline in private drives and walkways. Riding the red snowblower reminded Bootie of playing dodg'ems at the county fair, and Tom, who charged eight an hour, let Bootie keep half of that. It wasn't much, but as his mother never made good on her threat to charge him rent, and as he was paid in cash, Bootie pocketed the lot, a fat and floating stack of tattered ones and fives that he kept, secured by an elastic, in a brown manila envelope in his dresser drawer.

He had, when he left Watertown, four hundred and eighty-eight dollars there, along with the six hundred and some dollars remaining in his savings account, the money his mother said was from his father and which she'd once told him she hoped he would use to travel to Europe. With this much money—it seemed to him an important sum, even though he knew that it wouldn't go far, and certainly not as far as he imagined—he'd decided to keep the Honda, a portable hotel, as he saw it, and even to take his desktop computer. In so doing, he caused in Judy Tubb a sorrowful confusion after he'd departed, when she stepped into his bedroom and found his desk bare. Bootie had not quaintly imagined this maternal dismay: his mother had told him of it during their first phone conversation after he left.

"Is there something you're not telling me, Bootie?" she'd asked.

He was annoyed, hunched at a pay phone at a rest stop on the New York State Thruway, near Utica, where he'd pulled over for a cup of coffee and a slice of bad pizza, but he didn't let on, merely narrowed his eyes at the plastic case full of carnival toys in front of him (a game, whereby for only a dollar you could vainly attempt, with a metal claw, to retrieve the purple plush monkey or the bug-eyed Raggedy Ann), shuffled his feet on the ash-smeared tile and said, "No, Ma. There's nothing."

Because what he'd told his mother before he left, which wasn't untrue, was that he was going to Amherst, in Massachusetts, to visit his friend Donald, a year ahead of him in high school and now a sophomore at U Mass, studying History. He didn't tell her about New York, about the need to stake a claim with Murray. She wouldn't have liked it, or allowed it. She would have stymied his escape.

"What does Donald want you for now?" his mother had asked, only vaguely incredulous, as she shredded lettuce into the salad bowl. "It's basically exam time."

"He's got papers, not exams, Mom. And he lives off campus, in a big house. He invited me"—this was true: Donald had—"so I've got to assume I won't be in the way."

"How long will you be gone?"

"I don't know exactly. Maybe a little while. He's got some plans, maybe, for the summer."

"The *summer*?"

To which Bootie told his only bare-faced lie: "He's got some plans for me, to help me get into U Mass, maybe, for the fall."

"With your school record, I wouldn't think there'd be any problem," said his mother, cheering visibly.

"Yeah, but he can help me, maybe, get some credit for the stuff at Oswego."

"Really?"

"So I'd only be, you know, a semester behind." Bootie was almost sorrowful at how pleased his mother looked at this news, her blue eyes crinkling in her round face, and a glimmer of eager tooth showing between her lips. She was a school-teacher, for God's sake; if she'd stopped to think properly about what he was saying for even a minute she would've known it for horseshit. There was no way magically to turn Oswego incompletes into U Mass credits—no way without enrolling in summer school, a prospect he hadn't mooted. "Never mind now," he went on. "I'll let you know what pans out, if anything.

I mean, I'll be calling you all the time—it's not like I'm going to Africa or anything."

"No, sweetie. I know." She said she thought it was good that he had a project, and great that he was going to see Donald, who'd been such a good friend over the years, and that she'd miss him but she knew it wouldn't be for long. He didn't mention New York, nor did he mention his autodidactic program, nor did he mention the word "forever." He left clothes in his drawers and hanging in the cupboard, and he left most of his books, including the David Foster Wallace, which he'd never finished and had never returned to the library, and *Gravity's Rainbow,* at which a quick glance had told him he would not read soon, but not Emerson, nor *War and Peace,* and even a half-used tube of toothpaste and his red toothbrush, on purpose, because they were easy to replace and he could imagine her, in the bathroom that they shared, taking nightly consolation in these items in the mug on the sink's rim, a small suggestion of his impending return.

Three weeks later, Bootie was only marginally closer to New York than he had been, and he was considerably poorer. Almost all of his snow-blowing money had been spent, much of it in a dimly lit barn of a bar on the edge of the U Mass campus called The Hangar. More than once he'd found himself standing rounds for Donald and his roommates, as only seemed fair when he made no other contribution to his room and board. The school semester was basically over, and Donald and his friends felt the need, again understandable, to celebrate their successes.

Bootie had slipped comfortably into Donald's household and its routines. The four young men—five, counting Bootie—lived in squalor in a white clapboard house near the center of the town of Amherst, in a little gravel enclave behind another building, off the street. The house, only desultorily furnished, smelled of dirty laundry and open garbage bags. Bootie slept in the living room on the brown checked sofa, which was pilled and cigarette-burned, hidden from the passing world by a pair of grubby bedsheets tacked over the windows. None of the young men laid claim to the housekeeping, and the kitchen and bathroom were permanently grimed, the former by dishes and the remnants of food, the latter by engrained soap scum, shaving bristles, and spatters of urine. The fridge in the kitchen, when opened, emanated a swampy stink, on account of the vegetables that had rotted to slime in the crisper not long after Bootie's arrival. He had, gingerly, removed the bag of oozing lettuce, the split tomatoes, the squelching cucumber, and in so doing had felt sufficiently heroic: he had not, however, removed the crisper box and scoured it in the sink, as he knew his mother would have done—they were not, after all, his vegetables—and so merely plugged his nose when retrieving the milk jug (they bought it by the gallon, full fat) or the margarine tub. Like Donald, he lived largely on cereal (Frosted Flakes and Golden Grahams), and toast with peanut butter, and macaroni and cheese from a box, of the chemically orange sort. He, like his hosts, stayed up late, sometimes till first light, and slept until the early afternoon, barely aware of the orderly rhythms of the town outside their walls. But this student life did not depress him in the way dorm life at Oswego had: Donald and his three friends were not half-witted pretenders; they were serious students, whose hours at The Hangar were the reward for months of earnest labor, and who bent over their plastic cups of weak beer discussing Galileo and Hobbes, metaphor and prosody.

Donald, small and wiry with an oversized head, with long arms and bulky forearms like Popeye's, with an almost pretty, stubbled face, had grown his light brown hair to his shoulders and wore, daily, the same pair of Adidas sweatpants and the same crusty sneakers, changing only his T-shirts, of which he had a seemingly endless supply. When he talked about the Reformation, or about Fourierism, his eyes took on the beady zeal that Bootie recognized from his former roommates Lurk and Jerk—except that they had focused thus only on drink and girls. Joey, Ted, and Robert, who was known as Jump and who was, like Bootie, of a pale and spreading plumpness, were literature and philosophy majors, all ungainly, largely pimpled, and, to Bootie, at least at first, a delight.

In the first fortnight, when they were all determinedly lugging around textbooks and writing lengthy term papers, Bootie had thought, in spite of himself, that this might be a place for him, that he had rushed to judgment in his determination to be eternally and only a student of the world. Perhaps he should investigate enrollment, he had thought, and find a room in a house such as this one, in which to hunker for the next four years. He spent afternoons in the hush of the university library, wandering the stacks and taking notes from heavy volumes that he abandoned, at the end of the day, for someone else to reshelve. It had been luxurious, blissful. But now that school was done, he could tell that his fellows' interest was waning, that their intellects were slipping into hibernation, that their pedestrian summer jobs, soon to start, increasingly preoccupied them: Donald was to work for a local arts project, writing press releases and fund-raising grants; Joey, who claimed a devotion to the land, was signed up to assist on a farm in nearby Hadley, picking fruit and manning a roadside stand; and Ted and Jump were heading off to internships in Worcester and Boston. They had had, the previous evening, a displeasing, grade-grubbing conversation, during which Jump had confessed that he'd been to see his Western Philosophy prof to ask her to bump his grade to an A in order that he might maintain his GPA, and Bootie had been painfully reminded of the hypocrisy of all institutional education, not least because the professor, so Jump said, had listened not unsympathetically to his plea.

Over breakfast, bowls of Golden Grahams eaten at lunchtime on the same sofa on which Bootie slept, his sleeping bag crumpled at their feet, Don had asked Bootie what his plans were: "You know, man, if you want to hang here for the summer, that's cool with me, I mean, more than cool. And with Joey, too, you know, he thinks you're great, man, worth it for the conversation alone, he said so, just the other day. And you can have Jump's room, if you want, because Zach, you remember, the bearded guy at the bar, he's going to take Ted's room through Labor Day, assuming Ted comes back. But the thing is, man, it's a question of logistics, of finances, you know?"

Bootie had said nothing, had concentrated on his spoon, flimsy and overly bent, on his bowl, chipped, shallow and widemouthed, and on fishing for the floating specks of cereal that remained in his puddle of milk.

"The thing is, man, the rent? I can help you get something, if you're interested, maybe over at the Monkey Bar, I know the manager, or at the supermarket, the Big Y on Route 9, or even the Stop & Shop, maybe, but it's three-fifty a month for Jump's room, and, like, we can't get by without it, you know?"

Bootie nodded, carefully placed his bowl on a pile of books on the floor, and toyed with his socks.

"Thing is, I've got to know soon, because there's this chick, Wendy, I don't think you know her, but she'll take the room if you don't want it, and I told her it was up to you, but she needs to know, you know? She's got to move in a week, out of where she is now, so—"

"I got you." Bootie looked up, blinked through his smeared glasses at his friend, noted the speck of cereal at the corner of Don's full and girlish lip, the greasy curl of his hair at his chin. "I hear what you're saying."

"You don't have to decide right this second, man." Don was sympathetic, clearly a little awkward, but Bootie did not feel like making it easier. "Maybe you could let me know tonight, yeah?"

"Sure, man. Tonight."

And he had stayed on the sofa, in his brown flannel pajamas, while Don padded down to the bathroom for a shower. He had watched the sun rippling on the bedsheet curtains, had surveyed the disorder of the room around him, the entrail spillage of his open duffel bag against the wainscoting behind the door to the kitchen, and next to it, the pile of hardware and cables that was his computer, waiting face to the wall. He heard the water running, heard Jump's—or was it Joey's?—thunderous tread overhead, and the distinct quaver of a bird outside the window. He had, he realized, deferred his plans, had, since his arrival, escaped not Watertown but himself. In the months

in Watertown, he'd grown accustomed to long hours of isolation, to silent days interrupted only by the buzz of the furnace,
the hushed patter of snow and his mother's occasional tender
nagging. Here, in this house, he had allowed himself to pretend
that Don's life was his, had taken it on like a suit of clothes,
rather than plotting, as he had expected to do, his next step.
For weeks, he'd behaved—it was so easy, so reassuring—like
someone bolstered by the falsity of course work and student ID
cards. He had wanted, instead, to be living like a philosopher,
the way Emerson said that Plato had, alone and invisible,
known to the world only through his work, through his considerable thought. He had to get to New York, for this: to his
as yet unalerted teacher and mentor. To Murray Thwaite.

What was it Emerson had written? He reached for the fat,
thumbed paperback from the stack on the floor, tipping over
his cereal bowl in the process, and he watched, idly, as a rivulet
of milk slithered along the blue rug. He mashed it into the pile
with his bare foot, wiped his foot with his hand, wiped his hand
on the sofa beside him. He riffled the book's pages, found what
he was looking for, the sentences highlighted in fluorescent ink:
"Great geniuses have the shortest biographies. Their cousins
can tell you nothing about them. They lived in their writings,
and so their house and street life was trivial and commonplace."

Now, as the working world's day drew to a close, Bootie sat on
the steps of the imposing Catholic church in the center of
town. After walking the length of the village green and back,
after buying himself a tuna-salad bagel—in defiant extravagance, with a five from his manila envelope—he had settled

there to eat, and then to think. He watched the devout pick their way up and down around him, mostly women, mostly Spanish-speaking, some Filipino, a few with small children, none of them, he surmised, on the way to mass (could there be mass at four-thirty in the afternoon, or five?) but rather, like he himself, seeking space for contemplation and answers to their unanswerable dilemmas. It was warm in the sun, and he rolled up the sleeves of his shirt to take the heat upon his milky arms. He had tried to think, and then had tried not to think, merely to observe the passersby, the young in their end-of-term jollity, their midriffs and thighs bared and their gaits newly lazy, and the adults, still harried, forging professionally through. But he kept coming back to the Emersonian pronouncement, and repeatedly, particularly, as if it were a sign, to the sentence, "Their cousins can tell you nothing about them."

His, it was true, could not have said where he was, nor what he was doing nor had done. Marina Thwaite was his only cousin, or the only one he knew of—nobody was sure what Uncle Peter, his father's brother, got up to out in Los Angeles—of an age to have dandled him when he was an infant with all the brief enthusiasm of a young adolescent, and then, there-after, a sulky sophisticate, to have paid him and his sister little heed on the Thwaites' rare visits to Watertown. Soon, of course, she had been off at college, and then never in Watertown at all. He had only been once, within memory, to see the family in New York, with his parents and his sister, years before. He remembered their apartment, as big as a house, opulently fur-nished, and the wilderness of the park at its doorstep, in which he had longed to lose himself but had refrained, made nervous by his mother's furrowed brow and her warnings of muggings in broad daylight, of bludgeoned corpses in the thickets or sprawled under the picturesque bridges, forgotten like garbage.

He had not glimpsed even his uncle Murray since his father's funeral, when the three of them, Murray, Annabel, and Marina, had flown up from the city in a bitter late November squall and had stood in their rich cloth coats in the sleet at his father's graveside, their hands clasped, impressively he'd thought, before them. Afterward, at the house, Uncle Murray had made much of him, had leaned by the fireplace in the living room with an elbow on the mantel and a scotch in hand, and had quizzed Bootie—he'd called him Fred—about what his plans were, after high school, and whether he'd thought about journalism. Bootie, in retrospect, could see himself as he had been, newly tall and—so briefly—almost thin, his cheeks bright from embarrassment and the heat of the fire, his tweed jacket, short in the sleeves, clutched nervously about him by his crossed arms, at once proud and ashamed, above all aware that this man, whom he barely knew, was widely celebrated and admired, famous before he was a relative at all. Marina, too, had made him shy on that visit, almost as tall as he and slender, her brilliant eyes wide with compassion as she'd hugged him and whispered condolences in his ear. He remembered the lemony scent of her neck, and the frailty of her ribcage, and the surprising smallness of her breasts, which he could barely feel pressed against his chest. He'd been fifteen, had anticipated the swell of them, had been quietly disappointed. Even Annabel, in her very niceness, had discomfited him, because he didn't feel he could believe it, the way she had rubbed his back and kissed Sarah's tearful cheek, not minding, apparently, taking the dampness on her painted lips, all the while standing, in her elegance, like a reproach to his plump and gray-haired mother, whose suit, like his own, had been purchased for a smaller self, and pulled visibly at the upper arms. He remembered, of Annabel, above all the glittering diamond on her ring finger, and the posh singsong of her high voice.

And yet, he thought, as he watched a couple, surely students, pause to neck on the sidewalk in front of the church, almost as if making a point against religion and restraint, he knew—had known all his life—that his uncle's family was his only hope, his ticket out. His uncle was a man who had chosen the path of the mind, who had opted for integrity over glory, even if it had brought him fame rather than the obscurity advocated by Emerson (then again, whatever he said about Plato, Emerson himself had been hardly obscure), and Bootie thought, on the church steps, of how to present himself to Murray Thwaite—as a kind of disciple, an independent follower. This line from Emerson surely was a sign, pointing him to his cousins, who did not yet know him.

One thing at least was certain: he hadn't left Watertown for the Big Y on Route 9, which was no different from the possibilities—Annie's Truck Stop, for example, off the Interstate—with which he had taunted his mother at home. He knew Don was trying to help, but his manner still, somehow, offended, as if suggesting that Bootie had outstayed his welcome, was sponging off his friend, was the subject of hissed conversations between the roommates upstairs after he had fallen asleep. Who did Don think Bootie was, after all? A busboy or checkout clerk in the making? His friend had missed the point of him entirely, was no true friend. Let Wendy, whoever she was, contend with the slime in the refrigerator drawers;

let Wendy try to tackle the defective flusher on the toilet, which required frequent arm-dunking into the murky cistern to retrieve the detached flusher chain, glinting like pirates' treasure at the bottom of a well. While he could accept the trivial in his daily life, Bootie felt he could do so only with the knowledge that the sacrifice had purpose: only a transcendental good could override the indignities. And Don made clear—and Jump, too, in his grade-grubbing, had made clear—that here there was only the illusion of transcendence. Like Una in *The Faerie Queene,* who had to know wickedness even in the guise of good, Bootie, too, needed to discern the route to wisdom. He was, he decided, like a pilgrim in the old days, a pilgrim in search of knowledge.

As he stood and stretched his cramped legs, extending his arms fully to the sky, he felt his stomach growl. He would buy his own box of mac and cheese at the CVS on the way home. He would call his uncle at dinnertime. He would tell Don thank you for the offer but that he was moving on. And if he did end up at The Hangar, he wouldn't buy anyone's drinks but his own; not because he was an ingrate, but because in New York he would need every penny that he had.

CHAPTER FOURTEEN

All for Love

"Julius Clarke, you are such a *girl*! Miss Julia Clarke, paging Miss Julia Clarke!" David was making fun of him, which Julius had trouble pretending he enjoyed. They were trapped in the Sunday afternoon traffic, in their sealed, air-conditioned Neon—vermilion outside, beige synthetic in, and a rental, needless to say—on their way back from Long Island. It had been a rather grueling weekend for Julius, among David's friends, not because he wasn't accustomed to the moneyed— Lord knew, he'd courted them long enough, from his first days at Brown onward—but because he wasn't accustomed to sacrificing all glamour, all thrill to the god Mammon. The clutch of barking drones who had peopled the only moderately lavish rented house, uncounted blocks from the water, had seemed an antigay advertisement: perhaps more muscled and better groomed than their heterosexual counterparts, certainly more scantily clad, more readily inclined to offer lines of coke along with the cocktails, and in these senses more apparently generous in both body and spirit, they were businessmen nevertheless, jabbering endlessly, exclusively, about the Nasdaq and the interest rates, about arcane internal politics at their tedious corporations. Not one of their fellow guests had raised a familiar eyebrow when Julius was introduced, as clear an indication as he could have wanted that there were no *Village Voice* readers in their midst: they were merely a posse of *Wall Street Journal*ers who might sneak a risqué peek at *Out* on weekends.

Somehow, he hadn't expected to be so fully David's sidekick, even though this was "the meeting" with at least a segment of David's social set. He'd imagined that his name would have some currency, however unfixed; that his persona might provoke a ripple of interest. But he was, instead, a wife, smiled upon and then ignored, unless it was a question of aesthetics or of which downtown bars were hippest or of where to find the best bathing suit. He'd been asked where he got his hair cut, what gym he went to, and whether he had a regular massage— as if primping were his career, as if he were some eighteenth-century Parisian courtesan. So that when, eventually, a very pale, very young stockbroker named Ian finally made, on Sunday morning, the social effort for which Julius had ostensibly been waiting, and drawled, as they stood side by side at the kitchen island dicing onions and peppers for omelets, "So, David tells me you write *reviews*. That must be fun. What do you *review*?," Julius could barely restrain his surging irritation and replied, "I'm a chef, actually; and if you don't mind, I'll take over on the chopping front, here."

Ian, mildly baffled, had retreated, apparently unaware of any slight; and in the end, this brunch that Julius had almost single-handedly prepared rendered successful all of itself his entrance onto David's scene.

But on the way home, Julius, although he knew the importance of this weekend, of his success in it, could not fully mask his pique: he didn't dare utter anything so naked as a complaint against irritating Ian, or boring Bob, or tedious Thomas, or buffoonish Barry, their plump and voluble host, who was the only other openly gay man on David's floor at Blake, Zellman and Weaver, and a year or two older than Julius—no, instead he couched his complaints in faint praise, in hidden jibes about the cars and clothes, the quality of the food (his own preparations excepted), and the roughness of the sheets. It was this last comment—"I thought they were frankly prickly, didn't you? If I were Barry, I'd say something to the landlord—I mean, for the fortune he's probably paying . . ."—that had prompted David to hoot with laughter and slap the steering wheel and pronounce Julius a girl.

Julius considered sulking at this, but instead batted his eyes, stroked his lover's forearm, and cooed, in a Southern accent, "Miss Julia Clarke, baby, at your service," before allowing his butterfly fingers to rove into David's khaki lap.

"Watch it—the trucks have eyes." David squirmed a little, visibly pleased, while indicating with his head the ogling passenger of the battered fruiterer's van at a standstill beside them.

Julius wouldn't have said that he was working hard on his relationship with David—although Danielle and Marina might have put it that way—but he would have acknowledged that he was being careful. Aware of his tendency to ask too much too quickly—had this not been his downfall more than once?—and aware, too, of his propensity to brood, too visibly to succumb to his interior demons and to freight each conversation, each outing, each sexual interaction, with greater import than could rationally be found in it—aware of all these failings, if failings they were, he was consciously striving, in this instance, to be Natasha rather than Pierre, to remain a sparkling, light-handed companion behind whose mercurial liveliness he had to trust David could discern, when he was ready, the makings of a devoted partner. It was vital not to seem to care too much, and yet to seem ready to care; vital to seem to give rather than to take; and vital to be amusing and amused in the face of adversity.

Julius hoped that it was working. He had made already countless accommodations, although again, he wouldn't have termed them thus; nor did he even feel, necessarily, that this is what they were. But with David, for the first time, the lure of domesticity seemed not just a fantasy. David was a man in every way *normal*—preppy, popular, handsome, successful—and yet—so sexy—with a twist. He seemed to want Julius with a straightforward, almost overwhelming, certainty. He wanted them to travel together, to eat dinner together, to go shopping together. He went out of his way to charm Julius, showering him with little gifts—shirts, CDs, an electric massager, almost all sweetly just off the mark (the shirt collars too wide, the CDs too mainstream, the massager ordered from *The Sharper Image* catalogue), but charming just for that reason, and David the more attractive for his calm assertion, so adult in his conviction. And he responded just as Julius would have fantasized—*had* fantasized—to Julius's own overtures, to his suggestion that David skip work and stay in bed, or his offer to take David to a particularly louche East Village art opening where no *Wall Street Journal* reader would be caught dead. David was like an imaginary lover made flesh: in every obvious way nice, but keenly naughty, too.

Suddenly, Julius's power to seduce brought him not just desire, in return, but a whole life, the promise that he could be embraced, taken care of, fully and properly adored. David was everything he had always known he wanted, with, to boot, an alluring edge of temper. He liked to drink; he liked, in an almost naïve way, the excitement of cocaine, the mechanics of it and the illicit aura. Julius, less naturally inclined to drugs, was interested, rather, in David's interest. And David thrilled to the notion that he was "keeping" Julius, that Julius was his "geisha"—it was a word used by David, vaguely offensive to Julius, Eurasian after all, in its random Orientalism, but he let it pass without comment—a subjugation enticing to David precisely because he had realized Julius's worth in a wider world, or another world, at least. The boyfriend apparently idle at home was, in some circles, an esteemed, even renowned figure: it was as if, then, David had purchased for his own private enjoyment a painting that had hung, to some acclaim, in a moderately famous gallery. He had said as much to Julius, or almost, and this without showing the slightest interest in Julius's supposedly artsy friends; and while the implication was clearly that Julius was some class of trophy wife, he had chosen to take the status, at least most of the time, as a compliment.

And as a means to an end, to—he would have insisted—his own ends. In some complex web that he, Julius, could not for all his verbal facility quite have articulated, the two were united for their mutual worldly benefit. David had large, plush towels and heavy silverware, as well as a daunting square footage (was it 1,400?); but Julius had in mind more than these crass material comforts. He could not have said, at that early stage of what he envisaged as a lifelong partnership (but was this not precisely the Pierre in him, the stolid, brooding monogamist?) what more it was he could expect from his lover.

When, in the wake of his geisha maneuver in the Neon, Julius heard David suggesting, blithely, almost as if without thinking, that Julius should probably sublet his studio as he was never there anyway, and frankly move his things into David's apartment—there was, after all, an entire empty closet in the second bedroom—he could hide his delight only with as strenuous an effort as earlier he had hidden his irritation.

"Do you really think it's a good idea?" he asked, eyeing David sidelong: the slightly arched nose, the soulful dark eye.

"Don't you?" David turned, suddenly. Julius could tell, or thought he could, that David was nervous, afraid he had betrayed too much. Although perhaps this was merely Julius, projecting.

"Keep watching the road, sugar. I just want to be sure."

"Sure of what?" David sounded mildly petulant. "You live there already anyway."

"Sure it's what you want, that's all. Sure we're not rushing."

To which David said, eyes all the while on the traffic, "What's wrong with a little rush?"

And in this way, several days later, Julius found himself in his studio, packing all that seemed most personal to him: his clothes, a selection of his books—did he need his college edition of *Swann's Way* in French? He wavered; decided instead to take the highlights of his postcard collection, long attached to his walls with Blu-Tack and now gingerly removed. He left behind not only Proust but the untouched two-volume Musil filched, years before, from the books department at the *Voice;* and he left, too, the long-abandoned manuscript of his novel, begun at about the time Marina had signed her famous book contract. He took a couple of photographs from the collage on his fridge, ones of his family; the rest he stacked in a shoebox and stuffed on top of the fridge, at the back. He packed his favorite blanket—a green woolen one he'd brought from Michigan, and had had with him since college—but he did so hesitantly, aware that it was ratty, and originally from Sears, and not an item whose arrival David would applaud.

When he was done, the apartment looked like what it was: a cheap, near-student rental, with its unevenly whitewashed walls and pocked floors, its grayed futon shrouded in a faded Indian print upon the linoleum. The red curtains he had hung to hide the toilet (no door) and the cupboard (ditto) shone lurid and ghastly in the early afternoon light, an oblique but penetrating illumination that revealed a faint layer of dust along the countertops and a smattering of black spiderweb tendrils dangling from the popcorn ceiling. He had never once let David come to this apartment, and David had shown no inclination to do so.

Julius had no sublettor, for the time being, though he had put out the word. It had to be a friend, or a friend of a friend, someone prepared to lie to the landlord, to keep the answering machine message unchanged, to receive mail elsewhere. That tenant had yet to be found. In the meantime, in his trammeled jubilation—Don't let it show! Don't let it show!—Julius focused on the realization of one of his fantasies: moving in with his boyfriend. He repeated to himself: "I'm moving in with my boyfriend. *My* boyfriend. My *boy*friend. Mine."

Which of course was more complicated than it might have been. Julius's apartment lay deeply embedded in the Lower East Side, so far from fashion, on a narrow stretch named Pitt Street lined upon its other side by housing projects, big brick towers arranged around concrete courtyards, behind chain-link fences, and upon his own by crumbling tenements such as that which housed him, upon which no gleaming profiteer's eye had yet alighted, and no taxis ever jounced along the potholed pavement. Julius had to line up his boxes and bags—a paltry few, for a near-midlife accumulation—inside his building's front door, and pay the super's wife, a large and slow-moving woman in a dirty smock, with shiny olive skin and a disconcerting wandering eye, to watch over them, and then he had to walk several blocks to hail a cab, and direct the driver back to his place, to wait while he loaded his stuff (the driver, a hairy Russian, popped the trunk without moving from his seat and chomped imperiously upon a sandwich while Julius, slight and sweating, hauled out his belongings; the super's wife, too, sat upon a stool outside the building and, while occasionally admonishing him to "be careful, now," attended largely to the fanning of her fleshy cheeks with a tattered magazine), and then drive him uptown, across town, to the comparative social Everest that was Chelsea.

Unpacking, Julius was beset by strange fears: Did his books, or his blanket, smell? Did they carry must and deprivation, or a hint of mildew, in their folds? Were his clothes too threadbare to have brought? More than once David had fussed about his collars, or the shine of his trousers, had proposed a trip to Barneys, which Julius, divided—he wanted to look smart, and David had the cash; but still, but still—had coyly deflected; and yet, in order to play the role of David's partner—and this was the role apparently on offer: a visit to the senior Cohens in Scarsdale had been proposed—a whole new wardrobe was perhaps necessary.

As David had told him he must, he claimed the second bedroom's closet, and found that it held his belongings with considerable space to spare. The few books he'd brought he kept out of the cupboard, along with the pictures. He would wait until David came home, and ask him where he might put these things, if not frankly on display then at least accessible. He didn't allow himself to reflect on the strangeness of this, of having to ask where he might position his family snapshots or his encyclopedia of film so as not to disrupt the decor; and he knew, instinctively, that asking was, in this case, appropriate. He could anticipate the dozy indulgence with which David, having loosened his tie and shed his jacket, would ruffle Julius's hair and say, "You are *too* cute, Jules. *Too* cute. You didn't need to ask." But if he didn't ask, and merely made a space for Frank and Thu Clarke between David's sister's wedding pictures and the posed Cohen family portrait, taken when fourteen-year-old David sported glasses and braces both—if he took the liberty supposedly his, Julius could not imagine David's reaction. By which one so adept, indeed, often too adept, at imagining, knew he ought to refrain.

CHAPTER FIFTEEN

Do You, Napoleon?

"So you're glad you came?"

"Wouldn't have missed it." Ludovic Seeley's smile revealed the hint of a vulpine incisor. "A chance to take on New York?" He shrugged his narrow shoulders.

Danielle toyed with her fork and smiled at the window beside them, at her reflection and beyond, at the pedestrians passing on the other side of the glass, a million miles away, at a homeless man, dread-headed, tattered, teetering across the avenue from the park opposite. "If that's how you see it. You said 'revolution,' back in Sydney. Does it still seem that way?"

"We'll see, hey? Mustn't give the game away before it's started."

"That's rather cryptic of you."

"Mystery breeds interest." Seeley made a temple beneath his chin of his elegant fingers. "As a producer, you know that. I assume."

"I've certainly been told." Danielle turned her gaze to the gleaming empty plate before her, in which her shadowed reflection was again visible. She had decided that she would not let him play her, that she would present a forceful and direct front. She didn't want him ever to suspect that his movements had an almost physical hold over her, as if she were unwillingly his marionette. "But it seems to me it's sometimes stronger still, and more exciting, to shove everything out in the open from the outset. Blow everyone away, you know?"

Seeley curled his lip. He didn't look Australian to her; he looked English, or possibly French.

"By which I suppose I mean that you might have still more success—"

"If I told everyone, and in particular you, I'm guessing, exactly what *The Monitor* will be and how it will differ from the rest."

"Well, yes." She paused. "After all, Ludovic—"

"Ludo, please."

She nodded, vaguely. "After all, the economy isn't what it was six months ago, and a far cry from what it was a year ago, and the signs, as they say, aren't good. I mean, I know a lot of people in dot-coms who've lost their jobs, and it's still going on—and I guess my point is simply that in a market like this, you know, people actually *do* want something to believe in, something to look forward to. I can see that it's not the easiest time to start a new publication, but if you get the word out, and pitch it right, then you've got a whole new population of the disenchanted to draw upon—I mean, if revolution is what you're selling."

"Do you not suppose," Seeley spoke slowly, "that this might have occurred to me?"

"Of course, sure, I didn't mean to suggest— It's just that the way you talk, or don't, I suppose—" Danielle, sensing the heat in her cheeks, put a hand up to cool and cover one. She wanted to feel annoyed, but found that she did not, could not.

"You thought, quite rightly, that I might welcome your opinion. Which I do, please don't misunderstand me. But I can't fail to suspect—" Seeley was interrupted by the arrival of their hors d'oeuvres, a diverse pair of glistening, wispy constructions adrift on oceans of white porcelain, hers a supposed chèvre–and–bell pepper mille-feuille (or Napoleon) and his recogniz-able as a salad only by the three emerging spears of well-oiled endive that stood guard over their huddled, intestinal beetroot and marinated onion core. When the near-invisible waiters had retreated, leaving not so much as a fingerprint on the giant plates, he resumed exactly where he had left off, a suspension at which Danielle, privately of course, marveled. "That your motives for speaking to me, indeed, your motives for inviting me to lunch—a delight, I must say, too long postponed, and one about which I'm thrilled, but nevertheless—these motives, surely, are not purely altruistic?"

"I suppose—"

"Forgive me the circumlocutions, please. What I'm saying, all I'm saying, is that we might speak more clearly and under-stand each other better if you were to tell me what it is you're hoping I can do for you."

"What makes you think I would want you to *do* something?" Danielle was truly taken aback, unsure of whether to take offense. And yet: to be direct had been her goal. Directness above all.

"Your repeated return, my dear Danielle, to the word 'revo-lution.' That's what makes me sure you want something more than the pleasure of my company."

"Well, yes." Part of her wanted to explain, although surely he knew it (was he not all but winking, after all?), that the professional chatter was only the mask to hide her desire, precisely, for the pleasure of his company; but she was not so askew in her grasp of reality as to do so: while in her imagination she had conducted conversations both intellectual and personal with this man, she held no illusions, knew this was their first sustained exchange; and knew, too, the importance of seeing it not through the rosy filter of their already long, imaginary friendship, but by the true light of day. She looked again at the window, strove to see through herself to the outside, where the beggar had taken up a station on the sidewalk and was shaking his scaly outstretched hand at the crowds. "You're quite right, absolutely. It's so important to be frank. I'm glad you asked. Let me explain."

As they each gingerly dismantled and consumed their fanciful dishes—in her case at least, a fancy that, Danielle thought but did not say, was less original and extraordinary than the restaurant's reputation and price had led her to expect, and therefore disappointing, as she had chosen the venue to impress—Danielle proceeded to explain that she had been taken with his use of the term, that she had, perhaps wrongly, heard in it a certain echo, the suggestion of an ethos that she thought might be found, to greater or lesser degrees, in certain other publications or presentations, and that she, in her producer's role, had thought to articulate into, well, a movement.

Seeing his eyebrow arch, and the wrinkles form on his high forehead, she continued, "Or not necessarily a movement, if it's not really one. But to compare your project to the others, and see how much or how little they actually correspond. It's not as though I'm trying to rig the answers. It really is about asking the questions. And for me, well, the germ for me was your use, that evening in Sydney, of the word 'revolution.' And I suppose from there, by looking at what you've done so far, I've tried to figure out what it is you meant by that word; and I have some ideas. But I'd really like, I suppose what I'd really like, is to hear it from you." She smiled at him broadly, with her lips shut, in a way she hoped inspired confidence. "But not now—I mean, not that ideally I wouldn't hear it now, but I find people rarely speak as well as they do the first time, so what I'd really like is to hear it from you on camera."

"So you'd like to be surprised?"

Danielle laughed. She hoped her laugh seemed spontaneous. "If that's what it comes down to, yes, sure. I'd like to— I'd be interested in making the film as much about you as you were willing to let me. I see you as the linchpin, really."

"You flatter me."

"Not at all. But the one thing is the timing: I do think it could be invaluable to your magazine if the program—if we do it of course—if it coincides with your launch, or certainly by the end of the year. Which is a really short turnaround in terms of our series, but I think I can convince them, if we get some footage, if you'll talk a bit to the camera, maybe? I mean, what are the stories right now, aside from all the layoffs? The biggest thing is Nicole Kidman in *Moulin Rouge*!"

"Nicole Kidman," Seeley murmured. "Newly single, newly a star."

"Right." Danielle worried now that she had been *too* direct, that she had seemed unimpressively, bulldozerishly, forthcoming. Usually, she was most confident in her presentations; but this time—the marionette problem—she had felt the control to be his, throughout. He was curling his lip—still? Again?—

but said nothing, and she didn't know what he was thinking. "Like I say, it'd be great for *The Monitor*. For your profile over here. I know it would. But you should have a think, see how you feel."

He bowed his head slightly. "I'm honored. And flattered. And certain you're right in many ways. But I'll take some time, just a little." He let his eyelids flutter slightly, before he resumed his heavy stare. "I find it's best, for me, to reflect. I'm only rarely impulsive."

Like a snake in the sunlight, Danielle thought. She said, "Great. How's the hiring going, by the way?"

"Ah." He threw up his hands in mock despair. "It's an agony!"

"But why?"

"The budget's never big enough; the times, as you said, are suddenly uncertain. Why leave an existing job for an imaginary one? A year ago, yes; now, it's not so easy."

"What about the woman at the Met?"

"Julie Chen?"

"That was Julie Chen? God, she was tiny!"

"But a viper. A tiny viper. The most powerful sort. And I urged her to reflect, the way you've urged me, but she declined."

"She'll regret it, I'm sure."

"Not nearly so sure as I am, believe me. But slowly, slowly. I'm getting a team together. A bloody good team."

Danielle nodded, tackled her *poussin*. Their starters had been removed and their entrées delivered without her fully having been aware of it. Full marks for the service, at least. She looked up at him and allowed herself a genuine smile, a slightly lopsided one she knew made her eyes crinkle and her nose a little more beaky; but it was a smile she felt was fully hers, and she had the impression that in the return of his gaze, jaunty, slightly lingering as it was, there was fondness, perhaps even attraction. There was, at least, and mercifully, flirtation. There was hope. "You know," she began in a different, more confidential tone (and later, although she would ask herself why she had embarked unbidden on this path, she would not satisfactorily be able to reply), "this may be way out of line, but I have a friend—she's really smart, and she's done a certain amount of freelance stuff—she was at *Vogue,* at one point, but that was ages ago, and she's much more serious, really, than that. Anyway, she's just finishing a book and she's looking for a job—"

"In journalism?"

"Yes, that would be right. I mean, I don't know what positions you're still looking to fill, but—"

Seeley shrugged. "It all depends."

"You met her, actually. The friend, my friend. At the Met."

Seeley raised both eyebrows at once. "Surely not your mother?"

"Don't be silly. The other one. Marina. Marina Thwaite. Do you remember? Dark hair, tall—well, she was sitting down—pretty?"

"Certainly, I remember."

"She *is* pretty," Danielle insisted, keen in spite of herself to get his opinion. He seemed vague on this score, however—almost gay in his indifference. Perhaps he was gay?

"Yes, of course," he said. "Pretty, yes. But tell me, because I wondered: she's not by any chance related to *the* Thwaite, is she?"

"Daughter."

"Thought she might be. Right age. Bone structure."

"It's been something of a burden for her."

"I'd imagine so. That lazy wombat of a man. He's been riding on reputation for as long as we've been alive. Hasn't got an original thought in his head."

"Do you think so? I think he's quite brilliant, actually."

Seeley snorted.

"Maybe there's no point discussing Marina, then, because she *really* thinks he's brilliant. She's her father's Anna Freud. I think she'd marry him if she could."

"You intrigue me. You may not mean to, but you do."

"How so?"

"She sounds an interesting candidate for, well—for revolution, as you'd like to put it. In a literal sense, maybe: for turning around. *The Monitor* might work wonders for her intellectual development."

"You make it sound like a sinister Frankensteinian experiment."

"Hardly."

"Or Orwellian."

"No, I think not. It's the television that's Orwellian. Your business, I'm afraid, not mine. I'm an old-fashioned fellow—I still believe in the printed word."

"As does Murray Thwaite."

Seeley inclined his head in ironic assent. "It's a matter, though, of the meaning of the words."

"Or of the words having any meaning at all, if we're getting po-mo about it."

"Quite. That's exactly right."

"Murray Thwaite thinks things do mean," Danielle went on. "And my sense is that you don't, really."

"It's not as simple as that—"

"Not that you don't think 'table' will suffice to indicate this thing between us, that's not what I'm saying—"

"It's more a matter of questioning the meaning of emotions," Seeley said, "or of asking what they are and how they color our reality. Of letting go of their falsehoods so you can see things for what they are."

Danielle waited for him to continue. The beggar had returned to his personalized festooned bench in the park across the avenue, and the sidewalk was calmer, relieved of its noontime hurry.

"That's what I hold against Thwaite—he's a sentimentalist. There's nothing clear-eyed about his analyses; they're rants, just empty rants. And people buy them because they subscribe to some antiquated notion that a passionate reporter is more valuable than a dispassionate one. Bollocks."

"Well, more interesting at least, don't you think?"

Seeley seemed illuminated, almost aquiver in his seat. Danielle thought again of a reptile, a beautiful but dangerous one. "No, precisely no!" He leaned forward over their coffee cups, his voice low and fervent. "What could be rarer, more precious, more compelling than unmasking these hacks for what they are? Than an instrument to trumpet that the emperor has no clothes, and the grand vizier has no clothes, and the empress is starkers, too—do you get my point? Debunk the lot of them."

"That's revolutionary, sure, but what are you left with?"

"The seething truths about these guys, the lot of them, these hereditary asses—you reveal what really gets them going."

"And then what? What do you give people instead?"

"You give them something bigger than private opinion. You give them something in its way more true, or certainly more real, if truth is a fungible term."

"Which is?"

"Think about Napoleon."

"What about him?"

"An important chap, my dear, particularly here, particularly now."

"So what did he say?"

"Let me share what was said *about* him—ultimately always key, don't you think?"

"Hmm."

"It was said that 'if Napoleon is France, if Napoleon is Europe, it is because the people whom he sways are little Napoleons.' "

"I see," said Danielle, not at all certain that she did.

"Show people that Murray Thwaite is the Wizard of Oz, a tiny, pointless man roaring behind a curtain. Then learn what they are, and show them themselves. What could be more compelling than that?"

"You're a big fan of Napoleon, then?"

Seeley's incisor once again caught the light as he replied. "Isn't everyone, in one way or another, a fan of Napoleon's?"

"I'm not sure you'd be the best employer for Marina."

Danielle said this laughingly, but not wholly in jest. She was both alarmed and attracted by Seeley's outburst. She didn't think he could be gay.

"Please, please," he said, laughing now, too. "Don't hold it against me. Have her ring me. I'd be delighted. Truly delighted."

As they were leaving the restaurant—among the last diners to depart; and why not, thought Danielle, at $123 plus tip— she felt his hand at her back and the warmth of his breath, his proximate body, as he leaned to whisper in her ear: at last, for her, the intimacy he bestowed so profligately upon others; and the knowledge tingled beneath her skin on a current all the way to her extremities. He said, "Just think of it as a taste."

"A taste?"

"Of what you might get on camera, if we were to go ahead."

And that night, among her Rothkos, Danielle, mint tea in hand, the downtown lights winking knowingly at the window, could not help but remember that taste, the electricity of him, the charisma, the focus. As if he were alight. And the hand, delicate but firm, not directing but engaging, somehow, a sensation that carried within it, surely not just for her, the promise of something—was it sex? Could it have been?—a promise that she carried away like an unopened present. For next time.

CHAPTER SIXTEEN

The Fat Man Cometh

When her mother came down the corridor, Marina was sitting cross-legged on the carpet in shorts and a tank top, her back firmly against the wall, collating and labeling the articles she had downloaded and printed out for her father. In front of her lay the entrance to Murray's study, its door half ajar, and from that seclusion emanated the scent of burning tobacco and the occasional clicking of fingers on the computer keyboard. This was as close as Murray would allow anyone to loiter while he worked; and it was, for his daughter, a special dispensation. Aurora, the maid, was not permitted, he joked, within a hundred yards of his office. Marina, for her part, was grateful to be busy at a necessary task that was not her own book. Serving as her father's amanuensis pleased her more, she knew, than it ought; and more, certainly, than she would ever have admitted to the highly critical Danielle.

"For God's sake," Annabel said as she approached, "turn on a light! What are you doing on the floor?"

"I'll be done in a sec. Dad asked for these in a hurry, and I thought this way he could get each one as soon as it's done."

"I'm not criticizing, sweetie; I'm just worried you'll go blind." Saying which, Marina's mother swept into her husband's room with a peremptory rap on the door. She left a trail of bergamot and neroli oil in her wake—her summer perfume.

"Murray, dear," Marina heard her say, in a tone that suggested that Annabel expected, but would not brook, resistance.

Marina could tell from her father's voice that, in the first instance, he didn't even look up from his screen. She could picture his half-moon glasses, slipped, pinching his nostrils. He said, "Can it wait, beloved? I'm just in the throes of—"

"No, dear. I'm afraid it really can't wait. I do need to have a word now."

Marina, who had stopped shuffling papers, heard the creak of her father's chair as he swiveled. He sighed. Marina could see his thigh and shoulder through the doorway, but could not fully read their posture.

"That was your nephew on the phone," Annabel said.

"Judy's boy?"

"Is there any other?" Annabel was herself an only child.

"Everything okay up there?"

"Fine, Judy's fine. No, it seems he wants to come for a visit."

Marina stood, avoiding her papers, and slid frankly into the doorway. "Fat Freddie?" she said. "Coming here?"

Annabel, whose arms were crossed, nodded.

"What's wrong with that? Sounds like an excellent plan. How old is he?"

"Must be nineteen," said Marina. "Maybe twenty. Depends on his birthday."

"That's what I told him," said Annabel. "That we thought it was an excellent idea."

"When, and for how long?" Murray had already turned back to his computer, by way of dismissal, when he asked.

"Hence the word, Murray, dear. I just thought you should be informed. He's coming Thursday—"

"The day after tomorrow?" Murray looked over his shoulder, peering over his glasses.

"And I'm not sure he has any plans to move on."

"What does that mean?" Marina asked.

"It means he told me that he's thinking of settling here— interpret that for yourselves—and he just needs a place to stay while he figures things out."

Murray grunted.

"And he's very sorry to impose—he's certainly polite—but he doesn't know where else to turn."

"He's like one of your clients, Mom. Like that kid—what's his name?"

"DeVaughn. I know. And do we know anywhere he can park his car cheaply, he asked."

"Tell him no and he'll have to push off after a couple of days," said Marina.

"He's a nice boy," said Murray, almost tenderly. "Or he seemed it, back at Bert's funeral."

"That was years ago, Dad."

"I know Judy's been worried about him, dropping out of college, no job, no prospects. A bright kid, though, she says."

"I'm sure all this is true, Murray, but are we really—"

"Aren't we off to Stockbridge in a few weeks? It's not so long to put up with him."

"Depends what he's like," Marina said. "I remember him as fat."

"He was quite thin at the funeral, actually," said Annabel. "But this isn't about his weight, or his shoe size, either."

"The boy is family. We'll just see how it goes," Murray said with finality, turning not only his head but his hands, fingers poised to type. "Marina, if you have those articles? To my left there would be great."

Marina trailed her mother back down the hallway and into the kitchen, a sheaf of as-yet-uncollated papers clasped to her bosom. "Are you pissed off?" she asked.

"No, not exactly."

"It *is* an imposition, though."

"Oh, sure." Annabel had turned her attention to supper, was rifling through the fridge. "I thought Aurora was making gazpacho?"

"Top shelf at the back. And the cold salmon's in foil down below. She made mayonnaise, too."

"Bless her."

"I'll bet he eats a lot."

"Who?"

"The boy."

"Your cousin? He's not 'the boy.' And it's been a long time."

"Where will he sleep?"

"I've told Aurora to make up the guest room down by your dad."

"At least I won't have to share the bathroom."

Annabel paused in her rummaging, for a corkscrew this time. "My, you are a spoiled little girl, aren't you? Glass of wine?"

"It's not chardonnay, is it?"

"Chablis, actually."

"That's very seventies of you. I just don't think it's *on,* that's all, descending on you guys indefinitely, like that."

"Like what? Like you, you mean?"

"That's not fair."

"I know, I'm teasing. But, sweetie, he's one of your only two cousins on the planet. It's strangely—I just think, like your father, that we should wait and see how it goes."

"But he'll probably bug Dad, of all people. He'll get in the way. He doesn't know what it's like to work at home."

"That's why I wanted your father to be prepared. But who knows? It may work out. Maybe he'll become your father's indispensable right hand."

"Careful, Mom. That's my job."

"Oh, really? I thought it had been mine, all these years. You're welcome to it, though."

CHAPTER SEVENTEEN

No Place Like Home

That evening after supper, Murray Thwaite retreated to his study, ostensibly to continue work on his current long article, but actually, he hoped, to steal a couple of hours uninterrupted on his book, with which he had been making only minimal progress. He blamed, obscurely, his daughter, whose presence was more a source of anxiety than a help, in spite of her eagerness. Marina, unlike her mother, had a habit of lurking; and while he knew there was nothing but goodwill in her, at least in her conscious mind, he felt dogged by her need, by a spirit that, even when she wasn't curled like a waiting python outside his door, was always hovering and hopeful. Sometimes, absurdly, he imagined that she wanted purely to consume him, eating his words and the air he breathed and spewing them out as her own. At other times, their dance seemed the most naked seduction, a mutual consumption, a strange passion of a kind he did not share even with his wife. She discomfited him, his lovely, his adored, daughter, and he blamed the distraction of her for his inability to pursue the book. Each time he thought his insight sufficiently crystallized, he found it in shards as he sat down to write. He'd been mulling for weeks the matter of independence, of independent thought and what, frankly, it might entail—an apt topic, he considered, for a man thought iconoclastic, and in some measure the heart of his book—and had felt himself ready to opine. But instead, this evening, with an oily stain on his shirt from Aurora's fine mayonnaise and a tumbler of scotch, ice melted, on the desk before him, in this hour when he ought to have felt most at his ease, he kept imagining that he heard Marina's soft, approaching tread, or the rhythm of her breath in the hallway. He opened his window to the street, to the racket of exhaust and jarring potholes, but these noises, too, disrupted, as he began to listen for patterns in the run and stop of the cars, in the city night's swelling and diminishing waves.

This boy's arrival might help. Then again, the opposite was possible, even likely. When Murray was trying to work, he could feel the egos, the ticking minds, of those who shared his space, as surely as if they were actual blimps, expanding, rising and compressing the little air in which his own soul might move. The notion that an additional self roaming Murray's hallways might free him seemed, in truth, fanciful; but if Frederick guzzled the air, he would simply have to go, and promptly. Harder, by far, to get Marina to clear out.

From which stemmed two divergent but near simultaneous threads of thought, the one concerning Frederick, the other (more or less) Marina. His nephew, only son of Murray's only sister. It occurred to him that he ought to telephone his sibling. Although they weren't close there was a familial bond between them, and he hadn't spoken to her since—since when? Some conversation about the endless snowstorms, about the impressive inches fallen upon Watertown, a dull but necessary exchange of familial pleasantries at some point well past the

new year, perhaps around Easter, and, he feared, at her insti-
gation. Now, at least, they'd have something to discuss: the boy
and his plans, what it was Murray might do for him, how long
he might stay.

The second thought alighted, via Marina, upon her friend,
the small girl who had come to supper back in March, with the
dark curls, soulful eyes, and fine breasts: Danielle. He didn't
have to hunt for her name; he merely pretended to himself to
have to do so, aware, rather, that she was all too readily in his
thoughts. Not improperly at all; but theirs was now an almost
lively e-mail correspondence, in which he played a professorial
role, recommending books, offering advice, reminiscing wisely
about when he was her age. He hadn't mentioned these
exchanges to Marina, and sensed, clearly, that Danielle hadn't
either; and from this shared secret he derived some erotic
charge.

But what struck him this evening, even as he felt, or imagined he did, Marina, breathing down his neck (an expression
too nearly literal to please him), was the possibility, even
inevitability, of enlisting Danielle in a further betrayal—no,
that wasn't the right word: a collusion. Much better. He wanted
her to collude with him for Marina's benefit. Murray Thwaite
found before him the excuse he'd hoped for since March, to
arrange to see Danielle again, and this time, to see her alone.
In all their e-mails, neither he nor Danielle had mentioned
Marina more than in passing (this, too, titillated, smacked of
the illicit), but now the time had come, he realized, to place
her firmly between them, as a topic of discussion.

"Dear Danielle," he began, tapping at his keyboard with his
two thick but swift forefingers. "I hope you won't mind if I

confide in you that I'm quite worried about our dear Marina. This may seem to come out of the blue, but as you will understand, Annabel's and my concern [good to mention Annabel here? He debated, decided that it was] dates back to last fall, when Marina came home to us. We'd been hoping that a rest and the support of the family might be enough to help her get back on her feet, but as the months pass"—he paused, sipped his scotch—"and as the year anniversary of her return is not so far away [a slight exaggeration, but warranted, he thought], I find myself increasingly troubled." He read what he had so far. Did it seem alarmist? Not unduly. He wanted Danielle to know that he had things to talk about; that this wasn't (wasn't it?) a trumped-up excuse. He tapped on, erasing half of what he wrote, wanting to be sure that he found the right tone, and with it the right inferences, connotations, shades of possible meaning. Because he wanted her to read the message several times, to worry—as he expected she would—about its propriety, only to be reassured, in every phrase, that there was nothing untoward to be found, that it was a message Annabel might as easily have written. And yet beneath this superficial smoothness, he wanted her to sense—he wanted her not to be able not to sense—that he needed her presence more than her advice; that he wanted above all to communicate with her, Danielle; and that Marina was, here, mere pretext (pretext not being a role, he realized, that his daughter was accustomed to playing).

He tinkered with and tweaked his message—a mere two paragraphs—until his glass of scotch was gone; then debated storing his effort in the "send later" file. At which the very thought of Marina—did he not hear her again? Had she crept up upon him like the bloody cat? Surely not—directed his finger to the transmission key, and the message was sent. Simple enough: Lunch, next week? Or would a drink be better? That was the gist of it. Simple enough.

He poured a little more scotch from the bottle in his drawer. He'd forgo the ice, this time, on account of the human risks involved in venturing to the kitchen. He checked his watch: not quite eleven. Surely not too late for Judy? He himself planned to work at least until one. He had to look up the number in his address book; and mused, in passing, on the strangeness of knowing Danielle's e-mail address by heart, and not his sister's phone number.

Her voice was thick, as if with cold.

"Did I waken you, Judes? I'm sorry—"

"No, I mean, I guess I drifted off. In front of the TV. But I'm not in bed or anything."

Murray made conversation, coaxing his sister fully into wakefulness. It was a type of chat in which he did not readily indulge, these days, a provincial small talk familiar from his childhood—not just about the weather, but about its consequences (Judy's son-in-law was already getting good business up in Alexandria Bay; if the summer went on like this, it'd be a boomer for him, even with the economy faltering), and about the minutiae with which Judy filled her time: only a month to the end of school, the municipal pool opening Memorial Day, the cost of gasoline, her old friend Susan—sure, he remembered Susan, the redhead—was coming down from Kingston, Ontario, for a couple of weeks; her husband? He owned Burger King franchises, two of them, and very successful, too: they'd built an indoor pool up at their house, with a retractable roof, no less. Eventually, because she didn't mention him of her own accord, Murray brought up Frederick: "So, we're going to get a look at your boy at last," he said.

"How do you mean?" Judy sniffed. Perhaps she did have a cold. "Are you up in Massachusetts?"

"No, no—we don't go up there for another couple of weeks. No, the boy's coming here, of course. Didn't you know?"

"Frederick, you mean? My Bootie? He's in Massachusetts."

"What's he doing there, for pete's sake?" Murray felt as though they were both yelling down an ancient trunk line, trapped in an echoing cave of miscommunication. He wished he hadn't called. "Listen, Judy, I didn't speak to him myself; it was Annabel, this afternoon. So maybe he's in Massachusetts, but he's coming here this week, for a visit."

"A visit?"

"Can you hear me all right? I thought he was home with you."

"He left about a month ago. To see about summer school in Massachusetts. At U Mass. Where is it—Amherst?"

"Right, right."

"But he can't be doing that if he's coming to you. The courses start in a couple of weeks. I mean—"

"Maybe he just needs a break before he settles down to study."

"I don't get it. I only spoke to him just two days ago." Judy sounded—what?—thick, still, and now full of blame, as if this misunderstanding were somehow Murray's fault. She always played the victim. "Just two days ago, and he didn't say anything about New York."

"I didn't speak to him, Judes. Annabel spoke to him. I thought he was home with you."

"Not for a month."

"I understand: he left a month ago for Massachusetts. I'm just saying that I didn't know."

"Why would you?"

"Quite."

There was a silence on the line, as if, Murray thought, both were attempting to martial their mutual irritation; or else, perhaps, as if there were nothing more to say.

"So we'll give you a call once he's arrived," Murray offered at last. "He can fill us in on all his plans. Probably he's run out of clean laundry up in Massachusetts, needs a place to wash his socks."

"Maybe," said Judy, quieter now, with another sniff. "I'll tell you, though, Murray, it's awful quiet since he left. More than when he went to Oswego. I guess because I worry about him. I don't know what he's thinking, you know? He really needs to get back to school."

"Mhmm. Although you know, Judes, there's more than one way to skin a cat."

"You're saying he *doesn't* need to get back to school?"

Murray paused again. "No—it's just that sometimes . . . no, nothing."

"What?"

"Nothing. Nothing. You're right, I'm sure. He should get back to school. And you'll see, he will."

"You'll talk to him, then?"

"Talk?"

"About school? Please, Murray."

"Sure. Sure, I'll talk to him."

"He really looks up to you, you know. And of course his own father isn't around anymore, so—"

"No, of course not."

When he hung up, Murray felt as though he had been twisted in a trap, like some stupid raccoon. Here he was, as ever, punished for his big-brotherly impulses: there existed no circumstances under which he would ever ask anything of his sister, not a thing; and yet each time they spoke—at Easter, he remembered now, it had been a small sum of money, something about the maintenance of their parents' graves—she contrived to gouge him for something. He shouldn't make it so easy for her; he shouldn't call her is what he shouldn't do. No wonder her son hadn't told her where he was going—who would? By which one had to infer, however hopefully, that the son was not like the mother. Those were not things he would say to anyone, not even to Annabel. He was a loyal brother, above all.

Murray was revisited, in his desk chair, with the subsiding roar of the late night traffic at his ear, by a vision of his childhood home, the paneled vestibule and dining room, the cramped darkness of it, and the meanness, everything spare and bleached and doubly worn, and only their mother, their beautiful mother, with her patrician profile and wavy dark hair, like Ingrid Bergman, his mother the fantasist, who in spite of her ability to peel and prune and scour and press, in spite of her eternal apron and hospital corners, read novels and magazines and dreamed for herself and her son: of wider vistas, of glittering cocktail parties on Park Avenue, of fancy hotel rooms and travel to Europe. Most important, of Harvard: she dreamed of Harvard—or Princeton, or Yale, but ideally Harvard—for her son, and told him so from the earliest years, so that he grew up

with, in his mind's eye, not whistling fire trucks or the policeman's shiny hardware, but the hushed reading rooms of the
Widener Library and the dappled walkways of Harvard Yard,
places he wouldn't see in life until he was sixteen and a student,
but that floated as magically as Atlantis in his darkened childhood bedroom. And all the while, his father and sister were
mired in the there-and-then, in Watertown, where of course
Judy had stayed, proving something (what?) to someone
(whom?), or perhaps proving only that she was not like her
brother. Crap about the Protestant work ethic, early to rise,
Christian humility—garbage, all of it, which had served to turn
Judy into a blousy, bland matron napping at night in front of
the set.

And yet, his mother: even in the last days, still the apron,
the hands gnarled with arthritis, the ironed lace antimacassar
on the chintz armchair. For all her dreams she'd been no different, in the end, and all she'd succeeded in doing was turning
her boy into someone, something, she couldn't understand, a
fact made literal by her Alzheimer's, so that in the mid-eight-
ies when he'd gone up alone to visit, he'd sat beside her at the
table, in his "old" place, and when she asked for Murray, he'd
taken her wasted hand, and Judy had said, "There he is, Mom,
right next to you," and she'd fixed her sunken eyes on him,
aglow with fear, and cried out, "That's not my Murray, that's
not my boy! Where is he? You promised he was coming!"

And so, to guard against that life, to guard against that ever
being his life, from earliest days and with—although she didn't
ever know what it meant, what it might permit—his mother's
blessing, the resolutions: not only for Harvard, but never an
office, never a timetable, never an alarm clock, always a new

day, a new city, a new person, a new drink, another discovery, always more life, *more*.

Had he said this clearly enough in his manuscript? It seemed childishly simple, as a philosophy to live by, and clearly he was not a simple man. Nor was he the direct, rebellious product of that narrow vestibule of his childhood, in which you could barely open the front door on account of the stairwell ahead, and the bald square yard in front (he remembered the smell, grown hideous to him even as it was tender, of the leafy clippings, on a summer Saturday morning, when his father stood upon the stepladder on the sidewalk and inched his way around, barbering the front hedge to an even shorn perfection, grimly matched by his own monk's tonsure, a thin and mousy gray). Such memories were part of Murray, and escape an inescapable part of them; but it was not in this mode, this running away, that he had lived, nor that he would encourage others to live. Perhaps if the thought of his life then, of his sister's life now, still had the power to tighten his throat and sour the air (another cigarette lit might clear it), then it was disingenuous not to say so? Wasn't irrelevance, smallness, the dutiful petty life what everyone ultimately wanted to shed? And wasn't shedding as important as embracing, in the formation of an adult self?

And then he thought of Marina, raised as he'd wished to have been raised, and stymied, now, by the very lack of smallness, by the absence of any limitations against which to rebel. Should she then be shedding a life of privilege, moving to some Watertown of the heart, to begin again, her lot, on account of her birthright, to be a Judy figure, in whom merit would accrue merely because she'd given up all she'd been given? Nonsense.

But he'd told her himself to get a job, advice he would neither have given himself, nor taken. And he'd meant it. Was he in some way acknowledging that his path was for the extraordinary only, and that his daughter, for all she was beautiful and deeply loved, was not—how to accept this?—entirely out of the ordinary? He couldn't ask that question, couldn't answer it.

He remembered his father's telling him—his father, small as he was himself tall, with sloping shoulders off which Murray feared, as a child, the braces might slip, a bow-tied little man with an almost Hitlerian mustache, softened from menace by its grayness, and by the softness, insidious softness, of his quiet voice, a softness that belied his rigidity and tireless industry, his humorless and ultimately charmless "goodness" (why had she married him? She'd been so beautiful, and such fun)—telling him, as he deliberated upon his path at Harvard, to choose statistics, or accounting, or economics, saying, with that dreaded certainty, "You see, Murray, I know you want to go out and write books, or something like that. But only geniuses can be writers, Murray, and frankly, son . . ." And Murray had slain his father, no question about it, so that the memory of him was slightly pathetic, almost endearing; laughable, above all. And who was Murray, who would he be, but a little man, to stand similarly in judgment upon his daughter, and declare her incapable of the greatness she so longed for? Better to say nothing; more than that, to venture nothing; to wait and see. She might yet, as he himself had done, take them by surprise.

And what, then, would this boy be like? Had his mother called him Bootie? What form of unkindness was that? Frederick was his given name. And if he admired Murray, there might be hope for him.

Murray decided to look once more at his e-mail before log-ging off, just in case. And yes, she had answered. So swiftly. His neck felt warm, his hands, too—the old, familiar thrill. Although this was no chase, surely? But he listened for his daughter's tread, just in case, before he opened the message. It was brief, and fairly formal: lunches were difficult, given her schedule; but of course she'd like to talk about helping her friend, and if a drink weren't out of the question, then Wednes-day might work. She never knew places, and was certain he would, so perhaps he might suggest something? All of which, in its very propriety, thrilled him, the way the thought of her slender, white neck, her tidy waist against the fullness of her curves, thrilled him, or the neck's pallor against the dark curls, the eyes for which the cliché "smoldering" came to mind— things he ought never to have remarked, in a friend of his daughter's, in so very close a friend of his daughter's—but there it was: more life, more. And as he reflected upon which bar to suggest, which atmosphere in which to bottle this minor fan-tasy, he heard his daughter scream across the hall, a choked, guttural emanation, so alarmingly close that he jerked in his chair, and almost neglected to close off the screen before rush-ing to her aid.

CHAPTER EIGHTEEN

The Pope's End

Marina had been trying all evening to make progress with her book. She had sat with her laptop on her knees on her bed, with copious notes and photographs and several library books, all pertaining to Chapter Five, on which she was ostensibly working, spread in disarray about her, a sea of print that engulfed her bed and made it look tiny. She felt tiny, in the face of it: surely if so much had already been said, she had nothing here to add? She was writing, in this chapter, about the long-standing Western habit of dressing a child like someone else: like an older child, or like a parent, or like someone else entirely; and she was comparing this to those ventriloquists whose dummies were attired to match them, among other things, and making, or attempting to, a broader point about how children have been seen as emanations of their parents, and she needed to fit in there somehow the inverse argument, based around, say, the Laura Ashley ensembles of the seventies, in which mother and daughter both were swathed in frilly floral smocks in a reenactment—or curiously ironic restatement, perhaps, in the era of women's sexual liberation—of Victorian girlhood, in which case the question was, were they all, mothers and daughters, celebrating the repression of their sexuality, or its untrammeling? Those pervy lace-up black boots, the flash of calf, the loose layers of muslin and chintz, the tumbling curls above: they made every one from five to fifty into the same, slightly disturbing, erotic prospect—whereupon she wanted to draw comparisons to the girls in the windows of the brothels of Amsterdam, although she hadn't personally seen them, but she'd heard they were dressed to satisfy all manner of fantasies: the schoolgirl, the nurse, the vixen, the headmistress. But maybe this didn't fit in at all? Like a puzzle piece, there in her scribbled notes, albeit with a question mark beside it, this analogy had to have been intended for Chapter Five. But the notes were several years old, and didn't readily serve their madeleine-like purpose of conjuring intellectual arguments entire, a few words opening a rich sack of thought. No, largely the scribbled phrases stood only for themselves, chicken scratches on paper, meager and disturbingly free of import. Marina felt, as she struggled to pull up not merely sentences but voluminous paragraphs from the records she had retained around her, that she was engaged in the archaeological excavation of a lost culture—the lost culture being, of course, her own earlier thoughts—and there seemed no certainty that her interpretation of the present artifacts would have any genuine logic at all. Should she go back to the sources? Back to the tomes in the public library, back to the archives at FIT and the Metropolitan, back through the past five years of her life, as if she'd never been there, and try again to compile the arguments that, in the early days, had seemed headily full of moment? She couldn't face it. The notes were what she had, and all she would have, and whatever reconstitution she could manage—was this analepsis? Was it catachresis? From some mist of memory emerged Greek words of a literary theory course at Brown and she wondered whether they pertained to this crisis—would have to do. But it would be no good. She felt this every time she sat to write, that her reconstituted ideas bore as little resemblance to the originals as did the vegetables in instant soup to their former, unshriveled selves. Analepsis, catachresis, no: the word she was after was "floundering." She could already write the review of her unwritten book: "Marina Thwaite flounders about in her subject, with little direction and still less progress." The entire enterprise had become—already long ago; she couldn't remember when it hadn't been so—like the anxiety dreams of her adolescence, in which she had to stand up naked before the class, or deliver lines in a play she didn't know, or offer an impromptu analysis of a book she hadn't read.

It filled her with despair, a literal leadening of her limbs, a glazing of the eyes, so that she could barely lift the sheets of paper around her, and certainly couldn't decipher what was written upon them. She couldn't speak to anyone about this, about the burden of failure that weighed daily upon her: Danielle would be censorious, then efficient, briskly trying to take over and buck her up; as would her mother, from whose lips the infuriating phrase "Buck up, duckie" had been known, all too often, to fall. To Julius, even if he hadn't vanished, her situation would be an excuse for pretending, for a round of afternoon martinis, an enjoyable enough remedy but one she knew, from now considerable experience, to be ineffective. And her father: how many times had she tried—or felt as if she had, at least—to speak to him about her mind's atrophy, about the apparent impossibility of fulfilling her promise, in every sense, with this undertaking? And he didn't understand, couldn't or wouldn't: he was more machine than human, in this regard, for all he loved her. He'd honored every contract of his life; he arrived on time even at events he had no desire to attend. He turned his mind on, like a miner's lamp, and merely proceeded, doing the necessary until it was done. He'd point to the mess of papers and their scratchings and say, "See? It's all here, right in front of you. You've done all the hard work, now just get on with it!"

In defiance of which, she went wandering around the apartment. Her mother had gone to bed promptly, expecting an early-morning call, and the lights were few and dim, the air-conditioning a soporific under-hum, faintly Freon-scented, along Marina's path. She paused longest in the kitchen, where she considered making tea—Danielle, she knew, drank tea every night before bed, and swore by its properties—and decided instead to eat a cookie or two, some French kind Aurora had picked up at the supermarket, made with superior chocolate. She poured some milk to go with the cookies and left the fridge door open while she did so, its narrow, spooky light the only one in the room. She carried her milk with her through the dining room, back to the hallway, along past her room, past her parents' room—she imagined she could hear her mother breathing, almost snoring, but didn't stay to listen, feeling vaguely embarrassed at the indignity—and onward, drawn like a moth to the chink of light from her father's study. Barefoot, she was aware of being quiet as a cat; aware, too, suddenly, of the possibility of cat vomit somewhere on the carpet. Although the Pope had been better lately, eating less but throwing up less too, and with a new hoarseness to her breathing that usually made her easy to track. And yet, in no room so far had Marina heard the token wheezing; nor had she brushed against the furred bone that the Pope had become, all prominent spine and gaunt head.

Marina paused at the door, peered through the hinges at her father's back, bent at his computer, and realized she'd already stood here, or almost here, just hours earlier. It was clearly pathetic, to hover on the edge of someone else's life, like a maid or a dog, and he her father, too. A child with a glass of milk, she might have been six instead of thirty.

Without a sound, she turned and walked the few steps to the room that would be Frederick's. Maybe it would be a good thing to have him around for a bit, not merely a distraction but a catalyst. Either that, or the occasion for still more impressive pretense, for letting on that she was an "It" girl (once upon a time, in the *Vogue* days, she had been, hadn't she?), with the aura of incipient success as bright around her as a halo, with a book almost written and a host of suitors, a glamorous, if currently somewhat curtailed, adulthood. He was young enough, Fat Freddie, that he might still buy it, might not be able to see through the dazzle of her looks; but she remembered him, too, as saturnine in his plumpness, with eyes that, behind their smeary glasses, seemed to peer all too intently, to see too much. It had been years; who knew? He might not even be fat. And who was he, a college dropout from Oswego, to judge her?

Efficient as ever, Aurora kept the room aired and dusted and vacuumed. She'd placed a coaster on the dresser, in readiness for a bunch of welcoming flowers (was he a guest who merited flowers? But better, Marina supposed, to stick with tradition), and the bed was made up with fresh sheets, a billowy, crisp white duvet, in the middle of which, like the tufting on a pouf, lay the sunken black button that was the Pope asleep.

What better place for an aged cat, Marina thought, envying the licensed idleness, the creature's ability to make herself disappear without leaving the premises and to do nothing without garnering disapproval. She perched at the edge of the pristine bed, placed her empty milk glass on the night table (from which the eagle-eyed Aurora would retrieve it before the guest's arrival), and reached out to stroke the elegant old curve of the Pope's curled back.

It did not at first feel different, although afterward she would say she knew at once. But the warmth of the fur kept her from discerning the chill of the flesh beneath. What she noticed, though, all but simultaneously, were that the Pope failed to twitch beneath her hand, an involuntary wrinkling of the skin intrinsic to the long history of their caresses, and that the room, but for the distant sough of the road noise and the central air, was completely quiet. No rasping, no rattle. No breath at all. And although a part of Marina was not particularly shocked, and registered simply: "Oh, so this is death," another part of her—the child, she would chide herself—recoiled, and emitted the choked cry that brought her father running.

"What is it? Why are you in the dark in here?" He cut a disheveled figure, shirt untucked, glasses at the end of his nose, his silver hair rising and feathered like a chick's, a cigarette rakishly behind his ear.

"I'm sorry, Daddy—it's just the Pope. She's not—I mean, she's dead."

"Oh."

The two of them stood side by side without approaching.

"You're quite sure?" Murray asked, scratching at the back of his head.

"Yep. Sure."

The cat, a black blot on the duvet, didn't move.

"Is your mother asleep?"

"Hours ago."

"Hmm. Worse things could happen than leaving her there for the night, don't you agree?"

The idea seemed somehow sacrilegious to Marina, though whether the offense was against the cat or the bed and its imminent occupant, she couldn't have said. "Don't dead things, you know, leak?"

"Not overnight, I wouldn't think. And it's pretty cool in here." Her father seemed unfazed, as if they were discussing a plant, or a book. "I just think your mother's the one to cope with this. Or Aurora." He paused. "Unless you want to do it?"

"Not much."

"Didn't think so. Come on, let's shut the door. It'll be as if you never came in here. Why did you come in here, incidentally?"

"I don't know. Thinking about Frederick, I guess."

"Ah. The boy. The unknown quantity. I called his mother tonight—"

"Aunt Judy?"

"She didn't even know he was coming."

"Wow."

"So who knows what bedraggled or embattled soul is on his way to us? We'll see soon enough." He made as if to return to his study.

"It doesn't seem a very good omen, does it?"

"What?"

"Having the Pope die on his bed."

"The cat was seventeen years old, my poppet."

"I know, but—"

"And you know I don't believe in omens. And you shouldn't either. No self-respecting atheist should believe in omens."

"No."

"Certainly not a pope's death."

"Very funny."

He nodded toward the closed bedroom door. "Your mother will deal with that first thing," he said. "Don't give it another thought."

But Marina, once in her own bed, beneath her own duvet, couldn't sleep for thinking about it, about the kitten she'd been given (instead of a horse, her parents had joked: more on the scale of their lives) and had marveled over, its spastic steps and zealous pounces, its questing tongue upon her hand. She'd abandoned the Pope for college, and for years thereafter of living elsewhere, had taken the cat for granted when she came home to visit, a sleek nudge at her calf, a warm muff on her knees, the broad yawns and the haughty incline of that elegant head. And by the time Marina had come back to live the year before, the cat was an invalid and an eyesore, scrawny, patchy, yowling, and, of course, vomiting, the relentless sour smell of it, and while Marina had occasionally been roused to pity she'd felt largely, with the brutality of the young, contempt for the animal's diminishing, and revulsion at her habits. A tear or two welled up in Marina's eyes and moistened her pillowcase, but she couldn't truthfully have said whether this was born of sorrow for the Pope's loss, or a sadness for herself at her actual callousness in the face of death, or indeed—and maybe this was the root of it—whether her tears, shed only now, were an indulgence licensed by the Pope but referring, in their quiet woe, to her earlier despair, to the burdens she still had inexorably to confront, while the cat, still and free and cushioned by the finest goose down, by the ironed Irish linen, had found repose.

CHAPTER NINETEEN

Bootie Takes New York

On the second Saturday of May, at nine-fifteen in the morning, Frederick Tubb sat on a bench in Central Park, a mere half block from the street, in the pleasing shade of new maple leaves, with a plastic shopping bag beside him and a book upon his lap. It was *War and Peace,* now, which he'd decided was indispensable, and upon which he was making every effort to concentrate. But it was hard. On account of the heat, for one: in spite of the morning's promise of warmth, its faint haze—a humidity that, inside the park, hung with tropical weight beneath the overhanging branches, illuminated by piercing pools of already brutal sunlight—Bootie had reasoned—the way, not so long ago, people reasoned that they should dress for dinner, or for church—that he was now in a major city and ought to dress up because of it. Prickled by sweat, his curls clinging already to his forehead, his glasses slick, he regretted his decision. He wore a checked shirt with a collar and cuffs, albeit unironed and, more recently, untucked, above his faintly grubby khakis. It was either khakis or jeans—he had only two pairs of pants—and he'd thought the former marginally cleaner. He wore sneakers, great white boats upon his feet, because he had, for the time being, nothing else (his dress shoes were still, and perhaps forever, in his Watertown bedroom), but judging from the footwear that passed him along the path, this was perfectly acceptable. The footwear, or rather the people in it, distracted too, a parade of such notable variety and, given the early hour, volume, that it was difficult to keep his eyes turned to the page for more than a brief stretch at a time. He caught tendrils of conversations—"She say she don't got it, but I *know* she steal it from me"; "If you'll just read it, baby, I really think it would change your life"; "You *know* how to dress, don't you? So what can I tell you?"—and peered discreetly through his hair to see that often the most animated conversations were telephonic, sometimes even conducted through earpieces along near-invisible wires, so that the speakers, like madmen, gesticulated and emoted wildly apparently to the open air. He marveled silently at the shapes in which New Yorkers came, skinny driven men and women, in work clothes or clinging sportsgear, their veins popping along their rigid necks or at their tiny, taut calves; great, unwieldy creatures of indeterminate sex, pillowed giants rolling and jiggling beneath their loose T-shirts, their glistening faces furrowed by the absorbing administration of locomotion; and every size and shape between; Russian, Chinese, African, Andean faces, all hues and proportions, a medley offered up to his occasional glance that was, to Bootie, his mother's Unicef calendar—a perennial part of his childhood, pinned to the wall by the kitchen telephone—brought to life.

A horde of round-limbed Latin children bustled by, squawking, keen for the playground, their mothers—so young, his age perhaps; could they be mothers? But yes—ambling far behind, bent over strollers in which other, smaller bodies lay splayed and snoozing beneath dangles of colorful toys, the women's voices an undulating river of Spanish, punctuated by calls to the escaping offspring. One of the mothers looked over at Bootie, caught his eye and, in spite of his tentative smile, turned rapidly away.

Bootie had, in his plastic bag, his thumbed copy of Emerson; a pair of sunglasses bought on the street in Amherst for five dollars; and an old apple juice bottle with a torn label filled with water from the Thwaites' kitchen tap. He'd considered taking some breakfast with him—Aunt Annabel had told him already several times to feel completely at home—but worried about dirtying dishes, making a mess. He knew himself—his mother always chided him for it—to be one who, however unwittingly, left traces, smears and fingerprints and dirty cups. Better not to touch anything.

He'd wanted to get up and out before his relatives stirred, before the apartment's impressive hush—so much more silent, in its hermetic seal, than his mother's rattling house—was broken. He couldn't quite bear their bonhomie, the warmth and near indifference of their welcome, the way they assumed (and the very rightness of the assumption rankled) that he was there because he wanted to be assimilated into their lives, to be a part of them. Already, the previous evening, not his first but, given his lateness on Thursday, essentially his first, they'd invited him to join them at a barbecue at a friend's place. He'd thought they were joking—a barbecue in New York City?—till they explained that it was a penthouse apartment with a wraparound terrace, and the main reason to come along was the fabulous view. He'd been torn; he'd said he was tired and would stay home, but could see in Annabel's face, in Murray's, both that they didn't mind if he preferred to retire with a book, and, more visibly, that they couldn't fathom the choice. What, then, was the point not only of being in New York but of being in the *Thwaites'* New York? So he'd gone, only to be—predictably, unbearably—baffled and flushed at the gathering, his shirt stained first by sweat and then by the red wine he fumblingly spilled on it.

Annabel, seeing him repeatedly alone on the wide swath of terrace, had taken him in hand, had leaned against the glass barrier (he couldn't look down) to show him the glorious skyline, its landmarks, the curves and rises of the park so densely green before them, the toylike towers of downtown rising like some child's fabulous Meccano madness, the glinting river and the ever-pinkening, purpling veil of dusk as it fell over the great sky and the buildings around them. She had the kindness not to seem bored, to evince animation at his comments—he knew them to be banal, and blushed again at this knowledge, blinking fretfully behind his glasses—and even, in a gesture that touched and surprised him, to place her hand on his back when pointing westward across the park to the place where the Thwaites, and now he, too, lived. Even then, he was aware of the sweat on his skin, of the fleshy swell of it, of the possible clamminess of his shirt beneath her fingers, and this shame rendered him stupid and nearly mute.

While listening to Annabel and surveying the vista, Bootie kept a surreptitious eye on the other Thwaites, on Marina and Murray, as they glided separately and together among the crowd upon the terrace. Murray stood taller than most, his hair brighter in its silver shock, and Bootie could catch, every so often, the phlegmy bass of his laughter, or the amused rise of his voice. He drifted in a near-constant trail of smoke, like thought bubbles, a running conversation of its own. More spritelike, Marina bobbed her head, gangled her delicate limbs as if awkwardness were, among the beauteous, the most graceful affectation. The failing light drew her eyes more brightly, and deepened the red of her lips, so that from afar she seemed to glow like a painted puppet on a stage. He couldn't help looking, couldn't help it although he knew she was precisely that, a woman watched, and that such women couldn't even see him. She glanced over once or twice, seemed, in conversation, to be talking about him, explaining his presence—"My fat cousin from upstate," he imagined her saying, "it's not my fault"—which projection made him ever more sullen, in addition to his shame, so that by the time they regrouped and withdrew from the party, Bootie, half-sodden, had turned from a benign to a belligerent statue, who, squashed into the aura of Marina's delectable lemon fragrance in the back of the taxicab, could barely muster a word of gratitude for his hosts.

"You must be exhausted," Annabel had consoled his folded brow, his clamped jaw. "Maybe it was too much? Sleep in tomorrow—we all will."

But he'd woken at dawn, unexorcised, irked still although he couldn't quite have said at what, and had planned his temporary escape. The Thwaites' New York society, after all, was not what he wanted. (Or was it? He couldn't be sure.) He wanted, instead, his uncle's pure life of the mind. He hankered for something less cushioned, more real, for a state of a piece with the education at hand: self-reliance, after all, was the goal. Again reading, or at least pretending to, his paperback drawn up to his nose as if to parody his myopia, he wondered how he looked, on the bench near the park's edge, to the Latina mother who did not smile, to the hurrying joggers, to the dawdling girls—always the women, he was aware; conscious that he didn't imagine the men saw him at all—and as he wondered, furtively peering over his pages to see if he was being seen, and of course, too, to see, because therein lay all his interest (how dull novels were, after all; even this one, this Tolstoy, though it was better than most).

Again, in the morning's brightness, Marina shone. Even if he hadn't known her, he would have looked, caught by the sheen of her. She wore shorts, a T-shirt, sneakers, like the rest of them, but they became her, somehow. To Bootie's chagrin, she saw him, too, in spite of, or perhaps because of, Tolstoy.

"Aren't you the bookworm," she said, toeing the dust before him. "What have you got in the bag?"

"Just a book."

"How long have you been here?"

"Not long."

"It's the perfect place for Dad to spy on you from his study, you know." She squinted into the trees, pointed at the building looming over them from across the street. "Better in winter, because of the leaves, but even now—that's his window. When I was a kid, I'd spend ages spying on people from there."

Bootie shuffled his hands, his book, made as if to stand.

"Don't worry, he's not looking. I'm just kidding. But he *could* see you, if he tried. Planning to spend the day here?"

"Of course not. I—"

"Because the bench probably isn't very comfortable."

"It's fine."

"I'll tell you what. I'm just going to my favorite outdoor

yoga class—it's in, like, five minutes—but after that I'm headed downtown." She paused, cocked her head so her hair fell over one eye. "Have you been downtown? SoHo? The Village?"

He shook his head.

"I could take you. I'm meeting a friend, because I've got to get something to wear for a formal thing next week, so you'll probably want to wander around on your own"—it was as delicately phrased a dismissal as he could have imagined—"but I'll show you where to go."

Aside from reading, he had no plans; and she glowed so. He nodded. "Thanks."

"I've got to run"—she was bouncing on the balls of her feet—"but I'll meet you upstairs at ten-thirty."

"Downstairs, maybe?"

"If you like. In the lobby."

"Or on the corner?"

She looked hard at him, seemed almost to smile, her lips a tight line. "In the lobby," she said again. "At ten-thirty. Okay?"

She made a point of taking him on the subway. So he'd know how to get home on his own, she said. Bootie had never ridden a subway before, except once in Washington, D.C., on a school trip with twenty other kids when he was twelve, and this bore no resemblance to that memory. He was at once fascinated and repelled by the crumbling girders, the prison grilles, the roar and the reek of it, piss and rot in the air even though it was still spring, not yet fully hot, and the icy, plastified blasts that erupted through the train itself. Again, as in the park, he wanted to gawp at all the forms and faces: elaborate cornrows, electric manicures, scraggly goatees and acne-scarred or whiskered chins. A bald man in a fine suit, with his eyes to the floor, as if out of modesty. A grande dame, elaborately, coquettishly painted, with a naked and disconcerting glare: something, maybe, was not quite right. A little too much makeup, maybe; an infinitesimal droop of her lip. No, she wasn't right at all. And maybe—yes, there were stains on her silk cuffs, her tweed skirt was fraying—maybe she was the one who smelled so. He stared back, slid his fingers up and down the smeared pole, aware of its peculiarly human greasiness. The train, or the air-conditioning, he wasn't sure which, gave a rising gnatlike whine as they accelerated, and at speed they rattled and bumped like a fairground spin; but Marina—who pressed her back against the cloudy glass of the door between stations rather than touch anything with her hands—seemed, like the rest, unfazed. When they stopped inexplicably in a tunnel in midtown, and idled there, belching, Bootie felt a panic skittering in him: the black corroded walls loomed too near the windows, the air grew immediately sparse and more fetid. Momentarily, the lights went out, and the train, like some dying beast, exhaled. His throat was closing. His neck burned, and his ears.

His alarm must have shown, because in the black gloom, Marina leaned forward—a hint of her lemon scent in the miasma—and said, "It's perfectly normal. We're outside Penn Station." And again, "You're not frightened, are you?"

To which he shook his head vigorously, faster, he thought, even than his heart was beating, and thus confused the jolt of the train starting, relit, reanimated, with his own, willful shock. He didn't think he would come home this way—he didn't think he could bear it—although he didn't know how else he might span the island. Perhaps there was a bus; perhaps he'd walk; but this subterranean inferno, in all its constrictions, he could not tolerate. He didn't say so, merely thanked her, blinked attentively as they climbed to the street, molelike, and set off into the light.

He should have been watching the pedestrian throng, a different mix again on these narrower, more lowly built streets, almost bumping into him, casually oblivious, chattering, it seemed, in many foreign languages as they ambled in and out of the plate-glass fronted shops; but he found himself watching his cousin. Her gait seemed slightly altered, and her hand rose more often to flick at her hair, as if she were more aware of herself here, performing. She pushed her chin out a little, pouted her lips. It occurred to him for the first time that her floating little camisole, of a lace-trimmed rose, was not an unraveling leftover retrieved from oblivion but an item of fashion. He tried to figure out whose attention she thought to attract—not his, obviously—and only then took in that the neighborhood oozed youth and beauty, a wealth of golden-skinned, long-limbed specimens in whose company Marina seemed naturally, but not extraordinarily, to belong.

The friend, then, came as a surprise: hunched over a bagel at Dean & DeLuca, she was small, bosomy, beaky, redeemed from plainness by the light of her eyes and her pillowy lips. When she grinned, lopsidedly, her face crinkled into something dearer, more accessible than beauty. He liked her then, and too, for the poorly blotted daub of cream cheese on her pale blue shirt.

"How're you liking Manhattan? First time, isn't it?"

"Not quite. First time as a grown-up." Even the word "grown-up" sounded childish to him as he said it. He tried to stifle his blush. He wished he'd said "adult."

"Mom and Dad dragged him to the Beavors' last night." Marina rolled her eyes. "You know, they've got that penthouse over the park I told you about."

The friend—Danielle, her name was Danielle—smiled vaguely.

"Awesome view. But everyone was so stiff. Poor Fred here looked like he was dying to escape."

"No, no. I was— Maybe a little— It was—different." He looked at his hands. He could feel the color rising, unstoppable.

"Hey, don't I know it." Danielle seemed to smile for him. Her teeth were very white. "I'm from Columbus, you know, not like Miss New York here, who couldn't imagine life anywhere else—"

"Not fair!" Marina protested.

"But who, as far as I can tell, had never been to Brooklyn until her junior year in college." Both Marina and Danielle laughed at this. Their history; a private joke. Bootie waited. "Anyway, my point is that I know exactly what it's like."

"What *is* it like, then?" Marina asked.

"It's disconcerting. It's like you know it and you don't know it, at the same time. You've seen it so often, the images, in movies, on TV—you feel as though it's yours. But of course it's different. The way something you've dreamed is different from the real thing."

"Is that true for you?" Marina appeared to wink at her cousin.

"I guess so." He moved his fingers off the table, where they loomed pale and enormous, and tucked his hands between his knees. "I mean, I've hardly been here. I took the car to Queens, and then—I haven't seen much so far."

"You'd have to say it *smells* real, though, wouldn't you? The subway?"

"Sure. Absolutely."

"Frederick, if you don't mind my asking—are you here, like, on vacation? Or is this something more long-term? Marina was a bit vague."

"I guess I've been vague. I'm the one. I mean, I don't want my mom to know—just in the sense that she's obsessed with school, she thinks I can't accomplish anything without some stupid, meaningless diploma, so . . ." He paused, regrouped, began again. "I'd like to stay. Not with your folks, obviously— I mean, Murray and Annabel have been amazing, it's not— But you know what I mean. The idea is to get a place sorted out, you know, and some kind of—"

"Job?" offered Danielle.

"Yeah, of course. But then to be studying."

"Oh, right. Great! Where?"

"Not in a school. I mean—" His knee started to jiggle, rocking the table. It shouldn't be so difficult to explain; surely the notion wasn't *so* radical? "I mean, I don't really trust institutions at this point. I think I get more out of it, you know, on my own."

"Wow," Danielle said, and Bootie couldn't tell what she meant by it. Marina just stared, with a fixed, bright smile, as though he had spoken gibberish.

"Do you have, I don't know, a sort of program in mind? Or is it more general, really?"

"You mean, is it bullshit? No, I have a program. My own reading lists. And I take notes, and I write stuff up, but you know . . ."

"Who reads it?" Marina asked.

He blinked. "So far—well, I guess so far I haven't really sorted that out. Me, so far."

"Maybe my dad could read your essays."

He scanned her face, the red lips, the violet eyes—was she laughing? Not that he could tell. "Do you mean it?"

"Well, I can't speak *for* him—"

"But almost," Danielle broke in.

"But I definitely think you should ask. Or I can ask. I mean, you're his nephew. And he loves— What's it called? Mentoring. He loves nurturing young minds, all that. Keeps him young, you know."

"What kinds of things are you studying?" Danielle had that patient, almost maternal look again. It rankled. "I mean, is it literature, or neuroscience, or whatever?"

He frowned. "Mostly whatever," he said, and felt bad as he did and so went on. "Right now, it's Emerson and Tolstoy."

"A little light reading." Marina laughed. "But great stuff, seriously. Which Tolstoy? I love *Anna Karenina*. It's one of my all-time favorites."

"*War and Peace,* actually."

"Right."

From the vigor of her nodding, Bootie wondered if she had perhaps not read *War and Peace.* He didn't want to catch her out, so he drank his coffee instead.

"On a completely different subject," Danielle said, reaching out to touch not Bootie's forearm but Marina's, "we might know somewhere for Frederick to live."

"Might we?"

"Think about it—what about the now vacant home of our incredible disappearing friend?"

"He does want to sublet, I remember him saying."

"What's this?"

They told Bootie about Julius, and about the recent domestic reversals. "It's like they're on some permanent honeymoon—you can't get through to them," Marina explained. "Or else it's us. This David guy—none of us has ever met him, and you know, Julius likes to compartmentalize, he always has, but this is ridiculous, it's like he doesn't think we're good enough for David, or something."

"Or else David's not good enough."

"Then why cling to him? No, no, it's about, you know, giving his lover what he wants. Which makes me hate the guy, even though I don't know him." Danielle had raised her voice, clapped her hand to her mouth. "What kind of man doesn't want to meet his lover's oldest friends? I mean, really. To spend some time with us and then reject our company would be one thing; but just to refuse to have dinner—"

"Has he refused to have dinner?" Bootie asked. He hadn't been party to such conversations since his sister was in high school—the endless, fruitless analysis struck him as deeply female, uncomfortably intimate, like lacy underthings.

"Not strictly speaking, no," explained Marina. "We just keep getting the brush off from Julius, and it's not entirely clear why. So we blame the Conehead, as we call him. His name's David Cohen."

"The cokehead is more like it," Danielle said. "That's my sense of things, anyway."

Bootie was moderately shocked and knew that he ought not to be, so said only, "Really."

"Well, Julius, even though he's pretty straight—except for being gay, of course, but you know what I mean—has always liked to imply that his life's a little, um, risqué. The sex and drugs and rock 'n' roll thing seems, is, glamorous to him."

"And glamour counts, for Julius—he's insecure that way," Marina said.

"But this time,"—Danielle shrugged—"this time there's something more—what would you say, M? Authentic. There's something unnervingly authentic about his references to drugs."

"We'll be worried when he doesn't mention them at all anymore," Marina said with sudden brusqueness, gathering the empty coffee cups and crumbed waxed paper scraps from the table before them. "But right now, Danny, we've got to go buy some dresses."

Bootie joined the movement to stand, aware once again of his fleshiness and height, as Danielle, when upright, proved quite small. He was aware, too, that the prospect of a place to live—Julius's place—had slipped from the conversation and hence from his grasp. He didn't yet have a job, had no money for such a thing; but still, it felt like a small loss; which, in the river of petty gossip about Julius's love life, signaled how far askew Marina's—and Danielle's—priorities had drifted. This was no better than Amherst, than Oswego—and this in a world he had imagined, somehow, to be higher. His hopes lay still with his uncle. But Marina, here before him, was so much prettier, a gazelle, a confection. And if she'd invited him to go dress shopping, instead of briskly pecking his cheek and pointing him in the direction of the World Trade Center—"You can take the elevator up to the top. Take pictures of the view. Everybody in New York should do it once"—he would readily have acquiesced. But she was keen to escape, he could sense it, in the slide of her violet eyes, in her slight breathlessness; and it was Danielle who said, with a laugh, "Or you could traipse through Armani and Anna Sui with us, if you want. Because I've never been up the Twin Towers myself, and as a girl from Columbus, I always think it's *not* doing the tourist things that most makes you a New Yorker."

To which Bootie smiled, and blinked behind his glasses, rebuffing, for his cousin's sake, the amiable overture. "It's better if I go," he said. And because this was not immediately logical, made no apparent sense, he lied: "I've always wanted to see it. The view, I mean."

CHAPTER TWENTY

Julius's Dilemma

The nerves tingled to the ends of his fingers, and his blood pulsed in his ears. Julius was misbehaving, radically, and it thrilled and frightened him in equal measure. Sunday evening, still light, and he was waiting, on the one hand, for David to return from a family visit to Scarsdale; waiting, although not imminently, for the click of the key in the lock. And yet, it could be imminent, couldn't it? David could always take an earlier train, could always choose to forgo his parents' routine Sunday Chinese, lured by the prospect of his endlessly available and—so Julius liked to fantasize—relentlessly inventive lover, whose hairless olive-tinged skin was drenched and scented by expensive bath oils, then pamperingly wrapped in a stolen hotel bathrobe. And at the same time, somehow and perversely no less in the realm of Julius's fantasy, although it was, in this instance, by far more certain, or at least more imminent, he awaited with equal excitement the arrival of another, unknown man, summoned over the Internet and known only as Dale, a stallion (or so he promised) and a fitness instructor (or so he claimed), a guy whose moniker was SweetCheeks and who had promised an encounter both sensational and discreet, with the added advantage that he lived (or so he asserted) a mere three blocks away, and so could be in and out (as it were) in the blink of an eye, and certainly—although who could be entirely certain? And wasn't that the point?—before David returned.

If Julius could have explained this behavior, he would have departed in several different directions. He was happier, in his love life, than he could remember ever being; and there was no clear motivation for his treachery, if you looked at it one way—the stolid, staid Marina or Danielle way; and yet; and yet. First of all there was the matter of habit: some people were addicted to eBay, and maybe Julius was addicted, similarly, to this—drawn, just like the bidders who purchased jelly jars from Alaska or Oriental rugs till they were thick on the ground, by the lure of possibility, the sense, each time, that the undiscovered held the Answer, that this mate, this flank, this heaving torso, this rough jaw might prove the long-sought panacea. How could anyone, how could Julius, be expected to relinquish all this, all these, for a single known trajectory, however fond he was of the curls at David's nape or the line of his buttocks, however thrilling their intimate life might be? Could one not be Pierre *and* Natasha at the same time?

Then, too, there was the distinct but also inseparable titillation of the risk of being caught. Living alone, he had all but forgotten that excitement, had felt it only in hurried, humid gropings in public places, or once in the lavatory at a rather elegant dinner party hosted by an old acquaintance from Brown. But *this*—this was a thrill on the order of his adolescence, a thrill of the kind he'd known back in Danville when, at fourteen and fifteen, his parents had thought him at the movies at the mall, while in reality he trawled the parking lot behind a bar called The Hub, where it was known men could find each other and share the warmth of their cars, and where boys, fresh as he was, were prized; but where, too, hovered the threat of a police bust (they knew the score, just like everyone else) and more frightening still, the faint possibility of marauding drunken youths with knives or baseball bats, and an angry eye for the faggots. In that pullulating white Midwestern sea, an Asian faggot, a teenage Asian faggot, wide-eyed, slight as a reed, would have come in for particular treatment. When Julius was fifteen, a married insurance salesman from three towns over had been beaten into a vegetable (an eggplant, Julius always imagined: purple, spongy) by three footballers, after one feigned seduction and lured him to the gravel pits, and a trap. Not that Julius fantasized about violence—no. But the faint twitch of fear, the way it had made the cold air of that long-ago parking lot colder still, the way it had drawn the outlines of buildings, scurvy trees and, above all, men's shadowed forms in superior relief—the way fear had been sexy, had made him eminently, absolutely alive—that was craveable, delicious. As a teenager, always the ultimate terror had been not of the gay-bashers, nor even of the cops, but of a known face, of the car door that would open to reveal a friend of his father's, or a member of the church; or of a miscalculation in timing that would have his father, driving by to pick up his boy at the multiplex just down the strip, glimpsing the adolescent's entwined and compromised form by the sulfurous flickering of a defective streetlight. The biggest fear had always been that Mom and Dad would find out; the greatest triumph the secret life that remained so long unknown to them. The secret life defined him. Until, of course, the day he was exposed.

As he waited for the buzzer to ring (why was Dale so slow? Surely not a mere few blocks away? In which case, not, perhaps, a fitness instructor? Nor, perhaps, discreet? And the suddenly expanding, exhilarating, horrifying possibility that Dale could be anyone, *anything*, could be the bat-wielding thug of his fifteen-year-old nightmare), Julius contemplated, too, albeit briefly, the consequences of being caught, not by his parents this time, but by David, in David's apartment, in David's bed. In his least realistic self, Julius imagined that David might see the whole scenario as a setup for their mutual pleasure; but this didn't actually seem likely. He tried to imagine David's rage, his disappointment, and found he couldn't—he didn't know what David might do—and this in itself excited him. The magnitude of his betrayal was unimaginable.

Because in the realm of fantasy, at least, Julius was well acquainted with betrayal and its consequences. Yet another motor for this escapade was his certainty—wholly unproven, untraced even, but a thrilling fear of another kind, and, in his imagination, as real—that David cheated, too. It wasn't a matter of a true, prolonged affair—he was convinced that David loved him, Julius, exclusively; not least because David wanted to keep him shackled to his side, lavishly spoiled and carefully imprisoned, his trophy wife, his Desdemona—but of encounters, of stolen minutes after business meetings, of clinches with tie salesmen in the Barneys' stockroom, or with waiters at Balthazar's back door, of dabbling in airports or hotel rooms when the exigent demands of Blake, Zellman and Weaver carried him (business class, of course) to Chicago or Dallas or L.A. Julius dreaded the notion of these encounters in David's life as much as he reveled in their prospect for himself.

This was, to him, perfectly logical; although not explicably so. He couldn't bear the image of David's mouth on another man's, of his penis, in its private glory, shared. Of David's crushing, heartbreaking behavior, he had no evidence but his own fancy, which he combated with his own, overlaid fantasy-made-real, the fantasy of Dale.

Dale, who summarily appeared. Neither thug nor Adonis, with little sweetness in him, he proved a pasty-faced man of Julius's own age, with a near-shaven head, a bristly dun tickler on his chin, and a speckling of metal studs around his lobes. His eyes were round and lidless, his pale skin flecked with pale stubble and a bright blip of razor burn. His expression tended to the mournful; and whether by nature or on account of his own fear (but surely that would have subsided at the sight, and indeed the perfumed smell, of Julius in his stolen robe?) he proved laconic in the extreme; accepted a single malt on the rocks, and proceeded, rather antsily, to disrobe.

Dale's penis, while not an embarrassment, was far from gargantuan; and while his lips were pleasingly full, his tiny goatee presented, for Julius, a site of displeasure, a prickling obstacle to arousal. Julius suggested a bath, a line or two of coke (this he had foreseen; and had separated a small portion of David's reserves for this use. He felt like his mother, fretting; but he hadn't wanted to countenance the possibility that the unknown Dale might go wild at the prospect of drugs in abundance, make a grab for the lot, deck his paramour, and flee), a porn video on the huge flat-screen TV hung on the living room wall. Dale, nearly monosyllabic, accepted all these offers, his features set, throughout, in weary mourning, and then he fell hungrily, and still soberly, to the escapades for which they had contrived to meet—rather like a Midwestern bulemic, Julius thought, before a box of Cinnabon buns. Upon the living room floor, they wrangled and nipped and sucked, determinedly. The unsavory tickler proved problematic to the last, scratching at Julius's cheek, his smooth chest, his tender scrotum. Even the cocaine could not render their coupling sweet or even—for Julius at least—exciting. He was, as so often, disappointed, and distracted himself by imagining David's key in the lock, his slightly uneven tread, his horrified intake of breath. But this, this at least was pure fantasy, with all of fantasy's reassurance. The bland Dale—surely a fitness instructor after all? So tight, so dull—washed hastily and withdrew, and seemed, in retrospect, a figment. Julius bathed, for the second time that afternoon, inspected himself in the steam-filled bathroom for minor, telltale abrasions, but found none. His eyes seemed wider than usual, as if popping with mendacity: he thought of it as the Pinocchio effect. He didn't exactly regret his misdemeanor; more, he rued that it had not satisfied. He plumped the sofa cushions; returned the DVD to its box and its box to its place on the shelf; washed and dried the scotch tumblers; sprayed the air with an expensive French lavender oil, and proceeded, still in his robe, to concoct an aphrodisiac Grand Marnier–frothed mousse in time for David's arrival.

In the wake of this encounter, Julius felt not sated, nor guilty—opposing but mutually viable emotions. Rather, he felt sad, and tired. This, while no part of the fantasy, inevitably became the reality: because whatever he yearned for—and even to be able to name it might have quelled the yearning—seemed always destined to elude him. It was like Zeno's paradox, the arrow that can never reach its destination, ever closer but never there. But for Julius, his arrow didn't even know its destination, knew only that it wanted one.

This, too, was the relief of David, whose wants seemed so transparent. With David, taken care of, sheltered, spoiled, Julius could relinquish—or try to—the unnameables. He could have nice things, flattering attentions, some kind of respite from his strange, unending struggle. But for that to stand a chance of working, he needed actually to be cared for; and where the hell was David now?

When, at ten-thirty, his lover finally returned—and where, oh where had he been? Impossible not to wonder about the potential men on the Metro North train, or those in the bar at Grand Central—Julius lay sprawled on the sofa, the universal remote upon his chest like a dead man's rosary beads, listening to La Wally at top volume and nursing his injured pride.

"So, you decided to show up after all," he snipped, flinching from David's embrace and flouncing from the room. "Big of you, I guess."

"Oh my God, Miss Clarke—forget it. My uncle Merv showed up. The one who sells annuities in White Plains? Wanted ice cream, so we ended up at Ben and Jerry's after the Panda Garden. It took time."

"Then you won't want any mousse, either."

"What are you talking about? Either?"

Julius flung, or flashed, a glare over his toweled shoulder. Angry, he was also camping up his rage. He didn't know himself how much he meant it. "I made your favorite, Grand Marnier. But consider that it's not on offer. And 'either' because I, so readily available all afternoon, am not on offer either. Not anymore."

There was, as he'd hoped even in his irritation, sufficient comedy in his act to provoke a lunge in response, rather than a row. Or rather, a lunge only tinged with anger, rather than an enraged pawing. And Julius did, then, proceed to enjoy eminently satisfying sex, a tad rough perhaps, but excitingly so, with the man who was absolutely his lover and—at least for now, as Dale's visit had amply proven—all that he should want.

CHAPTER TWENTY-ONE

Awards Night

Sometimes Danielle found it difficult not to envy Marina, in spite of Marina's shortcomings. In spite of the fact, for example, that Danielle remained secretly convinced that Marina was not as smart as Danielle herself. Nor as funny. Danielle knew her envy arose from her shallowest self—she wouldn't really have traded places with her friend for anything; to be thirty and so at sea!—but she couldn't suppress it. Buffeted by the throng in the lobby, the milling, crowing glitterati assembling for their annual fete, Danielle, so consciously small, filling so tightly her clinging crimson gown, aware with every breath of the trembling white exposure of her cleavage (Marina had chosen the dress; Danielle had allowed herself to be persuaded), caught sight of Marina on her father's arm and reeled from the unbidden emerald surge.

They were, in the crowd, a distinctive pair. Danielle could see the swell parting slightly around them—the guest of honor and his beautiful daughter—could see women with bare shoulders and upswept hair whispering to one another as the Thwaites passed. The large, ornate lobby in which everyone gathered, itself the grand hotel's sub-lobby, reserved precisely for such functions, had a slightly faux Victorian aura—

wedding-cake plaster trim on the Wedgwood blue walls, huge tinkly chandeliers, the carpet beneath their feet of a souklike complication, a colorful scramble—everything old in form but brand-spanking-new, the rug's floral twistings of an invasive brilliance. In this Hollywood version of old New York, Marina and Murray advanced with the authority, the noblesse oblige, of leading players. An insignificant subset of society it might be—Danielle cast a skeptical eye over the assembled writers and journalists, a rumpled and bulging lot even in their finery—but the Thwaites nevertheless had dominion over it: oh, to be so easy.

Marina's dress, diaphanous, of a pale, milky blue, floated the length of her frame, softening her boniness, flattering her thin arms, her slightly jutting hips, illuminating the effortless rose of her cheeks and her splendid eyes. Face lowered, head slightly cocked, Marina giggled, like a coy lover, at something her father whispered in her ear, and at the sight of his lips practically upon his daughter's hair, Danielle felt herself envious anew. She hadn't allowed herself fully to consider how she might respond to father and daughter together, now that she had, in some small, clandestine way, separate relationships with each of them. She'd known they would arrive together, that Marina attended this event only as her father's date; but somehow, she hadn't *really* known it. Nor had she fully remembered the face that lurked behind the e-mails: fierce but handsome, in its weatherbeaten age; pleasingly leathered by drink and cigarettes; with its appealing, slightly long, upper lip and mildly cleft chin; and, now that she really looked, clearly the forebear of Marina's fine features. This was the face, she was only too aware, with which she would be conversing *in private,* when they met for their drink, only two days hence. A meeting of which Marina had no inkling, nor would; which oddity struck Danielle, as she observed their intimacy unseen. Murray Thwaite surprised her (and again: so tall, so silver); and then spotted her, before his daughter did, and pointed and waved with a broad, guileless smile. Danielle's stomach turned—as if she entertained feelings for the man!—but even as it did, she found herself wondering, from the forthrightness of his expression, whether Murray Thwaite's interested correspondence had actually been purely, as he purported, in the service of his daughter's interest. Maybe Danielle had just imagined, invented—how pathetic!—the underlying flirtation? Although, as they approached, she could have sworn that his gaze did drop and linger, momentarily, upon the neckline and bodice of her dress.

"Mr. Thwaite." She extended a hand and leaned forward at once, and he both clasped her fingers and kissed her cheek—with, she felt again, an undue and possibly meaningful pressure. "Marina, you look gorgeous."

"Doesn't she always?" said Murray, with an indulgence that seemed more than paternal. "You're looking rather fetching yourself."

"I made her get the dress, Daddy," Marina slid an arm around Danielle's shoulder. "Doesn't it look great?"

Murray Thwaite smiled again.

"She wasn't even going to try it on. I took one look at it in the store and said, you've got to have the boobs for it, and Danny's got the boobs. Didn't I say that, Danny?"

"Mind, Marina—I think your friend is turning the color of

her dress." He fixed his eye on Danielle. "But she isn't wrong, you know."

Danielle composed herself sufficiently to laugh, and was about to reply, but Murray Thwaite had turned and been engaged by a small, monkey-faced bald man in a velvet tuxedo jacket.

"Editor," whispered Marina. "Uncool and totally boring. But weirdly powerful. You know how it is."

"Yep. Bar's over there. We might pass a waiter on the way."

Their progress was slow. The cacophony of air-kissing and gossip echoed around them.

"Julius isn't coming, is he?" Danielle asked, when finally they had collected champagne flutes from a young woman in a bow tie.

"He didn't mention it, so I guess not. Part of the ongoing Invisible Man act—imagine *him*, missing *this*? I'm seeing him later this week, though."

"You are?"

"Don't be like that. I'd invite you, but he said he wants to talk about stuff."

"Just not with me?"

"You're being silly."

Danielle shrugged. "I think I'm being cut out of his loop. I know, but even more than you are. Don't roll your eyes. Because you're a Thwaite, or something. Because you'll be more palatable to the Conehead."

"That's so paranoid. I haven't met him either."

"But I bet you will."

Marina made a vague theatrical gesture with her champagne flute, and only narrowly avoided grazing the shiny, shaven neck of an older gentleman beside her. "Julius has given up all this," she said. "It must be for something."

"What's to give up?" asked Danielle, who had already finished her champagne, and was scanning the crowd for the bow-tied waitress. "Look at these people. Do we really want to be like this? All smarmy and self-congratulatory?"

"They're giving Daddy an award, remember? We like them, tonight."

As a different waiter elbowed past, Danielle deposited her empty glass and retrieved a refill, without having to ask him to stop. "I know, I know. But can't we just tell the truth about it for one minute? Look at all these preening clowns, dolled up in their Sunday best, everyone wanting to be more important than the next guy—it's gross."

"Is it? Don't you want to be more important than the next guy? You, of all people?"

Danielle sighed. Marina was annoying her. This was a way Marina had, an obtuse devotion to the more obvious tokens of status. "Your dad would know what I mean," she said. "He's never given a shit what these people think, these armchair tyrants who've never left their tiny New York circles. He goes out and does his thing, writes and says what he needs to, and they come to him. So he really *is* important. Not like these vacuous nonentities, who spend their time at parties like this one."

"Whoa, Danny. What's eating you?"

The green-eyed monster, thought Danielle, is chomping at my nerves. But she merely sipped, smiled, adjusted her neckline.

"Besides, you're wrong about Daddy, you know. Of course he cares. He pretends not to care, because that's the person he wants to be. Or rather: that's the person they want him to be. But you have to care, or you won't succeed. I've watched long enough to know that's true. You won't succeed, for example, carping like that."

Danielle took a deep breath, closed her eyes. Just when you allowed yourself to believe that Marina was a tiny bit dim, she came out with some irritatingly sharp aperçu. Danielle and Julius had often talked about this—back when they talked, of course. And then there was no call for Marina to hector and patronize: such certainties were easy enough to espouse when you were Murray Thwaite's only child, and a beauty in the bargain. Perhaps Marina simply needed to care about success, Danielle thought bitterly, and barely to lift a finger. Danielle's investment in acclaim was a lot less important than the actual work she produced—work that at present seemed to be going nowhere fast. Her boss hadn't cared overly for the revolution pitch. "It just seems so outdated," Nicky had said. "So seventies. There isn't revolution in a little clever sarcasm, Danny. It takes a lot more than that." She'd tried again to explain what she saw as the nihilists' revolution all over New York, the particular purging cynicism of the boom on the cusp of its bust—she'd put it like that, and thought it sounded pretty good—but Nicky wasn't biting. He cared too much for success: couldn't she pick a winner? he'd asked laughingly.

"Don't you recognize that man from somewhere?" Marina's tone had shifted to the conspiratorial, as she pointed with her chewed forefinger to the slight, attenuated figure of Ludovic Seeley. His suit was impeccably cut, but he wasn't wearing black tie; he hadn't wanted, Danielle surmised, to grant this society the satisfaction.

"That's Ludovic Seeley. The Australian guy who's editing that new rag, *The Monitor.* You met him with me, when my mom was here."

"He's better looking than I remembered. He seemed a little scrawny, that day at the Met."

"Or maybe success has made him seem more . . . well, more." Danielle wasn't convinced that Marina would hear her irony. She gave up, changed her tone. "He's actually a pretty interesting guy. Something of a snake, I suspect, but interesting." She paused. "I told him he should offer you a job."

"What kind of a job, exactly?"

"One that would make your reputation, of course."

"What did he say to that?"

"Ask him yourself," said Danielle. "I think he's on his way over." And yet again she attempted, as surreptitiously as possible, to adjust her cleavage in its crimson casing, before Seeley was close enough to kiss the back of her hand.

"Danielle Minkoff," he said, his eyes fully and firmly and almost passionately on hers. "It's my lucky day."

"Why's that?"

"I just popped upstairs to go to the loo, and checked out the seating plan. Seems we're at the same table."

"Oh yes?"

"I took the liberty of switching cards, and now we'll be side by side."

"My, how flattering."

"Don't be flattered—I was sparing myself that dowager dragon from *The Observer.*" He turned to Marina, clicked his heels. "We've met, Ms. Thwaite—with Danielle, in fact. About a month ago. Ludovic Seeley."

"Of course."

Danielle could see something peculiar happening to Marina, a physical self-consciousness that made her more gangly, and less present. It was Marina's particular equivalent of Danielle's adjusting her neckline. Which meant she fancied him. And he? Danielle attempted to gauge the intensity of his gaze upon her friend, but deemed that, if anything, he proved less chivalrous, and less knowing—indeed, less flirtatious altogether—than he was with Danielle herself.

The three of them ascended the stairs together, pressed to intimacy by the bovine throng, which funneled from the lobby upward, spilling into the cavernous, chandeliered ballroom. Here, tables were so tightly crammed that to pass between them, once guests were seated, was all but impossible. In this larger space, the noise rose, echoed, fell again, like a blanket muffling all exchanges, and Marina's words to Seeley were lost to Danielle, who heard only "Catch you later. I'm off to join my date." Then Marina wafted off to the table of honor, behind which Murray Thwaite could be spotted hovering, unlit cigarette in hand, partially obscured by an explosive and garish display of flowers.

This arrangement—comprised of birds of paradise, waratahs and kangaroo paw (and this, mysteriously, in the brief season of peonies)—was repeated in smaller configurations at each of the tables, flowers that, in their bowed spindles and squat bulbosity, in their vulgar blips of red, orange, and violet, towered over the guests as if in parody of their grotesquerie.

"The dowager is more waratah," whispered Seeley to Danielle, "and that one's more bird of paradise." He indicated a tall, bony woman of forty-odd as she passed in search of her seat. Led by her Sitwellian proboscis, she wore an unfortunate draped jacket of yellow tie-dyed crinkled silk. The dowager, it was true, resembled the waratah: stout and bristling, encased in a vermilion ensemble whose lines and hue served only to accentuate the immensity of her bosom. Silver-haired, stony-faced, with the pouting lip of a bullfrog, she was named, incongruously, Serena Ballou. "The balloon I can see," remarked Seeley sotto voce. "The serenity unfortunately not."

"Watch it," said Danielle. "I'm wearing red myself."

"Crimson is altogether different. It's a beautiful dress; you look superb."

"Please." Danielle flushed. "Make fun of me outright. At least then I know what's what."

"You shun my efforts at gallantry? How shaming. But I'm utterly sincere. You've got the perfect eye for what suits you. Really."

"Marina chose the dress." Danielle spoke without thinking, then wished she hadn't.

"A good and useful friend," said Seeley. "Hang on to her."

"I intend to."

"I wonder if one could overlook the father for long," Seeley went on.

"We've been over that, haven't we?"

"Of course. But I have greater reason to malign him when the city's media luminaries come together like so many sheep in order publicly to reward his mediocrity. A mutual lovefest. Most unsavory."

"That makes it sound as though the media luminaries could have made a better choice."

"Couldn't they?"

"My point is that their choice is always despicable. We see the same thing from opposite sides: I approve of Murray Thwaite, and feel he's diminished by accepting this award, because these people, this jury of so-called peers, is so appalling and mediocre. You think Murray Thwaite is mediocre, and so feel the award itself, and maybe the jury, too, are somehow less because he's being celebrated. But that makes you a supporter of the establishment. Not a very radical position, is it?"

"Or perhaps I hold the award and its recipient equally in contempt, which makes me at least clear-eyed."

"Then why are you here, Ludovic?"

"Why, indeed, are you?"

Danielle raised her glass. "It's all grist to the mill, you know. You never know what you might learn, even here."

"Quite," agreed Seeley. "Observe the animals in their natural habitat."

"And you're the wolf in sheep's clothing?"

"Just a man grateful to have any clothes at all"—Seeley adjusted the knife and fork at his place—"when it seems so many among us are utterly unclad."

Danielle couldn't help but glance downward, suddenly and absurdly afraid that her dress might have discomposed itself, and more fully revealed a breast. "The nudity—even metaphorical—escapes me somewhat," she eventually replied. "Everyone dressed up to the nines."

"And in their very caring, exposed. Even those who break the code do so to make a point—"

"That would be you."

"Yes, yes, that would be me. And in seeking to make a point, we seek recognition from the crowd."

"But then even the people who choose not to come at all, who stay home and watch TV—even they are implicated, by your reckoning. They're making some other kind of point."

"Exactly."

"Well, if you can't escape the system in any way, then what's the good of even thinking about it?"

"You forget your Napoleon, Danielle, my dear."

"Here we go again."

"Don't roll your eyes. If you can't escape the system, you must simply *become* the system."

"Alter it from within."

"No, not at all. Not 'within.' The very notion is fallacious. We've been over *this* before: You become the system. You become what people want to be."

"If you can guess what that is."

Ludovic all but sneered. "Tonight, absurdly, it would seem to be Murray Thwaite."

Danielle sat up very straight in her chair. The wine and the warmth of the room had painted high spots of color on her cheeks—she could feel them. "I'd be pretty happy to be Murray Thwaite, myself. He's written a lot of important stuff, and honest."

"My point exactly. Even you would embrace him, the idle old charlatan."

"You wouldn't care to meet him, then?"

Seeley stretched a long arm along the back of Danielle's gilt faux-bamboo chair, and leaned toward her. His face, pale, oval, Nabokovian, had an unnervingly predatory air. "Are you offering?"

"Well, I could. But only if you promised to behave."

"Believe me, I know nothing if not my manners. My mother was very particular on that score. But I do absolutely yearn to observe that particular animal in his natural habitat. Oh yes, I do."

Danielle's opportunity to introduce Seeley and Thwaite did not arise for some time. First there were the prickly little salads and their raspberry vinaigrette, and their antennae-like cheese straws; then there were the filet medallions, glistening in their gravy, and the somewhat hardened turret of potatoes au gratin. There were wines red and white, waters flat and fizzy; and then, before dessert, a movement to speeches. A shrill man's voice silenced the room—it was, Danielle could see, the bald editor in velvet who had claimed Murray Thwaite during cocktails— and in echo droned and squeaked an annual recitation about the Journalists' Association and its marriage, back in the sixties, with the Writers Guild, giving birth to this unique organiza- tion in which writers of so many stripes might unite—"Where the waratah and the bird of paradise conjoin," whispered Seeley, nodding at Madame Ballou, whose weakened chin appeared to tremble over her red jacket and whose eyes grew heavy-lidded as the speech wore on; while behind her, several tables away but in an unimpeded visual line, sat the yellow silk torso he had noted earlier, topped by its long, eagerly quiver- ing nose. From an angle midway between Seeley and Danielle, the nose would appear to sprout from Serena Ballou's gunmetal crop. The pompous little man—only a vice chairman, as it transpired, because he had yet to introduce the blue sequined battleship who was the society's chairman ("or should I say, in her honor, chair*woman*," he corrected himself, with a nasal whinny)—meandered from the history to the present mission

("Aha," whispered Seeley. "You see: there is a mission! That in itself could be hijacked. Why not my mission, I wonder?") to the annual award, so carefully selected, to the individual whose contribution to the published word . . . ("A confusion of the mission," hissed Seeley, "or are you televisuals not eligible?") The little man, whose name was supposedly known, and so never once mentioned, eventually withdrew, slinking back to his seat beneath the acoustically augmented echoing roar of dutiful applause, to be replaced at the podium by the battle-ship, who spoke in a smiling lockjaw, as if her sentences were dragged from between powerfully resistant lips. Seeley mocked this too, quietly, and the prominence of her glittering shelflike bust. At least she held forth only briefly, an encomium to Murray Thwaite, and then sailed calmly back to berth behind the largest flower arrangement, at Thwaite's right hand.

"Bottom's turn," Seeley murmured. Danielle glared at him; flirtatiously, of course, but with a pang of guilt at her coyness. She experienced some confusion as she leaned back in her chair, and felt the feathered, unacknowledgeable presence of Seeley's hand at her nape. She was reminded of the evening of their first meeting, in Sydney, and of the way she'd seen him bend toward Moira—and of what she, Danielle, had experienced then. To countenance mockery of Murray Thwaite, quite in this way and from this man, surely constituted treachery, both to her dear friend and to the object of derision himself, so newly com-municant and hence real to her; and yet, for the prospect of this hand, this sardonic smile, she was apparently more than willing.

In truth, Murray Thwaite's speech *wasn't* particularly re-markable, or didn't seem so when heard in Seeley's shadow.

Danielle could picture Marina's rapt expression—one she knew well—and caught it mirrored in many of the women's faces around her, including, surprisingly, Serena Ballou's. Murray Thwaite spoke about the importance of integrity, about pursuing truth even when it wasn't fashionable. He spoke of changing times, of a culture increasingly preoccupied with form over substance, with the anointing of celebrities whom audiences were all too keen to worship.

"Please don't misunderstand me," he said. "I'm honored to be standing here tonight, and grateful beyond measure for the recognition you've all so kindly bestowed upon me." He paused, looked meaningfully and handsomely out at the assembly, with a raised eyebrow that prompted Seeley to hiss, "Kitsch. Pure kitsch," and went on: "But I grew up questioning the very notion of awards and prizes, the promise that any *received* ideas or individuals could be trusted. I was young in the fifties, and really came into my own in the sixties—a time some of you here are old enough to remember with me—when we believed in tearing it all down and beginning again. When any establishment, and certainly any organization like this one, was suspect. Recall, if you will, that slogan from Paris 'Sixty-eight: 'Rêve plus evolution equals Révolution'—dream plus evolution equals revolution. Heady stuff, back then. Naïve, too, and maybe ultimately, in its naïveté, pernicious; but there was a lot of good in those times, those views, and they've undeniably shaped me and the way I've pursued my calling." He paused again, coughed his impressive smoker's cough.

"Disgusting old ashtray," Seeley said. "And as time has amply shown us, dreaming brings about no revolution at all, matey."

"If I don't believe it, I won't say it, let alone write it. If I spot an untruth or an injustice, it's my job to correct it, or at least to try. I don't believe something's important simply because I'm told it's important; and the inverse, perhaps more crucially, is also true: something isn't unimportant simply because it's been largely overlooked by others. I'll stop lecturing, because I also believe in not being a bore"—here, everybody laughed, rather more energetically, Danielle thought, than was wholly appropriate—"but I have to take heart from this generous award"—he nodded at the battleship, who appeared to return the favor—"and hope that this old-fashioned way of seeing the world, of trying to see it truly, still holds some sway. Or at least, that you still need a few grumpy old naysayers like myself around, if only to liven things up." He grinned, appeared to wink. "Now I for one am going to say thank you and good night, because I'm desperate to step outside and have a good old-fashioned smoke."

"Was that really necessary?" asked Seeley during the applause. "Of a piece with the whole—so *tired.*"

"I don't know," Danielle said. "The smoking is tired, the speech perhaps a little, too, but if he means it? Isn't he right?"

"Means it? Please, my dear. It's not even what he thinks people want to hear—it's precisely what he thinks they *don't* want to hear, some sort of cod liver oil for the soul. They don't want to hear it, so it must be good for them. Preposterous. Studiedly insulting, which seems to me far worse than unwittingly insulting. He no more believes it than you or I."

"I thought I did believe it."

"You make me laugh."

Danielle reflected upon Marina's earlier comment about her

father, her implication that his persona was less, or more, than unselfconsciously authentic—something Danielle had, over the years, more than once obliquely suggested to her friend. What had only this evening become clear was that Marina saw transparently her father's bravado, his artificiality, had always seen it, and didn't care. Perhaps everyone saw it and didn't care, even though his principal virtue was supposed to be his vaunted authenticity. Was she herself attracted or repelled? Was Thwaite a hero or a hypocrite? Or both?

"You have to understand the game," Seeley was saying. "They—we—all want the cod-liver oil from Murray. We want him to chide us for our lack of seriousness, and we want to shake our heads and take our castigation manfully because then we feel absolved, supremely free to watch the Oscars on TV and enjoy it. The way Catholics are entitled to a good piss-up on Saturday night, as long as they're taking their wigging in the pew the next morning. Lets everybody feel serious and still have fun. He's a stooge. He knows it and we know it. We're all complicit. Now, do you think he's done with his fag? Could you take me over to pay my respects?"

As they made their way slowly through the throng—which had risen en masse from the faux-bamboo chairs and now swarmed more tightly even than it had in the lobby below—Danielle was aware of something like a spell upon her: what Seeley's genuine feelings about Thwaite might be she could not fathom, as he appeared so powerfully to disdain the older man, yet clamored to meet him. She was also dimly conscious of a category mistake, in her presumption—automatic, Thwaiteanly old-fashioned—that Seeley might be possessed of such things as "genuine" feelings; that, indeed, when it came to

Seeley, "genuine" was a word with any currency at all. She couldn't fully gauge what ethics powered such a man, although some code had to be in place, and although, too, she suspected that his way, opaque to her though it might be, was increasingly the common way. As she shouldered past the bird of paradise woman, a fixed smile on her face, Danielle thought, "Code. Napoleonic code," and this seemed, although in somewise far from apt, nevertheless perfectly to explain the man. This alternative morality, this still—to her at least—unreadable code, was Seeley's means to domination. To get everyone to see another way, his way, and then to make that way the standard. Then to have them—all of society's little Napoleons, all of us, she thought—under his sway. Her eagerness to dismiss Murray Thwaite's speech as absurd, to interpret his genuine courage in questioning the academy as a self-interested manipulation—this, she thought, was Seeley-speak seeping unbidden into her brain.

Or was this nonsense? Simply an ordinary case of a young Turk needing to slay his father—anxiety of influence, as her college profs would have called it—because why else did Seeley want to meet the man? She could see, now, Marina's back floating up ahead, the skinny arms contriving elegantly to gesticulate in spite of the crowd. But before she relinquished her train of thought, she wanted to grant Seeley the benefit of the doubt. God knew, she could be irritated by her mother, but she still loved her. So, too, Seeley could both admire and despise Thwaite, and could despise him all the more for having earlier admired him. It would explain his desire to meet him; and didn't make of him any more a monster than she was herself. It seemed that Seeley *wanted* her to entertain grandiose fantasies about him; he encouraged it. But that, perhaps, was as much a sham as, if not more so than, Thwaite's desire to stand against the establishment even while accepting its award.

"Daddy's downstairs," Marina breathed. "Promising to take us to the Oak Room at the Plaza. And then maybe back home with a crowd, if it seems fun. I know it's a school night, but come on, Danny, say yes?"

"Could Ludovic Seeley come, too? He'd like to meet"— Seeley caught up with them, laid the feathery, breathtaking hand upon her waist—"I was just saying, Ludovic, that you'd like to meet Marina's dad."

"I certainly would. He's a—an important figure in my formation."

"Don't tell him that." Marina laughed. "It just makes him feel old. Then again, he's a sucker for flattery, so maybe you should. I leave it up to you."

Which was tantamount to an invitation. The trio moved with the tidal swell, to the paved plaza outside the ballroom, and thence to a waiting town car among town cars, distinguishable only by its dapper driver.

"Hey, Hussein, can Ludovic sit up front with you?" Marina asked; and to the others, "Daddy just has to take a few more pats and plaudits, I'm sure, before he can break away. He won't be long."

"You don't smoke," observed Seeley to Marina, as they waited against the car, bathed in the evening's warm breeze.

"Is that a surprise?"

"Maybe."

"Besides, how do you know I don't?"

"Because even I could do with a fag after *that*." Seeley

nodded back toward the dispersing crowd, among whom the bird of paradise was even now visible.

"If you'd grown up in the fug of it like I did, you wouldn't pine for it, believe me."

"Fat Al smoked, didn't he?" offered Danielle, eager to be part of the banter.

"Mm-hmm."

"Who is Fat Al? A departed house pet?"

"Close. My almost fiancé. Once." Marina made a face, waved her arm. "Off in the ether somewhere now. Either smoking or not smoking, I don't know. But not my business anymore."

Seeley bit his thin lip. "Was he actually fat?"

"Depends on your standards. Looking at you—I'd say you would have called him fat."

"He *was* fat," said Danielle. She thought they both looked a little surprised; as if they were in the process of forgetting that she was there. "He wasn't obese, but he was definitely fat. Marina used to grab his flab and say it was why she loved him."

"I see," said Seeley.

"Here comes Daddy," Marina said, and they all turned to watch the great man saunter across the plaza, his tie shed and collar unbuttoned, his glinting hair all but aloft in the wind. He was surrounded by well-wishers who fell away one by one as if choreographed, without apparently disrupting his gait. A lit cigarette stuck in the corner of his mouth, he smiled, though for whom it was not clear.

"Like some kind of god," whispered Seeley. Danielle looked at him, and looked at Marina looking at him, and wondered what on earth he was really trying to say.

CHAPTER TWENTY-TWO

Enough About Us

"He just seems a little creepy to me," Marina explained as she stepped out of the path of a zealous Rollerblader. "I can't quite put my finger on why."

"Who?" Julius was having trouble following. The night had been very late, the sun's glare oppressed, and he was concentrating on not vomiting, although he hadn't had any breakfast. Perhaps because he hadn't. Instead, he'd lingered under a scalding shower, and knew that his bright skin and gleaming hair now gave no indication of his suffering. That said, Visine hadn't really helped his eyes; and his nose, as so often now, itched and ran.

"What do you mean, 'who'? Are you even listening, Jules?"

"Just tired, that's all. Don't give me that look. Tell me who."

"My cousin. Frederick. You know what his mother calls him? Bootie. He's an adult, for God's sake. He could put a stop to that."

"Booty? As in 'Shake Your'?"

"I don't think he's done much shaking, to judge by its substantial size."

"Hey, girlfriend—you *lived* with Fat Al and claimed he was sexy."

"For some reason he's on everybody's mind at the moment. You'll be interested to know that my current attraction is positively slight."

"That's new. I want more on that. But why does the cousin creep you?"

Marina went on to explain that on the evening of the awards dinner, when everyone had gone back to the apartment, late, around one-thirty, and sprawled in the living room—just six or seven people, pretty drunk, by then, in a festive way—she'd gotten up to get some water and had found him lurking in the darkened kitchen. Just standing there. "Sorry, did we wake you, I asked him, and he said no, no, he hadn't been asleep, he was just getting a drink, but then he stood there, he just stood there without moving, no drink visible, and he looms, you know, with these thick glasses and scary eyes, and he was staring at me like a space alien, so finally I said did he want to come join us—weird enough in itself, but manners dictated—and he says yes. Isn't *that* creepy?"

"Why?" Julius yawned. Their slow pace across the park— he'd come to her neck of the woods, most generously—was exhausting him further. He felt as though he were swimming instead of walking. They were not far from the museum. "Isn't the kid entitled to a flash of glamour? I mean, he's from Buffalo or something—"

"Watertown."

"And he's young, young. Remember what it's like? *He's* scared of *you*."

"That's what my mother always said about spiders."

"Seriously. Think about it."

Marina thought. "I was never scared. Not of people. I was brought up not to be."

"Maybe that's your problem."

"What's that supposed to mean?"

Julius shrugged. "I think I need some coffee, before I take in any art."

"I'm not going to pick a fight about that one, because I don't see you enough, and I can't afford to. But don't think it isn't noted for the record."

Julius, too, felt there were certain distances between them that there was little point attempting to bridge. Sometimes you had to deal with Marina as though she hailed from a foreign culture—which, up to a point, she did. "Good to know you don't change. Now find me a coffee shop."

"On Madison."

"I don't know how you can live up here."

"I don't. I live on the other side of the park."

"It's all death. Same thing."

"Says the oracle, lately of the projects but now from Chelsea's exclusive loft heaven."

"Ooh, aren't we bitchy?"

"Well, you haven't invited anyone around, and there's got to be a reason."

"Really?"

"Danielle and I have been thinking we're not male enough, or not gay enough, for your David."

"Please. Don't be ridiculous." He didn't want to have this conversation either. If she didn't understand, how could he explain? When someone moved away from his hometown to take a new job, his family and close friends didn't feel slighted.

They felt proud of a man's accomplishment. And wasn't a relationship—for God's sake, in Julius's life, the accomplishment
of a relationship, already of two months' standing—something
of which Marina and Danielle should feel supportive and
proud? There was a cost, he thought wearily, to everything.

"We prefer to think it's not because you think we're dull."

Julius sighed. "David's really busy. He has an important job,
unlike you or me. He doesn't have that much time for social-
izing, and when he *does* have time, there are a lot of people he
needs to see."

"Wants to, you mean."

"Fine, wants to. What's wrong with that?"

"You'd just think he'd want to meet his lover's oldest friends.
Not necessarily even hang out with them, but meet them."

"You know what it's like: we're finding the rhythm of *our*
relationship, just the two of us. There'll be time—lots of
time—for everyone to meet, and to become friends."

"It's been months already, Jules."

"Just two." He paused. "Remember the Natasha/Pierre dis-
tinction?"

"Christ. How could I forget?"

"Well, remember what happens to Natasha at the end? And
nobody ever likes it, they all say 'But where did the real Natasha
go?' But the point is that she likes it. She's happy. That's the
point."

Marina sighed. "How many times do I have to remind you,
Julius? I haven't read the fucking novel."

When they were settled in a booth—its aged vinyl and
Formica dizzying to Julius's parched eyes—Marina chose to
forgive him, largely, he thought, because she wanted to keep

talking. Apparently their brief exchange on the sidewalk had given her sufficient information about his new life, because she asked—for a long time, at least—no further questions.

"So maybe I'm interested in someone," she confided, leaning toward him with almost menacing excitement.

"So you implied earlier. Who is he, that he can meet your exacting standards?"

"Weirdly, he's slight, and losing his hair, and very, very dry—his sense of humor, I mean—"

"Sounds great."

"Spare me the sarcasm."

"No, about the sense of humor—I meant it. Not the bald shrimp part, of course."

"Not a shrimp. Tall and skinny—or rather, slender. That's the word for him, I think."

"Gay?"

Marina sat back sharply. "No! At least, I don't think so."

"Sounds gay."

"No. I'm pretty sure he's not gay. Australian, so a little hard to read, you know."

"Australians are macho, or they're gay. Or they're macho and gay, Village People style."

"Stop it."

"Sorry. If you think he's straight, he's probably straight. What does he do?"

"Well, that's the thing."

"What's the thing? He's a porn star or something?"

"Not funny, Jules. Give it up. No, the thing is, he might employ me."

"Employ you? Who in their right mind would employ you?"

Marina grimaced.

"Okay, okay. You clearly can't be teased on this one; so tell me the whole story. I had no idea *you* were looking for a *job*. Begin at the beginning for me? Did you meet him at an interview?"

Marina explained how she had first met Ludovic Seeley, and seen him again at the dinner; how he'd come along afterward, had sat next to her at the Oak Room, how they'd found much in common, from their admiration for Anne-Sofie Mutter to a predilection for sushi to a distaste for online shopping, because the experience of savoring an item, the use of all five senses, was essential. "And he's setting up this magazine—it launches in September—called *The Monitor*, and he asked, suddenly, just offhand, in the limo on the way back home, whether I'd be interested in a job."

"What kind of a job?"

"Not sweeping the floors, I don't think. Danny had recommended me to him, but he said I was even more riveting—'riveting' was his word—than she'd made me out to be."

"So what now?"

"He suggested an interview. A formal sort of meeting. But it was just in passing, and we were pretty far gone by then, all of us—several bottles in, you know—and then at the end, when he left, he said only 'Let's be in touch,' so now I don't know whether I should call him, or maybe he said a time and I'm just blanking, or—"

"Do you want to go to bed with him or work for him?"

"Couldn't I do both?"

Julius recalled his week of working for David: the thrill of it, the glances, the first brushing of their fingers, the enhanced tension of their first kiss on account of their roles. "No law against it. But not the best way to begin, maybe. Muddies the waters, and all that. Causes trouble down the line. Or straightaway, even."

"How so?"

"It's not my business, but I thought you didn't *want* a job. At least, not till the book was finished." Noting her furrowed brows, he went on, "Though maybe that's changed?" Always, it seemed, he was accommodating. Trying to figure out what other people thought and expected, what they hoped for. Even now, even this, was about gauging what Marina needed from him. He hated it. As if he were the poor relation. It seemed that the only life that he had, all of his very own, was his secret life, and he could keep it safely his only by keeping it secret. Marina would never know about it, and if she did, she wouldn't care. She was too mired in the trivial back and forth of her own days. The endlessly unwritten book.

"If you kept in better touch with your friends, Jules, you might know these things. It's been a huge crisis for me, these past couple of months, whether to get a job or not."

"Please." He rolled his eyes significantly. "No more about how I don't do enough for you. I've been available nonstop for ten years to hear about these things. And if I'm a few weeks out of touch, you break my balls about it? *Please.*" He shook his hair as if chasing a gnat. "So tell me, why the crisis?"

"What do you mean, why? You've had successes, so maybe you can't know what it's like."

"Please. Again, please. Don't talk to me about lack of success. My career has been going nowhere for the past two years, and until recently, I couldn't even claim to have had a decent relationship."

"If you know so well, then stop being so flippant about *my* life. I'm thirty and unemployed, and looking pretty unemployable, as time goes on. Even my dad seems to think it would be a good idea. But it can't be a stupid job, not something utterly menial and meaningless. Not something I take on only because I claim to need the money, or to get out of the house, or—"

"Nothing like temping, for example." Julius said this for his own ironic satisfaction.

"Exactly. Nothing completely stupid."

"And you're sure this wouldn't be? Is it writing, editing, what?"

"I don't know yet."

Julius winced, passed his hands over his face. Her stubborn, puppyish eagerness caused him almost physical discomfort. "Just tell me," he said. "Tell me that you're not wanting this mysteriously undefined job just because he'd be giving it, this skinny bald guy with the silly name?"

"Totally not."

"Okay, if you say so. Now tell me that he's not offering the job just because he wants to get in your pants."

"That's beneath you, and I'm going to disregard it."

"Tell me one other thing."

"What?"

"How does Danny feel about this guy?"

"She says he's huge in Australia, very smart but possibly a tad slippery. Ambitious, too. Young for how far he's got."

"That doesn't really answer my question."

"I don't get you."

"How does she *feel* about him?"

It was Marina's turn to put a hand to her face, which she did in a fluttery way, bringing her fingers to rest on the silver chain at her throat, with which she began to fiddle, attempting to bring it up over her chin. "I don't think she feels anything about him at all. They met in Sydney, she ran into him here, she's thinking of making a program that would feature him—something about iconoclasts or something."

"But she doesn't fancy him?"

"I don't think so." She looked at the table, at the window, as if wracking her brain. "No. She's suspicious of him. She doesn't fancy him, as you put it. She'd have told me, if she did."

"Does she tell you everything?" Julius couldn't keep the sarcasm out of his voice, but Marina did not rise to it.

"Everything to do with that, yes."

"So who does she fancy?"

"I don't know. Nobody. She hasn't been interested in anyone for ages. Since that grad student who ran off and got married."

"If you say so. Maybe she should go out with your cousin?"

"Very funny." They were silent for a moment. Then Marina reached for her wallet. "Art-time, now. Enough about us."

Us? thought Julius. Us? But he let it go. He even allowed himself to feel a rush of tenderness for Marina, who seemed to him so oblivious, so simple and oblivious. It was good to see her, easy, like going home. Familiar even in its irritations. He'd missed her. "If you want to see the guy, I vote you call him," he said. "No point in playing the shrinking violet. It won't get you anywhere. And the job will either pan out or it won't. Either way, you're no worse off."

CHAPTER TWENTY-THREE

A Helping Hand

Murray didn't have to make up any excuse in order to meet Danielle for a drink: Annabel was rarely home before eight; he had a lunch engagement with Boris, over from London, and she knew how he was. If Murray wasn't home when she got in, Annabel would assume he was still "at lunch" with Boris. And would make sure there was some supper left on the counter, in case he wanted it. Murray had always been grateful for her independence, and grateful, too, that he knew not to take it for indifference. Increasingly, in the years since Marina had gone off to college, and most of all now that Marina seemed to have come home again indefinitely, Annabel had devoted herself to her good works in the law, had found fulfillment in the sundered and unsettled families of the underprivileged. Sometimes Murray teased her, lamented that she'd forsaken him for a bony, battered housewife or burly, knuckleheaded truant. But it was in jest only: they had attained, he told anyone who asked, an optimal balance between independence and trust-filled union. She didn't need to know where he spent every hour—certainly not when he was traveling, on lecture or book tours—because she knew that he came home at night to her. And he knew that the world's unfortunates could never really supplant him in her heart. They still had great sex, often enough to reassure them both. And besides, what was a simple drink with a friend of Marina's, other than the healthy manifestation of a father's concern for his dear girl?

Justifications, justifications, he muttered as he shaved, meticulously. It was not the second time: he hadn't bothered to shave for Boris, who, of course, hadn't been bothered to shave for him either, two bleary men in the restaurant window, blinking across the brilliant white linen at each other, their beards—silver and white, respectively—glistening in the sun's unrelenting scrutiny. They'd perked up with drink, had reached a state of conviviality at about the hour the restaurant emptied of lunch clients; and close to four, Murray had had the satisfaction—rather like that of bringing a difficult woman to orgasm—of eliciting Boris's gargantuan roaring laugh, a fat, rolling rumble that moved his shoulders, shook the flesh inside his shirt and rattled his jowls before erupting, enormous, into the now-empty room. After this, at last, Murray could disentangle himself, head home before the cocktail crowd came through the door.

For this meeting, he shaved; and put on cologne—the gin-and-tonic smell that he considered his own, although he was in fact a scotch drinker—and a fresh shirt, a narrowly striped one of which he was particularly fond. His hands seemed to him slightly to tremble, as he brought the razor to his face, as he fastened his buttons, and he wondered whether this was merely the glut of his luncheon wearing off, a call, not infrequently heard, for the hair of the dog; or whether the tremor was born of genuine apprehension. This latter would surprise only because this ritual—the odd drink, the odd fling, the odd prolonged liaison—was as much a part of him as Annabel, or Marina, or—in an analogy that struck him as more apt—as the Pope had been. If he were more anxious than was usual—and it was true, his heart's rhythms suggested either nerves or incipient infarction—then it was because, he chastised himself with a rueful snort as he downed a small scotch before leaving, he ought not to be fantasizing about, ought not to be seducing, his daughter's best friend. Because she *would* be seduced, he was almost sure of it—something about her hesitation, in the foyer, at the dinner. Something about the tremble of her milky cleavage. A very fine dress indeed.

He saw her at once when he entered the bar, alone in the gloom at a table against the wall—where a booth would have been, had the bar not had pretensions. He would have preferred a booth—a glass of wine, red, at least, before her. She looked smaller, paler, plainer than his imagination's portrait, her nose rather more prominent and her hair, of itself a rippling dark glory, rather unflatteringly styled, parted far to one side so that her cheeks loomed strangely broad, slablike. But even these facts, which might have been deemed shortcomings, aroused him, and when she raised her eyes and smiled—shyly, he would have said—he had to pause and clear his throat.

"My dear," he began, bending to kiss her cheek, which was cool and sweet-smelling.

"I wasn't sure you'd come."

"Am I late?" He made a show of checking his watch. "I try to be punctual."

"No, it's not that—but we didn't speak of it the other evening, and I wasn't sure . . ."

"I don't forget a date." He smiled. "Especially when I've made it myself. I would never forget a date with you."

She licked her lip, studied the mosaic tabletop. "And you're worried about Marina."

"Aren't you? To be honest, aren't you?"

Danielle nodded. "I suggested—I've suggested several times—that she get a job."

"So she told me. Let me get a drink." He flagged the waitress, ordered, indicated that Danielle should continue.

"And the book—I don't know—"

"Frankly, my dear, do you really think she'll finish the book?"

"I don't know."

"It's rather a bad sign, I must say, that lingering manuscript, for those of us whose livelihoods depend on completion. I'd finish it for her, if I could."

"I think she wants it to be perfect, that's the trouble. No offense, but she's trying to live up to your reputation, and your expectations—she wants you to be proud of her—and it puts her under a lot of pressure."

"I always told her not to write. Take it from one who knows, I said, when she was just a child, do anything but, anything but this. Although it does enable you, at least some of the time, to sleep in in the mornings." Danielle's face was grave, and Murray reached out—this was either the worst moment, or ideal—to put his hand, large and reddened, upon her small, white one. "It was a joke. She always knew it for a joke. I'm proud of her whatever she does." She did not remove her hand; just moved it slightly beneath his, like a trapped bird. "It's her happiness that concerns me," he went on, conscious, above all, of the warmth of their contact, of the frailty, or seeming frailty, of Danielle's moving fingers. "Not some measure of worldly success."

Here she extricated her hand, gently, in order, it seemed, to tuck the great wave of her hair behind her ear. He found even her ears, which were oddly round, attractive. "I know, Mr. Thwaite."

"Murray, please. Murray." He said it emphatically.

She nodded, again at the mosaic table. "Murray, then. I know it is. I think it's in her, the problem. Self-esteem. I mean, I know she's confident, we all know that, but on some other level, she's not been—I suggested a job because I thought it'd help her confidence, her momentum. I guess I thought having some other work might help her finish the book." Murray raised an eyebrow. "Or not. Maybe not. But either way, she's not finishing the book as it is."

"No."

"And in fact, I may have found a job for her. I'm not sure."

"She hasn't spoken of it to me."

"No, it's not definite. It would be with Ludovic Seeley's new magazine."

"Seeley?"

"The Australian we were with the other evening."

"Is he your boyfriend?"

"Oh no, nothing like that," but he noticed that she blushed. "He's just someone I know. But the magazine, *The Monitor*, it launches in September."

"Did he name it?"

"I don't know. Why?"

"Because in addition to the Christian Science overtones, it

was Napoleon's paper, as it happens. Suggests the boy has ambitions."

"I think he does."

"He seemed a spindly, snide fellow to me."

Danielle shrugged, awkward.

"Are you quite sure he's not your beau? Your secret paramour?"

"I'm quite, quite sure."

"He'd be a lucky fellow."

"You flatter me."

"But of course." He paused. "So you say he may employ Marina? To do what, I wonder?"

"I'm not sure whether it's writing or editing."

"And you think it would be a good idea?"

Danielle was silent for a moment. "I honestly don't know."

"No." Murray examined the bottom of his empty tumbler. "One can't know, can one? And one can't make up her mind for her, in any event. Each of us must make our own decisions."

"Yes, I guess so."

"Would you like another? I'm going to have another."

"Well, I . . ."

"It hardly seems fateful."

"Oh." She laughed again, tucked the cascading hair behind her ear. The delicious ear. "You never know, though, do you? What will be fateful?" And looked vaguely embarrassed. "Why not? I'll have another. It's the Pinot Noir."

CHAPTER TWENTY-FOUR

A Helping Hand (2)

He had some explaining to do. That's what she kept telling herself as she dusted Bootie's forlorn bedroom. Her brother had some explaining to do. What was she to think about Bootie in New York in the first place? He was to have been home by now; and then she'd conceded, gracefully, over the summer courses, glimpsing as she did a proper enrollment—a four-year course, a degree—and the University of Massachusetts was nothing to sneeze at, she was quite sure some famous people had come out of there; and his friend, the boy from the high school, a spotty boy with a scrawny neck, whatever his name was, a year ahead and a good example—he was a studious kid, she'd had him in her class—he was there already.

A spiderweb, a faint gray fluff, dangled from the ceiling over Bootie's bed, like a shadow or an ill omen. It fluttered slightly in the breeze she created with her duster—that's why she noticed it. But she couldn't reach it unless she stood on the bed. She paused, contemplating. Somehow it seemed a treachery to tramp frankly, full-footed, on Bootie's mattress, as though it suggested he might not come back. She knew this was silly, not logical, and she wiped the rime of dust from his headboard, the headboard Bert had sanded and painted a lifetime ago, imperfectly, as it happened, so that the duster always caught on a jagged splinter, and left a cotton strand behind. Out the window, she could see Hilda ambling past with her ancient lab, whose gammy leg had him shuffling, seeming miserable. The pane was streaky, on the inside. Had she really not cleaned here properly since he left? When did he go? She remembered the filthy curls of snow, the pushing buds. A long time, now.

And so what was Murray doing, giving the boy a job? Paid employment? Madness. Maybe Bootie was lying, or at least bending the truth? Maybe she'd misunderstood? She often felt, these past weeks, that she wasn't hearing properly, or not absorbing information as she ought—for example, she'd completely confused the story Joan Swan had related at lunch last Wednesday, the story about Emma, or Irma, in the eleventh grade, whose father had killed himself. Or they thought he'd killed himself but it turned out he'd just died. Or the other way around, perhaps. Which was the point: not that Joan Swan was a particularly good storyteller, but Judy had been on some kind of autopilot—where had her mind been?—and couldn't even tell whether listening was the problem, that is, not listening; or whether her hearing was in trouble. Either way, same result: she'd asked Joan a question that had seemed to her obvious, but that Joan clearly thought was very off, and proof that she didn't have a clue. And maybe this had happened, now, on the phone with Bootie, although she didn't think so. She hadn't been thinking about other things—how could she, when speaking to her only boy? Although possibly, it's true, thinking about all she couldn't say—which boiled down to "Bootie, come home!"—rather than about what he was actually whispering (he did fairly whisper, because his voice was naturally low, and because he didn't want the Thwaites to be disturbed) in her addled ear.

Hilda and the dog were long gone from the smeared frame. The sun hung low, orange, and cast an almost holy light, illuminating small, chosen moments along the street, including the porch of the Randalls' house, sagging, with its windows boarded. So depressing. When she turned, Judy could no longer see the spiderweb over the bed; not without the light on. She didn't want to know it was still there. She didn't want to flick the switch. She quit the room for the hallway, for the stairs.

This, really, was the problem of late: since Bootie had left, she found her reality too changeable. She seemed to have too much control over it, in a way. There was nothing, or more precisely no one, to reflect her experience back to her, and so her experience had become her whole reality. Which she didn't trust. Sometimes it was fine—decide to ignore the spiderweb, and it's as if it never was. There would be no independent confirmation of the web's existence, nor even of the spider's. And sometimes, less fine, as at night when she awoke with a shudder in the blue gloom, and couldn't be sure, in spite of the thunder of her blood, of her *own* existence. As if the quiet house had swallowed her.

She hadn't felt this way when Bootie had been at Oswego, and hadn't expected to feel it this time. Then again, she hadn't expected him to go like this, running away from home in all but name. Amanuensis, Bootie had said—which must have been Murray's word. Trust Murray to use a ten-cent word when a regular one would do. He meant secretary. That's what her brilliant boy would be doing. No shame in it, he'd said. Pound did it for Yeats, you know. "My brother is no Yeats" had been her response, tart enough, she trusted, to suggest that she wasn't floundering in the conversation.

In the kitchen, in the dusk, she considered supper. The frozen chicken potpie would take too long, and leave leftovers. A salad involved chopping. Was she even peckish? She couldn't quite tell; but it was the hour. Which was stronger, ritual or indifference? Which more real? What could it matter? And now did she have to accept that Bootie would never come home again? In which case, she reflected, opening a can of baked beans and careful not to nick her thumb on the lid, she ought to send him his dress shoes. She'd noticed them just now, shiny as beetles, neatly pointing to the wall at the foot of his bed, in uncharacteristic order. They were, she suddenly understood by this incongruity, evidence of the nature of his plans before ever he left home. Not her imagination. She felt pretty sure this was reality.

CHAPTER TWENTY-FIVE

A Helping Hand (3)

"You probably don't see it, because it's so, I don't know, unlikely or something, but I think he's incredibly sexy. That's what I kept thinking, the whole way through. I was there for a couple of hours, and they just flew by. He's just—what is it?"

"Magnetic?"

"Exactly. He's magnetic. And there's a way he has of speaking to you as though you were the only person who could possibly understand—"

"Trot out the clichés for us."

"But not in a cloying way. He's wry, you know? Ironic. Very British."

"I know," said Danielle, "except that he's Australian." She sighed, closed the computer file in front of her. She'd been trying to generate a proposal that would please her boss, pull ratings, get her noticed. She'd thought Ludovic Seeley was a good bet; but maybe plastic surgery was better. Women dying in doctors' offices while having lunch-hour liposuction. It would raise some of the same questions about integrity and authenticity in a more dramatic fashion. "So tell me about the interview. What's the job on offer?"

"Oh, Danny, it's as if it was made for me. As if it *is* made for me. It's incredible." Danielle could tell from the slight gurgle in Marina's throat that she was lying on her back with her knees up, probably on her bed—a posture Danielle had known since freshman year, one at once feline and jubilant. Marina sat up when she wasn't happy.

"Did he offer you something?"

"He basically said it's mine if I want it. I told him I'd think, but—"

"What is it?"

"It's editing a cultural section. Not ditsy cultural, like listings—he wants essays, serious but controversial essays on cultural issues."

"Such as?"

"Such as anything, really. Questioning essays. Like, is PEN really a worthwhile institution, for example. Or a renegade appraisal of modern art, the New York art scene, is Matthew Barney a fraud, that kind of thing."

"Okay. Guaranteed to help you win friends and influence people."

"I won't write the pieces, unless I actually want to, until there's something that really grabs me."

"How convenient. In the meantime, you can encourage aspiring young writers to get hoisted on their own petards."

"Excuse me?"

"You can commission people with nothing—which means, everything—to lose, and have them write blistering exposés that will ruin their careers forever."

"Hey, you know—"

"Sort of the journalistic equivalent of being a meter maid. Sounds great."

"What's the matter with you?"

"Sorry. Bad day at work." Danielle bit a hangnail, went on. "It's just a risky undertaking, around this town."

"But somebody's got to tell people that the emperor has no clothes."

"Yeah, he gave me that line, too. It's oddly persuasive, for a minute or two."

"What's that supposed to mean? It's not a line. It's a passionate commitment. He's an extraordinary guy—if you spent any time with him . . ."

"We had lunch, remember? To talk about my idea for a show?"

"I know. But all the more reason he'd be guarded around you. The magazine is secret, right now—it's his baby, you know. He wants to take the world by surprise."

"Sure, of course."

"You should be happy for me. You're being really weird."

"Have you said yes, then?"

"Not yet. We're having supper tomorrow night, and I said I'd give him an answer then."

So that's how it was. Danielle tore at the hangnail with her teeth, could feel the skin pulling too far: a small, live pain. Of course it wouldn't have occurred to Marina that Danielle might be interested. Marina who had said once, drunk, freshman year, as they lay on their beds fully dressed, each with a foot, still shod, on the floor to slow the room's spinning: "You're so lucky, really, Danny."

"Why's that?"

"You never have to worry about whether guys like you for your looks or for you."

Danielle had made a joke of it; she'd teased Marina, so that it was one of their oldest shared comedies. But still. She ought to have known that Ludovic Seeley, in such matters, would be no more a revolutionary than the next guy. Of course they were having supper. And that hand, light and strong, would settle in the small of Marina's back in that numbing, spiderlike way he had; and he would manipulate her every way he wanted her.

"You know, I have an idea," Danielle said, hearing her voice and reassured by its normality. "You might consider commissioning your cousin for those pages."

"Bootie? You mean Frederick?"

"I mean the chubby guy with the glasses. Of course I do. He seems smart. And sweet. And a bit lost. He could do something on spec, say; and if it was any good, it could launch him. Don't you think?"

"Maybe."

"Don't sound that way. That's the point of a job like that—you get to nurture young talent. That's what you get known for."

"Hmm. I somehow don't think Frederick 'Bootie' Tubb is up to it."

"You never know until you try. Give the kid a break. He's your cousin."

"You mean, out of the goodness of my heart?"

"Something like that." Danielle paused. "After all, what's the worst that can happen? You commission him, it gives him some confidence, you spike it, but encouragingly, and next time he's readier to try. For someone else."

"Maybe."

"And you could commission Julius, too. For real, I mean."

"I could. He seems to need the work. Talk about lost. I just feel like he's *gone,* you know? Lights on but nobody's home? I've been trying to figure out whether he's really getting everything he's ever wanted from this guy, or whether he's so bound up with his fantasy—you know, a Long-Term Relationship—that he's in the middle of some massive delusion."

"How was that morning?"

Marina gave details of her outing with Julius. She said his eyes had been red, his nose runny. She said he looked gaunt. She said he hadn't wanted to eat, and had shown little interest in the paintings. "And he smelled a little funny to me."

"Smelled funny?"

"Like medicine, or something. Not dirty—just sick. Or something. Maybe it was just some new aftershave." She sighed. "I really don't think he's happy, you know. Even if he thinks he is. You know how you feel like people have strengths and weaknesses, and they can choose to develop one or the other? It's like he's going all weakness, right now. It's like his soul is evaporating."

"Maybe that's how it seems because we can't see enough of him to see him clearly."

"Well, whether his soul is actually evaporating or whether that's our experience of what's going on, doesn't it amount to much the same thing?"

"Not, M. Really not."

After Marina finally rang off, Danielle returned to her list of ideas, inspired, or almost: Update on AIDS, she typed. Who is most at risk today. Nicky wouldn't want it. The youth trap, she wrote: What's becoming of the new generation of college leavers, now that dot-coms are going bust? And again: What's happening to twenty-something paper millionaires laid off by their dot-coms? As if there weren't already a glut of such reports. She checked her e-mail. There was a message from Murray Thwaite. He was inviting her to meet a friend of his, an academic who was coming to town to lecture—something about a possible program idea, something worthy and expensive to pursue, about Guatemala. Useless to her. She checked the date on her calendar, and wrote back at once that she would love to come. Then she returned to her ideas file. Fathers and daughters, she wrote. Men and women. And again: Ethics?

CHAPTER TWENTY-SIX

A Helping Hand (4)

Less than two weeks in Manhattan and a new life was forming, organically, as if it were fated. Bootie couldn't quite believe that the path could be so smooth. He couldn't say he hadn't expected it, because in some deep, inexpressible core of himself, where he didn't feel awkward or uncertain, he had foreseen this. No: more than that, he'd willed it. This was the natural outcome of his flight from Watertown, of his plucked courage in calling the Thwaites from Amherst. Had he been given to imagining, this would've been the way he'd imagined it all.

First of all, there was Murray. No, okay, first of all, there was Marina. Inevitably, foolishly, he had fallen for her shine, her violet eyes, her throaty laugh. Her throat, even. She was at once natural, girlish, and then formal, almost fake. He loved just watching her, seeing her at an angle, from behind, the dip of her chin when she was thinking, or pretending to think; the way her hand came up thoughtlessly to play with her hair, then paused, as if she, or it, had suddenly observed itself; then continued, and performed the gesture anyway, in a completely different spirit. It was as though, he thought, he got to watch a girl becoming a woman in front of him. Or else, as though he saw a woman whose girlishness was irrepressible. She wasn't always nice to him—moody, brusque upon occasion—and even that he sort of loved. He would pass her in the hallway as she took coffee and part of the paper back to her room, and she'd barely acknowledge him. It seemed, then, as though she was being real, the opposite of his mother, who was always puffing and flailing and smiling and trying to make everybody else feel better, as though she owed nothing to her true self. Even Marina's indifference was sexy, and it suffused every night he slept at the Thwaites', every morning he awoke there, with a faint haze of longing.

And second, there was Murray. What Bootie's friend Don would call a stand-up guy. For some reason, that was the phrase that stuck in Bootie's head, for Murray, like Homer's rosy-fingered dawn, just the phrase that seemed to sum him up. He, like Marina, had a public way about him, a type of jokiness that seemed very New Yorky to Bootie, jaded and a little off-putting; but when you got to know him a little you could see that this was his way of protecting himself, because so many people wanted things from him, and he had to put them off, some of them, as smoothly as possible. Bootie could see, from the first night at the Beavors', on that giant terrace over the park, how much in demand his uncle was; and he'd resolved from the first not to bore or bother Murray with unnecessary questions or solicitations. He'd thought he would do his best quietly to observe, to see how his uncle worked, to try to glean, at the dinner table, the procedure of his thought, and from his movements, from his study, the daily nature of his intellectual practice. Bootie, that is to say, knew not to overstep. He considered himself a pilgrim; he would have to move on, clearly, as no life could be as blessed as this one; but in the meantime—

he'd thought from the beginning, which seemed, after so much emotion, far longer ago than a fortnight—he would be Murray Thwaite's finest and most discreet pupil.

But he hadn't been there a week, even—he'd been there five days, or just over, if one was precise—when, to his surprise, and joy, and all but tearful gratitude, Uncle Murray came to him. He did it so naturally, as though he weren't extending a life-saving hand but merely making polite conversation. But Bootie could tell that when Marina had told her father about Bootie's independent studies, Murray Thwaite had known exactly what Bootie was trying to do, exactly how meaningful, how vital, even, the undertaking was. He had known exactly.

Bootie had been lying on his downy bed, on his side, in the afternoon, sleepily reading Emerson. He was just beginning the essay "Nominalist and Realist"—"I cannot often enough say that a man is only a relative and representative nature . . ."— when a knock at the door, very gentle, prompted him to throw down his book, sit up, straighten his glasses and fuss at his hair, because fantasy—ah, fantasy!—had immediately proposed that it might be Marina.

But Murray had entered, stood near the highboy, ruffled his own hair, smiled. "Reading?" he asked.

"Yes, sir."

"Don't 'sir' me. Just wondered if you were getting a little sleepy, lying in here."

"Maybe a little."

"Come next door for a bit. I'll get you something to drink."

And Bootie had spent the next hour and a half in Murray's office, drinking scotch—very slowly; he didn't care for the taste—at teatime and talking to his uncle as he had only dreamed, before now, he would talk to anyone. "I feel like I need to read these novels," he said to Murray, "but I don't really enjoy a lot of them. It's just weird, you know, why aren't I reading, like, history? Which tells you more. I guess I figure I'll read that stuff anyway, and this is more like homework; but the thing is, I'm kind of drawn to them, novels, I mean; it's like a love-hate thing."

"You're absolutely right. You do need to read them," his uncle said. "That's what it means to be civilized. Novels, history, philosophy, science—the lot. You expose yourself to as much as possible, you absorb it, you forget most of it, but along the way it's changed you."

"But *you* don't forget things."

"Of course I do. Writing helps. When you write about something, when you really think about it, you know it in a different way."

"I know. I've been trying—for myself, just for myself, to write essays. You know, papers, like for school, about my reading." Bootie paused. Murray turned his tumbler in his hand. "I don't mean to be presumptuous, but—" Bootie had promised himself he wouldn't do this, exactly this. But he felt a compulsion, as if Murray were asking him to ask, as if Murray knew already—surely Marina had told him? She must have—and was keen to help; but required, as any decent mentor must, that Bootie stick his neck out.

"Ask, my friend," Murray finally allowed him. "Whatever it is. I can't say worse than 'no.' "

"I wondered if sometime you'd be willing to read, maybe just one, even. Because to have your opinion—well, it . . . well." Bootie looked at the floor.

"You flatter me. I'm no professor. Have you got one to give me now?"

"Now?" Again, Bootie had to stop. He hadn't imagined such generosity.

"I've got some time this afternoon, right now. We could go over it together."

Bootie pushed his glasses up his nose, fidgeted. "I'm just not . . . I mean, I'd love for you—but I want—" He took a deep breath. "I want to show you something I can be proud of. Something that's my best work." He felt himself blinking, as he did when fretful. "I don't think anything's quite right yet. Do you mind?"

Murray shrugged, smiled. He was so easy. As if all of life could be so comfortable. "Whenever you're ready," he said. "But why don't you tell me a little about you."

"About me?"

"Frederick Tubb. What you care about. Your ambitions. Your projects."

Bootie nodded. He didn't know what to say.

"Your mother told me you dropped out of school. But my sense is that you're deeply scholarly."

Bootie wondered only very much later whether there had been irony in his uncle's tone. At the time, he'd felt himself sit up, open, as if to a magic word. "Scholarly. Yes, I guess. The thing is," he said, "and my mother would never understand this, but school wasn't remotely scholarly. Not scholarly at all."

"Because?"

"Because the educational system is a farce." Bootie flushed: such a pronouncement, and perhaps he had no grounds to make it. And again: he hadn't, till now, told anyone what he thought. Nobody knew this much of him.

"A farce?" Murray repeated, in a gently encouraging way.

And Bootie told him. Not everything: even though he was powerfully drawn to tell about Harvard, he kept it to himself. Because he didn't want Murray to pity him. Not at any cost. And he didn't want Murray to think that Bootie envied him, that Bootie had been pining for something that Murray had. Better not to mention Harvard. But he did talk about Lurk and Jerk and Ellen Kovacs, and he talked about his revelation; and then he talked about his time at U Mass, how he'd felt tempted to stay, how he thought of it as a little like Christ in the wilderness (he thought Murray frowned, here), how that had prompted him to move on, but specifically to move toward Uncle Murray, who didn't have any truck with bullshit, whose life was a template, a proof that you didn't have to give in to the deceit and the mediocrity, ever. When he finished speaking, he felt hot all over. He could tell his cheeks were bright red.

"You flatter me," Murray said again. "Please don't. You'll only be disappointed. But the point here is you, and what lies ahead for you, the great future that's yours for the taking."

"I don't know about that." It seemed Murray might be laughing at his nephew's naked soul.

"Why wouldn't it be?"

"I don't know."

"It's all a question of attitude, Fred, my dear. Attitude."

At the end of the afternoon, when Murray, who needed to go over the galleys of an article, showed him out with a warm hand upon his shoulder, Bootie had felt at once giddy and relieved, as if he'd been teetering on a high ledge and had been reassured of the waiting net below. He had spoken, and been heard, been *understood*.

From this he had taken confidence. He'd been reading, since then, not just the books he'd assigned himself, but Murray's books, too—the essays in *The Fat Lady*, about public education, about illegal immigration, about the embattled legacy of civil rights, about the IRA and Sinn Fein (which was the first time he'd really understood about there being two countries in Ireland, with a border in the middle, and he'd learned, too, what they were fighting about, more or less)—and he'd been trying to write an essay about Pierre wandering after the fall of Moscow, about what it meant to be alone and at the limit in the middle of a historic event. It wasn't going very well, in part, he thought, because it was all an idea to him. He couldn't imagine being in the middle of a historic event, but felt it important that he try to understand it, in part because Murray Thwaite seemed to be so engaged with the world, to be linked somehow to every big event since about 1960, almost half a century ago. And he strove to listen, as much as possible, to what was said around him.

In this way, after Murray's award, when he'd been invited by Marina to join the party, he'd heard Marina's friend Danielle whisper to the sinister Australian guy while Murray was getting more wine from the kitchen, and Marina had gone to help, and five others were still talking volubly about Silvio Berlusconi, for some reason, she'd leaned over and whispered (or maybe he'd misheard? But he didn't think so), "So, do you still think he's a charlatan?" Bootie was almost positive she'd said "charlatan." And then he'd seen the guy smile a small, slow, cruel smile, and gently shake his head, not as if to say, "Of course I don't," but rather as if to express amused surprise that she would bring up Murray Thwaite's patent charlatanry in the man's own living room.

Loathing had come over Bootie in a wave. Like sickness. He couldn't fathom that Murray's favored and fortunate guests would speak of him this way. Unless "he" was someone else? But who else could he be? He'd scanned the room, could think of no one else. And their conspiratorial intimacy, their artificial, cloying manner—he'd tried not to assume the worst about them, Danielle had been kind to him, after all; though he could tell at a glance that he didn't like the Australian—made him powerfully aware of what he felt for his uncle. As if Murray were a limb, or the girl he loved. Bootie felt fiercely about the Thwaites. He wanted them to be his family.

The night following the awards supper, at the dinner table—just Annabel, Murray, and him, because Marina had been off somewhere—Annabel had asked about his work, his plans. Clearly she'd heard from Murray, some garbled version of his learning program—she seemed to think he was under the impression he could teach himself the sciences, chemistry and the like—and she asked him, in that hostessy way of hers, at once gentle and persistent, even probing, like Stella Woods, his childhood dentist, with her soft voice, her tongue depressor, and inescapable, ruthless, tiny pick. He'd explained again about his reading list, a little about the farce of Oswego, though less than he'd told Murray.

Murray remained silent, but was not uninvolved. Occasionally, one or other of them would cast a sidelong glance at his impassive face, focused on the prosciutto, the caprese salad, the frisée and walnuts, apparently oblivious. Bootie (when would he stop thinking of himself as Bootie? He cursed his mother for it, but Bootie was still the name that rose unbidden; it was, to his chagrin, *who he was*) knew that Murray could have rescued him, had the power to free his nephew from this embarrassing repetition. But Annabel continued to probe, and Bootie, albeit agonizingly, continued to divulge his secrets. They came perilously close to Harvard. There seemed something perverse—voyeuristic, or masochistic, or both—in the exercise. He even said, "Please, please don't tell my mother," and Annabel reached out a reassuring hand, which did not stretch as far as his arm but lingered, momentarily, on the polished table between them, like a visible thought. At this point Murray finally spoke, placing his knife and fork with great deliberation upon his plate.

"Your mother couldn't possibly be expected to understand the first thing about you," he'd said quietly. "She's a good woman, but she doesn't have any idea who you are." He then rummaged about his mouth with his tongue (a trapped prosciutto strand, Bootie had assumed, as he battled with his own) and resumed eating. Only when Murray's plate was clean did he insert himself again into the conversation. "I've been thinking, Fred. Annabel and I have talked about it. And I think there's something I can do to help you."

"You've already been so generous."

"I know where you're coming from, here, my boy. I grew up there myself. I might have ended up at Oswego, and if I had, I might have turned and run. I might"—more dental rummaging—"and I might not. But I can certainly appreciate the impulse."

"It's not so much running away, or at least I'd like to think not—it's—"

"Embracing the future. *Your* future. Self-determination."

"And self-reliance, too."

"Yes, but unless you've got a plot of land and are planning on subsistence farming"—Murray paused and blew smoke, dragonlike, through his nostrils—"excepting that rather improbable scenario, you'll need a job. You'll need to earn some money in order to finance your studies."

"I know."

"Not easy in this town. Not because there aren't jobs—although most of them are soul destroying, of course—but because it's so damned expensive. So why not go back to Watertown, where you can live at home and read in peace?"

Bootie pushed his glasses up his nose, took a deep breath. "I'm quite prepared to do a soul-destroying job," he said. "I'll clean toilets, or be a stevedore, or flip burgers. That's fine with me. But the point is to be in the city. To learn from the city. To learn from life, as much as from books."

"And there's no life in Watertown?"

"No, none. Not of the kind I'm after."

Murray smiled broadly, tipped his chair back. "Good for you, Fred. Good for you. I knew you'd say that. Getting out of that town at the first opportunity was the most important thing I ever did."

Annabel smiled, too, her eyes on the wall, but said nothing.

"So, Fred," continued Murray, "I'm your uncle. I can help you, if you'll let me. First, I've got a life lesson to impart, although it's not usually my way. You want to take them by surprise. That's the crucial thing. Always remember it." He cleared his throat for emphasis. "But you need to be well prepared. I want you to hear me out, and I want you seriously to consider what I propose. It occurred to me a few days ago. I know you, I know how you think, so let me say that it isn't charity. Not for a second."

Murray went on to say that he'd been needing a secretary for years. That he had long ago exhausted his wife's goodwill (Annabel smiled again here, patiently; by which Bootie knew that she was fully party to this proposal, had perhaps even devised it) and the housekeeper's, and had been saved only by the return of Marina to her parents' apartment. "She's done the work," he said, "and I think she even likes it. But it's perfectly clear to all of us—including Marina, I might add; I'm not betraying any confidences here—that she isn't going to finish her book until all impediments, but I mean all of them, are removed. Any excuse to procrastinate; and her aged pa has provided a very good excuse indeed."

Bootie nodded.

"I've told her she needs to get a job. But above all, Marina needs to stop working for me. I've spoken to her about this— she's got irons in the fire; you're not stealing from your cousin. I know you'd be too honorable for that." Murray paused again. "So I'd propose to hire you as my secretary. My amanuensis, shall we say. Like Pound and Yeats. At a living wage, of course. A real job. We'd have to find our way to it, you know, define it as we went along, because in all these years I've never *had* a secretary. It might take a little while to get the balance right. At the outset, mostly what I'm sure of is what I wouldn't want you to touch, if you see what I mean. No unrequested tidying in my study. No moving piles around. I've always said that being in my study is like being inside my brain. You've got to be respectful of that—I count on it. You'd have to learn the mess—memorize it—until it seemed as orderly to you as it does to me. But that's a challenge. And you might learn something along the way. You might meet some interesting people." Murray fell silent, stared at Bootie, who stared back expressionless, blinking frequently behind his glasses. "What do you think?"

"Amazing, sir."

"No 'sir.' You know better than that. "

"Murray. Uncle Murray. It's an amazing offer. I'm overwhelmed, is all."

"He means it," said Annabel. "Murray's very big on not saying things he doesn't mean."

"Of course I mean it. And don't worry about Marina. She might feel tinily usurped for a day or two, but she's got big plans, I'm told. It'll be for the best."

Bootie nodded.

"You'll do it, then?"

"I—I'm just—"

"Give the poor boy a minute," said Annabel. "Don't pressure him over dinner. I'm getting ice cream all around, okay?"

But Bootie had known, as soon as it was offered, that he would accept. Far more than passive observation, it seemed the ideal way to learn from his uncle, to learn his uncle, indeed, as though his uncle were a book. It was at once exhilarating and frightening: to have such help, not to be alone. To be able, really, to take them all by surprise.

Then, too, there was the ticklish question of a salary. Murray, in further discussions, seemed to think that $30,000—

a sum astronomical to Bootie—was a living wage, for starters. And the matter of living at the Thwaites. It was the one thing Bootie kept coming back to: he couldn't see himself living and working, all the time, in that apartment. Because he never felt at home there anyway, and because it seemed somehow—unhealthy. Almost unsanitary. To breathe always the same (cigarette-filled) air. He'd need to find another place to crash.

Here, too, the gods had smiled upon him. He had again mustered himself to confront Marina, the elusive, violet-eyed Marina, about her friend's place—was it James? Or Julian? And she'd looked blank at first, twirling a curl between index and forefinger, chewing lightly at her plump lip; but had erupted, delightedly—she seemed, quite suddenly, prone to delight—when she'd recalled the mention of Julius. His name, it seemed, was Julius, and his apartment was east of Alphabet City, miles downtown (this meant little to Bootie) with, she said, a dog of a commute to get up here.

They were standing in the Thwaites' pristine kitchen as they spoke. "You'd have to cross town and come all the way up—take the F from Delancey all the way to Rockefeller Center, and then the B up Central Park West. You'd have a little bit of a hike from his place. It's not even on a bus line, I don't think. I'll have to ask him how he ever got anywhere when he lived there. But if you didn't mind that?"

"Of course I wouldn't. Anything. It sounds perfect."

"It's a dive, actually. I went there only once, and that was enough. But it's cheap."

Bootie had nodded, trying not to betray his eagerness. He didn't want her to think he was irrationally attached to this possibility, even though it seemed, somehow, his only possibility.

"I have to warn you that even though he doesn't look it, Dad gets to work super early."

"Like how early?"

"You must have heard him in your room. Or smelled the first cigarette, at least."

"I'm a heavy sleeper."

"Well, by eight-thirty at the latest."

Bootie had hesitated, thinking of the rush-hour subway, that subterranean horror.

"But he might not want you around then. Usually that's his quiet writing time. Maybe he'd be happy for you to come at noon, or whatever."

"I'm sure we'll work it out." Bootie couldn't pretend any longer not to care about the apartment. "Do you really think your friend would rent me his place? Starting when, do you think?"

"I'll ask him," she said, "when I speak to him. But you know, it's empty now."

Bootie had been waiting only a couple of days but it seemed forever. He didn't want to plague Marina, but found that the matter of the apartment rose, in his mind, like a cork, whenever their paths crossed. So that now he was trying to avoid seeing her, lurking in his bedroom if she came down the hall, or darting out of the kitchen the back way, through the dining room, if he heard her coming out of the elevator, her particular ringing step on the parquet. He thought that she sensed his flight, once or twice, and figured she attributed it to his crush on her—because he knew that she knew his weakness. It was an unspoken conversation between them, and he knew it amused her. She wouldn't even think of the apartment, of how important it was to him. Perhaps she'd forgotten that discussion altogether. She might need to be reminded. And then he'd remember that exasperated expression. He didn't want to elicit it again. He turned in circles, following the trajectory of his anxiety, coming repeatedly back to the same place. This was not self-reliance, he knew. This was not the spirit in which he intended to live. Were he independent, he thought, he would scan the *Village Voice* classifieds, and craigslist, and find a flat to share with persons unknown. But somehow he couldn't bring himself to do it: his life felt unreal already, his very flesh a tenuous thing, grounded here and now only by the Thwaites, by the small, growing, strangely delicious degree to which he was *known*. He couldn't help but imagine himself disintegrating, falling away atom by atom into a million infinitesimal pieces, were he to allow himself to drift out the door into the vast unknowing unknownness of New York City. The sensation was new to him—the way his claustrophobia in the subway had been new to him, and akin, although diametrically opposed, to that experience. In both cases, it was about feeling self-less, an Alice in Wonderland feeling, an appalling, thrilling, unsustainable feeling, a hollowing out. And just as he'd realized that he needed to remain aboveground, he'd realized, too, that he needed to claim an apartment to which he had some logical, some traceable connection. Something that would keep him from drowning, or vanishing, or killing himself there. (You wouldn't slit your wrists in the home of someone you knew, or of someone who knew the people you knew. It wasn't done.) Not that he was suicidal; not at all. But afraid of—how to put it? Afraid of having no shadow, of leaving no trace. But he couldn't say this to Marina: I need that apartment in order to leave a shadow. That sounded like pure craziness.

While he waited to hear from her—waited for her to catch him, deliberately, in the kitchen, or to knock on his bedroom door—he tried, as Murray had instructed, to memorize the mess in his uncle's study. This, it became immediately clear, was a prerequisite for any assistance he might, in time, be able to provide, just as it was obvious that he couldn't undertake his memorization while his uncle was at work—at least not while Murray was at his desk. Mercifully, Murray's "work" entailed frequent engagements and appearances, limousines to television stations and luncheons and drinks, not to mention foreseeable junkets out of town, lectures on campuses and at libraries, and in public halls across the country, a host of labors that seemed, to Bootie, antithetical to any spirit of contemplation or ratiocination, and inimical, in some way, to the very notion of labor itself. But he didn't judge him for it (although he could hear, in the back of his mind, Seeley's judgment). This worldliness, he deemed, as he sat uncomfortably cross-legged on the floor of his uncle's study, was the price exacted for a serious and independent life. You couldn't ever be entirely free, and Murray's pound of flesh was gouged out in hours stolen by colleagues, editors, unknown congregants. The pile of correspondence in Bootie's hands was comprised of importunate letters, a year's worth, all unfiled, out of order, begging Murray's attendance at dinners from Los Angeles to Calgary to Austin and beyond, in classrooms in Northampton, Massachusetts, or Ann Arbor, Michigan, at retreats in rural Kentucky and Southern California, and at conferences of businessmen in Miami or religious believers in Arkansas. Upon each page,

however crumpled, Murray had marked, in his marginally leg-
ible hand, the nature of his reply, along with its date; and a large
calendar along one wall was blackened, equally meticulously,
in a spreading swarm of ink, by the agreed obligations. It was
not as if, Bootie knew, a man *wanted* to do this. It would not
be excusable, morally, to *want* this.

On this day, Murray was addressing a graduating class at a
college in Connecticut, as commencement speaker. Bootie had
wondered at the necessity of this engagement: the institution
was very minor, and its coffers presumably only modestly full;
so if neither for the honor nor the cash . . . it had fleetingly
occurred to Bootie that his uncle could be considered, in this,
complicit with the farce of failed education. But he didn't dwell
on it. He wondered instead whether Marina knew these piles
as he was learning them, and wondered, too, whether she was
in fact hiding from him even as he hid from her, annoyed by
his usurping her role.

The study smelled of old cigarettes and musty papers and,
too, of cooking dust arising from the computer that was never
turned off. Aurora, he knew, was permitted only to empty the
wastebasket and, in consequence, the rug, unvacuumed, was
matted into pilelessness, grayed with ash and crumbs. Papers
in hand, Bootie moved himself to his uncle's chair. Its leather
creaked a little, was cool through his trousers. Murray's desk
was almost invisible for the folders and papers, the scatterings
of ash, the ashtrays and tumblers all but stuck to the pocked
mahogany. The disorder, and his express instructions not to
right it, depressed Bootie a little: it was a strange kind of work,
as strange as Murray's, to examine someone else's mess and leave

it as he found it. But if that was his work, he would undertake it thoroughly.

This was how he found the manuscript, on his third official day, while Murray commenced in Connecticut. It occurred to him—how could it not?—that he was overstepping, probing more deeply into Murray's brain than he was meant to. But it was confusing: the pile of keys was on the desktop; the desk drawer, locked, cried out for investigation; the smallest key on the chain fit, turned, like magic. As if the whole thing were fated. After all, Bootie told himself, he needed to know his mentor's mind as fully as possible. As long as he didn't disrupt, as long as he was just looking, learning.

The only sheaf of handwritten pages: Bootie knew at once it was important; he knew it was a secret. He couldn't not know. And before he started to read, he even flickeringly imagined it might be pornography, or sentimentalism, or, more shocking still, an intimate diary, disclosing outré opinions about Murray's colleagues and peers, or about Annabel's breasts, or Marina's—or, indeed, about Bootie himself. (He imagined, if this were the case, that he'd be referred to as Bootie. He couldn't help it.)

Afterward, he wondered whether he had considered not opening the file, and was forced to acknowledge that he hadn't. Not really. Which suggested an ethical lapse of which he wasn't necessarily proud. But in the spirit of the free exchange of ideas, in the quest for truth and knowledge, he allowed himself to imagine that this would be what Murray would want. So that Bootie, his pupil, might learn the better from him, shape himself more finely in his uncle's image.

And the truth of the pages wasn't a disappointment: far from it. It intrigued. This unnamed manuscript, Bootie could tell, from the first sentences, was his uncle's greatest secret, his genuinely private endeavor, riskier by far than gossip, professional or personal, could ever be.

How to Live: isn't this the question that plagues each of us, albeit intermittently, from our first awakening into consciousness? To ask, as William James did, whether life is worth living, is to prompt the joker's reply: "It depends on the liver"; and my own, of course, is almost shot. But the spirit of the riposte is, at the least, correct. Only if you can settle satisfactorily the issue of how to live can you then decide whether this vale of tears is worth the trouble. Mercifully, the issue is endless and irresolvable— in a way that I hope this book will not be endless and irresolute—and thus we are carried, upon the crucial questions, well past life's midpoint and often to its end. Certainly in most cases, life can reach a Beckettian decrepitude, a cold grubbing for survival, spiked by the embers of loves lost, without the liver's giving out. Let it be said that the questions of suicide, of whether 'tis a nobler thing, etc., cannot concern me here; not because they are not germane, but because the a priori of what life is, of what one should do with it—these first questions must be, it seems to me, answered first. And in these pages, that is what I am attempting to address.

Murray Thwaite was here revealing himself—not his ideas, but his thought; him*self*—and this, if only Bootie could read it, would prove the measure of the man. But Bootie scanned only the first paragraph before hurriedly snapping the folder, replacing it, with infinite care, slightly crooked in the drawer. He feared discovery—not by Murray, who was surely chomping canapés and quaffing bad champagne at the college graduation along the farthest reaches of the Metro North line; but by Aurora, or, worst of all, by Marina. But he feared, above all, his own discovery: he feared what he might find. It might thrill and succor him, than which he had no greater desire. But—although he couldn't have articulated it, just then—he couldn't run the risk of disappointment.

CHAPTER TWENTY-SEVEN

Floating

Marina accepted the job with Ludovic Seeley a full week before their first kiss. He was ironic and suave in accepting her acceptance, wry in the way she had swiftly come to expect of him: "I'm thrilled. Because I have complete confidence in you. Because I know that you'll want what I want. Because I know how to make you want what I want, and I know that if I don't, you'll make me believe that I did. Which is, after all, the trick of it." The trick of it, in that moment, and in the full week following, had been successfully to skirt the recurring subtext of their professional exchanges. It was an exquisite torture, a kind of test. She wasn't entirely sure that he felt the same internal fizzing and frothing as she, but she was almost sure. Then, too, she was trying to gauge whether he would feel any advance to be a weakness, would consider the actual connection of their fingers, or limbs, or mouths, to represent the base failure of their minds fully to have clicked. She decided that she couldn't take the risk, couldn't make a first move. After what seemed an interminable stretch, during which she reported to Danielle each evening and in exhaustive detail their interactions in the office that day, when he did finally press his lips to hers, Marina was moved almost to tears by his awkwardness, by the rise of flush along his cheeks and the swiftly apparent clamminess of his fervent hands.

"I'm good at most things, but I'm not so good at this," he murmured, as he pressed her against the inside door of his office, as if cleaving to a tree trunk in a thunderstorm. She didn't know if he meant the pass itself, or the kiss, or something broader, such as sexuality in general.

"You seem pretty good at it to me." This seemed the thing to say, whatever he'd intended; and in this initial intimacy, at last, she felt not frothing and fizzing but an ache in her core, unexpected and unstoppable, which prompted her to stroke his cheek, his brow, with a tentative finger, to pull her head back and say, "I want to look at you. Just for a moment. Really."

All of which she relayed to Danielle later that evening, lying on her bed with her legs up and the familiar giggle in her voice. "It all sounds like so many lines, you know. I know that more than anybody. Even when I said it they sounded like lines. But I meant them, too."

"Mm-hmm."

Marina had the impression that her confidante was doing something else, and she strove not to be annoyed. "I think it was seeing him vulnerable, you know? He wasn't really good at it, he was right. Not the kissing, I mean the whole maneuver. This is a guy who can juggle ten jokes in an editorial meeting, keep a dozen journalists cowed and laughing at the same time. And then all of a sudden, he's a geek. So genuine. Honestly, tears welled up in my eyes. A tear, at least."

Danielle cleared her throat.

"What's that supposed to mean?"

"Nothing."

"Danny?"

"I just don't know that 'genuine' is an apt word here. The guy is an operator."

"That's my point. Publicly he so is, but this was different. I think he must really like me."

"I don't think he likes your dad much, just so you know."

"What?"

"I'd ask him about it, if you care. He just said some things to me—"

"Plenty of people disagree with my father. *You've* disagreed with stuff he's said or written, loads of times. You've told me I should be harder on him."

"True, but—"

"What gives here, Danny? I mean, you've been weird about this since almost the beginning. What's it really about?"

"I don't trust him. I'm not saying I don't like him. I just—"

"You don't want me to get hurt. Thank you so much for your concern. Those are lines, too, you know."

"I know."

"And it's not really about whether you trust Ludovic Seeley."

"It's not?"

"It's about whether you trust me, about whether you think I'm capable of making the decisions that are right for me." Marina paused. This, too, was a line. "I want you to be happy for me. Because I'm really happy right now. I'm floating." She paused again. "Are you still there, even?"

"Of course I am. And I'm happy for you. Really."

But Marina felt there was a strange quiet around Danielle's words, a silence in the line; and she decided that Danielle was just saying she was happy because it seemed the thing to say, because not to say it would be egregious. Marina wasn't sure whether there was merit simply in the saying: maybe sometimes pretense was the best you could hope for.

CHAPTER TWENTY-EIGHT

I See You

So what was she supposed to do, when Mr. Murray says always "Don't touch, don't touch," but then he gives the boy, the nephew, the okay for this? Mr. Murray always says his mess is to him like the tidiest house—don't talk about the stinking cigarettes and the bottle emptying in the drawer, he means he can find anything, he knows where it all is. And this boy, the nephew, maybe he says he can keep the mess as tidy as Mr. Murray just the same, but Aurora knows. She knows he's moved the piles, mixed them up, she knows just from looking he's opened the drawers, maybe the locks, and if something is wrong, Mr. Murray will come roaring, yes, to Mrs. Annabel, and he thinks Aurora doesn't notice, he thinks because he doesn't raise his voice with her that she doesn't know he yells, and yells about her, Aurora this and bloody that, but she has heard him, of course she has. They all live in the house and pretend he is easy and lovable but really he is difficult, he is demanding and selfish and often angry, usually about selfish things, like where's my sandwich and why isn't the blue shirt in the closet, I mean the one for cuff links, and where are the cuff links, too, and Annabel, or Marina, I told you we had to leave half an hour ago and what the hell is going on. And what is amazing is how much everybody loves him anyway. Maybe this is not so surprising; he is charming and funny and sometimes in the kitchen he takes her, Aurora, by the waist with his long arm and dances her around, laughing and twirling, so she is a little bit dizzy, and although this should bug her it is actually nice, it makes her shake the tea towel and say, come on Mr. Murray, this is silly, stop that now. He makes all the girls feel pretty, even when they are not. She has seen it. And when he doesn't make the effort, it is so clear to anyone who knows him and how he is, even a little. Like the friend of Mrs. Annabel who came yesterday with the boy, the woman she works with and the big black boy—DeVaughn, that's it. Aurora saw the way he looked at the woman, the social worker, and yes, she was not pretty, with a face like a witch, all red and bones, her hair like old straw and the chin pushing up and out both, and a wart on it, too, but she was polite, she has been before, and Aurora can tell he does not like her. He did not smile, or flirt, or seem even to remember her name. Miss Roberts. He was not, with her, a nice man. Mostly he did not like the boy, the black boy as big as a man, strong in the shoulders and fat in the middle, and the woman seemed to want the boy to stay, to wait for Mrs. Annabel, who would not be home till who knew when. She was insisting, and he tried very hard to keep his voice low, Aurora could see it in the line of his mouth and the flicker of his tongue, in the way the hand went to his hair, to his pocket, but never out in the open, so Miss Roberts would not see it was a fist.

The boy—fifteen, maybe?—black like ink, an island black or an African black, not an American black, she thought, with big eyes and plum-colored lips that trembled, just a little bit—

looked scared and angry and embarrassed, too. He knew that Mr. Murray didn't want him there, that nobody wanted him there (he didn't belong there, anybody could see it), and this was all worse because he didn't himself want to be there. It would be embarrassing not to be wanted in a place you didn't even want to be wanted; Aurora felt bad for him. But she had salmon fillets marinating and ready to bake and the other boy, the nephew's sheets to change, and Marina's bathtub to scour because of the bubble bath scum, so stubborn, and that just to begin, so she could not stand around watching; but when Mr. Murray asked her she said—it was true—she did not know when Mrs. Annabel would be home and no, she said, they did not have a bedroom now, because of the boy Frederick. Then Miss Roberts, all nose and chin and that wart, wanted DeVaughn to spend the night. But he did not speak, she could tell he would not speak unless Mrs. Annabel came home, which she would not do, and she, Aurora, went to do the salmon and the bathroom and the sheets, to start, and she tried to listen and not listen at the same time, but they never left the front hall and Mr. Murray's trick with his hand worked because he never raised his voice, and she did not know what they said but in between the sheets and the bathroom the bony red Miss Roberts and DeVaughn, too, were gone. By the time the bathroom was done, the other boy, the nephew, was back, and when she was mixing salad to put in the fridge (she hated washing lettuce, or actually she hated drying it, that spinning bowl), Marina came back, too, and Aurora did not know whether Mr. Murray would tell about the boy, DeVaughn, or whether he would be cross about the other boy, the nephew, moving things in the study; and she would not know unless she heard him yelling, and she would not tell anything unless they asked her, which they wouldn't. But wasn't it funny that everyone pretended that Mr. Murray was an easy man. Even with one another, they pretended.

CHAPTER TWENTY-NINE

For Shame

If shame is the result of the Fall, and clothes our answer to that shame, then the clothes in which we dress our children become our legacy to them, the shame that we pass on. Obviously, they are our pride, too—pride and shame being opposite sides of the same coin. When the Mrs. Ramsey of American fin-de-siècle scandal (not to be confused with the Mrs. Ramsay of Woolfian high modernism, and an interesting opposite to her) dressed her daughter in ruffles and patent leather, with ribbons and bows, with rouge and mascara, little JonBenet whose baby Barbie face we all came to know embodied, as many noted at the time, both her mother's shame and her pride. A former minor beauty queen herself, who had coarsened and thickened, with the shadow of a mustache along her upper lip, red-cheeked not with the fresh glow of youth but with the wear of middle age, the threat of broken capillaries over her nose, Mrs. Ramsey surely saw in the little girl, in her tutus and lace, her uncorrupted self, the perfection she could never attain. She invested enough, some contend, to kill: to need to bury her shame altogether. If you can't be a winner, you can make a winner, and if what you made is not what you wanted, then what, in the end, are you?

Marina felt that she was at last coming to the book anew. She believed obscurely, and unacknowledgeably, that when she and Ludovic had undressed, a new transparency, a luminous nakedness, had come into all her life. She felt she finally understood what "clothing" was about, in an Adamic—or would that be Edenic? And why not Evic?—sense: the masquerade, the charade of it all. The simultaneous need for the charade and its painful, embroiling futility. And how much more so with one's children: any parent, along with their society, foisted baggage galore upon a child, sartorial baggage being simply the most visible of an immense, stifling web of parental, or societal, projections and constructs. To be your own person, to find your own style—these were the quests of adolescence and young adulthood, pushed, in a youth-obsessed culture, well into middle age. She saw suddenly how strange it is that adults long to be young, when the young have not had time to become themselves and are therefore largely what the adults make of them, want them to be. What terrible pressure. What relentless falsehood. She remembered Danny once joking, as she packed up for the Salvation Army a set of tight angora cableknit sweaters in aqua and tangerine and watermelon, gifts from Randy, that it wasn't until her twenty-seventh birthday that, in the face of a particularly egregious garment from her mom, Danielle had finally realized not only that she could choose her own wardrobe but that she had a moral obligation to do so. The necessary break with one's parents—only now, as she talked things over with Ludovic, did she see how necessary it was—could take many forms. By the same token, just because Marina herself had felt free to come and go, free to dress as she pleased, since earliest adolescence (she'd had an eye for it, from early on—even her mother had said so) did not mean that she had fought her battles. It didn't mean she was free.

A new transparency: she felt that with Ludovic, beginning a new relationship from scratch in a way she hadn't for years (all her friends were old friends; and her first meeting with Fat Al irretrievably lost, as was Fat Al himself, in the mists of time), she had a chance, they had a chance, to be perfectly open with each other, to be pure and clear. They had talked about it, or at least, she had. She didn't know why it had come to her so urgently, this need for utter frankness, but he seemed wholly to understand. He'd seen at once that it had to do with her father.

"If we're talking about transparency, about light, really," he'd said, "then the metaphors, the clichés, they're all ready and waiting. You're in your father's shadow. You're hiding your light under a bushel. Need I go on?"

"Meaning what, exactly?"

"That it's impossible to see you clearly—for your own self, most of all—on account of the distortion of light created by your father."

And from there, deep in the night, on the giant, raftlike bed in his Gramercy Park apartment, with the windows open wide to the sweaty air (Ludo didn't care for a/c; he thought it was fake), and a faint, vegetal stink rising from the street-corner garbage or the communal garden or both, they had got talking about Marina's book, about its subject ("Extraordinary," said Ludo, with his lips to her bare shoulder. "I mean it. Such a rich topic—the surfaces and their depths; it's what we're all about. The tenor of our times") and about its necessity.

"Of course you've found it impossible—remember, your father's shadow? And you stepped right back under it. But how can you ever be free if you don't get this off your back? And again, the words are speaking for us: get this off your back, will mean getting him off your back. A relief almost sexual. Certainly emotional—depression, of course, being the monkey on your back. This is the way you'll escape the expectations you imagine that he has for you, and work your way toward being, well, free-standing."

"And what would that mean?"

"Who can know? And how thrilling."

"Seems a little scary to me."

"You won't be alone. You can always lean on me." His lips were between her breasts, where she knew her skin tasted of salt.

"I wouldn't be free-standing then, would I?"

He paused, shrugged, smiled in the gloom. "It's all a manner of speaking, my beauty." He sounded to her, in that moment, oddly like her father.

"But isn't that what we're trying to do, you and I, with each other, but also with the magazine, isn't that the point of *The Monitor*? I mean, to *not* speak in a manner of speaking? Precisely not to fall into the known pathways? You're the one who said the emperor has no clothes, right?"

"A particularly useful analogy, I would've thought, for your book. Perhaps that should be its title."

"It's a book about children, the way children are dressed."

"Well, there you go. *The Emperor's Children Have No Clothes.*"

"Doesn't that make it sound like it's about the starving off-spring of a Third World despot?"

"It's catchy. It's intriguing. Trust me."

"But does it make any sense?"

"You'll make it make sense. That's what writing—manipulating language, for God's sake—is all about. You just need to explain it to your reader. Who wants to trust you, by the way."

"Okay, smartypants, *you* explain it to me, then."

"It's not my book."

"But I want you to. Please?" She batted her eyes at him.

"Ah, Lady Violet Eyes—irresistible. For you I'll try. But I haven't actually read your book, my dear."

"Nobody has."

"Not even your father?"

"At this stage, not even him."

"Well, then." Ludovic sat up against the headboard, cleared his throat. "As parents, we visit our complexes, whatever they may be, upon our children—our neuroses, our hopes and fears, our discontents. Just the way our broader society is like a parent, and visits its complexes upon the citizenry, if you will."

"So far you haven't gone beyond the premise of the book proposal." She tweaked his pink nipple.

"Give me time. I'm just explaining the title, after all. Where was I? Marina Thwaite's groundbreaking debut book demystifies these complexes, unraveling them through the threads of our clothing, and more particularly of our children's clothes. In this brilliant analysis of who we are and the way it determines how our kids dress, Marina Thwaite reveals the forms and patterns that both are and lie beneath the fabric of our society. In so doing, she bares children, their parents, and our culture at large to an unprecedented and frank scrutiny, and in her truth-telling, shows us incontrovertibly that the emperor's children have no clothes."

Marina laughed, applauded. Then, in mock celebration, she went to get them each a bowl of black currant sorbet and a shot of iced vodka from Ludovic's otherwise empty freezer.

In the wake of this discussion, then, Marina had found new confidence in her endeavor. She tried to work regularly on the book, for a couple of hours each morning—she even installed her laptop in one of the largely empty rooms in Ludo's apartment, where very quickly she was spending most nights—and she tried to talk over its progress with Ludovic in the office at the end of the magazine's grueling day. For Ludovic, she could tell, it was a strain, sometimes, to focus his mind on the book, when the magazine demanded so much; and she worried a little that the creative energies he had intended her to expend on *The Monitor*'s culture section were being at least partially siphoned off by *The Emperor's Children*. But he was the person who assured her that she had to finish it; he was the one who, more than she herself, more than Murray, to be sure, had faith not only in the manuscript but in its author. And she was doing well for the magazine, too, coming up with ideas, suggesting contributors, matching topics and journalists. Whenever she faltered, or felt doubt—when, for example, she thought Lettie Abrams sneered at her proposed auction house corruption feature in the middle of the editorial meeting—Ludovic would summon her to his office, close the door, and bolster her with his evident desire. They didn't fool around behind his desk—

they were far too professional for that. But he wooed her, during the day, with words, with dizzying blandishments. He seemed even to adore her breasts, tiny hummocks that she had always felt verged on the plaintive; he praised their daintiness, and the tight points of their areolas when excited, "like some perfect, juicy little fruit," he said. "You're one of those rare creatures who was made not to wear clothes at all. Prelapsarian, my sweet. Everything about your beautiful, beautiful body should be celebrated, and illuminated, and adored."

"Oh, stop it, Ludo. You're making fun of me."

"Not at all. It's a supreme irony that you should be writing a book about clothing. You, of all people."

"It's about nakedness now, too, I think. Thanks to you."

"Then I've done something right with my life."

CHAPTER THIRTY

Merge

Against her better judgment, she let him do it. That was the sentence she repeated in her mind, but she knew it in no way represented the truth. It represented "the truth" she would save for Marina, if ever it came to that. Which she couldn't seriously contemplate, and knew she would have to prevent. But Marina was her first thought after he left. How could Danielle ever explain to anyone how distinct her relationship with Murray was, how separate, and yet—so swiftly—how intense? Through their correspondence—tentative but revelatory, never inappropriate—and then over drinks (twice), lunch (once), and (most fatefully) supper, she'd come to know him by that last day of May, that star-filled evening of supreme calm, in which he walked with her from the restaurant on Cornelia Street back up to her building and asked, as ever with great ease, as if nothing could be more natural, if he might come up (and, she noted, without pretext: he didn't say "for coffee," or "to see the view" or "to pick up that book I loaned you," which he might have; by which she further knew him, she felt, for a fundamentally honest man)—by then, in so short a space of time, she considered that their connection was almost eerie, a meeting of minds, a Platonic reunion of divided souls. To whom could you say such a thing? She might have said it frankly to him, were it not for Marina, and for Annabel. Not that he was afraid to talk about them—she loved this in him as well, and marveled to find herself loving anything, let alone so many things, in a man who had been for her so many things for so long, but not plausibly an object of passionate love.

He had admired the Rothkos. He had loomed shaggy and grand like a crumbling castle, a half ruin, in the semidarkness of her pristine apartment, his belt unbuckled and his bare torso monumental, and had held her to him so that she could hear his heart beating beneath the grayed fur against her cheek. When he spoke, his voice resounded in his chest, and entered her ear like an immense echo.

"They keep you sane, I'm guessing," he said.

"Who do?"

"The Rothkos. That's what they'd do for me. They stop everything, the washes of color, they pull you in. Keep you from jumping out the window."

"It's always a possibility," she said, pulling her head back to look at him.

"I know it. Every day you find the reason not to. As he did— Rothko—in the pictures." He paused. "Until the day he didn't anymore."

"Exactly," she said. "I wonder about it, wonder if that's why people have children, to stop asking the question."

"It's true it puts an end to it for a while. But only by ending it, if you see what I mean."

"I don't," she said. "I don't think."

"You have a child and you stop questioning the futility, true. For one thing, you're too fucking busy. For another, the question is answered, the futility is confirmed. You've passed it on to the next generation. They're essential, you no longer are."

"But you don't really believe that."

"I do and I don't," he said. She believed she knew exactly what he meant.

"All your work, everything you've written—"

"Every day the question. And sometimes, that's the answer."

"And sometimes this is?" She gestured at the room, at their half-clad bodies.

"Sometimes this is," he conceded, then frowned. "But often not. Because it can have the opposite effect."

"Does Annabel know?"

"She does and she doesn't."

"Don't ask, don't tell? How about Marina?"

His glance, here, was sharp. He turned to look out the window at the skyline, sparkling in the velvet night. "No, as far as I know. She doesn't need to. It's none of her business."

"I'm not sure about that," said Danielle. "But if it's any consolation, I don't think she does. She wouldn't imagine you capable of such things."

"Whereas you did."

"I wouldn't say that. I mean . . ."

"Of course you did. Or we wouldn't be here. *I* wouldn't be here." He grinned the broad, guileless grin. "But aren't you glad that I am?"

When he had left, Danielle lay on her bed, which smelled of them and faintly, too, of the gin-and-tonic cologne, and she thought first of Marina, and of what would have to be kept from her now. Danielle had never before had a secret that she couldn't confide in anyone, but this, she knew, was such a secret. She couldn't tell Randy, even, who so wanted her daughter to find love. If that was what she had found. She held in her mind two disparate realities: one was the fierce tenderness she felt for this disintegrating giant, the joy at his small kindnesses and vulnerabilities, the sense—overwhelming and surely false, even she could see—that she could anticipate all of them, that, like a blind person, she had developed some extra sense, where he was concerned, and could practically finish his sentences. The other was a certainty of wrong, a moral repugnance. This she experienced abstractly, with her mind; it was, consequently, the weaker of the two realities. She was fascinated by the internal conflict, or by the notion of it, because in truth, she didn't really contemplate renouncing him. The disgust was an idea, something she knew she ought to conjure, the way an autistic child can learn to smile at his mother to show happiness. Her bones, her flesh, the tickle of her scalp and the pads of her fingertips all spoke without prompting a chorus of desire. Pressed to his chest she'd felt safe and exhilarated at once, as if swept by a great internal breeze; and there seemed little point telling herself that this was immoral. Marina—or even Annabel—didn't come into it. This in the space of a week or two. She'd become a person she would never have anticipated being.

She couldn't look ahead at a future to this union. Nor, suddenly, could she imagine an end to it, either. Which left only a present. He'd given her his cell phone number, one he said almost nobody knew. He'd said he wanted to see her tomorrow—the first day of June. He'd said he wanted her to wear again the dress from the awards dinner—the dress, she couldn't help but think, that had had no effect on Ludovic Seeley. That was the night Marina had thrown herself at him; and now they were colleagues and lovers both. And Danielle, who should have seen it coming, had ditched her revolution project in favor of the plastic surgery piece. She was even considering tracking down a case of fatal liposuction. If you couldn't expose Seeley you could always join him, enact the perversities of his cynic's revolution and give the audience the trash they didn't yet know they wanted. Murray would disapprove. Or he would have, if he'd known the history of it; but as it stood, he was trying to persuade her to chase this Guatemalan story, and thought that lipo was the pressure from on high, Nicky's idea. She'd let him think it. She never would have pegged herself for a cynical dissembler, a liar so many times over. Thank goodness she wasn't seeing much of Julius these days: he'd be able to smell it on her, a dog sniffing fear. And that other boy, the cousin: Frederick. Bootie. Bootie Tubb. Who worked for Murray now. Even meeting him just twice she could tell that he was canny, and proud, and that he held the world to impossible standards. In that sense, she'd recognized him, and he her; and so he would see the change in her, if he were to see her. He didn't seem the sort to feel pity at another's fall; rage, rather. He'd already, somehow, been disappointed, although he could barely have been twenty, and he wanted to make someone pay. Murray would disappoint him, sooner or later, she was certain; it was this sixth sense, this new prescience. She didn't believe that Murray *could* disappoint her, because she knew him so utterly. Absently stroking her nape, she leaned against the wall as dawn broke in her window, watching the Rothkos bloom into their full colors; and she wondered idly whether maybe, suddenly, she'd been granted, along with passion, a gift of clear sight. She briefly considered, in the day's first flood of light, turning out to the sky, the roofs and the towers stretching in front of her, that there was nothing she could not divine, and that this, surely, would keep her—would keep them all—safe. And then the flare of gold settled into a hazy summer morning, and she curled her back to the window and went to sleep.

JULY

CHAPTER THIRTY-ONE

Booted

The room was hot. Sweat down your bare neck, steam on your glasses, air unmoving as an oven hot. The ceiling fan didn't work, and there was no possibility of cross ventilation as the apartment's three windows sat side by side, staring out at the narrow, airless street. In the cupboard next to the door, he'd found one oscillating fan (so close to "osculating," and yet so far; a word he'd recently learned and had no occasion to use), a smallish one, that he propped on a pile of books and trained closely upon himself, so that it dried, in patches, the sweatsoak over his skin. He kept a cup of ice on the table beside him, and sucked a cube periodically, which hurt his carious molar but at least lent him, however briefly, the illusion of being cool. The ice was ancient, and tasted of dust and the freezer.

This was, at last, Bootie's first night of his first weekend in the studio, the Saturday of this long-awaited weekend preceding Independence Day; and the temperature hovered up around 100 degrees. His mother had hoped he'd come home, but he'd sold the car to pay his rent (this he hadn't yet told her; she was liable to cry), and besides, it seemed appropriate, in the wavering experiment that his life seemed to have become, that he should spend Independence Day independently. Murray and Annabel had invited him up to Stockbridge, where they were going to their fancy house with Marina and her creepy boyfriend, Ludovic, but he could tell they didn't really want him to come. Besides, given what he was writing, he wouldn't have felt comfortable with them anyway. Not that he had anything against Annabel; and not that Murray had any inkling, yet, of what his nephew thought of him. Not, indeed, that even Bootie had known until, just the other day, the full extent of his rage. After all, as Murray himself said, you want to take them by surprise.

Great geniuses have the shortest biographies. Even their cousins know nothing about them. He would have given a great deal to return to a state of blissful ignorance where Murray was concerned. Every revelation only diminished further his uncle's fading glow. If Oswego had been a fiasco, what, Frederick wondered, was the word for this? He'd taken to thinking of himself again, quite consciously, as Bootie, because he intended to put the boot in, to give his uncle the boot. Marina had asked him—it seemed it had been originally Danielle's idea, in this seething nest of vipers: she, with the maternal smile, the chummy, condescending manner, and the most hideous secret—if he'd like to write an article on spec for *The Monitor*. He'd had to ask what "on spec" meant, and had at first been tongue-tied and overwhelmed that Marina had thought enough of him to extend the invitation. Then he'd found out about Danielle, and grown suspicious. Marina had said he could write about whatever he chose, as long as it fit the general rubric of "cultural exposé." She'd made a big deal about *The Monitor*'s being a new type of magazine, a no-holds-barred organ of truth in which anything—anything true, that is—would be welcome. That was weeks ago, before everything, certainly before he'd read all of the manuscript, and before he'd found even the first e-mail. He hadn't known what to suggest. "Don't worry." She'd flashed him that long-necked, gawky smile that was, on her, beyond alluring, intimate and mysterious at once. "Something will come to you. It's going to be great."

His first idea had been to write an essay about Murray Thwaite, and everything his uncle signified. He would keep it a secret, until it was done. He'd imagined it at first as a gift to the Thwaites, had imagined Marina's pleasure, and—when it was published, if it was published, his uncle's, too. Not an exposé, exactly, or only—so he'd thought—an exposé of his own heart. Maybe a personal, almost autobiographical account of what it was like to grow up in the long shadow of such a man, to know by his existence of what might be possible in life—to know, even as a boy in Watertown, what a life of the mind might be—and yet to feel always that this tantalizing possibility was too far removed really to touch. He'd envisaged it, at first, as a story with the happiest of endings: about coming, at last and alone, to the metropolis, about depending upon the kindness of relatives who were near strangers, of discovering, in their company, not so much the comfort of the body but the comfort—or maybe comfortable unease (or would that be disease?)—of the mind: here, in Murray, was an interlocutor and a mentor, here was greatness held close. The image in his head then, at the beginning of June, was of a kindly but formidable giant scooping up a mere boy in his enormous palm, and teaching him, little by little, to grow.

Unease, dis-ease: over the course of that infernal, stifling

month, Bootie came to understand the situation in a different
way. Things looked different; Murray looked different: still an
imposing façade, to be sure; but a hollow monument. Bootie
didn't like Ludovic Seeley any more than when first he'd met
him, but he came to wonder—uneasily—whether the Australian had a point. In which case, Seeley's magazine was the
obvious place to make that point. Marina, he came to believe,
either already saw the truth about her father, or should be made
to see it. It was her only hope for freedom from him—really to
let go of his myth. No matter what, she would be—should
be—grateful that someone, that he, Bootie, had the dispassionate rigor to speak out. This, Bootie believed, was what *The
Monitor* was for. This was his destiny.

It was cumulative. First, of course, he'd wondered about the
commencement in Connecticut. He couldn't have said whether
that, or Danielle and Seeley's whispered exchange, or both
together, had sowed the tiny seed of doubt. And then there was
the time, in perhaps the second week of working for Murray,
when his uncle called to him to hunt the clippings files for several articles he'd written, years before, about Bosnia. He was
writing about the Hague, the War Crimes Tribunal, and he
wanted, he said, to check some of his earlier facts and details.
But then Bootie, who read the earlier pieces, also read Murray's
new article, and found that in it, not merely phrases but entire
sentences and, in one case, a great, meaty paragraph, had been
lifted wholesale from the already published work and trans-
planted to the new.

Bootie worried overnight, found himself deliberating the
degree of deceit, or inadequacy, represented by this theft. He
wanted—as when hearing about Julius's drug use, for exam-

ple—to be able to feign worldliness, or at least indifference. But as he lay beneath the snowy eiderdown he couldn't let it go; and the next morning, fingers trembling, he stood in Murray's office and cleared his throat.

"Fred."

"Murray. I just. I have a question."

"Yes?"

"Your article."

"Yes?"

"The tribunal article. The one you just finished. With the history of the Bosnian conflict in it."

"Yes?"

"You wrote about that before. The conflict, I mean."

"I spent weeks in Sarajevo. I went to Kosovo. Srebreniça. Yes."

"But you wrote the same things."

"How do you mean? I thought the same things, more or less, then and now."

"But your descriptions."

"I saw these places, these events. I'm not sure I follow."

Bootie could see the papers in his hands trembling, so difficult did he find this. "But you used the same words. Exactly. The same descriptions. You plagiarized them."

"I wrote them."

"But then you wrote them again, the same."

Murray laughed, leaned back in his chair. "Oh, that's very good. I did. Yes, I did. I wrote them again the same." He lit a cigarette, tried—it was obvious he was trying—to keep a straight face. "Plagiarized. That's beautiful. Can one plagiarize oneself? Plunder, yes; recycle, certainly; but plagiarize?" When he laughed, his chest emitted a discreet rumble, as though a digger were turning over the earth inside him. "Do you really imagine," he said eventually, "that there are enough words in the world for them always to be new? Novelty among the young is greatly overrated. If you've worked to find the right words for what you want to say, then surely it would be foolhardy to discard them merely because of some sense of etiquette—some sense that it was rather shabby to repeat yourself. Do I ever give the same lecture twice? Of course I do. Do I have the same conversation more than once? It goes without saying. I am guilty of the tedium of repetition. I'm sorry—you're disappointed to find your uncle is an old bore. Alas." He said this last with a broad, winning smile, and in the moment Bootie felt he'd been ridiculous, muttered an apology, and moved on.

But later, he realized, it stayed with him. He went back to Emerson, whom he felt understood these things. "All persons exist to society by some shining trait of beauty or utility which they have. We borrow the proportions of the man from that one fine feature, and finish the portrait symmetrically; which is false, for the rest of this body is small or deformed." It was a disappointment, a deformation, albeit minor. His uncle was perhaps a little lazy, a little lax. He could forgive it, but he wouldn't forget.

And then there was the next thing, a scant week later. Murray, out for the afternoon, left him a list of things to do, among them a telephone call to a fund-raising dinner for a Harlem youth program at the end of June, at which he was to have given a speech. He asked Bootie to cancel it, to express his profuse regrets, but something urgent, he was to say, had come up. And then there was, next on the list of things to do, another phone call, an acceptance to a dinner given by the publisher of *The Action,* in honor of two Palestinian activists who were coming to town. Bootie had even heard of one of them, had read about him in the newspaper, knew he was important— and yet. And yet the two events were on the same day. Murray didn't say anything about it in his message, but he was blowing off the youth program for the Palestinian bigwigs, it was as easy as a simple sum. Bootie found himself deeply unsettled: each deformity was slight, but he began to worry that they added up to a grotesquerie. He didn't raise it with his uncle, who, he was sure, would only laugh charmingly again; but quietly, he adjusted his sights. Murray Thwaite looked less and less the shining giant.

Which was why—perverse as it might have seemed from the outside—Bootie was drawn back to the hidden manuscript. He'd hoped it would prove a vindication, that it would clarify and simplify his vision of his uncle. Seeing the private mind, he'd thought, would be the answer. He'd read it in fervent snatches, over lunch hours when Murray was in restaurants and in a long evening when all the Thwaites were out together. He read it hunched at Murray's desk, sweating, periodically wiping his hands on his trousers or his shirt to keep the dampness from marking the pages. The deception made him sweat, and its attendant fear; and then reading itself—the words on the page—made him sweat, too, as if he saw the man naked, saw the man's need and desire, and was repelled both by it and by his physical form. It was a powerful and tremblingly ghastly experience.

He couldn't have known beforehand how he would feel about it, that the manuscript would seem to him both pretentious and trite, that it would so fully clarify his vision of Murray that all he could see, now, was the small and deformed self, its grander outline vanished. He believed now that the Great Man had been an illusion all along, mere window dressing. Reluctantly, he slid into alignment with Ludovic Seeley: Murray Thwaite was one great con trick, a lazy, self-absorbed, star-fucking con trick.

And to be honest, it made him angry. Not a little bit, but a lifetime's worth of angry. It wasn't rational, he knew—Murray Thwaite was who he was; it was presumably all he could be—but Bootie felt betrayed, belittled, nullified. He'd pinned his hopes on a hollow man. And he realized this was the article Marina wanted him to write, even though she didn't know it. This was the article he'd been sent to Manhattan by some greater power (Emerson, maybe?) to write. This was his fate and his calling—not an essay for himself on Pierre wandering Moscow, but an essay about Murray in New York.

And then, as if he weren't riled enough, he opened by mistake an e-mail from Danielle to Murray. He hadn't realized that Murray had left open his personal e-mail account, had thought the mailbox on the screen would contain professional correspondence only. And while the message said nothing scandalous, he just knew, he suddenly knew. From the tone, from its brevity. He was young but he wasn't a fool. He just knew. And the deformation was irrevocable and complete.

And now, as he worked on his secret piece for Marina, he realized that Marina had been right. Over the better part of a month, a topic had certainly come to him. He wasn't going to write an ad hominem attack: that wouldn't be worthy, would betray the very standards to which he wished to hold his uncle.

He would, he'd decided, write a thorough and thoughtful analysis of the manuscript, an exposé of the secret book: because it was when Murray drew his own intellectual self-portrait, Bootie believed, that he unwittingly revealed his gaping flaws, and rendered a picture more morally accurate than he knew. Bootie was going to tell this truth, show the world the man as he was. It was going to be devastating; and, as Marina had flippantly suggested, it was going to be great. Telling the truth: what could be more important? There was grandeur in the undertaking, and perhaps sacrifice, too—he knew people might be annoyed about it, angry, even at least at first—but he was called, morally called; and he could feel nothing but swelling excitement about that.

So here he was, washed in sweat, his jockey shorts sticking to his skin, the rest of him palely bare to the ugly room and its oscillating fan, penning the article that would change the world. Or change his world, for sure. This was revolution for you. More Dostoyevksy than Tolstoy (he'd still not made it to the end of *War and Peace,* but *Crime and Punishment,* now there was a novel!).

Bootie had contemplated guilt, and rejected it: Murray must have wanted him, if not to *read* the manuscript then at least to know it was there. Either that, or he'd devised some deliberate test of his nephew's honor, along the lines of "I shouldn't have to hide the keys to my desk when I wouldn't ordinarily. I have to trust, I will trust, that the young man will not abuse his position." That would be very like Murray: self-serving pomposity in the name of an insouciant high-mindedness. In which case, Bootie had failed the test. But Murray would have known that he would fail it—he had to have known, or else why set it? And although these things were unsaid and unsayable, Bootie fancied that his uncle had been looking at him differently of late, an ironic, inquisitive look, as much as to indicate that he was waiting, good-humoredly, for his nephew's reaction. When he thought about it, Bootie could imagine that if he had been, as he'd so hoped to be, awed by his uncle's book, struck by its depths and wisdom, then he would have had to say so, sooner or later. In that circumstance, he would have been scanning for an opening, a way to share his elation and lay praise at the great man's feet.

What had so disappointed him? He was trying to articulate this sorrow as clearly as he could, but found it slippery. His article, in its first draft at least, was suffering because of this. He didn't want to come right out with his concomitant discovery—Murray Thwaite's personal antics might make him a scumbag, but were they *relevant*?—but this, the e-mails, the knowledge that up in Stockbridge along with the Thwaites, Danielle Minkoff might be putting in an appearance at any moment, under false pretenses, this colored, for Bootie, every sentence of his uncle's prose, and made it hard for him impartially to dissect the book's shortcomings.

Bootie ran his hands through his sticky hair, chewed the dusty ice, stood up and circled the tiny room. In addition to its terrible heat, it was ill lit: a puddle of light on the table, a dim, reddish bedside lamp on the floor by the futon, a sickly fluorescent strip over the kitchen counter. He could see a couple of cockroaches, little ones, stretching their antennae in the sink. Out for a walk, like he was. He stuck his head out the window. He could hear yelling and music, salsa music, from one of the other apartments over the way and, seemingly far off, traffic. Few cars came down this street, which stank of sweet rot and old stone. He was all but naked and aware that he could be seen if anyone cared to look, and this unusually didn't bother him. He had a feeling of being down in it, in the shit, he would've said, stuck in the refuse of lower Manhattan, far from anything living but in the thick of life. He heard a cab pull up, and drunken hooting. Bootie breathed deeply, the stink of it, and of himself, his hours of sweat, repelled and impressed in equal measure.

And then there was a clamor and a scuffle on the stairs, and impossibly the door fell open, a sudden burst into the room of limbs and laughter. Bootie cowered, his hands over his near nakedness, and blinked, his back to the window. He felt a new eruption of sweat upon himself, cold this time.

"Who the fuck are you?" asked one of the men, still a blur to Bootie, his arms seemingly entwined with the other man's torso, but a figure notably pop-eyed, and very gay. "And what the fuck are you doing in my house?"

A light in the fog. "Julian? You must be Julian."

"Julius. Shit. I know who you are. Shake Your Booty. Marina's cousin, right?"

Bootie nodded, sidled crabwise toward the futon, his discarded clothes.

"Sorry. What's your name? I mean, your real name?"

"Frederick."

"Man, I'm sorry. I totally forgot. I thought it was next week. That you were coming."

"No. Today."

"Evidently." There was a silence, during which Bootie put

on his jeans and a T-shirt he had filched from Donald, in Amherst.

"This is Lewis," Julius offered, indicating the other half of his four-armed creature.

"Hey, man." Bootie blinked solemnly at the muscular youth, at his fine, shaven head, his mocha skin, his bare biceps. He felt they were engaged in a silent standoff. He couldn't tell whether Julius was drunk, or high. Bootie didn't want to get on the wrong side of any potentially volatile cokehead; but then again, he didn't have anywhere else to go.

"I don't have anywhere else to go," he said eventually, quietly. "Or I would go there."

The salsa music from over the way bounced along unperturbed. As much as to invite him to the party. He could hear voices that went with the music, a gathering.

"That's okay, Frederick. That's okay." But Julius just stood, skinny, staring, bug-eyed.

"Let's go, man. Julius? Man? Let's go." Lewis put his fine arm on Julius's thinner, paler one.

Julius shook his head slightly, as if waking. "She never mentioned you were fat," he said.

"Excuse me?"

"I'd never pictured my tenant as fat."

"Man, that isn't necessary." Lewis led Julius back out into the stairwell. "Don't go harassing the kid like that. He's done nothing to you," Bootie heard Lewis say, and then Julius whispered something in return. Lewis stuck his head back through the door. "Sorry about the mix-up, okay? Have a good one." He closed the door very carefully, almost without a sound. Bootie heard their footsteps retreat down the stairs, and a moment later, in a break between salsa numbers, heard them muttering to each other in the street below as they walked away toward the avenue.

Bootie knew that Lewis was not Julius's boyfriend. The Conehead. Where was he? And who was Lewis? He took a deep breath. He didn't need to approve of his landlord's behavior. Here he was, in the shit of it, in the heart of life, right? When he was sure they were gone, he took off the jeans and the T-shirt, which was already damp, and lay down on the futon. If he didn't care so much what Marina thought, all this would be easier. If he hadn't wanted Murray to impress him, perhaps he would have been less disappointed. As it was, he was going to write the article. He would make it so good that in spite of everything, Marina would have to publish it. Would *want* to publish it. Because the truth will out. Whenever the salsa music stopped, he imagined he heard the cockroaches dancing in the sink.

CHAPTER THIRTY-TWO

Exposé

It was just before dawn when he left. On his way out in the elevator, Julius rubbed his eyes, coughed. Felt like shit. His heart was thundering, in the back of his head, it seemed. His dick and his thigh muscles and his throat were all sore. And he felt as though the cigarette smoke had settled, along with the sweat, in a film upon him. If he'd known that Lewis lived three blocks from his and David's apartment, he wouldn't have pursued him with quite as much gusto. When he'd gone to the bar, almost all the way to his old neighborhood, it hadn't occurred to him that the day's catch could live in the building next to David's gym. Even racing—he'd been up, up last night—he'd had the wit not to foul the nest, he'd headed for Pitt Street—if he were honest, he'd have to admit that he'd planned it all beforehand— only to find that fat naked fuck practically wanking on his futon. He couldn't really remember what Shake Your Booty looked like, just the glasses and the thin spread of hair on his chest and the womanly spill of flesh over his BVD elastic. The kid had been trying to shrink his bulk into the window frame, hands over his underpants like someone in a torture photo, as if Julius had been wielding a water cannon or a BB gun. He'd been scared. And Julius had been mean to him. Which he felt bad about, in the middle of feeling like shit; but he'd been angry. The whole thing a colossal fuck-up.

Julius wallowed in the despair of his hangover: What the fuck was he doing with his life? With himself? He had meant to be sorting out his career this year; had been diverted—so thoroughly—by love; and now he wasn't even any good at that. He was an asshole, a selfish, screwed-up jerk. He was supposed to take the ten-thirty train out to Scarsdale for an extended weekend of Cohen-charming. He thought of David's mother, a far cry from his own delicate parent with her fears and hesitations, her flowery indirection. Mrs. Cohen was small, but a force; and she had plans for this holiday. David, who'd gone out there yesterday to placate her, had snickered down the phone about her new patriotic melamine plates (all stars) and cups (all stripes). She'd bought Chinese lanterns with American flags on them, and the caterer was bringing a kosher feast, including a cake with blue icing. The Cohens didn't keep kosher, but Adele's cousins from Albany did, and they were going to be there. "It never hurts to make an effort," Adele had told David. "What do you think of my manicure?" Which, David had said, gleamed a jingoistic red.

Julius was dreading it all just a little: the goy, the Asian, the fag. They meant well, but couldn't really be pleased about it, and Adele always manifested her displeasure by failing to hear what Julius said and promptly forgetting all information concerning him.

"Is it Ohio?" she'd ask. "Illinois?"

"Michigan, actually."

"Come again?"

"Michigan."

"Of course. I had a boyfriend from Michigan once. But I could never have lived there. No future in it." And then: "Your mother must have had a hard time adjusting. It's all so different in Korea, isn't it?"

"Vietnam, actually."

And then she'd throw up her hands with their glittering nails: "Of course, doll. Of course, that's it." And again: "What does your father do?"

"Coaches."

"He what?"

"Coaches. Sports. Football, actually."

"Don't tell me. We're not good at sports, none of us. But I thought he drove a bus—coach, bus, you know?"

"Ha. Right, Mrs. Cohen."

"Adele, Adele. Of course, Adele."

In order to limit the time with Adele, and with Samuel, her slight and effacing husband, who would once have been handsome like his son but who had, now, the aspect of fruit withered on the vine, a lesser specimen, Julius had pleaded work. He did in fact have a commission of sorts, his first of the summer (he'd been too busy working on his marriage to chase up commissions), vague though it was. Marina had suggested he write something for *The Monitor*, not for the launch issue (that one was already "sealed." She'd used the word "sealed" and it had annoyed him. It didn't seem to him the right word, and he suspected it was Seeley's) but for one soon after. With a weekly magazine, there was a lot of space to fill. Marina hadn't said the piece was on spec, but he surmised as much from her vagueness: no set topic, no contract, the promise of emolument unspecified, but certainly less grandiose than he might hope.

She wanted some class of cultural exposé, or so she said, although it wasn't entirely clear that she knew what she meant. Nor, for that matter, did Julius: "exposé" suggested revelation. The sight of Shake Your Booty in his undies was an exposé of an insalubrious kind; or the sight, mercifully unrecorded (except, he thought flinchingly, by said Tubb) of Julius in Lewis's most capable arms was an exposé, too. But Marina wanted something other, and while he was doing his best to oblige, he hadn't come up with it yet. In this sense, he'd told a small lie to the Cohen parents, and even—insofar as he had implied he would get started on something—to David. Julius thought David had narrowed his eyes reprovingly; and then, just before he left, had said, "You know, Miss Clarke, that no blow is going to help you write any piece at all, or even to get started."

"Are you something of a saint, now?" Julius had stuck out his tongue—like a queen, like the bitch he was, he thought. But he'd been genuinely angry, the beginning of the anger that, well fueled, had had him insulting Marina's stupid cousin.

And now Julius would absolutely have to make the ten-thirty train, to smile for Adele Cohen, to choke down the blue Independence Day cake without a hint of exhaustion on him. Worse still, he'd have to have something to show for his truant night, an article topic at the very least. He sighed, which did nothing to slow the thundering of his blood. He would have to leave the topic to his unconscious. There were still four hours till he had to leave for the station. Or maybe he would do a little more of the stuff and power straight on through.

Exposé. Exposé. *Julius sera exposé. Julius a été exposé. Julius a voulu être exposé.* There was a man leaning against the wall outside his apartment building who looked at once familiar and unfamiliar. His spiky hair was gray and white, not intermingled but distinctively speckled, like a hen's, discrete islands of gray and white. He gave Julius a look, worrying to him in its length and intensity. Perhaps he was a spy, hired by David to monitor Julius's comings and goings? That was an insane thought. Or was it? He reminded Julius of someone. Of whom? Not of Adele. Adele. Scarsdale. Ten-thirty. Grand Central. He must take a shower; he must shave. There was no time. There was plenty of time. Had he left these lights on in the apartment? It would seem that he had. He shouldn't have insulted the fat boy. He should not have had sex with Lewis. How sore he was. He should not have stayed up all night. All he needed was a topic. Exposé. Not of himself, but of another. And maybe just an hour's sleep. Just an hour.

CHAPTER THIRTY-THREE

Affianced

The fragrant haze of early morning drifted over the pergola at the end of the garden, peculiarly enticing. Marina slipped from her bed—shared, without parental comment, with Ludo, whose lean back was turned against the rising light, a bubbled bony ridge not unlike the late Pope's—and knelt at the open window, through which breathed a whisper of honeysuckled air. She watched her mother, in her lavender dressing gown, step barefoot across the overgrown lawn, leaving flattened shadows in her wake on the emerald sea. Annabel carried a mug—doubtless tea, probably jasmine—and with her other hand she gathered the hem of her gown to her knee, as if she were a maiden, as if there were dew. The powdery light, promise of heat, seemed from above to soften and cloud her fair hair, so that Marina had the fleeting illusion that her mother was a girl from a storybook, uncorruptible and free; or was, indeed, some avatar of Marina herself, some liberated alternative incarnation. She was tempted to call out, but didn't want to disturb the morning's spell. Barefoot also, she threw on the sundress that lay crumpled on the floor, closed the bedroom door behind her, and skittered down the prickly, sisal-covered steps to join her mother outside.

Annabel's smile, slow and finite, suggested that she was not surprised by her daughter's arrival. Marina looked back at the sleeping house. "It's beautiful here, Mama."

"Always."

"Actually, in the winter, it was pretty creepy. Cold and isolated."

"That can be beautiful, too."

"I imagined a sniper hiding out here, night after night, spying on me." Marina ran her hand over the slatted bench, brushing away the dust and leaf droppings before she sat.

"My silly girl."

"It seems such a long time ago."

"March?"

"So much has changed."

"Ludovic."

"Ludo, the magazine, even the book. I'm going to finish it, you know. It's basically done."

"I know."

"You say that as if it had always been perfectly clear, but it wasn't. In March it wasn't."

"Ludovic," her mother said again.

"Mama, I'm going to marry him."

Annabel sipped her tea.

"You don't say anything?"

"I'm thrilled for you, baby doll."

"But?"

"No 'but.' You believe in him—"

"He believes in *me*."

"It's mutual, then. It's very thrilling. But you mustn't—"

"I knew there was a 'but.' "

"You mustn't idealize, that's all. That's all I wanted to say. You'll marry a man, not an idea of one."

"Of course. I know it's been quick, but I'm not a fool."

"Far from it." Annabel stroked Marina's cheek, and her fingers were warm from cupping her tea. "You're still my little girl and I want to protect you. It's allowed. It's my job."

"Ludo protects me, more than anyone. You don't like him, do you?"

"He reminds me, in some ways, of your father."

"Daddy doesn't like him."

"I don't suppose he does. But that's not the point."

"What has Daddy said to you?"

Annabel's eyes flickered with reproach. Marina was reminded, as she had been periodically and exasperatingly throughout her life, that there were times when her parents' relationship superseded her, was closed to her.

"It's just that, you know, that's so important to me, about Ludo. We're completely transparent and honest with each other. Not like *our* house, where we all pretend that we're honest but actually it's all bullshit."

Annabel gazed intently at the lawn, sipped her tea.

"I'm sorry. You came out here for the peace of it, and I've spoiled things. But I want you to be happy for me."

"Of course I'm happy for you, darling. You're alight with it. You're beautifully alive."

"But what?"

"When are you thinking to marry?"

"Labor Day weekend, we thought. The magazine launches about ten days after that, and it would feel different—right— for us to be formally together before then."

"That's soon. A bit like getting married before the baby is born?"

"Like that."

Annabel set her mug down on the bench, crossed her arms. She was still watching the house, its half-pulled blinds. She didn't look at Marina. "You know how I adore your father," she said.

"Never a cross word," Marina repeated an old family line; but it was true. They never did argue. She spoke sharply to him on occasion, when he indulged in some particularly tyrannical rant or bluster; and then he might sulk, vaguely, or bolt, even, for a short while; and then it would pass. But they didn't argue. Now that Marina thought about it, this was her mother's doing, wholly, as Murray Thwaite could be querulous, even petulant. Danielle had long ago joked—to Marina's abiding annoyance—that Annabel seemed, sometimes, like Murray's mother. The unspoken corollary to which was, of course, that Marina seemed like his lover. It had annoyed her because it seemed on the one hand right, a private familial delight, for Marina if not for her mother; and at the same time, unspeakable, totally private. She'd been annoyed because Danielle seemed at once to expose and to sully a truth held secretly dear.

"So keep in mind," Annabel was saying, "that it's different, in time."

"Sorry? I'm sorry, Mama. I was just thinking."

"It doesn't matter. You'll have to see for yourself. But I loved him for his mind, for his ideals—oh, of course for his looks, too, all that, he was to die for, and a bit older, so all the more dashing—but you have to see, he was someone extraordinary and I loved him already for what he wrote and said and did;

and it would have been enough for me, then, to love him from afar." She laughed. "Or *almost* enough. Okay, not really. But you understand what I'm saying?"

"I guess."

"I'm saying that although I thought I knew him well when we married, my picture was colored by what I believed him to be."

"Mm-hmm."

"He didn't make any false promises. He was never other than who he is. But I had to learn to see him clearly, and learn not to be disappointed."

Marina felt her mother was trying to convey something in particular. She did not want to have this conversation. "I don't think Ludo is some comic book hero, you know."

"I'm sure not. I'm sure not." Annabel stood and put her arms around Marina, holding until her daughter softened, like a child, in her embrace. "I want my baby doll to be very happy. Will you be married here, maybe?"

"Yes, please."

"In this very pergola. With flowers in your hair."

"On the Saturday of Labor Day weekend. The end of summer and the beginning of the rest of our lives. What do you think?"

"It'll be beautiful. Is his family coming?"

"Just his mother. I mean, there is just his mother. He's got a younger brother, but they don't get on. He doesn't think Darius will come."

"Darius? That's the brother?"

"He's a journalist in Sydney. Not as successful as Ludo. I think it's awkward."

"Mm-hmm."

They were silent for a few moments, listening to the morning birdsong and the rustling leaves as the heat began to rise. There were faint sounds, as of banging, from the house.

"Someone's up," Annabel observed.

"Not Ludo, I don't think."

"Who'll be your bridesmaids?"

"Just Danielle." Marina bit her fingernail. "It's weird, though. She basically set us up, Ludo and me, but she's been very strange about it all. About us."

"In what way?"

"Snippy. As if she's envious, or as if she doesn't like him. Or both. I don't know."

"Maybe it is both. Why don't you ask her?"

"I'm not twenty-one, Mama. We don't have time in life to start that kind of endless conversation. Besides, I don't know if I want to know. All my life people have been jealous of me for one thing or another, and I'm tired of pretending that I don't notice, and I'm tired of feeling guilty about it. And the whole point about Danielle was that I never had to pretend before. I don't want to be pretending."

"Do you think she wants to get married herself?"

"Of course she does. We're thirty, for God's sake. And I feel bad that she's on her own, but it's not my fault."

"No."

"It isn't, is it?"

"No."

"And I think she's sorry that I have a job, and a good job, too; and I think she's sorry that I'm going to finish my book. She's *sorry*. Can you believe that?"

"Maybe she shouldn't be your bridesmaid."

"There's nobody else I'd want. She's my best friend."

"Well, I'm sure it will all pass. These things do."

"But you know I invited her to come now, for the holiday. And she said no."

"Just because she's come three summers in a row doesn't make her automatically free the fourth."

"But I'm pretty sure she *is* free, that's the thing. She wasn't going to her mom's, or her dad's, and she doesn't have a boyfriend—I mean, maybe she's working, but then she chose work over us, you know? I'm a little bit hurt. More than a little bit. She knew it was important."

"Does she know about you and Ludovic?"

"About getting married? Not yet." Marina scrunched up her face. "You're the first person I've told. I haven't even told Daddy yet."

Annabel nodded toward the house, where a large robed shape was visible in the shadow of the French doors. "He's just coming now, so you can if you want."

Marina pulled close to her mother's side, took her arm. "But I want him to be happy about it. Like I want Danielle to be happy about it. You'd think the people who love you best could behave a little less selfishly, wouldn't you? Like you, I mean. Why can't they behave like you, and be genuinely happy for me?"

"Try them. Try him."

"Not right now, Mama." Marina unfurled herself, tiptoed out onto the lawn with her arms akimbo. "Morning, lazybones."

"Not as lazy as your young man, it seems."

"But he doesn't know, yet, what it's like to wake up here, and you do."

"I do." Murray stretched, bearish in the bulky robe, for all he was a lean man. "If I were a believer, I'd call it a blessing. But as it is, I'll just say it's damn nice."

"Ah, my wordsmith," Annabel spoke lazily, without moving from her bench. "Is that the best you can do?"

Murray took the pergola steps in one and zealously embraced his wife. "Actions," he said. "Actions speak louder."

Annabel giggled. Marina watched them for a moment with the strange old sensation of envy, that feeling of childhood, and then turned and ran back to the house, aware that the grass was already dry and warming beneath her feet. When she reached the door, she heard her father calling, "Hey! Hey, missy! Where'd you go?" But she didn't turn around.

CHAPTER THIRTY-FOUR

Fireworks in Stockbridge

Danielle spent Sunday morning in her office, sweating because the a/c was off, looking through a file of color photographs showing the bottoms and thighs of botched liposuction recipients. The photographs mostly did not show faces, just endless angles of lumpen, bulging, purpled limbs, limbs with strange indentations, limbs that looked like badly stuffed pillows. Buttocks protruded at implausible angles, or sagged without delineation into legs. But above all the distress was of texture and color. Danielle had brought breakfast—a cranberry muffin in a waxed paper bag—but found she couldn't eat it. Even her water, fizzy, made her gag a little. She knew that at the bottom of the file were pictures of the patient who had subsequently died, an only moderately plump mother of three from Tampa. Mid-forties. Her husband had agreed to talk. So had several of the women whose rear ends Danielle was ogling. Nicky was into this story. It was a good one. Danielle had known it before, but looking through the pictures, sickened and compelled, sullied but unable to turn away, Danielle felt certain, almost triumphant. If she did this well, if the ratings were good, Nicky would let her have any story she wanted: reparations for

Aborigines; nihilist revolution in the media; heck, why not a full hour on something crazy, like women terrorists?

She should have been in Stockbridge. Only in flashes—or were they waves?—was she aware of the enormity of what she had embarked upon, and the impossibility of it ending well. She'd unthinkingly imagined that she'd spend every Fourth of July with Marina, waking in the blue and white bedroom under the eaves that Marina actually referred to as Danny's room, to the sound of blackbirds and cicadas and the kiss of the hot, grassy air among the maples. And of course it was different this year because of Seeley, and perhaps on his account she might have stayed away (not that she felt any regret or residual attraction for him—no, quite the opposite—but because she'd been used by him, and falsely; and because she suspected him of using Marina, although she couldn't have said what for); but in the event there had been no question of her going, and she realized, in some horror, that she'd probably never spend that holiday in that place again.

In years past, Murray and Annabel had been elsewhere in July—California, Tuscany, hiking in Canada—but even had they not been at the house, Danielle wasn't sure she could have wandered happily among their joint belongings. Everything had a different color, now. Given that they were there, it was naturally out of the question. Rationally, she marveled that a few unexpected turns should so thoroughly have upended her life—had the Chinese dinner at the Thwaites' apartment been a mere four months ago?—but she was not, mostly, rational.

Like an addict—no, she *was* an addict. She thought about him all the time, or else thought about thinking about him, and the fact that she shouldn't. She smelled him on her clothes, the biscuity waft of cigarettes that now permeated her once-clean studio and all its contents. Sitting at her desk, or on the subway, she recalled, beneath her fingers, the texture of his skin, its poignant sag, its aged coarsening. She prickled at the sound, or the thought of the sound, of his voice. She, who had scoffed at cell phones, now took no step without hers charged and at the ready for his unexpected call. She had endured the exquisite torture of hearing the phone ring in her bag while she walked idly up Hudson with Marina on a syrupy Thursday afternoon, as a thunderstorm gathered; of knowing, without checking, that it was Murray; and of leaving the apparatus to tinkle and whimper in her bag, her heart to thump treacherously at her ribs, while she rolled her eyes and drawled, "Nicky seems to think he can bug me about anything, anytime, these days. It's *so* annoying." She checked her e-mail as she might worry a chipped tooth. And when the contact finally came, she feigned nonchalance, near indifference; just as she dressed three times each morning, as she used to do in high school, in a meticulous effort to project the right tone: I look great but I'm not dressed up. I'm not dressed as though I *expected* to see you; I'm so casually, so naturally, stylish simply because it's my way.

The photographs, sickening, had taken her mind off him for a time; and yet, even knowing that he would not ring, could not ring, she found herself listening to the silence, hoping. There was nobody else in the office on this Sunday morning, no buzz of machines, no chatter, simply the airless, sticky quiet into which his silence, deepening, fell. When she was at home, even the Rothkos seemed to wait for him. She kept the fancy sheets on her bed all the time (so this was why she'd bought them!); and the apartment's tidiness no longer presaged a meditative solitude, speaking, instead, anticipation of her visitor. It was a different, slightly more studied tidiness. Her apartment now struck her as the stage set for a play, a site awaiting action. As if it weren't quite real on its own any longer. She now kept a bottle of Lagavulin in the cupboard over the fridge and behind it, hidden, a symbolic, as yet unopened, carton of Marlboros. She kept on hand packets of heavily salted pretzels, which she was beginning herself to appreciate, and Altoids, for which he had a weakness. She felt simultaneously proud and ashamed of these accommodations.

Sometimes, she worried that she bored him. She worried that she seemed to him young, insignificant, ignorant, naïve. At other times, she worried that she didn't bore him, worried that this signified a lowering of his standards, that his oft-voiced appreciation of her breasts, her hair, her wrists, stood in the way; that she, least likely candidate, was being objectified, diminished: just a woman, and a young one, and available. She wasn't a complete ninny, didn't flatter herself that Murray had been an adultery virgin. Alternately, she longed to hear about his other conquests in order to rank herself among them; and longed to shut out all intimation of their existence. She was jealous of them as she could not be jealous of Annabel, nor even of Marina, and she, like he himself, insisted that they speak quite normally about these two, that they not shunt them artificially to the periphery. To her surprise, Danielle found this, most of the time, peculiarly supportable, as if these two, her ultimate rivals, dear friends and nemeses, were so far to the fore in life's picture that they might have been anyone, dissolved into an undistinguished blur. Far more disturbing were his evasions when she asked, "Have there been many?" and

"Am I the youngest?" and "How long did the longest last?" She wanted, of course, to ask, "Did you love her?" In spite of its predictability. In spite of the horror she would feel at any possible reply. But she was learning the limits, knew not to ask this. He had—was this not part of the appeal?—a mania for honesty as he saw it. (Which was not to be confused with allowable delusion: he really believed that a cup of coffee at the end of a night's booze could sober you up for the drive.) If she were to ask him even the most outré of questions (for example, and impossible, "Do you love *me*?"), he would reply without regard for her brittle heart, her tender ears. So that she must, in this love, be her own guardian. She did not stop to question this, which seemed to her a lesson for her own maturity rather than any possible selfishness on his part.

She considered all these things, she considered *him,* all the time. Every possible waking moment. And they waited for her, like patient wounds, when she was in meetings, or society, waited to assail her as soon as she was again free. She wanted to be free of this dis-ease; and yet she loved it, yes, like an addict.

Marina hadn't believed her when she'd said she had too much work to do. Danielle knew that Marina thought it was all about Seeley.

"They can't ask you to work on this weekend out of all weekends. It's practically the biggest holiday of the year."

"They're not *asking* me to. It's not kindergarten."

"So?"

"So, I haven't managed to get a film idea into production all year. And I'm supposed to pitch in a week. It's important."

"You wouldn't be left on your own, you know."

"I know."

"It's the chance for you and Ludo to get to know each other. My two MIs."

"Two mes?"

"Two Most Importants."

"You know I'd love to."

"And my parents. They're dying to see you. Mom was asking again yesterday if you'd be coming."

This suggestion had made Danielle shudder. She was relieved, in her amorous fog, still to have the decency to be appalled. "Please tell her I'm sorry. You know I wouldn't miss it if I didn't have to."

Marina was quiet for a moment. "I'm wondering why you don't want to make the effort for someone so important to me."

"Oh, M." Danielle could anticipate, then hear, her own faint-heartedness. "Please don't be that way. I promise it isn't about Ludovic. I'd do anything to be there this weekend." And this, at least, she meant, "But I really can't."

"You don't have some tryst lined up, do you? Some secret blind date?"

"How long have you known me?"

"I just thought I'd ask."

And now, in the silence in the office, the phone rang, almost causing Danielle to upend her water onto the glossy, disconsolate buttocks and thighs. She had so willed his call that it never occurred to her that it could be anyone besides Murray. "Beloved," she whispered into the receiver.

"Glad to know you care," Marina replied. "You're busted, big time, baby."

"What do you mean?"

"I mean that you may be working, just like you said, but I call expecting a sad sack and get a lovebird instead."

"Hardly."

"Who's the mystery man? Who's beloved?"

"I thought it was going to be my mom. She's feeling a bit down, and I told her to call me here."

"And Randy Minkoff is beloved?"

"Is that so strange?"

"Girlfriend, we've got some talking to do. If you're in love, you're excused from the Thwaites' annual Independence shindig, no questions asked—I absolutely believe in love, especially these days, as you know. But there must be something wrong with the guy, if you haven't told me about him."

"There *is* no guy."

"And your mother is beloved?"

"You already asked me that. You're haranguing me."

"I bet you're blushing."

"Come on, Marina. I'm just trying to do a little work here, is all."

"And your mother is beloved."

"Yes."

"Bless her leopard-print heart."

"What did you want, besides to check that I was really here?"

"That's not very nice."

"I'm teasing. You tease me, after all."

"You know I don't like to be teased."

"Who does?"

"I wanted you to be the first person after my parents to know. We're getting married."

"Oh, Marina." And a deep breath. "I'm so happy for you. That's—amazing news."

"Isn't it? I always told Julius I was the uxorious type at heart."

"He'll scream."

"He'd beat me to the altar if he could. Him and the Cone-head. Who is Pierre, who is Natasha? Handy dandy, which is the justice, which is the thief?"

"So when's it going to be?"

"He can't possibly beat me, if that's what you mean. We're having a whirlwind romance, if not a shotgun wedding. Labor Day weekend. And yes, in spite of everything, the bride will wear white."

"You sound almost high."

"I *am* almost high. Come off it, my life was in free fall, and now look."

"Don't tell me that you owe it all to me?"

"But I do. Ludo said so again just this morning."

"You don't owe anything to me."

"Ah, beloved . . ."

"Who are the bridesmaids? Julius and David?"

"I only want one, and you know who she is."

"I'm honored."

"So get your butt in gear and get to the train station on Tuesday afternoon."

"Because?"

"Because even if you don't take four days, which even lazy me can understand, you can still take off the Fourth of July. There are going to be fireworks in Stockbridge. Consider it the engagement party."

"But I don't—"

"I don't take no for an answer, here. There's a train getting in to Albany at 7:42 on Tuesday. One of us will be there."

"But M—"

"This you can't deny me. I'm getting married in less than six weeks. We'll see you Tuesday."

She could not deny her. Danielle considered it, bent again over the wattled, mottled limbs. Was there any way to call him? Did he know what was going on? Might he pick her up at the station? And could she stomach it?

Out on the street, the humidity squatted like a toad upon the afternoon. There would be rain, but not yet. She decided to walk, did not expect, on so quiet and heavy a day, to encounter anyone that she knew, but near Astor Place caught sight of Marina's cousin, truffling toward the subway with a pile of papers under his arm. Even in the heat, he wore a dress shirt, though somewhat limp, with the sleeves rolled up, and his forehead was slick with sweat. When she called out to him—"Frederick? It is Frederick, isn't it?"—he stopped, raised his head, blinked, like some underground creature just emerging into the light. "Marina's cousin, right? It's Danielle—we met."

"I know. Hello." He stood without smiling, still blinking. His eyes were huge behind his glasses, thickly lashed like a cow's.

"You didn't go to Stockbridge?"

He pursed his lips. "You didn't either."

"Too much work, you know. I usually do. It looks like I'll go just for the Fourth."

Frederick Tubb shuffled his feet, adjusted his pile of papers. He looked back down at the ground.

"You're working for Marina's dad now, aren't you?"

"For Murray." He said his uncle's name with a challenge in his voice. "Yes. I'm working for Murray these days. Probably not for long."

"How come?"

Frederick shrugged. Danielle tried a different tack: "How are your studies coming along? Are you finding time for them?"

"I'm writing an article. For Marina. For *The Monitor.*"

"That's great news. I—"

"She said you told her to ask me."

"Well, all I did was suggest . . ."

"So I guess I owe you a thank-you." He didn't sound grateful.

"You don't owe me anything at all. I'm glad it worked out."

"It hasn't yet."

"I'm sorry?"

"Nothing's worked out yet. I'm writing the article, but it's 'on spec.' Do you know what that means?"

"I do."

"So maybe they won't publish it."

"And maybe they will. What's it about?"

Now he looked her straight in the eye, and did not blink. "It's a secret. It's going to be big, though." He nodded, solemnly.

"Wow." Danielle laughed, more a bark. "That sounds interesting."

"Yes. It is. You'll see." He wiped his brow with a balled cloth hankie pulled from the pocket of his shorts. Danielle noticed, looking down, that his shorts looked like truncated trousers, stained baggy twill reaching to just above his knees, and that he wore dark socks with his sneakers. His calves, pale, solid, hairy, and forlorn, loomed brightly. He looked as though he'd lost his long pants on his way to the office and was wandering the streets half-dressed. He looked a little crazy. Unwell.

"Good luck with that, then."

He nodded, head down, and shuffled off.

CHAPTER THIRTY-FIVE

Notes from Underground

Bootie had been feeling soul-sick anyway and the unexpected encounter with Danielle made him feel worse. The apartment, after Julius and Lewis withdrew, had remained an infernal heatbox; only it seemed, in addition, a place scarred by malevolence. Bootie had thought he could enjoy the space, in spite of its crumminess, but then its owner had caught him all but naked and had insulted him, had called him fat to his face; and as he lay in the darkness on the damp futon on the floor, hearing still the salsa music over the road and the fan's bland whir and listening, in spite of himself and fruitlessly, for the scuttle of cockroaches, he had felt the room, with its flaking stucco and cloying furnace air, to be hostile. He couldn't sleep—for his rage, for the heat—for a long time, and drifted off near dawn, when the music had finally stopped. He awoke around noon with a pall over him, not merely the coating of dried sweat, but the horror, swiftly recalled, of the night before. Julius had been on drugs, or drunk, but still, Bootie couldn't fathom the ill will. It was like kicking a dog in the street. And the heat: the apartment felt hotter, if possible, as if it were a repository for the sticky stillness, a deliberate storage trunk for misery.

He decided after some minor deliberation to go to the

Thwaites'. At least for the day and possibly for longer. They were all away. He had a key. The air-conditioning would be on. He'd walk up to get a copy of Murray's third book at the Astor Place Barnes & Noble, then take the subway, which could not alarm him on this quiet summer Sunday. He'd take his notes, the beginning of his draft, and he wouldn't leave their apartment until his masterful analysis of Murray was complete.

And yet, calmly en route to his destination, the N and R stop at Eighth Street, he'd been waylaid by Danielle. He wanted to loathe her—in principle, he knew he loathed her—but her manner was kind, and sincere, and even though he maintained his chill (surely to her mystification, because how could she guess what he knew?), he'd felt guilty about it. He'd wondered whether the e-mail he'd read—inadvertently, of course—had been a figment. Perhaps he didn't know what he knew he knew? And if he did, then was she not doubly a villain, to smile and chat in the July haze on that steaming street-corner, as though the world were still in its place? It was like the endless news, the scandal in Washington, the missing intern—Chandra Levy—and the congressman. He married, she just a picture, dark curls and a charming white smile. Now look. He should have said to Danielle, "Think of Chandra Levy. It isn't worth it." He should have warned her. Because in the end, one way or another, the man was always the culprit. Just like some greedy child, demanding a second dessert while still hoarding the first, taking a mere bite, discarding it. Danielle ought to know this. She shouldn't have let him, shouldn't be hurting her friend, or her friend's mother, in this way. He, Bootie, bore a responsibility in this mess. Knowledge brought responsibility. But he wasn't yet entirely sure of how to proceed. What was public, and what private? What his to contend with, and what his simply, painfully, to know?

And why, in the summer, was the air beyond the turnstiles quite so fetid, a blooming composite reek of piss and sweat and enveloping garbage rot, borne on furious steaming gusts through the foul tunnels? The woman beside him covered her nose with her manicured hand, squinting toward the tunnel mouth. Flat and small, she wore a red sundress pulled tight across her breastbone, carried a beachbag; perhaps she, too, was on her way to an illicit tryst. The entire city was doubtless rife with deceit, with rot, like the rot in the subway air. Murray Thwaite claimed that honesty was paramount; but the word had, for him, only his own meaning. He claimed that he fought injustice, that his life had been devoted to what he deemed a "moral journalism." He claimed that he lived for and by his independence, his own wits. He presumed to opine on paper about how life should be led, about the very meaning of the word, when he was evidently—Bootie meant this in all seriousness: Bootie had *evidence*—someone for whom words had no fixed meaning. Somebody needed to make this clear, and public.

Sitting on the train, the malodor around him leached somewhat by the climate control, Bootie perused the papers in his lap. He had copied out quotations from Murray's manuscript, some inspiring, some silly, but all of them problematic in context, and tried to make order out of them. Interspersed among the Thwaiteisms, Bootie had recorded his own comments, ranging from the exploratory ("Is it actually possible for intention and actuality fully, purely, to overlap? Can we really be who we want to be?") to the vituperative ("MT is a liar. This is a bare-faced lie"). When Bootie had begun his article draft, the day before, he had done so in a state of high emotion. He could see that now. As the train rattled along its track, he reread his introduction and caught in its rhythms the keening of sentimentality, the weakness of a disciple wronged. No: for the article to be any good, it had to do precisely the things of which Murray wrote so admiringly and with such promise, but which he himself did not live up to. It had to be precise, and calm and clear. It had to be patient, frank, substantiated. It had to be accessible and germane. It had to be true.

He realized his adjectives had been chosen to match the train's music. He realized that the train was slowing, in the tunnel. That the train was stopped.

He looked up, peered through the greasy window at the tunnel wall, its close blackness. They must be outside Times Square, where he would change trains. He always remembered, in such moments, Marina's soothing nonchalance as she assured him, on that first subway ride, that the trains always stopped in the tunnels outside the big stations. It was perfectly normal.

Perfectly normal, too, when the lights flickered, then went out. It had happened before, and while he didn't much care for it—did not like it at all—he could handle it. He concentrated on his breathing, the swish in his nostrils, which had replaced the fans' whirring. The fan, like the lights, had died. A wan emergency bulb strobed near him, an epileptic's nightmare. Down the carriage, in the gloom, two older women spoke quietly to each other in Spanish. The woman in the sundress coughed—it was a fake cough, Bootie thought, nerves—and rummaged in her bag. The lights did not come back on.

Already, the carriage grew hot, a particular windless, stagnant heat. There were no fetid gusts, no bursts of furnace air, just a slow seepage of weight, a feeling that the air sat on them, on his legs and arms and above all his neck, the heat licking at his throat and closing it, little by little, making it hard to breathe. Still the lights did not come on. No trains rumbled past in neighboring alleys. There was no audible movement outside the carriage.

Inside the carriage, though, passengers moved in small, furtive, anxious ways. A cocoa-skinned youth in massive, dragging jeans stood, muttered, made as if to move, sat again, stood and stomped to the end of the aisle. As he yanked the door, and the next door, making his way to the trapped room beyond, he cursed. "Fuck this shit, man. Fuck this shit."

Bootie checked his watch. It had been only a few minutes; less than five. The carriage held its breath. The air weighed. Bootie licked his teeth, again and again, the inside of them, with the tip of his tongue. His glasses, slick, slipped down his nose. His fingers slithered against one another. The woman in the sundress had been fishing, so furiously, for her Walkman, and now clutched the headphones to her ears. She kept her eyes shut, and the muffled bounce of her music filtered along the carriage. Something sunny. Maybe she was pretending to be at the beach.

Bootie, like the others, started at the crackle of the PA. A fresh clamminess sprang along his palms. A man's voice, sharp and high like a dog's, spoke largely unintelligibly. His last words were "as soon as possible." These he repeated two times. When silence fell again, Bootie could hear people asking one another, quietly, what had been said. He did not himself ask. It wasn't clear that anyone knew the answer. He, like the woman with the Walkman, closed his eyes. He concentrated again on his breath, tried to measure his breath to slow his heart. His heart made more noise, more sweat, than anything else in the carriage. He couldn't let himself think about all the possible outcomes—fire and explosions chief among them—that might be causing their stop. He must not think about the walls pressing in, about the earth weighing down, about the train like a burrowing earthworm, arrested, eminently squashable. Bootie's throat was very tight now, the noise in his ears thunderous, so loud that when the barking conductor came again over the PA, Bootie was barely aware of it. He screwed his eyes shut; he dug his nails into his palms; he tried again to concentrate on his lost breathing. He was still breathing.

Twenty-three minutes. They were stopped twenty-three sweltering minutes, like lost miners, like spelunkers without egress, like dead men. For Bootie, it was a mind-altering experience: he wasn't at once sure exactly how he had been changed by it, sure merely that he would always be different. He knew something he hadn't known before, about himself and his limitations. He would never, never allow that to happen to him again. But at least, he thought as he walked, at speed and with great determination, up Sixth Avenue the two good miles to the Thwaites' apartment, gulping almost the thick air, so relieved to find it around him, in abundance, however soupily, at least he hadn't given in and screamed. He had drawn blood on his left palm from the force of his gouging, and had brought on a headache of migraine proportions from the screaming inside his head; but he'd kept his mouth closed and his eyes closed, had concentrated on the swish in his nostrils (he could still hear it, the way a shorebound sailor feels the roll of the earth), and had made it through. That nobody in the carriage could tell how close he had come to eruption, insanity—not even, he imagined, the young woman in the red sundress, who had smiled conspiratorially at him as they disembarked— struck Bootie as a near miracle.

He'd often imagined, as a boy, that his parents or teachers, Big Brother–like, could penetrate his skull and eavesdrop on his thoughts, could even, conceivably, usurp his self; and even in adulthood, he carried a vestigial faith in and fear of trans- parency. But his Earthworm Hour, as he came to think of it, reinforced for him the opacity and isolation of his soul, and of everyone else's. It made clear to him the need to speak clearly, to try to be heard above all the blood rushing in people's ears. Nobody should be allowed to be the woman with the Walk- man, willfully, artificially blocking out experience and truth: it was Bootie's job to engage, and to speak. Not unintelligibly, like the conductor, but in the clear voice of reason. But the whole thing drove him half crazy, no two ways about that.

CHAPTER THIRTY-SIX

On the Grill

"I somehow never pictured you barbecuing." Seeley leaned against the doorjamb, his long, candy-striped torso curved against the oxblood wall. His shirt was crisp. Everything about him looked faggy.

"You'd be amazed at what falls to the paterfamilias," Murray replied, without taking the cigarette from his mouth. Some ash floated down into the grill. Murray was sweating. "You'll do it, too, in your time, even though you swear you won't."

Seeley narrowed his hooded eyes and appeared to smirk. As much as to say "never." Murray felt like a bear beside him, felt like grabbing him by the collar and shaking him senseless. Danielle thought this guy was a snake; but all he could get out of Annabel was that mild, faintly PC acquiescence: whatever makes our baby happy.

"What are you going to do if that magazine of yours flops?"

"It won't."

"Of course it won't. But it might."

"There's always another outlet. But *The Monitor* is going to change the scene."

Murray flipped a slab of steak with his greasy tongs. Fat spattered on the front of his shirt. He felt that this in itself was manly. "You know," he said, "there's a very successful British sandwich joint that's been trying to set up shop in Manhattan. But Americans eat differently. They want their food customized."

Seeley adjusted the curve of his spine, crossed his arms over his narrow chest.

"I'm not saying it's a good thing. We're all obese over here, I know that. But it's the way it is. Just because it's a relatively new and changeable place doesn't mean we don't have a culture."

"I'm Australian, not British."

"Meaning?"

"Meaning, I know."

Marina appeared around the side of the house with a colander full of beans. She had a muddy streak across her forehead that looked as though the makeup department had planted it there, to designate a young maiden fresh from the meadow. The beans were just picked, a dusty heap. "My two favorite men in the whole wide world."

"Steak's almost done. Chicken takes longer." Murray dropped his cigarette end through the grill onto the coals.

"That's disgusting, Daddy."

"Gives new meaning to secondhand smoking," Murray replied. "The meat will thank me."

"Don't do that when Danny comes, okay? She's a very clean person, and probably wouldn't be able to eat supper."

"Your friend Danielle is coming here?" Murray reached for the scotch tumbler perched upon the patio wall. "I thought she couldn't make it this year."

"I bullied her. Just for the day on Wednesday. But I bet I can get her to stay the night." Marina had put the colander on the table and wrapped her arms around Seeley's waist. "I told her it was our engagement party, on Independence Day." After a moment of silence in which the meat sizzled oppressively, Marina said, "I thought you liked her, Daddy."

"I do. I like her very much. She's an extremely pleasant young woman."

"Pleasant? She'd *cry*, Daddy, to hear you call her that. She's brilliant, actually. You got a sense of that, Ludo, didn't you? She's really brilliant, and her work is very important."

"Something in films, isn't it?"

"How can you never remember *anything*? She was going to make a documentary about Ludo, remember?"

"But thought better of it," Ludo added, pulling himself upright and out of Marina's embrace. "Let me get the platter for those steaks." He slipped back into the house.

"Daddy, are you even happy for me?"

"Of course I am, princess. It seems very fast."

"Romantic speed. It's at romantic speed. But if we're both sure, why would we wait?"

"Indeed." Murray, fiddling with the tin foil around the corncobs, burned his fingertips. "Shit," he said. "Shit, shit, shit." Now he understood why his cell phone had shown four messages. He hadn't yet had a chance to ring her back, but had been worrying—in a passive, intermittent way—that some injury had befallen her. That, and he'd been annoyed. Because they'd had an understanding that she wouldn't call him this weekend, that he'd call if he could, but to please leave well enough alone. And there he'd been thinking that they can never wait, women, and never really listen. But he'd maligned her and now felt remorseful. As well as faintly unsettled. He knew he was up to the acting job—a role as much as any of his others, as much as the barbecuing paterfamilias or benignly doting papa—but for Danielle it would be a test. She seemed very truthful—it was one of the traits that had attracted him, and now he felt almost constrictingly fond of the girl, a low but constant flame that could easily be kindled—and she might not care for the drama—very sexy, he'd always thought—of deception. It was always about limits, the right ones: the quick, wordless clinch in the pantry being something to strive for, and the anxious exchange of glances to be avoided at all costs.

Had he done this before? Yes and no, never so egregiously. He wincingly transferred the corncobs to the steak platter, which prompted, from Marina, a cluck of affectionate exasperation, and she sent Seeley back to the kitchen for a second receptacle. He'd never had an affair with a friend of his daughter's, everything so perilously—so delectably—near to the surface. And what was he thinking, to allow this reunion in Stockbridge, up till now always a sacred family ground? And the degree of his fondness: he was losing control, as he'd known that he must, as he always, on some level, wanted to do. Like taking the nth scotch against his better judgment. He loved thinking about her—the skin, a certain hopeful tenderness, the weight of her curls, the weight of her breast in his hand—and that was as it should be. But he should be capable of not-thinking, and there he was beginning to fail. Her voice should not be so readily breathing at his ear. Recklessness would lead to mistakes and in this instance—he glanced at his daughter, the smudge now wiped from her radiant brow, her hands again and with unseemly zeal upon the torso of her intended—the stakes were too high.

The air smelled of citronella, and the late light was pleasingly colorless. A swarm of midges hovered over the lawn. Annabel, across the table, looked down at her plate, at her cob and slab of steak, with a furrowed brow.

"What, besides the humidity and the bugs, could possibly be wrong, my love?"

She shook her head. "DeVaughn."

"Again?"

"I just got the call. He's been arrested for attempted arson. His stepfather's car."

"Maybe it's a good sign," Marina offered. Seeley appeared to stifle mirth.

"How so?"

"Well, don't people burn things for insurance, usually? So maybe he was cooperating with his stepfather. And that would be a good thing."

"Do you really think this is a time for jokes?" Annabel helped herself to the green beans, rather too energetically. "I'm going to have to go down there. He'll be arraigned in the morning."

"You can't go down there," Marina said. "This is our family holiday. The Fourth! Our engagement. It's special."

"Who'll go if I don't?"

"Hasn't he got a social worker or something?"

"Well, actually, I am his lawyer."

"I can't believe this."

"Marina," Murray said, "you claim you want to do something important with your life. Your mother does something important. You'd do well to emulate her."

"We're celebrating my engagement. Ludo's and mine. I am your only child."

"I should be back on Wednesday. I could even bring back Danielle, you know. There's always a silver lining."

Marina pouted, in an exaggerated way, both to indulge her petulance and to seem to mock it.

"How many cases do you take on, at any given time?" Seeley asked.

"It's not the number of them—there aren't that many. It's somehow the boy has gotten under my skin."

"Because you can help him?"

Annabel looked Seeley frankly in the face. "Because I *can't,* actually. Because no matter what I do, it won't be enough. His life is unbearable. He can't be saved."

"The appeal of the lost cause," observed Seeley.

"We're big on them at our house." Murray picked at the corn in his teeth. He hated corn. "I don't think we know any other kind."

"That's rather sentimental, isn't it?"

Marina stared at Seeley as if she didn't know him. Murray, however, was not surprised. "No sentimentalists around here, my friend. No religionists, either."

"We can agree on that, at least," said Seeley. "Although I'd maintain that there are those for whom religion is essential. That we want them to have it."

"We? They?"

"Marx was quite right: an opiate. It's necessary. Let's not be sentimental, but practical, instead. Wouldn't DeVaughn be better off if he got God? Wouldn't his stepfather? If there's any way out of their appalling quagmire, wouldn't that be it?"

"I'm aware that for many people in tough circumstances, faith is what pulls them through," Annabel said. She spread her ten fingers wide and flat on the table, and seemed to be pressing hard against its surface. "And I have great respect for that. I don't believe, myself, and I'd never encourage anyone to put store in something that seems to me clearly a figment. It would be a false hope."

"But why?" Seeley leaned forward over the glass table, his long fingers appearing to caress the citronella air. "Why is any hope not better than none? Who's to say you're not wrong? And who are you to deprive DeVaughn even of that?"

"To hand him a Bible in his prison cell? There are priests whose job that is. For me, it would be unprincipled. If I'm not an honest broker, then what am I?"

"Ah." Seeley sat back, smiled. "As I say, you're a sentimentalist."

Annabel shook her head.

"Because, really, you think you know what's best for him. Or worse: you *presume* that what's best for you would be best for him, would somehow serve some figment—your word—of objective truth to which you subscribe; when in reality, his life and yours are so far divorced that the same truths simply cannot pertain."

"Pure sophistry, my friend," Murray said, folding his napkin. His bonhomie was as real and as fake as Marina's earlier petulance. "Marina, it's not too late to change your mind."

She glared at him. Seeley laughed. "I'm not trying to distress anyone. Far from unprincipled, I'm advocating the prescription of a proven cure. Religion can perform miracles."

"But not for you?"

"I don't happen to believe. But clearly, for those who believe, it can. Put it another way: Could DeVaughn be any worse off?"

"Can we talk about something else?" Marina stacked the plates. "Did any of you see the little fawn and her mother that are living just in the woods over there? And who wants watermelon?"

"I've got one thing to say to young Ludovic, here—"

"Daddy, you don't always have to have the last word. I asked about the deer."

"They're living at the back of the Jaspers' property," Annabel said. "Evelyn was complaining because nothing keeps them out of the vegetable garden. They've ravaged her lettuces, in spite of the chicken wire."

"But not our beans? That's weird. Do you think they don't like beans?"

Murray could see that Seeley was still trembling slightly, and his eyes had a feverish glow. Like an animal interrupted in the middle of a hunt. "More beans for us," Murray said, with a broad smile that could be seen as conciliatory. "Isn't that right, Ludovic? All the more beans for us."

CHAPTER THIRTY-SEVEN

After Supper

"You mustn't mind Daddy," Marina said. "He's old-fashioned, in his way. He'd be furious to hear me say it."

"I don't mind him at all. He entertains me greatly."

"I did think you were a bit hard on my mom," she said. She inspected his features for some response. They were lying in bed, naked but under covers in spite of the heat: Murray, to Ludovic's unvoiced but discernible annoyance, had turned on the air-conditioning, and the house was hermetically chilly. The windows had been sealed against the tree frogs' song, the rustling branches.

"I didn't mean to be," Seeley said. "I was merely trying to explain my point of view."

"Your point of view is a very moveable thing."

"Mutability is my hallmark. It's healthy. It's vital."

"If you say so."

"She wasn't offended, was she?"

"Would you care if she was?"

"Of course I would. I think she's a very dignified woman."

"And my father?"

"You know."

"You've never said. You wanted so much to meet him, but you disagree with him about everything."

"Do I?"

"You know, before you marry me, you'll have to accept that I'm my father's daughter in most things."

"Meaning?"

"Meaning I agree with him, mostly. I understand him better than anybody else."

"I don't think so."

"You don't think I understand him?"

"I don't think you resemble him. Not at all. I think that's an illusion he has tried very hard to maintain, because it suits him."

"How so?"

"We've talked about this. About how well you reflect on him. About how problematic it is to be reflecting at all. You are a beautiful, highly intelligent, talented woman in your own right. I wouldn't be about to marry you if you weren't."

Marina sighed, wriggled slightly beneath the sheet. "You certainly know how to make a girl feel special."

"Seriously, my darling. You need to separate yourself from your father. Put some distance between you."

"Move to Australia?"

"Not at this point, but maybe, someday. You need to take a stand."

"On principle?"

Seeley shrugged. "Because I say so. And because I'm always right."

"I see. How could I forget?"

"I don't rightly know."

"I'm cold."

"Then come closer. I am ready to envelop you."

"To what?"

"Give in, my girl. Give in."

CHAPTER THIRTY-EIGHT

"Murray Thwaite: A Disappointed Portrait"

In the interests of full disclosure, let me say that Murray Thwaite is my uncle. My mother's older brother. He is also, at the moment, my employer. I serve as his amanuensis (his word) or secretary (mine), working in his office, which is located in his apartment on New York's Upper West Side. It is a very nice apartment. Let me say, too, that he and his wife, my uncle and aunt, have been nothing but kind and generous with me. They have housed and fed me (although I live on my own now) and, obviously, they have employed me. And so the question is, Why is Murray Thwaite such a disappointment to me?

Even though our families were not especially close when I was growing up in Watertown, New York, I have always been proud of my uncle's accomplishments. His intelligence and erudition impressed me from an early age, and I have been a devoted reader of his books and articles since I could begin to understand them. It is fair to say that he has been my hero.

Bootie felt okay about this introduction, although he wasn't entirely sure about the word "hero," which seemed to imply feats of daring. He'd considered "idol," a word in which the falsity was inherently implicit, the connotation always already faintly pejorative, but he wanted to convey the innocence and sincerity of his admiration. "Hero" was better for this, suggesting as it did the Greeks, or firefighters. He was not in Murray's study, nor at the dining room table, but comfortably set up in his former bedroom, in the grave quiet, on the broad bed. He'd found a leftover lamb stew in the freezer for supper, which he'd microwaved; and some melon chunks in a plastic box that, though slightly fizzy on the tongue, were perfectly edible. Their remains lay congealed on a plate on the dresser top, and the bedroom had taken on a faintly gamey smell. He had also spilled a few drops of stew on the white duvet: after wiping, they looked unfortunately like trails of excrement.

Murray Thwaite has built his reputation on being a straight shooter. On telling it like it is. From the civil rights movement and Vietnam right down through Iran Contra and Operation Desert Storm, from education policy to workers' rights and welfare to abortion rights to capital punishment—Murray Thwaite has voiced significant opinions. We have believed him, and believed in him.

Bootie hesitated over the section that followed: he wanted to make specific mention of Murray's most influential contributions, as far as he, Bootie, was concerned. It was hard not to make it sound like a laundry list or a fanzine; but maybe it

would be okay to seem to be a wholehearted disciple. Maybe
it would be rhetorically powerful, and strengthen the effect of
the second half of the piece.

Of course, even though he felt passionate about it, the whole
undertaking had a strangely artificial feeling. Bootie had never
written an article before, let alone for a real publication. He
wasn't quite sure what should be in it, wasn't sure either about
the balance of facts and opinion. It seemed that he could put
forward his opinion pretty succinctly, in a few hundred words,
and that in some fundamental way it would not require any
substantiation: the authority of his conviction ought to suffice.
For example, everybody would know what he meant when
he called Murray "a straight shooter," or "the country's liberal
conscience." Perhaps they needed some guidance in order
to comprehend Murray's lesser known idiosyncracies—his
comparative fiscal conservatism, which dated way back; his
particular closeness to and popularity among the black community, at least on paper, which was a holdover from the old
civil rights business; but basically, Bootie figured you could take
a lot for granted. Or not? Maybe *Monitor* readers would have
only the vaguest sense who Murray Thwaite even was. Which
would mean that Bootie should begin at the beginning, in
Watertown, and provide all the background stuff: more fact,
less opinion.

Yes, that would be the way to bulk it out. A sort of mini-
biography. He realized that he didn't really know all that much
about his uncle, in *that* way. Not where he'd lived or what he'd
done, exactly, when. He knew other stuff: the family myth, the
aura, the Thwaite household atmosphere. For the rest, he could
ask his mother—which he wouldn't do—or rely on the research

of others. Leaving the lamby room for Murray's study and its residual nicotine breeze, Bootie sat down to Google his uncle. Knowing the man as he now did, he felt disappointingly certain that Murray, sitting in this chair, would have more than once Googled himself. One of the items near the top of the list was a profile from the Columbia University student newspaper, by one Roanne Levine. When he read it, Bootie found himself wondering, given its gush, whether she, too, had been seduced by his uncle. He could almost hear her breathlessness in the article's sentences. He, himself, needed a different, cooler tone.

Bootie worked on his article all night and past dawn. Several times he foraged for sustenance in the kitchen, finding, among other things, a Mars bar so long hidden behind the phone book that the chocolate had turned white. As he ate it, he thought about whose it might be: which Thwaite hid candy? Perhaps it had once been Aurora's. He consumed, also, two fruit yogurts, a bowl of cereal, and half of a large bag of potato chips, the expensive kind, in a heavy paper bag, of some elaborate flavor that approximated sour cream and onion. At about 6:30 a.m., before he finally went to sleep, he ambled back to the kitchen and finished the bag. Not because he was hungry, because at that point he was really only sleepy, but because it seemed a quiet aggression, a gesture against Murray that would never even be remarked. It satisfied him, anyway.

After considering the possibilities carefully, Bootie had decided not to mention Danielle in the piece. It was his concession to Annabel, of whom he was quite fond; and to Marina, too. She didn't deserve the double blow of her father's and her best friend's villainy revealed at once. He couldn't leave it out altogether, but had drawn the line at vague innuendo. He was quite pleased with his formulation, slipped into a passage about Murray's purported transparency, which in fact (according to Bootie) masked a willful and powerful obfuscation, not to say dishonesty. He'd put an entire little sentence in parentheses, between two other sentences: "(Murray Thwaite is similarly complicated and opaque when it comes to his personal life, a series of emotional entanglements pursued with Machiavellian efficiency for maximum personal benefit.)" Bootie liked the use of "Machiavellian," which to him evoked a lot of gleeful hand-rubbing. He didn't think any but the most astute would understand what he was really trying to say.

Bootie hadn't been asleep long when he was wakened by someone moving in the apartment. Opening and shutting doors, running water. Frankly banging things. At first he didn't know where he was. Then he didn't know what time it was—eight a.m.—and still further, he couldn't place the noises. It occurred to him that perhaps one of the doormen—maybe Milos, the burly Serb—made use of the Thwaites' apartment when they were away. But something about the racket struck him as angry. At the least, irked. Someone was making a point.

Bootie put on his glasses and rubbed at his curls. He went to see. As he made his way down the hall, he observed that he had not perhaps comported himself like an ideal guest. His shoes and socks lay strewn across the corridor. In the living room, the sofa cushions were piled upon the floor—he'd tried, briefly, to find a comfortable position there in which to work. An empty yogurt container and a sticky spoon were stuck to the glass coffee table. He ventured over to the kitchen: some-one had spirited his greasy plate from his bedroom and placed it by the sink. While he was sleeping. Someone had swept up the potato chips he had spilled on the floor, and had left them in a reproachful mound near the stove. The empty milk carton lurked balefully upon the counter, next to the coffeemaker, through which fresh coffee was actually trickling. Puffy, bleary, sickish, Bootie understood that someone—female—had come home. Unexpectedly.

He poured coffee for himself, sniffled, waited. She would certainly soon appear. He considered that everywhere he laid his head he was essentially unwelcome. With luck he would not, just now, be insulted. She would not call him fat. But he could with justification be accused of gross slobbery. He stepped on some Special K, pulverizing it beneath his bare heel. The abandoned Mars bar wrapper fluttered forlornly on the countertop in the air-conditioning wind. Poor Bootie, he thought. Nobody wants me. Poor Bootie. Then he thought of his mother, who did want him. He thought of her as a grasping, winged monster, her glittering, sorrowful eyes teary, her badly permed hair a fright, her spreading body swollen into all of Watertown, the ugly, dilapidated maw of it, trying to swallow him up, bring him home. He cleared his throat. He would rather be alone and unwanted than ordinary. He thought he would. But he hadn't imagined a loneliness like this. He hadn't known it could exist, nor that it would make him so sad and angry.

"Bootie. You're up."

"Annabel." Recently showered, she was dressed for work, lean and beige, leafing through papers as she entered the room.

"It was a surprise," she said, without looking up. "I somehow thought you'd found a place."

"I'm sorry. It's just—I was working on stuff and it's a long way back, and it's so *hot*."

"Better today, actually. I drove from Stockbridge this morning, and it was pretty fresh up there."

Bootie nodded, but she still wasn't looking at him. She frowned, quite strongly, at something she saw in her papers.

"I'm off to court right now," she said. And here she glanced at him at last. "Are you here for supper?"

"Not—I don't think so. I mean, definitely not."

"Okay, well, we'll see you soon, then. But could you please pick up before you go?"

Bootie started to mumble—he wanted her to understand that he hadn't known she would be coming, that he wouldn't have made a mess if he had.

"Because it's, you know, a holiday for Aurora, too."

At the front door, she apparently relented, and called to him, "Are you absolutely sure you don't want to come out to Stockbridge tomorrow? I'm driving back, probably with Marina's friend Danielle."

He went to join her as she waited for the elevator. "Thanks, but I can't. Too busy with this article."

"Article?"

"For Marina. She asked. For her magazine."

Annabel, distracted, smiled halfway. "They're getting married, you know. Isn't that exciting?"

"Who?"

"Marina and Ludo." The elevator doors opened, and Milos rose from his stool to hold the machinery still while they finished their conversation. "We're celebrating tomorrow."

"They're getting married?"

"Not tomorrow. In September. Soon enough."

Bootie didn't know what to say.

"It'd be great if you could get that duvet cover in the machine," Annabel added as Milos moved to close the door. "Just spray some Shout on it, on those stains."

"They're lamb," he said. It seemed important that she know. But she'd gone.

Bootie, wounded by Annabel's briskness, tried to tidy as effectively as he could. He knew—his mother always complained of it—that he had no talent for cleanliness. "It's about learning to see the dirt," his mother always said, as if dirt were language, or music.

This news about Marina: he couldn't let it go. He wanted to believe that there was some misunderstanding, but knew better. He had watched Marina—when was he not watching Marina? The pleasure, and the sorrow, that her movements caused him, was physical—and had seen her hands turn to birds at her throat, her eyes open wider and brighten, her broad mouth seem itself to lift—all this in conversation with Seeley, Ludovic, that long lying lover, his aristocratic slouch not unlike the first letter of his name, as though he were always oozing earthward, slinking away. At first, that very first night when she'd met him, when Bootie had joined the group in the living room after Murray's awards dinner, even then he'd seen on her face as she followed Seeley the particular eagerness, the luminous attention, which she tried—just as he, Bootie, always tried, when speaking to Marina—and failed, to conceal. He'd thought, then, that Danielle was envious, that the two women vied for Seeley's attention; but in retrospect, he must have been wrong. He should have been keeping an eye on Murray. He'd been a naïf, all those weeks ago, and the possibility of such goatishness hadn't occurred to him. He'd still been a believer.

Bootie lingered in the living room after picking up the cushions, the yogurt container, its attendant spoon: remembered the quality of the lamplight, that early evening, the enticing way the women's hair gleamed in its glow, the peachy pool, like warmth, on the white sofas. He had come out of his room when he'd heard the voices, the laughter, and had slid down the hall in shadow, had lurked, eavesdropping, in the kitchen; until Marina, surprising him there, had invited him to join them. It had felt like Christmas. He'd known she was just being polite, but her kindness, like Annabel's, moved him, made him feel as though something, some small cog in his chest, actually shifted. He'd been that grateful. And then he had watched, watched everything from a hard chair just outside the illuminated circle, had hovered, unnoticed, like some privileged ghost. He'd half-listened, too, but his excitement and anxiety had been such, and the voice in his head so loud—This is it. This, at last. Here the heady salons of wisdom and the freedom of intellectual discourse; the thrill of the life of the mind, of the life so long imagined, so meatily conjured, just like *this,* when lying in the mustard yellow bathtub in his mother's house in Watertown, always fearing that Life would never come to him, or he to it, and here It was, in its subdued but beautiful splendor, a small group, all ages, talking, laughing, smoking, listening, as if in Madame de Staël's living room, or in the court of Catherine the Great, or at Rahv's house after a *Partisan Review* meeting. The thinkers of the ages had always done this, the Life, this, its purpose—that he had barely taken in what was actually discussed. Nobody spoke to him, after the introductions, but

Danielle had smiled encouragingly his way a few times, in that manner he found both reassuring and irritating. Even the exchange between Danielle and Ludovic hadn't spoiled it for him. They had all seemed witty and he'd felt as though he were slightly deaf, or listening to a language he knew only imperfectly, as though he were missing phrases, references, piecing together a brightly colored, impressionistic whole from only partial information. He couldn't have known how partial: how much he'd learned about Murray since that star-struck night; and here, not so very long after, Marina and Ludovic Seeley were to marry.

CHAPTER THIRTY-NINE

The Fourth of July (1)

Julius couldn't quite believe he hadn't gone. Or rather, he had gone to bed for what was to have been an hour, and had been wakened four hours later by David, on the cell, from the Metro North station out in Westchester, wondering where the hell he was, his sexy irascibility erupted into full-blown ire. Julius had been able honestly to croak, to cough, to lament his throbbing headache, his fluctuating body temperature, his streaming nose.

"It's some kind of summer flu, you know? It's really bizarre. I was up most of the night. I set the alarm to call you, but I must have slept through."

"So you didn't work on your article after all?" David's contempt was clear.

"Come home and take care of me, baby. I'm sick as the proverbial dog."

"This is unbelievable. My mother—"

"All mother-son relationships are sick. She'll be thrilled to have you to herself."

"You have no idea how much trouble she's gone to."

"Look, if you really want Typhoid Mary, I can drag myself

out of my rank bed, here, and lurch toward you on winds of vomit."

"Great."

"Even sick, I am your love slave."

"That's good to know. But you're hugely letting me down."

"I'll make it up to you. You know I will."

"You can come tomorrow."

"Exactly. I can come tomorrow."

But on the morrow, Julius claimed to be no better. He couldn't entirely have explained why. He stayed in, he cooked an omelet, he had a long, cool bath. The day after, he contemplated again reneging, but, recognizing that his momentary yen for peace and solitude could easily result in the end of his relationship, he relented.

The Cohen celebration of July Fourth was less difficult than it might have been. They had a swimming pool, which helped, and a selection of seven cousins aged from nine to seventy-three, many of them good-looking, like David. A number of neighbors were also in attendance, bearing trays of smoked salmon and bowls of potato salad. The Cohens served Prosecco alongside the canonical beer, and in the brief hour before it began to rain and they all moved inside, Julius was able to joke, to a still grumpy David, that lounging poolside with a flute of bubbly made him a queen in mud. This was when David coined the nickname Queen Muck, or Lady Muck, which he subsequently, and to Julius's irritation, eagerly employed, almost like a weapon.

After the storms had passed, they gathered, damp but unbowed, and watched the local fireworks, he and David hand in hand on the lawn by the Scarsdale pool, theirs an intimacy that the Cohen parents graciously ignored (Frank Clarke loved his boy, but Julius knew no self-respecting Midwestern football coach could stand for two boys holding hands in public. On his own familial territory he would never have dared such a thing), and they slept—in twin beds—in David's childhood room. Julius put on his best show of manners, charming Mrs. Cohen's aunt and giving piggyback rides to the littlest cousin, a sturdy boy with buck teeth, named Owen.

In the train on the way back, on Thursday morning, Julius told David he'd had a wonderful time. "Your parents couldn't have been more welcoming. Thank you."

David looked up from the Business section of the *Times*. "They could have been more welcoming, actually. They would have. They wanted to. Two days' more welcoming, as you well know. But you didn't show up."

"That's not fair. I was sick. I wasn't making it up."

"Fine, you were sick. But you don't seem to appreciate what a big deal this was for my mother."

"Or for you, it seems like."

David's hair was rumpled, his eyes behind his glasses wide, his skin office-pale. "Or for me. I guess that's right."

"If I'd known I had the power to enrage you, I would've done it sooner. It's very attractive."

David looked over his shoulder at this.

"Afraid Daddy's on the train? Or Daddy's Westchester golf buddies? Don't worry, sweetheart, they all know you're a big old fag."

"Please," David said, looking back to the paper. "Not here. Not now."

"You surprise me," Julius persisted. "Are you afraid of being outed to a bunch of men in suits? Or is it that you might know them? What is it, Davey? You can tell me."

"If you don't shut up right now, I'm going to move seats and pretend that I don't know you. Seriously."

Julius could tell he wasn't joking. "Two can play at that game, sweetheart," he said, and held the Arts section up to his nose. He saw at once that one of his erstwhile rivals in the *Village Voice* office, a plain, plump woman named Sophie—still plain and plump, in her headshot—was having her first novel reviewed. Favorably. She was three years younger than he. He wanted very powerfully, in that moment, to be with Marina or Danielle. With people who would understand all the different ways at once in which he felt horrible. But just then, it felt that he would never get them back: he'd made his bargain, had chosen David, and now that's all there was. No career. No novel, that was for sure. No friends. Just David, who didn't understand.

CHAPTER FORTY

The Fourth of July (2)

Danielle had been anxious about the car ride with Annabel. She didn't know what they'd say to each other, given how changed, and how charged, their relationship, or nonrelationship, now was. Danielle felt overwhelmed by Thwaites, and by guilt, of course. Annabel had always been kind to her. She contemplated taking the train instead, but decided both that this would seem too peculiar, and also that fate must have thrown her together with Annabel for a reason. Certainly her mother would have thought so.

In the event, she need not have worried. It transpired, in the car at least, that Danielle's repressive mechanisms were Yale-tight: if Annabel had no doubts, and if, for Annabel, their relationship remained unchanged, then surely it remained, for all intents and purposes, precisely that? It was, yet again, a matter of fact and perception, and the question of which constituted reality. Danielle deemed it both pleasant and uncomplicated to inhabit Annabel's prelapsarian vision, and discovered, to her surprise and satisfaction, that she was able to do so entirely without complication, without, indeed, any sense whatsoever that she was perpetrating a deception. Their ride together was, inspiringly, as their conversations had ever been.

Danielle in fact remembered their talk, the spring night of the Chinese food, the night, as she saw it, when "it" all began, a chat about Annabel's client, the troubled boy, and recognized the outlines of that case in the scenario Annabel was here describing. The previous morning, before the judge, had not gone so well, and the boy was in the custody of the court. The only way this could possibly have been avoided, Annabel thought, would have been for her to offer to take him home for the week.

"The judge just might have agreed," she said. "But I didn't ask. It's a moral failing, I feel, but—"

"It's the Fourth of July. And Marina's engagement."

"Oh, there are so many reasons. But mostly it was the look on Murray's face that I kept picturing. I don't know that his sense of humor would extend to Independence Day in Stockbridge with DeVaughn."

Danielle almost said something then—something innocuous like "I bet he wouldn't like it"—but she worried that the tone might seem strange, or her inflection brittle, and so instead she looked through the windscreen at the asphalt ahead and smiled in a vague but agreeable way. She sensed that Annabel was deeply embarrassed with herself, that she felt she had failed a test.

"Ludovic was saying the other night that I'm wrong to impose my values, my belief, my culture on someone like DeVaughn. I disagreed with him then, but maybe he's right. I think it would've been better to bring DeVaughn to Stockbridge rather than have him spend the holiday in jail—because that's essentially where he'll be—but for whom would it have been better? Certainly not for any of us—I suppose you could say I chose my daughter's well-being over DeVaughn's—and maybe not even for him. What do you think?"

"I think Ludovic is very good at making us all doubt ourselves and second-guess our decisions. But if it works, hey, who's to complain?"

Annabel didn't reply.

"I mean that if his fluid logic helps you to understand and feel okay about leaving DeVaughn in the system, then that's great."

Annabel still did not speak, perhaps because of a knot of traffic, but it was hard to be sure. Danielle, tortured, elaborated further. She wished she knew whether Annabel liked or disliked Seeley. She was always cagey about such things. "I don't mean that you're *justifying*—or, well, if I do, I don't mean that you're justifying without justification. It's just that it seems to be a tactic of his."

"What does?"

"Seeley—he seems to want to make you feel good. One, I mean. But actually, I always think he's imposing his vision of the world while giving you the illusion that it's your own. He wants to be Napoleon, you know."

"My goodness. A bit late for that, isn't it?"

"Not literally, of course. But that's the effect. He wants people to follow him. He wants to revolutionize and control their whole lives."

"Are we talking about the same Ludovic Seeley who is so good at helping in the kitchen and is going to marry my daughter?"

"I know it doesn't seem possible. But he's very frank about his ambitions. Ask him."

Annabel laughed. "I think he wants to be the most successful magazine editor in New York. He wants to outdo Tina Brown at her height. That's my impression."

Danielle smiled again at the road, vaguely. There were a great many trees along the highway, and they were oppressively lush. The light was hazy. She marveled, faintly, at her own forthrightness with Annabel. Somehow, because of Murray perhaps, she felt she'd made a generational shift: as if she were Marina's aunt, instead of her friend, or at the same time as she was her friend. Danielle felt she was a palimpsest, many people, all at once.

"Which is not to say that he has no substance," Annabel went on. "Politically, obviously, he's not in the same camp as Murray, or even me. But he has integrity."

"Wow. I'm not sure that's a word I would've used in connection with him."

The trees loomed as they went by, trees upon trees, endless and verdant.

"If you feel strongly about him, maybe you should say something to Marina. She *is* planning to marry him, after all."

"I know. It's not very easy."

"If I felt my best friend was about to make a fatal mistake—"

"Yes, but then you'd be guilty all over again of what Seeley accuses you of. You'd be imposing your point of view, without considering whether it was best for your friend."

"So Seeley might, in your opinion, be a bad man but good for Marina?"

"I'm not saying that. I'm saying that he would say it was possible." Danielle paused. "And I suppose I'm saying that right now I don't think I'd say anything to her about my feelings. They're just my feelings."

"Feelings." Annabel sniffed. "It's all we've got to go on. And I'm feeling terrible about DeVaughn."

"He would've been miserable in this car. And at your house. Miserable."

"But we don't *know* that."

"Yes, we do."

Annabel and Danielle arrived at Stockbridge just before noon. It had started to spit with rain, and the blown branches were showing their undersides, heralding a storm.

"Not quite what we envisaged," Annabel said as they pulled up the drive. "No barbecue today."

"No naps in the pergola, either," said Danielle. It had always been one of her favorite things to do at the Thwaites' country house, to retreat behind the screens with a book and a glass of lemonade and end up dozing on the bench, which was at once uncomfortable and oddly pleasing. "Maybe we'll all play Monopoly."

"Maybe," said Annabel. "Something like that."

At least Murray wasn't around when they went in. Ludovic was reading in an armchair by the French doors to the garden, and Marina lay stretched along the sofa, eating half a bagel. She licked the melting butter off her fingers like a cat.

"You're here!" She sprang up and, without relinquishing the bagel, threw her arms around Danielle's neck. Danielle wondered if she was getting butter in her hair. "It's such a relief. There's practically a tornado watch on."

"Your mother drove like the wind."

"She never does. I was betting Ludo you wouldn't make it before lunch."

"Where's your father?" Annabel was already on her way upstairs.

"Working, I think. In your room."

It was easier not to witness the Thwaites' reunion. Danielle wanted their affection—or lack of it—to be hidden from her.

"Got anything for lunch?" she said, half as a joke—on account of the bagel—aware, as she did so, that she and Ludovic had not directly greeted each other. As if he knew what she thought of him. Or as if he thought the same of her. She touched his shoulder, deliberately. "Hey, congratulations, you two."

He all but clicked his heels. Hard to do, in flip-flops, she wanted to tell someone but couldn't.

"September, eh? That's very soon."

"We're going to hear that a lot. But the plan is to have a JP, have it here, so it shouldn't be difficult to organize."

They were discussing plans at the kitchen table when eventually Murray came downstairs. Danielle heard his tread, thought she could feel herself flush. When he came into the room, she stood and turned, but slowly, in order fully to compose herself, and found herself mysteriously, guttingly, faced with the Murray Thwaite she had known for years, the amiable, distracted patrician patriarch whose unfocused but benevolent gaze seemed to slide over her like water. He shook her hand and kissed her cheek, and in these gestures she sought some acknowledgment—an extra pressure, a single whispered word, even a lingering glance—but his mask was so complete, so impenetrable, that Danielle wondered, fleetingly, if their intimacy were merely her imagining; wondered, too, if he thought she was a whore—somehow there was an insult implicit in the very success of his play-acting—and whether this whole thing, in all its madness, were invention. He moved on, poured coffee, lit a cigarette, asked about arrangements for the afternoon ("If I'm not grilling, I need to know what my task is"), asked Ludovic what he'd been reading, planted a kiss effortlessly (enviably) upon the crown of his daughter's head— in so doing he allowed his eyes, for an infinitesimal moment, to meet Danielle's, a moment that, in optimism, she took to designate the kiss as hers although it fell upon Marina—and vanished back up the stairs.

Only after he had left the room did Danielle breathe normally again; or so it seemed. She could smell his gin-and-tonic smell even after he had gone. She realized that she didn't know what Marina was saying, and that she'd been holding her mug of iced tea to her mouth possibly for minutes, as if it were warm and as if it were winter, as if steaming her cheeks. The prospect of twenty-four hours seemed suddenly long indeed.

"What color flowers for the bouquet?" she asked. "Or what kind of flowers, anyway?"

"Well," Marina said, "I'm torn between a bunch of late wildflowers—you know, Queen Anne's lace and coneflowers and salvia, something like that that's really from here, you know, that shows the beauty of this place; or else something more sophisticated, like, I don't know, half a dozen calla lilies tied with a ribbon."

As she said "lilies," Seeley, yawning, nodded and pointed a finger.

"I'm not sure the groom is supposed to decide on the bouquet."

"Oh, I'll have my finger in every pie," Seeley replied, with his languid smile. "As you know, it's my little way."

"Will you choose the dress, too?"

"If I could." He grinned, took a cherry from the bowl in the center of the table, and placed it roundly in his mouth. "But Marina is a paragon of taste, and if she's choosing the right bouquet, she'll definitely get the dress right." He spat the pit into his closed hand and magicked it away. "It's everyone else's attire that perturbs me."

Danielle was hardly listening, and her smile felt stuck. It was the most peculiar sensation: Was this what going mad was like? She might have imagined his glance, not seen it; and failing that, he hadn't in any way acknowledged her. She told herself she hadn't expected him to, but how could she not have? Till now, she hadn't fully accepted the force of her desire, and in this context it was not only shameful, as an adulterous affair must be, but just plain embarrassing, too. As if she were in love with her father. Marina's father is who he was here, not the ironic, ursine courtier who visited her apartment alone and at odd hours, or who half-rose from his chair in his shambolic aristocratic way when she entered a bar or restaurant. Danielle was blushing—the memory of her cheek upon his chest, the texture of his earlobe, with its minute fuzz, the edible smell of him—and Seeley laughed.

"I'm not impugning your fashion sense," he said. "Granted, you're not at your best today, Danielle, but by and large you do quite well."

"That's big of you."

"Although you should wear heels. You're small."

"Thanks a lot. That's what my mother says, too."

"Danny's mother is a trip. Her name is Randy."

"Randy by name, randy by nature."

"If you can believe it, the joke's been made before. But it couldn't be further from the truth."

"I met her," said Seeley, ingesting another cherry. "At the Metropolitan. When I first met you." He gazed, with affected longing, at Marina.

"Oh fateful day," Danielle said. "It sure seems a long time ago."

"Even though it isn't," Marina said. "It isn't long ago at all."

All afternoon, Danielle had the weird, sparkling sensation that something was about to happen. Because how could it not? So much emotion was pent up in her that surely it must—like telepathy, like ghosts—move furniture, people, events. A catalytic emotion. But this anticipation was hers alone: she could sense, albeit dimly, that for the rest of the household (except, of course, for Murray, conveniently sequestered, at work on a piece), this was truly a day of rest. Intermittently, Marina and Seeley twined themselves together like snakes. They read. Played Monopoly. Watched the rain. Engaged in desultory chat. Annabel came and went; made an apple pie; put on an anorak and plastic clogs and fetched lettuce from the garden. They all gathered in the great room (again with the exception of Murray; she dreaded seeing him among them, but couldn't bear not to. How could he be in a room directly overhead, seconds away, and so utterly inaccessible?) to watch the biggest afternoon thunderstorm. The trees bent double. The screens in the pergola flashed. The house was so tightly sealed—"Like a ship," Annabel said. "We had them build it like a ship"—that the storm seemed strangely silent, a dumbshow of writhing foliage and driving rain, punctuated only by the thunder, which seemed to boom through the floorboards and vibrate in their feet. It was simultaneously involving and irrelevant, Danielle thought, as the firmament flickered. Above all, explosive. Like her feelings for Murray. Perhaps this was her telepathic effect; in which case, while not auspicious, it was at least not wantonly destructive. As she thought this, a large branch at the bottom of the garden snapped and dropped, narrowly missing the pergola.

Murray emerged only later, like the brief flash of sunshine that slid between the afternoon clouds. He stood, cigarette in hand, on the slick stone patio, surveying the garden. "Looks like I'll be called upon to grill after all," he said. "So I'll go get in another hour before I do. Joseph wants to run this piece about the ramifications of pulling out of Kyoto ahead of the talks in Bonn."

"Your father is obsessed with the barbecue," Seeley observed when he'd gone.

"It's the only cooking he's ever done, and he's very proud of it."

"I might go have a nap." Danielle thought it was now or never.

"You've got at least an hour." Marina gave her one of her smiles. "I'll come and wake you up. We can have some girl time."

"Talk about me, you mean," said Seeley.

"You wish." Marina kissed him on the cheek.

Danielle knew where he ought to be, in which room. It was

at the opposite end of the hall from hers, around a corner. There was no other reason to go there but him. Inevitably, the door was shut. Danielle stood outside it, aware of the thick pile of the carpet beneath her feet, looking at the clouds blowing past through the hallway's small, high window. She listened. She contemplated knocking. But if Annabel were there—she might just have heard voices behind the door, softly, although he could always be speaking to himself; she'd heard him do it— then what would she say? She couldn't pretend to be lost, after all these years visiting. She could have a question, but didn't. If he knew she were in her room for an hour he would come to her, wouldn't he, even for a few moments? Just for an innocent word. Just for a fleeting embrace. Or not. Because it was possible he'd all but forgotten that she was there, or that her being there was significant. Men were good at this sort of thing, Randy always said. "Look at your father," she used to say. "Compartmentalizing. It's like cows having four stomachs. It seems like sophistication but actually it's the sign of a more primitive organism."

Danielle sighed (audibly, she hoped, even as she hoped not) and retreated to her little blue bedroom, with its toile de Jouy draperies and cushions, its turned-post single bed, the blue rag rug underfoot a little more frayed than the previous year, all of it suddenly a cozy celebration of her spinsterhood, her supposed celibacy. There was another unused bedroom, at the front of the house, a green room, with a double bed. But they'd never put her there. It had never seemed pointed until now.

When Marina woke Danielle she was drooling and had the quilt stitching imprinted on her cheek. The weather had passed and the late sun sent shafts of fierce light across the lawn.

Danielle opened the window, and the air smelled washed, in the momentary way of high summer after a storm. Marina plumped herself at the end of the bed, fiddled with the bed-posts, while Danielle fought her way back to alertness.

"Why don't you like him?" Marina asked.

"Who?"

"Come off it, Danny."

"I like him, I like him. I don't *know* him, for God's sakes."

"You really wanted me to meet him—and now you wish you hadn't arranged it."

"That's ridiculous."

"I feel as though we're drifting, you know?"

"You're in love, silly. You forget: it's consuming. And if we drift a little, well, isn't that in the nature of things?"

"We've known each other more than ten years."

"Look at Julius. Maybe it's just that time of life. You know. People get married."

"Not you, though."

"Not yet. Who knows, maybe never."

"But you're not even trying."

"What's that supposed to mean? I didn't realize you'd been trying."

"You know what I'm saying. I worry that you're too wrapped up in your career to let go."

"You mean, I'm too uptight to fall in love?"

Marina, legs crossed, cocked her head prettily. She looked intolerably smug. Danielle couldn't bear it. "What if I told you I *am* in love?"

Marina grabbed at Danielle's ankles with both hands. "I knew it. 'Beloved! Come to me, beloved!' Who is he?"

"That's absurd. That's my mother I was expecting. No, the point about being in love—it's inappropriate."

"What does that mean?"

"It's—it's—unrequited. That's the word I want."

"Oh. I'm sorry."

"No, don't be. It's also—I mean, it's also inappropriate. So better that it's unrequited."

"Is he eighteen?" Marina's voice took on a gleeful pitch. "Is he older? He's not married, is he?"

Danielle shrugged. "I shouldn't have said anything. It doesn't matter."

"Of course it does. You can always talk to me." Marina, Danielle could tell, was itching to hear more, partly because she felt genuine anguish for her friend (if only she knew) and partly because she loved gossip.

"End of story. There is no story. Just don't think I have no heart, or anything. It's just that my affections are misdirected."

"That sounds serious. I'll get it out of you, you know."

"Why don't you find me someone suitable instead?"

"Because if you're really smitten, that will never work, will it? It's not Nicky, is it?"

"Please." Danielle pulled a face. "It's not Julius either, in case you wondered."

"Do I know him?"

"I don't think so. Let's leave it alone, okay?"

Marina still had her hands on Danielle's bare ankles, and she gave them a squeeze before letting go.

Before supper—if the curious holiday meal served in the late afternoon could be called supper: it represented a disruption of mealtimes that occurred also at Thanksgiving, and clearly at

Christmas for those who celebrated it, and that always unsettled Danielle, who relied on a strong innate order in the unfolding of her days—expensive champagne was produced, with which to toast the happy couple. Danielle drank two glasses rather quickly and felt herself, in her dizzy float, better able to cope with, indeed to ignore, the surrounding strangeness. She helped Annabel to set the table outside, which first involved much mopping with tea towels, and then, in what, for all her detachment, approached desperation, she ambled over to Murray, who stood and smoked by the barbecue.

"You seem a dab hand at this," she said.

He glanced at her, barely. "That I am. Marina probably told you, it's my chief culinary expertise." His voice sounded as though it were being recorded for radio, an iota too hearty. She wondered whether anyone else would have noticed.

"She did tell me, in fact." Danielle couldn't think what else to say. She waited for Murray to volunteer something.

"Shame you don't smoke," he said at last. "Marina said you'd object to my smoking over the meat."

"It doesn't really bother me. I find one can get used to anything." She was looking at the grill, now, and not at him, but she thought his eyes were on her.

"That's the spirit," he said. "Adapt to the circumstances at hand." She stood a moment longer, made as if to go. "She wants you to be her bridesmaid, I think."

"Yes, I think so."

"An honorary member of the family."

"I hadn't really thought of it that way." She waited again, but he seemed to be done, wholly absorbed in the turning of chicken legs and hamburgers.

She drifted back into the kitchen, aware that her limbs moved loosely, that her demeanor projected—must project—cool indifference. This was the exquisite torture: not guilt, as she had anticipated. Not awkwardness either with Marina or her mother, as those relationships seemed—were!—unchanged. No, the alien was her intimate, the man she felt she so thoroughly understood, with whom she would now reluctantly have conceded she was in love (and how foolish was that?), who seemed, infuriatingly, impossibly, inevitably, to be able to turn her off like a switch, to relegate her to the realm of the irrelevant, a playmate for his daughter merely to be tolerated, and, ideally, escaped. She wanted to repeat his blandishments aloud at the table. The shock of it. She wanted to remind him, whether his family was there or not. She wanted. And wanted. And endured in her wanting: the damp seat, the dry chicken, more champagne, the headache the champagne brought, the midges, the chat, his failure, no, refusal, to look, look at me, I caused a thunderstorm with my passion and I sit here shaking under my skin and you don't notice because you're trying so hard not to notice, but of all the people at the table there are really only you and me and you know it, the air is charged with it, it's a heat, a hot wind, and Marina and Seeley are a sham next to it, Annabel ceases to exist, is simply obliterated in the gale of it, this isn't a fantasy, not my imagination, I can tell by the way you lift your fork, by the set of your jaw, by that sixth cigarette, you are smoking me, or would if you could; but how long can we sustain it, how long till the eruption, till the storm returns again and they can all see what it is, what it really is?

"You're very quiet tonight, Danny," observed Annabel.

"Must be the nap. I sleep so well here. I think I never woke up properly from my nap."

"It may be the barometric pressure," said Seeley. "It affects some people."

"And some people claim that caffeine keeps them awake at night, too," said Murray, extinguishing the sixth cigarette, like the rest, half-smoked.

Danielle suddenly saw, through the fog, or storm, of her will, how very little Murray liked the man his daughter was going to marry. They were not alone at the table, or in the world. Ordinary as it was, the recognition pained her—she didn't want to admit the ordinary—and released her.

Later, by herself, she sat at the table and watched the fireflies flicker across the lawn in the dusk, and breathed the damp blue air. Murray, fetching the grill tongs to be washed, paused a moment behind her in the dark, and placed his hand full on her crown like a warm cap. He said nothing, and was gone; but it was all she had wanted; benison.

CHAPTER FORTY-ONE

The Fourth of July (3)

"I think Danny's in love with you," Marina told Ludovic as they undressed.

"With me?"

"She's in love with someone inappropriate, she says. It's unrequited. And she won't tell me who he is."

"Maybe 'he' is a 'she'?"

"Seriously, Ludo. It just occurred to me—all her talk about you before we met, and she wanted to make that movie about you, and then when we started going out, she maybe couldn't bear it—that would explain how weird she's been." Marina was rubbing lemon-scented lotion into her calves. "You know, Julius even suggested it. He asked me if Danielle was in love with you, and I laughed. My God, I feel so bad."

"Why would you feel bad?"

"She, you know, entertained hopes. She still does. She's in love, she told me so."

"It may well be some other inappropriate choice. I'm sure there are plenty of them."

"But if it's you?"

"Then she fails to take into account the emotions of the

person whom she loves. She is, therefore, a poor lover, and your sympathy should be limited."

"That's not very nice of you."

"Seriously. It's narcissism, to love a wall and resent it for not loving you back. It's perversity. Love is mutual, it flourishes in reciprocity. You can't have real love without a return of affection—otherwise, it's just obsession, and projection. It's childish."

"So in fact, I should feel mild irritation at her, for not growing up."

"Something like that."

"You have a way, don't you? You turn everything on its head."

"I have a way, yes." He laughed, drily. "Your friend Danielle calls it my revolution. It's just my desire that people should see things more clearly."

"Or your way. Depending on how you look at it."

"It always depends on *that*. For the record, I don't think your friend is in love with me. I'm not just being modest. There seemed an initial, faint signal of interest, which I nobly and appropriately ignored—"

"Why?"

"Because she's not my type. Because I was waiting for you. And since then, nothing. A heart of stone. If anything, she's angry with me."

"Now *that's* preposterous."

"For taking you away from her. No, I'm not saying anything strange here. She's your best friend, accustomed to having unlimited access and, let's face it, in some ways accustomed to having a life more fully organized than yours—the apparently successful job, the apartment. And then suddenly, you're not just more beautiful and more interesting, you're also engaged and employed and on to the next stage. You don't need her advice anymore. It has to be painful." Leaning back in bed, Ludovic put his hands behind his head. "Maybe *you're* her inappropriate love object. Did you ever think of that? Not sexually, necessarily, although I wouldn't rule that out. But either way, you were at the center of her world, and now you aren't."

"Have I been a bad friend?"

"For the first time in living memory, you've been following your own path. There is only right in that."

"You've saved my life."

"The mission isn't accomplished yet. After all, we're still in your father's house." He embraced her, stroked her brown arm. "But not for long, my sweet. Not for long."

CHAPTER FORTY-TWO

Let Go

Recovering from the misfortunes of the Fourth was, for Julius and David, a somewhat mixed effort. On the one hand, their routines resumed—David's long hours at the office; the passionate reunions in the evenings; the summer social whirl of cocktails, suppers, parties—and on another, Julius, at least, felt that things were altered. Perhaps his own ardor had cooled. Or rather, one branch of it had. He no longer tingled with the same anticipation, no longer found David's possessiveness, his Othello-like grip, erotic. It felt, instead, the tiniest bit oppressive. It was like waking from a dream: he looked back and could see the way he'd felt, but couldn't exactly feel it again. He couldn't be a stay-at-home wife forever: somehow, he and David would have to renegotiate their dynamic. He needed more room. And yet still, inevitably, the thought of David with someone else appalled, infuriated; and the evenings when David was late, failed to call, Julius fretted, then pouted, and, when he was cooking, deliberately sabotaged the meal. Burned stew, soggy asparagus, separated sauces: look what you made me do.

Just over two weeks after their trip to Scarsdale, on a Friday, David did not come home, nor did he call. They'd planned to

dine in, take it easy, then to stroll over to a party at a neighborhood bar, the Florentine, around eleven. Julius, after a
couple of glasses of wine, after a line or two, dialed David's cell
phone and hung up on the tinny digital recording. Eventually,
after eating half of the green duck curry he'd prepared, and after
tossing the rest maliciously in the garbage, Julius, in high dudg-
eon, rang the office. But it was Friday and everyone had gone
home. He tried David's cell one more time, and one more time
after that. He dressed for the party—it was a party given by
David's friends Ned and Tristan, so surely David would put in
an appearance there—in true Natasha style: he tried on six
shirts before he found one that pleased him, one of David's,
Italian and close-fitting with a gleaming azure cross thread, and
he left the other five not simply on the floor but trampled
underfoot. He threw towels on the bathroom floor; he
deposited gelatinous globs of shaving cream, speckled with
beard bristles, in the sink, along with chalky toothpaste spittle.
He tried on jackets as he had tried on shirts, collecting, at his
ankles, a swirling flood of expensive cloth that he kicked at with
his shiny black shoes. For good measure, he shot his foot at a
stack of glossy magazines on David's side of the bed, and they
slipped, with the ease of a trickling fountain, into the fray. He
opened dresser drawers—the chic, handleless dresser with
modern lines to which David was partial—and discarded their
contents and left the drawers open.

Contained in the bedroom, the signs of his pique were discreet, Julius felt. David, fickle and self-absorbed, merited
worse. By the time Julius left for the Florentine, at half past
eleven, David was six unannounced hours late.

David's friends never skimped—there were Belvedere martinis at the bar, and kir royales for the faint-hearted; there were bowls of immense, pinkly gleaming shrimp and extended mar- tial rows of black and white sushi. A cornucopia of cut fruit spilled artfully onto a table at the back of the room. Even in the blue gloom, Julius could tell that the flower arrangements were elaborate. The music, at first, allowed conversation; and then, as if the DJ concurred with Julius about the pointlessness of talking to this group, he turned up the volume. Dancing was presumably encouraged: a woman, no longer young, with a salt-and-pepper mane and a prominent nose, a woman squeezed into a T-shirt manifestly too small, from which her arms bulged, seized Ned by the wrist and dragged him to the room's most open space, where she twirled him like a puppet. It was, Julius recalled, Ned's birthday.

After midnight and a couple of lemon vodka martinis, Julius wandered outside and stood, along with a few inveterate smok- ers, on the street corner. The neighborhood, on a Friday, was much traveled, and groups jostled enthusiastically, as if head- ing somewhere. A friend of David's, now out of the din, touched Julius's shoulder and asked after him.

"I don't know. I thought he'd be here."

"That's weird," David's friend said. "That's not like him. Punctilious David."

Was it unlike him? Julius hadn't considered David's absence as anything other than a fact; but he supposed, if he did, that David was considerably more reliable than he himself, by the world's standards, and that it was strange indeed that he had not appeared.

"Is he, like, sick?"

"I don't think so." He shrugged. "I'm sure something just came up."

"Hmm." The fellow—Julius couldn't summon his name— eyed Julius with apparent suspicion and then drifted back inside. Julius, who didn't smoke, bummed a cigarette from the little woman next to him (her tiny wife-beater, her slicked hair, her attempt to be butch, struck him as poignant) and crossed the avenue to smoke it by himself, while pretending to examine the contents of an antiques store window.

It said something unnerving about him that he hadn't considered the possibility that something was wrong. He had imagined—he still imagined—that David simply fancied a change, a little irresponsibility. Lord knew, Julius was familiar with that feeling, even if he didn't readily pardon it in others. Of late, Julius seemed to experience nothing but that feeling, a constant push, a jangling restlessness that tickled at his skin from the moment he woke in the morning. If he thought about it, he supposed he was unhappy, but couldn't make sense of this, because he had, at last, almost all that he had wanted. It was true that even as he'd been perfecting his soufflés, he hadn't been improving his chances for greatness. He had written few pieces since the beginning of the summer, and had let certain commissions slide. He needed to make calls, to butter up the magazine editors scattered around New York and the country upon whose goodwill his livelihood depended. He hadn't given a thought to his future, aside from his domestic future. He, who always read, wasn't even reading a book.

Julius didn't like to think that David might, however unwittingly, be responsible for this unhappiness—because, as Julius examined through glass the outlines of an art deco armchair with cowhide upholstery, he gave his physical anxiety the name "unhappiness," thereby allowing it immediately to grow and change shape—and nor did he care to think that David might also be unhappy. If he, Julius, was unhappy, did it mean that they both were? Or was that merely projection? It didn't seem likely, somehow, that Julius would be unhappy and David perfectly content, but how could one tell? He realized he'd assumed that David's absence was due to philandering because his own—a few weeks earlier, for example, with the handsome Lewis—had been due to just that. But David's nameless friend was right: David didn't usually fail to show up altogether. Unhappy though Julius might be, he had a responsibility to his lover. He might need to call police stations, hospitals.

It was getting on for one when Julius turned the key in the lock. The apartment smelled of French fries and gin. David sat at the table, his sleeves rolled up, his violet tie loosened and spotted with ketchup that looked like blood. David's eyes behind their glasses were blurry. He had before him a huge hamburger and fries upon a sheet of crumpled wax paper, and a glass of Tanqueray on ice. Julius knew it was Tanqueray because the bottle was also open on the table, and almost half empty.

"Look what the cat dragged in," said Julius, hands on hips.

"I could say the same to you." David daubed vaguely at his chin with an already greasy napkin.

"*I've* just been representing both of us at Ned and Tristan's *odious* party," snapped Julius. "You're the one who's been AWOL."

"I've had a bad day."

"Well, clearly not as bad as it could have been. Not bad

enough to actually call and tell me about it. Here I've been, worried about whether you'd been hit by a car."

"Not too worried to go to the party." David narrowed his blurry eyes. "Not too worried to trash the bedroom. Or to wear my shirt without asking."

"Are we eight years old, to be so proprietorial?"

"No," said David, with parodic dignity. "We are merely observing a fact." He took a careful swallow of his drink, clicking the ice cubes against his teeth. "What's with the bedroom?"

"It doesn't matter now. I made dinner, you know. Duck curry."

"That's funny. There wasn't anything to eat when I got here. I went out again to get this."

"I can't believe we're having this conversation. Like I'm some kind of fifties housewife, and you have a right to be pissed off because when you show up over six hours late there isn't dinner on the table? Is this a joke?"

"All I said was that there was no dinner when I came in. Just a place that looked like it had been ransacked by thieves. And no Julius. Which, given how my day's gone, wasn't very nice."

"You keep harping on it, so you'd better come out and tell me why your day was so bad. Did Rosalie burn your coffee? Have the markets been in turmoil?"

"I got fired." David said this with a mouth full of hamburger, and Julius thought he might have misheard. He held his hands out in a gesture of incomprehension. David calmly finished chewing, swallowed, took a gulp of gin. "You heard me. I got fired."

"How come?"

"Not 'I'm so sorry'?"

"Of course I'm sorry. You know I am. But what's the reason? Can we fight it?"

"Did they fire me because I'm gay? Sorry, not this time. They fired me because they're not making any money. They fired nine of us on the floor."

"How did they decide? Why you?"

"It doesn't matter. I don't know. There's no way to know. Was I too expensive? Unproductive? I don't think so. Bad personality? Tell me, no."

"Maybe they fired you for being best dressed."

"Maybe."

"Baby, I'm sorry." Julius hugged David, who was still sitting, from behind. "I had no idea. Poor you. That is the worst day. The worst." It fleetingly occurred to Julius that he was not, for now at least, permitted to indulge his own unhappiness. It was, suddenly, time to buck up, be brave. With which he had not had much experience, to date.

David mumbled something, drank a little more gin.

"I'd offer to get you a drink, but I think you've been taking pretty good care of that yourself."

"I haven't been drinking long. I got this bottle on the way home. I took the Circle Line tour. It was relaxing, and kind of beautiful. Reminded me of the elusive pleasures of Manhattan."

"Have you had anything to eat?"

"A lot of peanuts. And this burger. I'm going to bed now."

"Let me help you." Julius fumbled at David's buttons, but David brushed him away. "We'll have to go, you know," he said, as he wandered toward the sea of cloth beyond the bedroom door.

"Go where?"

"If I don't get another job right away, we'll have to leave this apartment." He paused, and spoke slowly and clearly. "The rent here is very expensive, Lady Muck."

"Let me clean up, quickly." Julius bustled past him, with much swinging of limbs: put shirts back on hangers, socks, briefs, sweaters in drawers, while David looked on. He threw the shirts badly dampened by wet towels into the laundry basket. David stood by, pale and sleepy, occasionally rubbing his nose. When he was done, Julius hugged David against him. "I'm really sorry, beast. You should've called me."

David waved his hand.

"I was home. You should've called me."

"I'm going to sleep. I drank a lot of that gin." David belched quietly and shuffled into the bathroom. He peed noisily with the door open.

It struck Julius that David, drunk, was moving like a fat man. The whole scene was vaguely depressing: the smell of hamburger fat and fries had followed them into the bedroom. He couldn't imagine David without his job. It was a new type of nakedness, one that Julius felt he should not be displeased to see; but instead he was worrying, already: about bills, about rent, about the costs of restaurants and clothes. About his unwritten piece for *The Monitor*, a couple of grand right there. "We can always go to Pitt Street," he said. "Kick Marina's cousin out. If we have to."

David didn't answer. He dropped his trousers, wrestled with his tie, climbed into bed with his shirt still on. He put his glasses carefully on the night table and turned his back to Julius who stood, still, in the middle of the room.

"Can I give you a kiss?" Julius asked. "Just a little one?"

"If you want to," David said, without turning over. "I've had a really bad day."

CHAPTER FORTY-THREE

Finished

Not very long after announcing her engagement, not very long after her willful insistence that Danielle should join them for the Fourth, and immediately upon his return to New York and to work, Marina delivered to her father a modestly sized but apparently complete manuscript, upon the title page of which was typed THE EMPEROR'S CHILDREN HAVE NO CLOTHES. The page that followed this rather fatuous heading was, apparently, the dedication; and it, too, rankled: "For my parents, who taught me everything," it said, and then, "And for Ludovic, who taught me more." Murray could see perfectly clearly his daughter's sentimental impulses, but this didn't excuse the simple sloppiness of it. It didn't make logical sense. Everything and more. It made no sense at all.

His perturbation at these initial words constituted, to Annabel and to Danielle (albeit separately), his resistance to reading the book; but in his heart of hearts, he knew he hadn't ever wanted to read it, had been perfectly content to imagine that it would never be finished. He couldn't say to anyone—not even to young Frederick, whose rabidly exacting, almost demented standards amused him; here was a young man who could, and did, quibble with Tolstoy—that he shirked, for a fortnight, his duty to read the book because he suspected that it wouldn't be any good. This wasn't the same as thinking that it might bore him—the subject seemed at once so frivolous and so abstruse that Marina would have had to accomplish a major feat in order not to bore him. Rather, he realized that all his anxieties about Marina's intellectual abilities, about her gravitas, clustered around this pile of paper like a lingering dank smell. Turning the pages, reading them, might clear the air; but then again . . .

For over a week, Murray kept the manuscript at the top left-hand corner of his desk, with the copy shop's elastic band still tight around its middle. Periodically, Frederick would ask him "Have you read that yet, by any chance?" and if he wasn't already smoking, Murray would light a cigarette before replying. "Not quite. Very busy. You know."

The fourth or fifth time they had this exchange, Frederick coughed, slightly, at Murray's answer and said, "I think it would mean a lot to her."

"I'll read it the minute I can."

"When you were at lunch yesterday, she came in to look at it. She didn't say anything, but I know she could tell—I could tell she could tell—that it hadn't been moved."

"Then let's move the damn thing." And Murray had picked it up, snapped off the elastic, ruffled the pages, and stowed it in his bottom drawer. "I cannot have the whole world breathing down my neck," he said. "It makes for a very unnatural reading."

Frederick had raised his eyebrows and retreated, and this, too, had irritated Murray. He tried to explain it to Danielle when they met at her apartment at lunchtime the next day. "I know Marina's waiting for my judgment," he said. "She's been waiting for it for her whole life, and now, it would seem, is the moment of truth. I cannot tell a lie—"

"Can't you?"

"Not about something so important. Do you realize, she hasn't even given you a copy? Just me and the boyfriend. That's it."

"Of course I realize it. But you shouldn't be so— First of all, what makes you think you'll be anything but proud? She's written her book, at last—it's been almost all of our adult lives." Danielle massaged Murray's agitated shoulders with her thumbs, rubbed him with her small, cool palms. "That in itself—well. And even if you have reservations, you'll have compliments, too; and then, I bet, without lying at all, you'll be able to, you know, accentuate the positive. She really does want your feedback, not just your praise."

Murray made a face.

"Okay, mostly she wants praise. But not only praise. She's bigger than that."

They were quiet for a moment, and the midday honking and rumbling seeped through the room. The Rothkos seemed to Murray to have their eyes shut.

"I'll say this once and then never again. My only child has followed in my footsteps, than which there can be no greater flattery, and has written a book. But then again, my daughter has written a book about children's clothes. A book. About children's clothes."

"Come on, here. It's about the significance of children's clothes, the way they reflect our cultural mores. It's not—"

"It is a book about children's clothes." He sighed. "Which

either means that the footsteps in which she follows are peculiarly, unexpectedly small, or at least that she sees them as small, in which case, how gravely I have failed, on all fronts. Or else it means that her own feet aren't very big."

"Does this have to be about you, beloved?"

"Her diminutive feet are not 'about me.' But they can't help but disappoint." He paused. "I shouldn't say these things to you. You're her best friend. You don't want to know that her crusty old father thinks her book's junk."

"You haven't even read it. Have you gotten beyond the title page yet?"

"The dedication. To her parents—that's me—and the boyfriend. Or should I say the fiancé."

"Are you worried that he's somehow changed it?"

"The book or the girl?"

"Both, really. I just wondered."

Murray sighed again. "How would one know? About the book."

"He spurred her to finish it. He named it. She told me. I think he's read it along the way."

"But he didn't write it."

"Didn't he? Strictly speaking, he didn't. But . . ." Danielle shrugged.

"You think he's a real Svengali."

"I think he's Napoleon. And I think he's your enemy. And I think Marina is his Trojan horse."

"Please go on, my child. This delicious mixing of martial figures. Are we at war? I wasn't aware."

"He wants something from you. He desperately wanted to

meet you. He liked the idea of Marina because she was your daughter, at least in part."

"So really he wants to go to bed with me, you think?"

"I don't know whether he wants to subdue and convert you, or to crush you, but in some unsayable way, I think it's all about you in the end. Not about Marina."

"I thought you just said that it wasn't all about me. You were quite adamant."

"Don't make fun of me."

"I'm not making fun. Far from it."

"You don't see the danger, do you?"

"What danger could there possibly be? Or, put it another way: What could be more dangerous to me than this?" He gestured to the bed, themselves in it, the bright summer sunlight through the window, painting broad golden stripes along the floor.

"Forget it, then. Don't say you haven't been warned."

"When the sky falls in, Chicken Little?"

Danielle pulled on a T-shirt, crossed her arms. "You've got to read the book," she said. "As soon as you can."

So Murray, in the two days that followed, read the book. He took it out of the apartment in a plastic supermarket bag and he set himself up in a bar over on Amsterdam, with fish and chips and a scotch, and he stayed the first afternoon in his gloomy, sticky booth until he had reached the midpoint, and he stayed the second afternoon until he'd turned the last page. His emotion, as he stacked the pages back together, wheedled their elastic round, and wrapped them in plastic, was akin to anger, although it wasn't anger proper. He couldn't detach himself, couldn't entirely tell whether he would have thought badly of the book if he hadn't expected to think badly of it. At certain points, he'd been impressed by her facility, her turns of phrase, and had thought that she could really write, could even find the apt metaphor without stretching too far. But that was neither here nor there, in light of the content. A lot of frothy waffle, repetitive opining swirling around a string of utterly unrevealing facts, about the size of the children's clothing market in North America, or about the age at which children now bare their midriffs versus when they have sex, or trite garbage, introductory sociology garbage, about the nineteenth-century invention of childhood (how before that they were just miniature adults, as we can tell from the portraits) and about how we now, as a nation, never want to grow up. That was exactly what he yearned to bark at his daughter: Grow up, grow up! There were the depradations of rampant capitalism, the atrocities in Bosnia or Rwanda, the melting polar caps to attend to: and his daughter was busy investigating the cost of velvet-collared winter coats at Best and Company. The book as a whole struck him as an artfully wrapped gift box, a flurry of elegant paper and ribbons that, when opened, proved to be empty. Perhaps not entirely empty: a few glittering, worthless marbles rolled around in the bottom of the box. This was the analogy he prepared for Annabel, for Danielle, for Frederick, if he were interested.

For Marina, he required a subtler approach. Praise—he must begin with praise. He'd done enough teaching to know this. And then, adulterated, the truth. He couldn't avoid telling her the fundamental truth, which was that she should not publish the book at all. There was no way to sugarcoat this news; but somehow, he needed to deliver it in such a way that she would follow his advice. She owed herself more than this—perhaps that was the formula. She was capable of so much more. She had so illustrious a future in store (maybe this was overstating the case—she was, after all, thirty years old, with precious little to show for it) that she shouldn't undermine her (as yet non-existent) reputation merely for the sake of a little attention. Once a book is published, it can't be taken back, he would tell her. It will always be your first book.

Or your last. Impossible not to think, in the booth, in the bar, in those moments before the tab was tallied and the check delivered, impossible not to recall his own hidden manuscript, a work that similarly, as he saw it, walked the line between seriousness and popularity, more successfully, if he were fortunate, but confronting some of the same risks. There would be no one to tell him not to publish, no reader upon whose frankness he could rely. In this sense, he consoled himself for the brutal blow he had to deliver, Marina was lucky. To have a reader who so loved her, and who cared so much.

He called her at Seeley's. She was almost always at Seeley's, now; and Murray found that he missed her, the little attentions, her sweet-smelling wake. He missed some sense of urgency that she carried with her, a feeling that he had to live up to her expectations, had to be the myth. He got this a bit from Danielle, this unvoiced but discriminating adulation, but with Danielle it was different. Danielle, after all, wasn't permanent, wasn't family. He called Marina at Seeley's and invited her to go to lunch with him. He made a reservation at San Domenico, where the curious and surely lascivious publisher had taken her all those years before. On the morning, exceptionally, he shaved before noon, and was careful to comb his hair. He asked

Annabel what he ought to wear, and she chose for him a jacket and a shirt, both of which, in earlier years, Marina had given him as presents. (Without Annabel, needless to say, he would not have remembered this.) Annabel worried that he would upset Marina, but he promised her he would be tactful.

"You've never been much of a diplomat," Annabel said. "Would you like me to come along?"

"She'd smell a rat," he said, and laughed; but in the taxi, his hands were shaking a little. Danielle, too, had prepped him: "Your opinion means everything to her," she'd said. "Be careful."

"If that were true," he'd replied, "then she wouldn't be marrying the fiancé. She wouldn't say he'd taught her more than everything."

"A little boy in a sulk," she'd said. "Try to be a good father, as well as a good reader."

"Crap," he said to himself, smoking a last cigarette before crossing the threshold. Marina was already there, although she hadn't yet seen him. Her dark hair fell over her face as she scanned the menu. Even from afar, through glass, he could admire the line of her back, the elegance of her slender bare arm upon the table. She was, indubitably, lovelier to behold than Danielle. Less sexy, perhaps, but lovely. It was incredible to think, still, that this dark swan was of his making.

She stood, when he approached, and smiled her big, goofy smile. "Did you ever think, Daddy, that I'd come from my office to meet you for lunch? Did you ever think I'd have a job?"

"And a book, both." He embraced her. "You've done it."

Her downward glance was modest, a false modesty he knew because she was so like him; and the very poignancy of that false modesty struck him as the hardest thing to bear. Far easier to have her angry with him—throwing plates, even—than to have to witness—to cause—the dismantling of her careful defenses.

But it was a matter of principle, and of parental responsibility, and he would do it. After talk about *The Monitor,* after some discussion—cursory—of the wedding plans, after the ordering and the first drink, he said, "I've read your book." He paused, she straightened, he could tell she thought he paused too long, and that this was an ill omen. He wanted to reassure her, but couldn't. "There's some great stuff in there," he said. "You write beautifully."

"But?" Her smile was wide, and tight. "There's always 'but.'"

"You're right. There's always 'but.' At least, when someone loves you as much as I do, there's always a 'but.' Because I think I've raised a girl who wants to know the truth."

"I want to know what you think, yes. It means a lot to me."

And so he told her. He tried to couch his opinion as best he could; but then again, it was important that she not go away with the impression that a little tinkering, or even a good bit of tinkering, would suffice.

"You're telling me that I shouldn't publish my book?"

"I'm suggesting that with a little revision to make them stand alone, one or two chapters, appearing in magazines, might more effectively and economically convey what you have to say."

"You're telling me not to publish my book."

Murray took a deep breath. "I am being completely frank

with you because you are my only, adored child. It is simply not clear to me that there is a book in your book."

"What is that supposed to mean?"

"Call me old-fashioned, but in my world a book—if only on account of the trees chopped down to produce it; but for many other reasons as well—should justify its existence. It must have a *raison d'être*. I just don't see one here. I'm sorry."

"You're saying that you think my editor will reject it?"

"No, of course not. Not for a second."

She looked momentarily relieved.

"I'm saying that in spite of the fact that I'm sure they would cheerfully publish it, I think you should find the inner fortitude to resist the temptation. I don't think you should allow this book to be published."

"Because you think it's trivial?"

Murray raised his shoulders, stuck out his lower lip: *"C'est evident."* He was desperate for a cigarette, but drank his drink instead. Their lunches were in front of them, largely uneaten. It was as if the food, and the restaurant, had been swept away and they were conducting their conversation in a vacuum.

Marina had not raised her voice, nor did she do so now. But the sounds came as if strangled out of her mouth. "If you thought it was a worthless project, why didn't you say so before? You've had seven years, Daddy. It's quite a long time."

Murray sighed. There were so many answers to this, none of them flattering. What had seemed a minor but not shameful undertaking for a girl of twenty-three was no longer appropriate for an adult of thirty. He had long ago stopped believing that she would complete it, and so had not worried about its futility: he had seen the project as a Beckettian emblem of

Marina's interminable, incontrovertible malaise. He couldn't have known until he read the manuscript how fully silly it would be. He hadn't judged the topic (or not wholly) but rather her interpretation of it. But what he said was, "You never asked for my opinion about the project. But you did ask my opinion about the book."

Marina, looking down—but not, now, with charming false modesty—nodded. "I see," she said.

"Don't cry, my dear girl. Please don't cry."

"I'm not crying." She looked him in the eye, and he could not rightly read her expression. "It's just very interesting to me, Daddy."

"What is?"

"Ludo warned me you'd be hostile. All this time, he's said that you don't really want me to succeed with my writing, that you want me in your shadow. I told him that was ridiculous. It's just very interesting."

"That *is* ridiculous. Nobody wants your success more than I do." Murray watched while Marina, with great concentration, ate. She did not look up. Eventually he said, "Would you have wanted me to tell a lie? Would that have been the father you respect?"

"Ah, respect," she said, and now there was certainly bitterness in her voice. It seemed to Murray as though the sound had a color: greenish. "How could I forget the Thwaite family watchword? Except it's not clear to me, Daddy, that you have respect for anyone at all. I just don't think you do."

"You're upset."

"Of course I'm upset. Why wouldn't I be?"

"I'm not telling you what to do, I'm just letting you know what I would do. That's all."

"You've made your point. Can we talk about something else?"

They endured a strained and prolonged silence, in which Murray knew they both fought their impulses to speak. The hushed burble of other conversations became again audible around them. A waiter dropped a fork. But this was what restaurants were for: the public repression of strong emotions. Murray asked her again, in more detail, about *The Monitor* and its progress; and in stricken monosyllables, in a near whisper, she replied. Thus they dragged themselves to coffee, and through it. They would not be seen to argue; and both, perhaps wrongly, were aware once again of being seen. A talk-radio fellow, a handsome but minor man in his forties with a voice like a butter knife and a shirt the color of the Mediterranean, stopped by the table to glad-hand. He put his palm on Murray's shoulder, stared frankly at Marina, was visibly thrilled to learn she was daughter rather than protégée, clearly because this, in some strange universe, gave him hope. His obsequious bobbing and grinning served, in some measure, to dampen the tension: Marina couldn't help but smile at Murray after the man— whose name, to their mutual amusement, was Baz—retreated.

CHAPTER FORTY-FOUR

Weird

"It doesn't surprise me, I have to say. I'm afraid it doesn't surprise me at all."

Upon her return from lunch, Marina, her crisp, sleeveless shirt wilted by misery and the heat, had immediately shut herself in Ludovic's office to await his return. Unshod, stretched on his leather sofa, she had contemplated tears, but decided to save them until the venting of her indignation inevitably brought them forth. She didn't need tears to express her misery to herself.

When at last Ludo came back from his own extravagant lunch—something with the marketing department and advertisers: they were setting up a corporate sponsor for the launch party—free booze in return for a plug on the invitations—Marina told him what her father had said. This was when he claimed not to be surprised.

"What did *I* tell you about your book?"

"You said you liked it."

"More than that. I said it's brilliant. It'll be a hit. Trust me. Your father is woefully out of touch."

"He didn't say it was no good. He said not to publish it. Ludo: he said it's worthless."

"How many times do I have to tell you that your father's sense of his own importance is deeply involved with keeping you down? He'll do anything to keep from feeling like a has-been, and using you—or in this case, abusing you—is just a minor necessity in his schema."

"You make it sound as though he's deliberately malicious."

"I don't mean to." He held her to him and she turned her nose to his slender neck, a position simultaneously safe and awkward. Something was askew in the curve of her spine. "He doesn't know what he's doing. He thinks he has the best of intentions. But he's a very angry and hostile person."

"I don't believe—"

"I'm serious. You need to break away from him. You need to ignore his bullshit—because that's what it is."

Marina nuzzled Ludovic's shoulder. It smelled of ironing. He sent his shirts to the cleaners.

"Will you promise me that?" he said.

"What?"

"That you'll break away from him."

"I don't even know what that would mean."

"It would mean acknowledging the truth about him. Seeing that he's not some great mythical god, but just a mediocre journalist with a mysteriously high-flown sense of himself." Ludo paused for emphasis. "Your book is a more important work of thought and scholarship than anything he's produced in more than twenty years."

"Really, Ludo." Marina took a deep breath, and they stared at each other in silence. Eventually, she said, "This shouldn't be an excuse for you to attack my father. It isn't about him, I don't think. It's about my book."

"Exactly right. And you have to learn to call a spade a spade." Which Marina, somewhat bemusedly, insisted that she would do.

Later, at her yoga class, when the time came for shavasana, corpse pose, Marina finally found herself crying. The tears slipped out of the corners of her closed eyes and rolled hotly down into her hair near her ears. She cried silently, grateful for the dimmed lights, the soft drone of the teacher's voice leading the group through relaxation. The sorrow Marina felt was like an internal howling, as though some organ had been plucked from her. Was this what it meant to grow up, this vast loneliness? And like her anger in the restaurant—that beautifully somber place, now forever spoiled for her—she could control the feeling, push it to one side, just as she could brush away the tears before the lights were turned back on; but she did not know if the force of it would ever abate.

"It was awful, Danny," she said that night on the telephone. She sat on the kitchen floor, near the apartment's service door, with her knees to her chest. Ludovic had shaken his head in dismay and taken his glass of wine through to watch CNN.

"What did he say?" Danielle seemed to be eating something while she listened to Marina's account of the lunch. Marina tried not to let this annoy her. It reminded her of how much it irritated her to hear the change in her father's breathing and realize he was smoking while speaking to her on the phone.

These were selfish distractions: surely her best friend ought to be able to listen, and listen only, for the short time in which Marina needed her?

"I'm so sorry," said Danielle. "I kind of can't believe he would do that."

"Only kind of?"

"You know what I mean. I believe you but it seems unbelievable."

"Tell me about it."

"What are you going to do now?"

"What do you mean? I'm going to send my book to my editor and let him decide."

"Why do you think he said that?"

"I don't know, Danny. Because he's a self-absorbed asshole, is why. Because it's not the kind of book he would ever write, so he doesn't see the point of it." She sighed. "Let's not talk about it anymore."

"But you don't—I mean, I know you're angry, but you don't think he *wanted* to help?"

"What's that supposed to mean?"

"Nothing. It seems sad, is all. You and he have always been so close."

Marina made a snorting in her nose. "Maybe it's been a proximity under false pretenses," she said, feeling again and briefly the gape in her chest. "Ludovic points out that everybody else had to lose their illusions about their parents earlier, but because society—or our segment of society, at least—agrees with and reinforces my parental illusions, I've been able to hang on to them for much longer."

"It's an idea."

"What would you suggest?"

"I don't know, M. I'm just wondering whether you misheard, or misunderstood, or . . . I don't know. Your father adores you. He'd never willingly hurt you."

"You're the one who always used to tease me about worshiping him. He's not God, you used to say."

"But he's a smart guy, with your best interests at heart."

"I don't think it's that simple, actually. I see things more clearly now."

"Are you sure?"

"It just makes me wonder about the wedding. About having it in Stockbridge. I mean, maybe we should just go for a restaurant here in the city and be done with it."

"How come?"

"Do I really want him to give me away, and on his property? Do you know what I'm saying? It's not like I'm some crazed feminist, but under the circumstances . . ."

"I don't know." Danielle laughed. "Maybe you're precisely ready for him to give you away."

"That's not funny. I'm not an old book, you know."

"When can I read *the* book, by the way?"

"Soon." Marina did and didn't want Danielle to read the book. Or, put another way, she both cared and did not care what Danielle thought of it. "When it's ready."

After a pause, Danielle said, "I'm so proud of you, you know. You've done it."

"Then why do I feel so depressed?"

"PPD," Danielle said. "Not post-party, like in college, but the real thing. Post-partem. Perfectly natural."

"None of this is natural," Marina said. "This is the weirdest time in my life so far."

"Good weird, or bad weird?"

"Just weird."

CHAPTER FORTY-FIVE

"Murray Thwaite: A Portrait"
by Frederick Tubb

The article had proven much trickier than Bootie could have imagined. He was obsessed with it: every evening for two weeks, leaving the Thwaites' for the lengthy above-ground trip home to Pitt Street, he found himself thinking through the events and exchanges of the day, wondering whether he should amend his portrait in light of a kindness, or a brusqueness. He'd rewritten the piece, by hand, a dozen times, hunched at the table in the Pitt Street apartment, often with his shirt off, always half-expecting Julius to reappear. He didn't think about its publishability—whatever that might mean—but focused instead on its truthfulness. If he could make it utterly true, then its force would necessitate its publication: as his mother always said, the Truth will out.

The Murray Thwaite he hoped he had drawn was rightly complex—but he'd reached a point where he was no longer sure. He knew, for example, that Murray's entanglement with Danielle (he couldn't really picture them going to bed together, although he'd tried; and who knew if it was an actual physical affair, and what did it matter? They were involved, regardless, in inappropriately intimate communication) had colored his emotions, and Bootie couldn't tell whether his moral dismay had inadvertently suffused his prose. When Murray took so long to read Marina's manuscript—and his own daughter had written a book!—Bootie felt his anger at his uncle seep through the week's drafts; but then, when he did tackle her work, Murray simply cancelled all his appointments in order to devote himself solely to it, for which he regained some of Bootie's respect. Then there was Murray's reaction, regarding which Bootie was of two minds: he wanted only success for Marina, but he also suspected that Murray wasn't exaggerating when he called the book silly (it was a silly topic, after all). He suspected, too, that Ludovic Seeley had falsely bolstered his girlfriend, and had probably had a hand in muddying the manuscript as well.

Bootie knew it was irrational, but he was inclined to blame Ludovic Seeley for many things—even more so than Murray Thwaite. Uncle Murray, after all, paid Bootie for times he didn't work, and plied him with review copies of books, and had even—oh, long abandoned project!—offered to read his autodidact's essays, if ever essays there were.

But writing about Murray, over and over again, had become Bootie's most consuming project. There was no time for fat library books with scolding titles, let alone for the hectoring tomes of Musil that glared at him from Julius's bookshelf. He had come to think of Murray as his, somehow, as an idea rather than the man, and sometimes the man surprised him, like something forgotten and rediscovered: the smell of him, the echo of his voice on the telephone.

By the end of July, he'd reached the point where his written Murray, blurred though he was, superseded the man in the

room, became stronger than he. This was the time, Bootie realized, to let him go, to send this Murray Thwaite out into the
world. He felt it was crucial to be honest, fully honest, as
he took this step. He didn't want anyone to feel he'd been
hypocritical or deceptive. He must precisely redeem the
shortcomings of his uncle. He typed up his final version on his
own computer, in Julius's apartment, and e-mailed it to himself, so he could print it at Kinko's. It seemed more honest, for
example, to print it at Kinko's rather than at the Thwaites',
when they might not be pleased with its contents: he would
not use their printer, their electricity, their paper. He then had
three copies made and, allowing himself to indulge a small
vanity, had them bound in plastic covers, one red, one navy,
and one black. The red one was for Marina, because he wanted
her to take note of it, of him. The navy one was for his mother,
because it seemed a safely sober color, an announcement of the
seriousness of his endeavor. And the black one was for Murray
(and for Annabel, of course, should he choose to share it),
because he wanted, in all things, to be straightforward, and it
was imperative that Murray should know what Bootie had been
up to. Black seemed appropriately mournful: it expressed the
sorrow with which he delivered his blow.

Strangely, he would think afterward, Bootie didn't consider
that this gesture of openness might cost him his livelihood, and
indeed, his family connections. He couldn't have said what he
thought might happen, because he didn't waste time imagining the outcome. He did what he needed to do.

Curiously, his mother responded first. He sent her the essay
by Express Mail, and she, doubtless impressed by the urgency

of the packaging, read it at once. She rang him at Julius's, in the evening, caught him dozing flat on the futon.

"What in the Sam Hill has gotten into you, Bootie?" she asked.

"How do you mean?"

"Well, I haven't read Murray's unpublished book, but I'd guess he didn't want me to. That's not what he hired you for, I don't think: to bite the hand that feeds you. Are you going crazy on me, Bootie? What on earth is going on?"

"Nothing, Ma." He explained that Marina had asked for a cultural exposé, and that this was it. He did not explain that he still, secretly, harbored the hope that this essay might make Marina love him. Even though he knew better than to hope, he was sure, in his fantasy, that if only she really looked his way, understood his mind, then this could not fail to transpire.

"I'm going to call your uncle. Has he seen this?"

"I gave it to him. I doubt he's read it yet. He took ages to read Marina's manuscript."

"He's a busy man, Bootie. Jeez. You know, it's time for you to pack in this crazy nonsense and get back to school. They sent some papers from Oswego. I opened them. It's time to register. I can write the check tomorrow."

"I'm so far beyond that, Ma."

"Beyond a college education? What's that supposed to mean?"

"I don't know how to explain it, except to say that I'm in the middle of *life*. But really in the middle of it. There's no turning back now."

"You're losing your marbles. Bootie, do I need to come and get you?"

"I'm an adult. I am *all grown up*. I am *living my life*."

His mother sighed. "There is no need to raise your voice at me," she said. "I think this is all crazy, but I love you just the same."

"I love you, too, Ma."

"He's going to be very upset, you know. I sometimes don't think I know my brother too well, but I know that much. He can have a miserable temper. He always did. And what you've done is terrible."

"Somebody has to tell the truth. Somebody has to call it like it is."

"What makes you so sure it's the truth? And why does it have to be you, I wonder? Are you trying to ruin your life?"

"It'll be fine. You'll see. It'll be fine." He was accustomed to reassuring her in this way, although it did occur to him then that it might not be entirely fine.

Marina called him two hours later. He was reading Emerson when she rang: "This goiter of egotism is so frequent among notable persons that we must infer some strong necessity in nature which it subserves; such as we see in the sexual attraction. The preservation of the species was a point of such necessity that nature has secured it at all hazards by immensely overloading the passion, at the risk of perpetual crime and disorder. So egotism has its root in the cardinal necessity by which each individual persists to be what he is."

"Frederick," she said. "Is this some kind of joke?"

"It's a cultural exposé."

"It's an insane rant against my father."

"I don't see it that way at all. That wasn't my intention. Maybe the tone isn't clear?" He thought a second. "I've never written for publication before. I thought you could help me edit it."

"You didn't really think I'd publish this, did you?"

"Somebody's got to tell the truth. And people who do, usually get punished. It's not the way to make friends, I know that."

"What's the truth here, Frederick? Except that you don't like my father?"

"I actually sometimes like him a lot. He's been really kind to me, like with the job. It's a nuanced portrait."

"Nuanced?"

"I thought you of all people would be able to see it."

"Because I'm angry with him right now, you mean?"

"Because you see him." Bootie sat hunched on the floor holding the phone between his shoulder and head, examining his toes while he spoke. He ran his fingers around them as if he were tracing them with a crayon on the floor. He felt that this helped him from getting too upset. "Has Ludovic read it?" he asked.

"He has, actually." She made a sort of low whistling sound, an intake of breath through her teeth. "I'll have you know you've caused one of our biggest disagreements ever."

"You fought about me?"

"He has some idea that your article—I don't even want to call it an article—is, not the truth, but a truth, your truth. That's what he says. He sees validity in that. He figures *The Monitor* should run it, get people talking. It's a start, he says."

"And you don't?"

"Frederick, hello? You're attacking my father for a manuscript he's working on that nobody has seen. I haven't seen it. My mother hasn't seen it. It's private."

"It was right there in his desk drawer. It still is."

"You're family. He trusted you. Don't you get it? You're just like Ludo. It's not that you *can't* ruin his life, it's that you choose not to, because you care about him, about our family. Haven't we been nice to you?"

"Extremely." Bootie traced his feet faster and faster. "I don't think it's going to ruin his life."

"He cares more about this book than about anything. It's his life project, and you make fun of it."

"He wasn't so nice about your book, as I recall."

"That's got nothing to do with it."

"You forgive him, if you do, because he believed he was help-ing you."

"He didn't publish his opinion in the paper. He took me out to lunch. And no offense, Bootie, but you're a long way from being my father. He has a right to his opinions."

"And on life's fundamental questions, he has no opinions to speak of," said Bootie, holding his feet as if to stop them run-ning away. "That isn't an opinion, it's a fact." He paused. "Nobody wanted that manuscript to be brilliant more than me," he said, quietly. "He's been my hero for my whole life."

"At least he never needs to know," she said. "We can put an end to this right now."

"Oh no," Bootie said. "He has his own copy."

"He what?"

"I gave him a copy. I left it with him yesterday afternoon when I was going home. Today he told me he'd try to get to it tonight." In the silence that followed, Bootie imagined that

Marina was trying, like something out of *Tom & Jerry* or *Road Runner*, to figure out how she could steal the folder back without Murray ever reading it. "He knows it's for you," he said. "He knows other people have it."

"Does he know what it's about?"

"I didn't mention, no."

Murray Thwaite didn't call Bootie at Julius's that evening, although Bootie sat up until two in the morning just in case. He didn't want to be caught napping. Bootie assumed this was because Murray hadn't had a chance to read it, or didn't feel like it, in any event. The way he'd skated over Marina's book for so long. But when Bootie arrived shortly after nine, swaggering as cheerily as he was able, Murray met him in the hallway and asked him to come into his office and sit down. By which Bootie knew he had been read.

Murray appeared grave, but eminently avuncular: reassuringly rumpled, he leaned back, crossed his long legs, lit a cigarette, fiddled for a while with a bit of silver paper from the cigarette box, tossed it in the wastepaper basket, missed. Bootie didn't realize at first that the glass from which Murray intermittently sipped was filled, copiously, with scotch. Bootie was aware of his own physical disadvantage: of his glasses slipping down his nose, of his broad thighs sticking out awkwardly, of his inability to sit comfortably on the small sofa among piles of papers. At least he could rest his feet firmly on the floor; but they were shod in sneakers, and could not console him.

"You are a very young man," Murray said. "Which is a fine thing. Ambitious, serious, independent."

Bootie kept his face expressionless, blinked behind his glasses.

"You don't think much of me. That's your job, your generation's job, but as my nephew, closest thing I've got to a son, it's specifically yours, too." He smoked, coughed slightly. He was drawing this out on purpose, torturing Bootie. "In time, you'll do your great things," he said; and Bootie thought that he had been right to reassure his mother: it would be fine. "Or else you won't," Murray went on. Then he stopped and stubbed out his cigarette and leaned forward so his elbows were on his knees and he turned his eyes on Bootie and his look was mean, a mean glimmer in the puff and sag of his older man's face, beneath the impressive shelf of his eyebrows. "But where the fuck do you get off, you little nullity, you common little piece of shit, snooping around in my papers and crapping all over them? What has been going on here all this time, exactly? Hmm?" He leaned forward. "Hmm? Hmm?"

"Nothing, sir."

"Quite clearly nothing. Nothing in the line of real work. I've paid you a king's ransom, my wife opened our house to you, my daughter took you under her wing and this is how you repay us?"

"No, sir."

"What the hell does that mean? And don't fucking call me sir."

"I'm very grateful. What you've done for me—I can't—"

"Oh, I see. It's just that you had to go through my private papers and publicly voice your highly authoritative opinion to the fucking world? Do you know what you are? You're a little shit, a nothing, you have the intellect of a moth. You're a speck of filth from Watertown, New York, which is itself a speck of filth. You're a nothing. And do you know how I know? Because I was just like you, Christ, I was you, except I wasn't fat. But I knew my place, I knew what I had to earn, I buckled down and kept my mouth shut and I listened and I learned and I worked, you little asshole, I worked until I'd made something of myself." He paused, drank a thick gulp. "And people paid attention to me not because I was some trumped-up little shithead, not because I was related to so-and-so or kissed the ass of this one or that one. They paid attention because I'd done my homework and I knew my stuff. Facts, not opinions. You're not entitled to have opinions until you know the facts."

"With all due respect, sir—"

"Respect? That would be precisely what you're lacking, I believe."

"Please, I just want to say that my opinions were formed on the basis of facts."

"Facts?"

"Your manuscript—*How to Live*—it's a fact."

Murray looked stunned, for only a moment. He sat up, and leaned forward again. His hands, to Bootie, loomed enormous. "A fact? A fact? The earliest notes toward a long-term project, scattered scratchings that may never see the light of day, that will certainly never, in their current form, see the light of day? This, you call a fact? And if I rummaged through the insalubrious sea of detritus you cart around with you and turned up your diary, I suppose that would constitute a public document?"

"A book manuscript exists. If you died tomorrow, someone would publish it."

"I would see to it that they couldn't. But that's beside the point."

"To your readers, the manuscript is very precious. Even more precious because it's not published. I'm just telling people what it is."

"No, young man. You're shitting on me from a great height. Which, you don't seem to understand, I can immediately put a stop to. A wave of my hand, and you simply cease to exist."

"So I'm fired?"

"It means simply this: that as far as I'm concerned, and, with me, the thinking portion of this city, and by extension, of this nation, you will simply cease to exist."

"What will you tell my mother?"

"What will *you* tell your mother?"

Bootie, numbed, nodded slowly, stood up to leave. He didn't have anything to gather together but made a semblance of looking, playing for time. He hadn't imagined that things would turn out this way. Then again, he simply hadn't imagined. He had been very certain, certain at least that Marina would want to publish his article. He had worked so hard to make it true. The rest, he'd thought, would fall into place, as long as he conducted himself honorably. Before he got to the door, he said, "You know that Ludovic Seeley isn't on your side, don't you? You know that he'd like to publish it?"

"Is that what he said?"

"Not directly. But I have it on good authority."

"Rubbish."

But Bootie thought that Murray looked disconcerted, which, childishly, pleased him. He'd been made to feel like a scrabbling animal. It made him want to bite. "Just one last question, sir? Before I go?"

"What?" Murray, standing, menaced. He was lighting another cigarette, and wielded the match as if he wanted to set Bootie's clothes, or his hair, alight.

"Didn't you leave it there for me?"

"What are you talking about?"

"I have to say I thought I was only doing what you wanted me to. Following instructions, almost. It's just that I responded differently to your manuscript than you'd hoped."

Beneath his great brows, Murray said nothing, blew smoke through his nose like a dragon. Bootie almost laughed, partly from nerves, partly because the situation struck him as funny, absurd. He was waiting for Murray to break into a grin, clap him on the shoulder and say something like "Enough of this silliness. Now let's get back to what matters, okay?" It would irritate Bootie a little (nobody likes their efforts to be dismissed), but would pleasingly restore order. In order to help this scenario unfold, Bootie offered—although it felt silly even as he spoke—"You've always been my hero, you know. I said so in the piece."

Murray emitted a snort that brought further trails of smoke from his nostrils. "I think you'd better get out," he said, and moved toward Bootie, forcing Bootie to retreat backward into the hall. "Right now."

CHAPTER FORTY-SIX

The Cuckoo in the Nest

Marina said that she'd cried when she read it, had raged at Bootie when he called, but felt sorry for him, too, because he really didn't know what he was doing. Marina also said that she and Seeley had had their worst-ever argument—she may have even said "first real argument"—and it was clear that the discord still rankled: the possibility lingered that the piece might yet appear. Seeley was, after all, *The Monitor*'s editor; he was, in this matter, Marina's boss. Marina said, too, that the most uncomfortable part about it was her own *schadenfreude:* "Daddy did this to me, you know, just a week ago, and now it's officially forgotten and all lovey-dovey, and I'm just supposed to suck it up. But Bootie's given him a dose of his own medicine, hasn't he? He's essentially telling Daddy not to publish this book. His secret book."

"I guess it isn't brunch recipes after all," Danielle had said. Neither Murray nor Marina would show her Bootie's article.

"And another thing," Marina went on. "Another thing I keep thinking is that Bootie—Frederick—is weird and sometimes even creepy—the way he looks at me, if you could see—but he also isn't stupid, you know? He actually seems pretty smart, even though his article's a bit confusing. It's confusing because it's like he was writing in code, for people who already know the manuscript and know my dad, and of course nobody has actually seen it, not even me. Bootie, you know, stole it from Daddy's desk. But my point is that I found myself wondering whether his criticisms are legitimate, and maybe actually in this book the great Murray Thwaite really does reveal himself to be, I don't know, less thoughtful, or less interestingly thoughtful—I mean, he suggests he's even a little bit shallow. And what if he's right?"

"Don't you think someone might have noticed it before now?"

"Ludo thinks Daddy is shallow, as a pundit, and narrow, too. Like he says, it doesn't interfere with his affection for him, it's not about the man but his work."

"And Ludo's some disinterested authority?"

"Ludo would love to admire Daddy's work. He says he admires the older stuff, before Daddy got lazy."

"Your father isn't lazy."

"Don't you think I know him better than you do?"

"All I know, M, is that Ludo wanted to meet you *because* you were Murray's daughter. And he went on and on about despising Murray before that."

"What's your point?"

"No point. But I think you have to take what he says with a grain or two of salt. I don't know what his motives are, but they're not straightforward."

"This is my husband-to-be you're talking about."

"I'm sorry, Marina."

"You've been in love with him since you first met him in Sydney, and you'll do anything to try to ruin it for me."

"That's preposterous."

And then Marina had cried, but at least she hadn't hung up, and Danielle had finally persuaded her that they should talk about things face to face, and they had met at Union Square and walked about under the trees, back and forth, back and forth for well over an hour, eventually arm in arm, while Danielle listened to Marina speak about how difficult it was to be her father's daughter, and how wearing it was when people were always envious of you, in fact there was nothing to be done about it but you couldn't help but feel resentful because your problems were genuine but nobody wanted to believe in them. Marina came back to the matter, ultimately unexplored over the telephone, of whether Bootie might actually be right; and Danielle could tell that Seeley's sway had all but turned her.

"Think about it: there's nothing worse than pretension, and false pretension is the bottom of the barrel. Daddy despises my book because he thinks its goals are too frivolous, somehow not fitting for *his* child. Meaning, by the way, that it's not about me but about him. Which is another story. He's like the monster that ate Manhattan, he thinks it's all, always, all about him." She sniffed. "But my point is that isn't it worse to be doing something pretentious and bad, rather than unpretentious and totally decent? I don't think I'm Flaubert, here, or, I don't know, Dr. Spock or Gloria Steinem or whatever, making ground-breaking pronouncements. But *he* does. All this time, if we believe Bootie, Daddy's been holed up reinventing the wheel. Live decently. Don't lose your temper. Embrace Beauty and Truth. Above all, Truth. Blah blah blah. Please. He's offering up tired maxims as if they were original gems. Just because he imagines he's a thinker doesn't mean he can suddenly turn into one."

Danielle made only a vague noncommittal noise at this juncture.

"Ludo believes in debunking. He always says—and he's so right—that it's a nobler thing to do to write a good book about, say, cheese—a useful, plain-speaking guide to cheese—than another crappy novel. Or worse, than some pompous tome of pseudo-philosophy." Marina had stopped circling the park to deliver this, and fluttered her arms in the air. A homeless woman lying on a nearby bench, alarmed by the outburst, muttered obscenities.

"So what are you saying?"

"I don't know." Marina started to walk again. "I'm saying that nobody ever does to Daddy what Bootie's just done. Nobody reminds him that he's mortal. He gets away with murder. And so it has to be a good thing. That's what I'm saying, I think." She stopped again, momentarily. "Which doesn't mean I think the article should be published. I'm my father's daughter, for God's sake. It isn't even a very good article. But I'm glad Daddy had to read it. Glad for Daddy, in the long run. Not glad for Bootie."

"No. What happened to him?" In truth, Danielle didn't need to ask what had happened to Bootie. In a differently slanted account of events, Murray had, with a type of laughter that communicated his discomfort, told Danielle about kicking the boy out.

"Filthy manners," he'd said. "That's what it comes down to. I don't know what happened up in Watertown, but not socialization as civilized people understand it. The kid's a creep. He stayed with us for ages. Ate our food. We took him around. Marina found him a place to live. I fucking hired him, because he was my nephew. And when Annabel had to come back to town around the Fourth, she found him holed up in our house, and everything turned upside down. That's what she said. We should've known. The cuckoo in the nest. We just laughed about it. And then he felt free to shit on us, I mean, really shit on us. Pathetic little fucker." Murray had been physically restless in the recounting, huge in Danielle's studio, the same way Marina was restless out of doors. Both paced.

"I'm so sorry," Danielle had said.

"Why? Why would you be sorry? I'm sorry to learn that my own flesh and blood is a sociopath. Or a psychopath. Or maybe it's plain old Asperger's, what do I know? But he's a cursed little shit, either way."

"He was trying to get close to you, don't you think?"

"Is that how you win friends and influence people? Pardon me for my poor response. I guess I went to the wrong schools."

"No," Danielle said. "You know perfectly well that he did."

Murray had not been amused.

"I feel sorry for the kid," Danielle had tried to explain. Later, she didn't try, with Marina, because she didn't think it made sense to either of them, father or daughter. To Murray, she'd said, "He's young, and smart, and ambitious, and he's from Watertown. I was from Columbus, for pete's sake, and that's a damn sight more auspicious than Watertown. And what has he got to pull him out of there? Nothing but you guys. You're his ticket, his hope."

"So he shits on us."

"Because it's complicated. The more he loves you, the more you do for him, the more he hates you, too."

"Then he's an ass. It doesn't matter. I won't be seeing him again."

"Does your sister know yet?"

"Judy? She's so narrow-minded, all she'll care about is whether he's coming home to go to that godforsaken college at Labor Day."

"Is he?"

"I don't know. I doubt it."

"You'll never speak to him again?"

"Try me in a decade. But right now, I'd say no." But later, after scotch, and supper, and sex (Annabel was up in the country, gardening; and although Murray refused, on principle, to stay the night, because he and Annabel spoke daily from their respective beds, he had no curfew, no immediate call), when they dressed and went up to the building's roof terrace to admire the skyline and the great velvet canopy of summer night, Murray had said, "And of course, how can I help it, there's a tiny part of my brain wondering whether this kid is right. Whether he's the only one brave enough and dumb enough to tell me the truth."

"You know that's not how it is. He's envious, he's expecting the world, and—"

"And why shouldn't he? And if it's a heap of crap, why shouldn't he say so?"

"It's your private manuscript, and the first draft."

"It's my fantasy book. The book I wish I were capable of writing, by the man I wish I were."

"I have the greatest respect for the man that you are. And I like reading your books."

"Do you think we'd any of us get anywhere without pretense? Without pretensions, too? Frederick Tubb would still be in Watertown." Murray gestured away toward the Hudson. Following his arm, Danielle was struck again by the glory of the city around them, its glittering stalagmites and arterial avenues, strung with the beaded headlights of the ever-starting, ever-stopping traffic. Even the dark patches, the flat rooftops of the brick and brownstone buildings to the immediate south and west, or the hollow she knew to be a playground by day— even these ellipses were vital to the pattern. Farther downtown, a cluster of skyscrapers rose, alight, into the night, stolid mercantile reassurance in the mad whimsy of the city.

"Watertown," she said. "And everyone might have been the happier for it. So you're fretful about the book, and he's made it worse."

"I won't publish it now."

"It's not finished."

"No. I mean that I expect I simply will not publish it. I've never done this before."

"It's a long way from being finished."

"It's a self-parody, as he says. It's a fake."

"I don't believe that."

"Did you see the little plane?" A tiny flashing light, like a firefly, jounced low across the speckling skyline just beyond the end of the island. It appeared almost to weave among the buildings, a light flashing between lights. "Someday I'll take you up in one of those things. Or to do the helicopter ride. It's a tourist gig, but the view's stupendous. I took some visiting Kurds, a few years ago."

"Manhattan from above?"

"Best done at night."

After a while, Danielle said, "Do you think he's all by himself? Your nephew?"

"How would I know?"

"He doesn't have any friends. He's in love with Marina."

"It's an interesting twist, isn't it: the fellows who don't care for me all fancy my daughter."

"And her best friend fancies you."

"So it would seem."

Danielle couldn't repeat any of this to Marina, pacing the dappled, tree-draped circuit near the farmers' market; but she wanted to shout that she understood, she felt she saw them all, as if she were the audience and they players upon the stage, this peculiar sense of clear vision that she'd had since things with Murray began, that her world unfurled before her in illuminated palimpsest, and she knew, she felt, why Bootie said this, or that, and what he really meant by it, and knew, too, the dance between Murray and Marina as if she had choreographed it herself. She wondered briefly whether this was what it was like to be Annabel, and dismissed the thought. She had no desire to usurp Annabel. And what she saw and knew differed—if only in its quality, its particular, crystalline nature—from whatever it was that stirred the other woman.

Walking beneath the trees, in the green-gray shadow, when at last Marina seemed to have calmed and they prepared to part company, Marina asked whether Danielle had heard Julius's news.

"We think we've got troubles. He sent me an e-mail because he really wants to do a piece for me. I'd told him to but he couldn't come up with a topic, because as far as I can tell he's too busy with the parties. In fact, I told him he could write about the downtown parties, you know, a fun piece about, I don't know, what their significance is among the twenty-some-things versus the thirty-somethings, because there really does seem to be a cultural, like, a generational shift. Isn't that pathetic? He's agreed to do it—*our* Julius, writing style garbage like that. I swear, I almost cried. So anyway, the thing is, David's lost his job."

"My heart bleeds."

"That's not very nice."

"How can I care about someone I've never even met, who has essentially declined to meet me?"

"You can care about Julius, can't you?"

"Of course I care. What are they going to do?"

"If they don't sort things out pretty quickly, they'll have to move, it sounds like."

"Back to Julius's place."

"I guess."

After a moment's silent walking, Danielle asked, "But what about your cousin?"

"Bootie?" Marina shrugged. "I don't know. I hadn't thought about it. Maybe he'll go home to Watertown."

"Wow. Do you really think so?"

"Well, he won't be going back to my parents', that's for sure."

SEPTEMBER

CHAPTER FORTY-SEVEN

The Man Without Qualities

Bootie spent the last day of August, which was a Friday, vigorously erasing himself from the Pitt Street apartment. He couldn't be sure how spotless or grubby it had been when he'd moved in two months before, but Julius struck him as both nasty and probably fastidious, and he very much needed the return of his full security deposit. He was moving into a shared apartment in Fort Greene, Brooklyn, found after all in the *Village Voice,* where Julius had suggested Bootie look, when he called—he was civil about it, after all—to tell him that he, Julius, needed to reclaim his place and that Bootie would need to vacate it. Bootie scrubbed and mopped and dusted; threw away his extra papers; packed the remainder of his belongings. He had the sense that he was frequently required to eliminate himself. Everyone just wished he would go away. On his last night, he went to get a burrito at the taqueria a few blocks over; and when he brought it back, he sat at the table and let its smell pervade the room. He ate it with a glass of water. He would have wanted a beer but didn't have the extra money.

He'd already placed his thumbed Emerson, its back cover now torn, in the bottom of his suitcase, along with the rest of his books. He'd only barely managed to zip the case and didn't want to spew his clothes out again across the floor. Instead, to keep him company while he ate, he took from Julius's shelf the first volume of Musil. *The Man Without Qualities*. It was clearly German, and although he hadn't heard of it, he could tell it was considered a classic by the way it was published: the blurry, evasive photograph on the front cover, in black and white, showed a mournful, dark-eyed face. Indistinct, it nevertheless seemed to demand Bootie's—specifically Bootie's—attention. Bootie might earlier have claimed, in jest, that his uncle was the man without qualities; but the man's expression and his own sentiments intimated strongly that Bootie, in fact, was he. He had withstood, he felt, severe blows. He hadn't spoken to the Thwaites in weeks, and even Marina had only called twice since his argument with Murray, to see that Bootie was okay. Which he wasn't, really, needless to say; but both times he'd spoken as cheerfully and vaguely as possible. He didn't want Marina to think there was nothing in his life. He'd pretended to his mother, who had of course exhorted him to come home, that he was gainfully employed (in a restaurant, he'd said; which wasn't entirely untrue: he'd worked three days as a busboy in a chic place on lower Fifth Avenue, but he'd dropped a full tray of dishes on the third day and it had made a great deal of noise) and that he was looking into courses at the New School.

"What's that?" she'd barked. "I've never heard of it."

"It's precisely for people like me, Ma. For people who are studying at the same time as they have to work."

"Some kind of community college, then?"

"Different from that. It's a good school. Ask anybody."

"I'd like to know who it is in that city I'm supposed to ask, now I'm not speaking to your uncle."

"You don't need to not speak to him, you know."

"Why would I want to speak to him? The way he treated you. His own flesh and blood."

"Please, Ma."

"I'm not denying that thing you wrote was terrible, a terrible thing to write. But nobody's ever going to read it, so what difference does it make? I mean—"

"Ma. They might publish it. *The Monitor.* They still might."

"Don't be ridiculous, Bootie. I should hope not. Marina's got more sense than that, I'd like to think."

But he couldn't talk about Marina with his mother, even though Bootie longed to talk, and talk about Marina, just to say her name to someone. He had changed the subject, back to school—"Maybe I'll take Russian, Ma." "Russian?" "Why not?"—and done his best to calm her dismay.

He was, actually, on the verge of gainful employment. He felt that September was the beginning of a new chapter in his life, a fresh start even if there was no one there to see it. He was moving off the radar: great geniuses have the shortest biographies. Their cousins can tell you nothing about them. And, as his uncle had exhorted, in a moment of striking wisdom, "take them by surprise." He'd found his room in Fort Greene without any help. He'd found a temp agency with which to register (although, to be fair, it was nasty Julius who had also suggested this possible avenue of employment, had even given him the name of the agency) and now was slated to begin work with some downtown financial company the day after Labor Day. Bootie wasn't a fast typist, but he'd taken the agency tests and they'd told him he was very accurate with numbers ("Speed is important, but accuracy is what really counts," the billowy frosted blonde had informed him with a waggle of her pointed chin. "What use would speed be, without accuracy?") and that he would be easy to place. He didn't have to wear a suit (thank goodness, because he didn't have one) but he was expected to wear a jacket and tie. Bootie hadn't asked about footwear. He knew they wanted lace-ups. But all he had were his sneakers. The dress shoes were in Watertown: he could picture them exactly, toes against the wall as if he'd walked out of them and right through it, like a ghost. His mother, with her propensity for shrine-building, would not have moved them. As for the work itself, he didn't know exactly what he'd be doing; but he would be paid, the frosted lady assured him, at the end of each week. Only a week until payday. This was real life, he told himself. This was doing it alone.

In the morning, when he'd taken his things downstairs and had assembled them, computer included, on the sidewalk, and was wondering how he would lug them up to the avenue, he watched a taxi pull up. Julius got out—scrubbed and gangly, his lavender polo shirt neatly pressed—and behind him, a man with, behind his glasses, haunting eyes, a Musil-like blurriness, who had to be the Conehead.

"Bootie, right?" Julius, so civilized, held out a hand, as if this encounter were their first. "I'll get the cab to wait for you."

"Thanks."

"They're hard to get over here," Julius went on, as the Conehead hovered behind him, carrying bags. "David, this is Marina's cousin—"

"Frederick."

"Right. I only know you by your nickname, of course."

Bootie looked at David, whose wrists and forearms were

white and hairy like his own, but bony, too. They looked unhealthy. David looked unhealthy. "You guys both moving in?" Bootie asked.

"Both of us. Just till we, you know, find somewhere." Julius was all affability. "Just for a little while."

"Cool." Bootie felt he should say something about how much he'd enjoyed staying there, but he couldn't bring himself to lie so brazenly. He couldn't even claim that it was a pleasant apartment. It was horrid. "I'd better not keep this guy waiting." He gestured at the cabbie, who was reading Friday's *Post*. "Thanks again," he said, which seemed generally positive but not ingratiating. As he stowed his suitcase, his duffel, his plastic bags in the dank cavern of the taxi's trunk, alongside an oily spare tire and a pair of vicious wrenches, Bootie watched Julius and David disappear with their luggage into the dark stairwell. He had the impression, perhaps false, that Julius was holding David's hand, leading the way.

The new room smelled funny: a lingering must, emanating perhaps from the closet. Spacious, plain, it was on the top floor of a brownstone on South Oxford Street, with a view to the back of rooftops and, if you stood with your nose to the window and looked down, of scrubby gardens and fences. The lemon-colored paint was peeling and the floorboards had been scuffed of their shine around a central rectangle where a rug—pale blue, shaggy; he'd seen it when he visited—had long lain. In a corner by the window, the boards were badly watermarked, blackened and leached. Perhaps there had been a plant there.

He couldn't remember. Warped, the cupboard door didn't shut, and dangled stupidly like a dropped lip.

There was a bathroom on the same floor, and two other bedrooms, occupied by women, both of whom Bootie had briefly met but would not necessarily have recognized on the street, one a midwife who had warned that she would keep odd hours, and the other a graduate student from India with an earnest manner whose field and indeed institutional affiliation remained unknown to him. He recalled that both women had been small and dark, one spreading rather, in the behind, and the other precise, tight, tiny. Neither had been attractive, which suited him fine.

Downstairs, on the middle floor, there were two larger bedrooms, inhabited by the tenants of longer standing, who had placed the ad and interviewed him: a long and limber yoga instructor named Joe, of Roman profile and luxuriant curls, whose walls were lined with ropes and pulleys and props of various kinds, like some medieval torture chamber. Joe had the bay window overlooking the street and had been proud to show his room, whereas his companion, Ernesto, a hulking and swarthy fellow with bulging cheeks and a shaven head about whom Bootie had garnered virtually no information, did not volunteer to open his door. Bootie was aware that his own room lay on top of Ernesto's, and wondered whether all his movements could be heard. He thought of Ernesto as Mayakovsky, on account of a photograph he had once seen. He wished he had someone to say this to, but in this new, this self-reliant, life, did not.

Bootie, of course, had no furniture, and no money with which to buy any. He had swiped a sheet from Julius, so that he could make a bedroll in which to sleep; and over the months since leaving home he had accumulated a few postcards—Beckett, smoking; a Paul Klee painting that he'd chosen for its title: "Dance, You Monster, To My Soft Song"; and a skyline shot of Manhattan at dusk—that he taped to the yellow walls. Aside from that, his personal effects did not register upon the room. He put his duffel and bags in the closet, placed the tangle of the computer tidily in the corner, initially over the water stain, on top of the blue towel he'd filched from Julius along with the sheet, until he realized that this was his only towel and reclaimed it. He then worried a little about the computer's contact with the water stain (it didn't look recent—but who knew its source?), and ended up moving the computer to an alcove behind the door. He stacked his small collection of books into a tower alongside the computer. Their spines were the most colorful things in the space. The room looked as though it had been cleared for a dance class, or else to be painted. It didn't seem that even dust bunnies could gather there.

All in good time, Bootie told himself. Off the radar. New beginning. He had no telephone. He had only his keys. He sat, cross-legged, in the middle of the darker patch where the rug had been, and looked out the window: a low line of brick wall, topped by chimney pots; a lone pillowy cloud; a pair of spreading branches, like the image on a Japanese screen; the light, the perfect light, and the sky. He closed his eyes, hung his head. He could see Marina, then, in snatches, although he couldn't hear her voice. If he strained to hear her voice, then he lost sight of her: it was as if his brain needed to remind him that she was an illusion, that she wasn't really there. Sometimes Murray came into the picture; sometimes Annabel. He did not allow

Ludovic Seeley. He did not allow Danielle. He believed that without them, everything would have unfolded differently. There had to be blame attributed somewhere, someone to loathe. Because in spite of everything, he loved the Thwaites, all of them, Murray in his own way almost best of all. The thought of Marina actually spurred an ache behind his ribs—this was it, this must be "heartache"—a palpable agony. He was resigned to his loss—this was real life, he'd always known in his deepest self, that it would be this way—and at the same time, not resigned. The wedding was to be that very afternoon. It couldn't be stopped, and yet it couldn't happen. His eyes closed, he watched her moving, her funny gait, the boyish bump in her throat, the smile. The violet eyes. Her hair against her ear. Those hands. He knew it all better than he could have acknowledged. He knew her, the way he felt he knew Murray, too, but more so. They were his own flesh and blood; they were his; they comprised his whole world. They were lost. All that he had wanted, lost. All that he had wanted them to be. It hurt, but he kept his eyes closed and he kept watching them move behind his eyelids, so beautiful, in the middle of his empty room, in the perfect light of his lone window.

CHAPTER FORTY-EIGHT

Getting Ready

Preparing for your wedding should be a pleasure, the greatest pleasure, surely, short of the wedding itself. But four days before the nuptials, Marina was struggling. Her dress, Jil Sander, off the rack, was being altered. A small Spanish woman, with a tight chignon and a peculiar wen by her right ear, scrabbled about on her knees at Marina's feet on the gray carpet, her mouth full of pins. The dress had already been fitted once; but doubtless in the flurry, Marina had lost a pound or two, and now, in the dressmaker's mirror, she could see the cloth sagging at her ribs, where it was intended to cleave to her, and sliding loosely at the hips, where it was to have molded. The dress, columnar, simple, was blue, not white, which seemed to Marina departure enough from tradition, a pale greeny-blue that might, in the trade, have been referred to as sea foam. She had the shoes (their heels were silver, and very high: she worried, although only fleetingly, that one would sink into the lawn and stick there as she processed upon her father's arm); she'd ordered the flowers (calla lilies, after all); she knew how she would arrange her hair (upswept, though less tightly than her dressmaker's, and with a lily tucked into its waves). Food had been organized, and seating, and a marquee beneath which the guests would sit, so that neither sun nor rain could spoil things; and even the decorations for the pergola had been finalized. There wouldn't be so many guests—just a hundred—but those there were had had their lodgings organized, in and around Stockbridge.

In the event, Ludovic's family wouldn't be represented at all, although he'd put her on the phone to his mother, whose accent was, to Marina's ear, primly British; whose voice, faintly tremulous; and whose tone, if Marina were frank (which, with Ludovic, she was not), chilly. The exchange had been brief and formal: Marina had gushed, in her best social manner, about how very much she wished her future mother-in-law were coming and how immensely she was looking forward to meeting her; in reply to which Mrs. Seeley had said only that unfortunately circumstances (unspecified) prevented her from making the journey. Marina had paused to consider that her mother-in-law might be a nightmare, but had concluded that the distance between them meant it didn't so much matter. Ludovic, in passing, had suggested they might take a week in Sydney once the magazine was launched.

"The mater doesn't do well on airplanes," he said. "Nor on the telephone, really. But she's quite sweet. You'll see."

Marina had merely smiled.

Her struggles were not born of the predictable emotions. She had no reservations about her intended, although it seemed that everyone else did. She felt no rancor at the fact that organizing the wedding had been left entirely to her and Annabel, even as she'd been preparing her own section for the launch issue of *The Monitor:* she understood the magnitude of Ludovic's commitment, and that he had now, of all times, to fulfill it. His ambition, inevitably, was a part of his appeal. Her struggles lay, it seemed, in other quarters. Except with Annabel: she had no quarrel with her mother. Her mother was genuinely happy for her, she felt. But on every other front: she was to be given away by a man she still hadn't forgiven; accompanied by a maid of honor whose disapproval leaked from her like a scent. Julius was hemming and hawing about whether he would even be able to attend, on account of his move, and of the Cone-head's "commitments," and how could she not be mortally offended by that? And then, in a recurring flight of imagination that made her shudder, she feared, inexplicably, that her cousin, tacitly disinvited, might burst upon them on the day and wreak some sort of vengeance. Set the house on fire. Shoot her father. Kidnap her. It was crazy, she knew, to entertain such wild implausibilities.

"Mama," she'd whispered one recent evening, at her parents' bedroom door, "tell me I'm insane, but Bootie isn't going to hunt us down and kill us, is he? On my wedding day?"

And her mother had emerged from her closet to say, in a soothing maternal whoosh, "No, no, darling, don't be silly. Not at all. I imagine he's just sad, poor boy. He's a troubled one." A blouse over her arm, she had shaken her head wistfully. "It's just because it feels peculiar. Like having a tooth out. I'm sure in time it will come right again; but for now, we just have to live with it."

"But he won't try to kill us?"

"I don't think so, darling. I think his article about Daddy was as close as he could come."

That article, that article: just the other day, waiting for Ludo in his office, she'd noticed that it still existed, in the personal queue of his computer. Evidently, Ludo had had the article scanned—or conceivably even typed in, by Lizbeth, that smarmy princess of a secretary, forty-eight, fleshless and sinisterly demure, who always looked at Marina as though she pitied her—and had kept it. As though, although they hadn't spoken of it for weeks, their lives weren't sufficiently fraught without that, too—nominally already dealt with—returning to complicate. Who needed a prenuptial blowout? Instead, when he'd come in (Lizbeth clicking tidily and glossily behind him like a well-groomed poodle), Marina had asked about the launch party—set for the thirteenth—and they'd gone yet again over the list of local celebs who had RSVPed. It was what Ludo cared most about, at that point, more than the wedding, it sometimes felt, even though to a significant degree the guest lists overlapped. He cared about the celebrities, the ones only on the party list: "No reply from Sontag's secretary," he'd complained. "Even though Lizbeth has rung over there twice. Don't you think you could expect a bloody answer? Even a no? And frankly, she should be there. I could make her hot again, if she'd let me. But at least Renée Zellweger is a yes." Maybe it had been a mistake to have the two events so close together. Marina couldn't remember now why it had seemed so important. The urgency of their passion, doubtless. But she couldn't have foreseen the obstacles, or her barely controlled anger at almost all involved.

In the last week of August, in the quiet of the city, she'd met with Scott, her book editor, and he had pronounced himself thrilled with the manuscript. They would publish the following September; there would be fanfare of a relatively grave sort ("It's sexy but serious," Scott kept repeating. "That's my mar-

keting pitch: sexy but serious. We could run the first serial in
Vogue, or *The New Yorker*—maybe both?"). They would adver-
tise, and tour her, and "it's also a natural for TV," he'd gone on.
"Maybe *Rosie,* maybe *Oprah*—that's what we're thinking." She
would in time have to strategize with the publicity department:
they would want "a really great head shot," he said. "You're gorgeous. You're a young celebrity. Let's make the most of it." In
the office, she had bubbled, thrilled, a tingle of triumph on her
spine; but as soon as she regained the street it struck her that
only Ludo would be happy, and that even he was otherwise preoccupied. She wouldn't tell her father—not yet, anyway. The
wound, still unscabbed, couldn't take it. He didn't believe in
her, or not in the book; would merely warn her against being
manipulated. She could play the conversation in her mind, and
certainly did not need actually to conduct it. But even the
imagining incensed, as she walked back down Broadway
through the jumbled, zinging hubbub of Times Square. The
late summer tourists, all encumbered and gawping, their loose
shorts flapping like flags, ambled, slung with bags and cameras,
beneath the neon cacophony, eager and clueless, while bike
messengers wove in and out, skimming the curbs, and locals—
still so many of them, even after lunch at the end of August,
the quietest hour, sidewalks thick with them, like herded sheep,
in the stink of exhaust and sweat and sausages—nattered,
waved, pushed, argued, like hammy extras on a film set, and
generally enraged her. By the time she crossed to calmer
Chelsea, wondering whether she might, fortuitously, glimpse
Julius and with him, perhaps, the elusive Cohen, she bristled
anew at Murray's intransigence, reliving their San Domenico
exchanges, as if she were but some spinoff of his own enterprise

and her output his to control; as if—this, really, was always his
way, when she thought about it, and why (she dug with her
foot, crossed against the light, roundly scolded by a cabbie's
horn), let's be serious, why had she not thought about it before?
Marina the diligent daughter, his right hand, who else could
finish his work, even his sentences if need be, and never ques-
tioned, never asked, when he might make room for her,
because—it was so obvious; how could she have needed Ludo
to show her, and even, too, the missteps of poor Bootie
Tubb?—to him it was all about Murray Thwaite, always. There
was nobody else. And the rage welled up in her again at the
dressmaker's, perched upon her silver heels, her arms out to her
sides: could she let him give her away, she wondered; but could
not countenance the breach if she denied him. Not now. It
would have to be as they had planned, but always, always, she
would hold in her heart the memory of her buried rancor, the
chemical taste of it, and it would taint and corrode the wedding and its recollection, invisibly but as surely as an acid bath.

Not to mention Danielle, or Julius, her closest friends gone
AWOL, lost in their own selfishnesses at this, Marina's most
important moment. Danielle, who had accused her husband-
to-be of every dishonesty, of charlatanism, almost, out of some
unspeakable coil of envy which Marina knew she ought to be
able to forgive (poor Danielle, with her secretive and failed
infatuations; it had to be hard, after all, stranded alone, to see
Marina blissful) but couldn't, quite, yet. Her maid of honor:
Danielle, too, would process, part of the parade of clandestine
ill will. It seemed an intolerable prospect, for all Danielle had
retracted her harsh words, had tried to paper over. No wonder
Marina feared Bootie's bursting in: these tiny, skewering

dramas seemed impossible to control, to contain: there had to be an eruption, some eruption, whether her own or someone else's; at which point Bootie was the safest, most expendable among them.

When she got home, she tried to explain this to Ludo, who dabbled abstractedly in his plate of sushi, but she was bound by loyalties and confidences and did not, above all, want to pain him or suggest to him that those around her welcomed him anything less than wholeheartedly, and thus he didn't really understand what she was trying to say and dismissed it, tediously, as the "archetypal jitters." "Don't be predictable, my sweet," he said with a wave of his chopsticks. "It's so unlike you. We've got such important things to focus on, just now."

CHAPTER FORTY-NINE

Home Again

David lay on the futon with his eyes shut. "I can't believe this," he said.

"You can't believe what?"

"What do you think I mean?"

Julius sat at the table with his chin in his hands. The room was really very small, especially for two people; and after David's place, parodically dingy. "You can see why I never invited you here," he said.

"I can't see, though, why you ever lived here in the first place. It's disgusting. What does it say about you that this is your home?"

"It's very cheap."

"Standards, Lady Muck. You of all people know a body needs standards."

"It's very cheap. We can afford it. When we strike it rich, we can go again."

"Which is worse, do you think: this place together, or this place alone?"

Julius sniffed. "I lived here for six years on my own and perfectly well."

"But not happily."

Julius shrugged. He wasn't sure, at this point, what happiness might entail. Perhaps all these years he had been happy without knowing. It seemed perfectly possible.

"Because it feels unhappy. You know, there are animals that go off by themselves to die? I don't know which ones, but there are. It feels like a place you might go to die."

"Thanks a lot."

"Seriously, the vibe is bizarre."

"Maybe it was the boy, Marina's cousin."

"Dank."

Julius nodded, but felt guilty about it. The boy had contrived to inspire nothing but guilt since the first unfortunate encounter. "He's not so bad, I hear."

"From whom, exactly?"

"Okay. He's dank."

"Do you really want me to go to this wedding? I'm not sure I can face it."

"She's one of my best friends. Maybe my best friend. And oldest."

"I know, I know. The gorgeous WASP in the cafeteria line on the second day of college. It'll all be so fancy, the incredible guest list. I know, I know."

"I've been to plenty of things for you." Now, more than ever, Julius was aware of this. Aware of all he had relinquished—willingly, it was true; but still. This wedding was non-negotiable.

"What's with you and your college friends? It's like you never moved on."

"I never needed to."

"Is that the benefit or the drawback of going to such a fancy school?"

"Since when is Union not fancy?"

"It's not hobnobbing with the jetset."

"She's not the jetset, David. Believe me." He couldn't resist: "That you could mistake Marina for the jetset shows you haven't got a clue."

"My point exactly."

"I am asking you to do this. And I'm asking you to drive the car, and we have to pick it up in an hour. The wedding is at six, and it takes two and a half hours to get there, and I wanted to check in to the hotel first."

"I think I let the movers take my tux. It's in storage, by now—can't get it till Monday. Oops. Sorry."

"Then your regular black suit will be fine."

"Fine? I don't think so."

"I packed for you." Julius pointed at the two suit bags by the door. "Everything we need, including lotion and breath mints."

David still had his eyes shut, his arms over his head. "Shaving cream?"

"Toothpaste, too."

"A bedtime story?"

"Also."

"I'm still not sure I can go. Just the thought of it upsets my stomach. It's like all your friends are members of Mensa or something. Like you have to pass some stupid test to join the club."

"I should have made you meet them before."

"Why?"

"You wouldn't dread it, then. You might even be looking forward to it."

"I'm not dreading it. I mean, who *are* these people?"

"Her dad is actually pretty famous, you know."

"In pretentious magazines nobody reads."

"Does it matter? She's my best friend."

"Doesn't that make it worse? She's had so much of you, for such a long time. I can't really stand it. And you're mine, now."

"I'm not anybody's, Mister Man. As you well know."

"You don't love me." David sat up, put on a miserable grimace, like a clown's unhappy face. His hair was appealingly tousled. "If you loved me, you'd spare me this. You'd stay here with me."

"Come with me. At least as far as Stockbridge. You have to drive the car. The hotel will be cute—Marina promised. And then decide."

David stood. "It has to be cuter than this hole."

Julius batted playfully at his arm. "This is my home. Ever so humble, and all that. If *you* love *me,* you'll suck it up."

"I'll drive you to Stockbridge." He sighed, a gargantuan mockery of a sigh. "Who ever thought I'd end up like this. Lady Muck's humble chauffeur, and keeper of the Muck Hovel."

"I'm not joking," Julius said, in a joking voice. "I really can't be doing with that."

"Oh no, oh please, Lady Muck, forgive me!"

"I really can't, David." Julius, too, was standing, and thin-lipped, and google-eyed. He was still trying to pretend that he was in jest, because although they both knew otherwise, the pretense seemed important. "So why don't you go shine up the Bentley, and we'll be off."

David made a noise in between a snort and a giggle, an ultimately unparseable noise that further irritated Julius; but he moved to the door and shouldered his bag even as he made the noise and Julius knew that this first step, at least, he had won.

"You'll have a good time, I know it," he said in the close stairwell, where the old and odorous air hung unmoving. Then amended: "Or an interesting time, at least. I can promise you an interesting time. And interesting is good, right?"

"May you live in interesting times? Is that good? I thought it was a Confucian curse, not a blessing."

"Well, sweetheart." Julius briefly slipped an arm around David's waist as they stepped onto the street, but pulled it immediately away because he thought he could feel David flinch, because he knew David didn't want their intimacy to be seen. "No worries on that score, at least. Whatever else they may be, our times are almost criminally uninteresting. The dullest times ever."

"We can make them exciting, Lady Muck," David said, suddenly apparently more cheerful. "Just getting out of that place is a start. Look, the sun is shining. Look, the world is still here."

"It's not that bad."

"It is, too. Don't pout. It is, too. Out here in the wider world, even Stockbridge seems possible. It's that place, I'm telling you. Where animals go to die."

CHAPTER FIFTY

Lady in Waiting

This time seemed as though it would be much worse than the Fourth of July. It had to be. She was the only one who wasn't family—aside from Seeley, who couldn't, in this context, count—staying in the house. The spinster room, of course, as ever. But that wasn't the challenge. The challenge was the thickness of the air. She, who had felt she saw so clearly that it hurt, had felt that the truth, crystalline, was, with Murray, granted her (though not through his help, or anything he did: but just by his presence; as though, indeed, he were but a part of her that had been lost, a magnificent Platonic epiphany repeated, and daily repeated: this, surely, was love!), felt, now, that the weight of emotion lay like a veil, a fine mist. No exchange, however simple, was untainted. Paradoxically, only Ludovic seemed the same, his lightly mutable self in the face of all crises, flitting into and out of conversations with a sardonic flick of the tongue. Marina was a mess. Her mother, the indomitable Annabel, had fallen into frantic distraction: so busy doing (where were the boutonnières? Now please, now—and the disposition of the chairs, in their slightly arced rows, before the pergola; and the tying up of the marquee's sides, on account of the clement weather; and the scudding cumulus clouds in the sky, were they, too, something to be done?) that she couldn't listen. She and her daughter repeatedly presented to Danielle the tableau of supplicant child, trailing, anguished, in her mother's wake. This vision—repeated on the lawn, in the kitchen, the bathroom—forced Danielle to reconsider the Thwaite family dynamic, or rather, like the trick of an Escher drawing, to see the same thing in reverse. Always, Danielle had seen Annabel as the odd one out, taking forlorn care of a husband and daughter whose passionate bond had no place for her. But on this day she felt enlightened: maybe, in fact, Marina and Murray so greatly needed Annabel, desired her attentions more than anything, that, unrequited, they turned to each other for consolation because the great, nurturing force of her was so widely dispersed—upon the running of their worlds, the making of weddings, the salvation of DeVaughn and others like DeVaughn, always the kind word, the palm upon the shoulder, the extra, and meaningful effort—that they were left ravenous for more, clinging satellites to her sun. Danielle had seen Annabel as dispensable where in fact she was—Marina tripped up the stairs behind her mother, all but reaching for her hem— The Family incarnate.

Which made Danielle smart. Because by this logic, she too was consolation, not the respite and final fulfillment she had all this time imagined. Murray turned to her not heliotropically, but in the small and sorry spirit of diversion. This didn't seem possible—given what they shared, their private realm of truth among the Rothkos—but once imagined, it didn't any longer seem impossible, either, and gnawed at her, on the wedding day, till—even in the midst of makeup, the hairdresser, fetching sparkling water for Marina, laughing, the two of them in their underwear after they'd both run their stockings and decided to do without them—she could think of nothing else.

Murray kept well out of things. His study was off their bedroom, and even on the morning of Marina's wedding he sequestered himself there, supposedly finishing a newspaper column, or was it a magazine essay, Marina wasn't quite sure, but told Danielle they weren't to bother him—not even about the champagne or the ice, which were his jobs—until after noon.

At lunchtime, the caterer set out sandwiches, chips, watermelon, and lemonade on the kitchen island, and everyone foraged, each taking his portion on a paper plate to a remote corner. Marina, suddenly overcome with superstition, retreated to her bedroom so as not to see Ludovic (who, in a parody of propriety which Marina herself had requested, had been moved, for two nights, to solitary confinement in the other, double, guestroom) and told Danielle she needed some time by herself to think. Which is how Danielle came to be in the pergola, with her mozzarella, basil, and tomato on focaccia, her back to the house, aware of the late bees against the screen and only at the last, and suddenly, of Murray joining her.

"May I?"

"Perhaps not a good idea."

"My family would think it odd if I didn't flirt with you just a little. I have a reputation to live up to."

"I'm finding it pretty weird, all this."

"I'm staying out of it." He sat, on the bench opposite her, as far away as he could be. It felt as if her skin were attempting to move her body, to close the gap: yearning.

"Hard to do when you're Best Woman. It's my job to be involved."

"Quite."

"I haven't asked a lot, have I?"

"What on earth do you mean? You can ask whatever you want."

"I want the night. A night, any one. Just all of it."

"Yes. That would be . . . yes."

"You'd have to lie. You won't want to."

He looked up at her, through his hair, like a boy.

"You could say you were traveling. A talk. You forgot, someone reminded you, you have to go."

"When?"

"Soon."

"Why now?"

"Because." She sighed. She couldn't say that it was because she had been struck with the fear that he loved his wife. In their discourse, so mature, it was a laudable trait, to love your wife. He spoke of it often, and she played along, taking it for the necessary rhetoric of a man over thirty years married. But he was, in his way, a truth-teller—that, above all, was what she had idealized, had wanted—and in this newly imagined light, he meant each word as it was said. Only her skills as a reader were at fault. "Because I want you to; and I've never asked you anything like it. Nor will I, ever again."

"Don't promise too much." He, too, sighed. She wished she knew the meaning of the sigh, which seemed, suddenly, open to many interpretations, few of them favorable to her. Then he said, very quietly, "Don't you know yet that the more we have, the more we'll want?"

And she felt a flush of delight.

He stood, holding his untouched plate in front of him like an offering. He ran his hand through his hair, in his boyish way. She wanted to kiss him, looked down at her watermelon instead.

"I have a lecture in Chicago next Monday that's been postponed," he said. "I found out yesterday. It's on the calendar. I'm officially out of town."

"Would you do that?"

"I'm officially out of town," he said. And as he was leaving, "Do you want some vodka in your lemonade to get you through? Easily done, no one would know."

"I'll be fine," she said, swallowing the "now."

CHAPTER FIFTY-ONE

"Vows by Lisa Solomon"
Special to the *New York Times*

When the bride strolled down the aisle on her father's arm, gasps were audible among the assembly. Swathed in a close-fitting seafoam chiffon, she carried a profusion of calla lilies, and wore two more entwined in her raven hair. Her smile, one guest observed, was like a second sun in the glorious late summer afternoon: "She's always been that way. A ray of sunshine." The vows, written by the couple themselves, were exchanged on the steps of a romantic summer house at the bottom of the garden at the bride's family's country home in western Massachusetts, under the authority of Judith Rohmer, a local justice of the peace and longtime family friend. The bride teared visibly, and the couple held hands throughout.

"The whole wedding was *so* Marina," according to her friend the critic Julius Clarke, who has known her since their college days at Brown. "We all knew that when she got married, she'd do it more beautifully than anyone. She's always been an 'it' girl, her whole life." A journalist and author of the forthcoming book *The Emperor's Children Have No Clothes*, Marina Thwaite, 30, is the daughter of the celebrated journalist Murray Thwaite, and has attracted attention as an intellectual and socialite since her high school days, when she was both an organizer of the national movement for high school students against apartheid and a sometime model for *Elle* and *Seventeen*.

Her husband, Ludovic Seeley, 36—himself an "it" man, featured last month in *New York* magazine's article on eligible bachelors—agrees: "It was love at first sight, for me," he maintains. "We met through a friend of hers [Danielle Minkoff, a producer for public television, who was also "best woman"], and the moment we were introduced I knew she was the one." This was an introduction in passing at the Metropolitan Museum, "tellingly, over food, not art," Marina laughs. It took them some weeks to meet again—at a gala honoring Marina's father—but once they did, in May of this year, things moved very quickly.

"We knew we were destined to be together," Marina explains. "So what was the point of waiting?"

The irony, for this young couple, is that they have to bring their first "baby" into the world in just two weeks: Mr. Seeley, originally from Sydney, Australia, moved to New York city earlier this year to take the helm of the new Merton Publications weekly, *The Monitor,* which launches on September thirteenth. Marina Thwaite is cultural editor for the magazine. "It's very exciting to be working together on this amazing new publication," Marina says. "It's really going to wow people. Ludo is an amazing editor."

Her husband returns the compliment. "Marina just came on board over the summer, and she's done a phenomenal job. It's a superlative team, and I think readers are going to be surprised by the magazine—it's something completely new."

The launch party, rather like this wedding and only fractionally less exclusive, is slated to be one of the fall calendar's major social bashes. "It'll be a little flashier," Ludo confesses. "We wanted our wedding to be low-key and intimate."

The bride's father, Murray Thwaite (author, most recently of *When the Fat Lady Sings*), hasn't yet seen any of *The Monitor*'s articles. "I've been hearing about it, though. It's going to be unlike anything else. It's going to be great."

If the wedding is anything to judge by, that's certainly true. The familiar faces of New York and Washington intelligentsia sipped champagne and nibbled at caviar blinis on the rolling lawn while a chamber ensemble played Mozart in the twilight. The tree frogs serenaded the party, too; and as night fell, the guests were ushered to splendidly decorated tables under a grand marquee. When the time came to cut the cake, Ms. Thwaite and Mr. Seeley returned to the folly where they had made their vows, and embraced in front of a cheering crowd.

It wasn't staid elegance, however: once the dancing got underway, Ms. Thwaite kicked off her heels and spun out onto the grass, her dapper husband, his bow-tie loosened, right behind her. "It just feels incredible," she said.

"Whoever knew that getting married could feel so liberating?"

"It's all a matter of finding the right editor," Mr. Seeley quipped, as he twirled his bride to the samba beat.

CHAPTER FIFTY-TWO

Bedtime

"We got through it." Murray lay on the bed with his eyes closed, hands clasped behind his head. "We did it. Let me say, *you* did it. You did it all. Brava."

"Not really. I'm glad it went off well."

"They're still cleaning up. Four-thirty."

"That's a good wedding."

"Is anyone else still here? I mean, have we got any guests around?"

"I think Danielle left with Julius and his boyfriend. I told her to stay, but I guess she thought it would be weird, to have breakfast with just you and me. Too much parents."

Murray didn't open his eyes. He pictured her in her apartment, the light across her cheek. He sighed. "She's a good kid. She loves Marina."

"She didn't want her to marry Ludovic, though."

"Who did?"

"Come off it, you. Nobody could have passed your tests. He adores her."

"Does he? He's a slippery fish."

"That's what Danielle thinks."

"It's a package, isn't it, what he's bought."

"Bought?"

"Won. However you want to put it. He's hooked our Marina, and ended up related to me at the same time."

"That's a little self-absorbed even for you, my darling."

Murray straightened, opened his eyes, and began to unbutton his shirt. "I wish I thought so. He's pure ambition, that slinky snaky so-and-so, with his too-tight shirts. He wants to do something spectacular, and believe me, doing away with me would be good enough. The closer he gets, the more mortal the blow."

"What are you talking about?"

"The article. The boy's article."

"What about it?"

"He told me himself, the kid, he told me that Seeley wanted to publish it. Probably still does. I'm not demented, you know."

"I'm sure he was just making it up to get back at you. Bootie. Frederick. That poor kid. He worshiped you."

"And had a bloody peculiar way of showing it."

Annabel stepped out of her dress and stood in her slip, in a pool of silk. "They love each other. It's their time now."

"My time ain't over yet, baby." Murray wrapped his arms around his wife, lifted her off the ground, out of her dress, and dropped her, with a bounce, onto the bed.

"No, I don't imagine it is," she said, and laughed. "But it's four-thirty in the morning."

"We have eternity for sleeping. There's no rush."

CHAPTER FIFTY-THREE

Tiger Woods

Danielle woke up on the floor of Julius and David's hotel room, at the end of their bed, wrapped in their bedspread, slightly clammy, and in her underwear. They were still sleeping, one of them snoring softly, and Julius's foot dangled in the air perilously near her head. Something—either the bedspread or the carpet, of a fading crimson, patterned with large escutcheons, and very close to her cheek—smelled musty. She contemplated leaving, slipping out discreetly before they stirred; only to remember that she was trapped in Stockbridge and reliant on their help. Everyone—Marina and Annabel, that is—had expected her to stay on at the Thwaites' after the newlyweds had departed, in their festooned, chauffeur-driven car, for a fancy hotel in Lenox. Perhaps they'd imagined, too, that she'd ride back to the city with Murray and Annabel, making cheerful conversation from the backseat. She couldn't have done it. In the shower, she remembered the night before in snatches: the ceremony, the speeches, the spat between bride and groom in the stairwell when they thought no one was there. Marina had been tense, almost angry, at the beginning of the party— Danielle figured it had to do with Murray, with her ambivalence about her father—but had put on her best social face, and Danielle had watched as she'd slowly melted into her role, until she was the exuberant carefree beauty she appeared to be. The spat on the stairs seemed to be about the woman from the *Times* Style section. Seeley was telling Marina not to blow her off. "It's good for *The Monitor*," he was saying. "Keep it in mind."

"It's our fucking wedding, Ludo. I don't want to keep talking to that crazy bat with her notebook."

"It's the *New York Times*."

"I don't give a fuck. It's bad enough that she's here at all. Let her watch us all she wants. I don't want to talk to her."

Whereupon Danielle had revealed herself, made a joke, and offered to mop up the journalist if they wanted her to.

"She just asked for five minutes to speak to Marina," Seeley said, tight-lipped. The rose in his lapel seemed to quiver with exasperation. "It isn't much."

"Hey, M"—Danielle, against her better instincts, opted to palliate—"five minutes? For the smooth unfolding of your wedding night? Go on, you can do it. For Ludo, here. For love?"

The look Marina gave her was peculiar, as though she thought Danielle was making fun, or judging. As though, Danielle thought in the shower, Marina thought that Danielle thought that Seeley was revealing his true cynic's colors. For him, even the wedding was about advancing his career. She hadn't considered it at the time; and maybe she was projecting. In any event, Marina had recomposed her features, sallied forth, smiling, and fulfilled her duties to love and to *The Monitor*.

And of the evening, above all she remembered, inevitably,

Murray. After their lunchtime conversation, they had barely exchanged a word, but she'd been always aware of him, as if he were electronically tagged, aware from afar of the terrifying expertise of his apparent indifference, of his impeccable ability to play the necessary role. He and Marina, two of a kind.

And, too, there'd been Julius, the long-lost, only mildly sheepish on the arm of his beau. David seemed fine. In fact, David seemed, to Danielle, a matter of no possible significance, a young—definitely younger—perfectly polite, handsome-enough, sort of boring-seeming guy from Westchester, a businessy type, the kind of guy, back in college, to whom you cheerfully said hello at the salad bar, with a genuine smile, even, but with whom you never bothered further, because you sensed—from the clothes, the friends, the haircut, the major (probably Political Science, or Economics), even from the tenor of his voice—that he didn't have anything interesting to say. His most intriguing feature, to Danielle's mind, was the degree to which he seemed ordinary, urnormal, even heterosexual: the chino'ed center of the privileged nation. Which might explain at least part of Julius's attraction, of course; but as for its intensity, its prolonged secrecy—Danielle was mystified. David didn't seem hostile, after all—"I've heard a lot about you, yeah, great," he offered, along with his rather feeble hand, upon their introduction—merely irrelevant. More generously put, he remained amiably reserved. She noticed that he didn't dance, a certain type, and instead sat on the sidelines with a bourbon on the rocks and a tolerant but weary expression while Danielle and Julius spun and dipped in front of him. She'd expected, given the history, that Julius would kowtow to his lover, focus, above all, on David in this gathering of old friends that didn't include him, but Julius proved refreshingly, Julius-ly, callous on that score, and abandoned David for long stretches to gossip with people he hadn't seen for years.

Tanya Reed, for example: Danielle had never especially liked her, and everyone had always claimed her sourness was born of insecurity—Danielle didn't buy such excuses: "We're all insecure," she would say, "and then some people are polite and some people are rude." It was a firm tenet of Randy Minkoff's. But success had rendered Tanya, while more expensively dressed and coiffed (with the result that she looked less of a pinhead, her horsily narrow face now balanced by a pouffy brown bubble), no less of a lemon; and after Julius spent ten minutes catching up on her career (*Newsweek,* book contract, an invitation to teach at Georgetown), Danielle stood back and watched Tanya's attempts, rather spastic, to move her body in time to the music, an irregular jerking and flailing in a lavender sateen suit, and whispered, to Julius, upon his return from dancing, "There goes one bony-assed white woman."

Which Julius then repeated to David, who laughed with a zeal Danielle deemed misogynistic: he was laughing, she felt, at the wrong thing. But he seemed to like Danielle better after that, and made more effort to converse.

He hadn't been pleased, however, about sharing his hotel room. Julius and he had engaged in some close whispering, after Danielle had asked Julius the favor. She knew it was a big one—she suspected they'd envisaged their stay in the clattery old New England inn as a romantic getaway rather than a slumber party—but she felt she had no alternative. As the two men conferred, she saw Julius shake his head; and at one point it seemed he was on the verge of shaking his finger. Of course she

was welcome, he assured her afterward. It was no trouble at all.
And David gamely helped her carry her things from the little
blue room to their waiting silver Grand Am, "a Budget beauty,"
David drawled, with a roll of his eyes.

When she came out of the bathroom, dressed in clean
clothes and with her hair wet, David was sitting up in bed, his
torso naked, his back against the wooden headboard. He was
wearing glasses, which he hadn't done the night before. Julius,
still asleep, twitched mildly.

"I can drive you to the train, if you like," he said.

"Right now?"

David shrugged. "No time like the present."

"I don't know the schedules."

"Amtrak? They'll be regular."

"It's Sunday, too."

"Still, morning, noon, you know."

"You'd like to take me *now*."

"It seems the most convenient."

Danielle was almost impressed. He was quite pleasant about
it, in his way, but clearly David would brook no opposition. He
wanted her gone before the day—his day with Julius—was
begun. "Whatever suits you," she said. She wasn't going to
struggle against it—after all, she'd barged into their romantic
retreat uninvited—but nor would she forget. Nor was she meant
to forget, she realized: the boundaries were being set. She was
being tacitly informed that she ought not to intrude thus again.

The station, at Albany, was almost an hour away. David drove
fast, with music on—something current, vaguely familiar, but

Danielle couldn't place it. He wasn't particularly inclined to talk, but Danielle, intermittently, insisted.

"How's the job search going?" she asked, at one point.

He flicked a glance at her, as though he couldn't quite believe she would ask that, of all questions. "Okay," he said. "I guess. I mean, who knows, really? Not okay, in that I don't have a job."

"No."

He didn't volunteer anything more. After a while, she said, "What do you think of Julius's place?"

"Grim," he said. "Famously grim. Lethally grim."

She nodded. "I haven't been there in ages, but it always has been."

"Unsalvageably grim. Not fit for human habitation."

"Surely not that bad?"

"I saw the tenant moving out yesterday morning. Tall, plump kid with big glasses, moon-faced on the street corner. Looked like he barely made it out alive."

"That's Bootie—Frederick—Tubb. Marina's cousin. He looked that way for other reasons. Nothing to do with the apartment, I swear."

"And they would be?"

"Julius didn't talk about it?"

"Hard as it may be to believe, the life of Bootie Tubb is not a big topic at our house."

"It's a long story. He would've been at the wedding, but he's had a falling out."

"With Marina?"

"With all of them." Now it was Danielle's turn not to want

to talk. "He's just a kid," she said. "A brainy, fucked-up kid. Like we all were."

"Speak for yourself."

"Which do you think you weren't?"

He gave her a withering glare. The silence fell again.

"What did you major in, in college?" she ventured again, after a time.

"Poli Sci."

"Mm-hmm."

"You must have been English, right?"

"Does it show that badly? We all were. I was double, English and Philosophy. I don't remember a thing."

"Who does?"

"Seriously, though, I look at the books on my shelves and it's clear that I read them, back then, but I can't remember ever doing it, and I don't have the first idea what they might be about."

"Read them again, then?"

Danielle sighed. "Not now. Maybe someday. I look at them and wonder who I was, you know? It's a long time ago. I'm *thirty.*"

"You should throw those books away."

"Like, in the garbage?"

"Like that."

"Sacrilege. It would be."

"Do you hang on to clothes you haven't worn for ten years? Or bags of pasta, or cans of beans?"

Danielle did not need to answer.

"What is it about books? Perfectly rational people get crazy about their books. Who has time for that?"

"I measure my life out in books."

"You should be measuring your life by living. Correction: you shouldn't be measuring your life. What's the point?"

"Julius measures his, too."

"I don't think so."

"He used to."

"We all change. Thank God."

Danielle, marginally offended on Julius's behalf, took a deep breath. "Speaking of which, you got him a new suit."

"Before I got the ax. Yeah. Nice, isn't it? Italian."

"The cuffs aren't frayed. I missed the old Agnès B., his so-called 'signature,' i.e., only, suit. But he looks good in the new one."

"He looks a bit like Tiger Woods, don't you think?"

"It never occurred to me." Danielle thought for a second. "I guess, a little bit." She chewed her lip. "Do you follow golf, then?"

"I play it, too."

"Wow. I don't think I've ever really known a golfer before."

"Is it so hilarious?"

"Not at all—I just, I didn't know people, younger people, really played anymore."

David said nothing.

"I know, that sounds idiotic. I just never thought about it. Clearly." The car, with its powerful a/c and new plastic smell, lapsed into mechanically augmented silence. Danielle reflected that growing up, coupling, was a process of growing away from mirth, as if, like an amphibian, one ceased to breathe in the same way: laughter, once vital sustenance, protean relief and all that made isolation and struggle and fear bearable, was replaced by the stolid matter of stability: nominally content, resigned and unafraid, one grew to fear jokes and their capacity to unsettle. Where there had been laughter, there came a cold breeze. What, after all, was Julius doing shacked up with a golf-loving businessman? A year ago, he would himself have guffawed at the notion. All of them, all three of them: a year ago, they'd been still linked, inexorably and, they'd thought, forever. It was supposedly better this way—each of them had found her heart's desire—but did they laugh as they had done for so many years? Would they ever laugh that way again, or was it over, now, in the Realm of Adult Sobriety?

As they drove, at speed, along the highway, she watched David, as much as possible without appearing to do so. He didn't look as though he'd ever been much of a laugher. He looked as though he'd been a golf-playing businessman even in short pants. It seemed hard to credit that this person made Julius's joy, that he was either Pierre or Natasha to Julius's Pierre or Natasha. Whatever she had against Ludovic Seeley, she didn't think him a nonentity. He, at least, would make Marina laugh; or he should. He was evil incarnate, though nobody but she, it seemed, could tell, but in that very extremity, he was worth the trouble. And Murray: for one thing, she was biased; for another, he was funny. Marina had always said, from the beginning, that he made them all laugh. Prone to antics.

The wedding had been powerfully antic-free. No fisticuffs; no unexpected tears; all the speeches the right side of good taste, her own included. She kept waiting for someone to mention Bootie Tubb—early on, when Marina was getting dressed, one of the catering staff had come upstairs to tell them that there was a young man at the door, and Marina had been obsessed that it would be Bootie; but it was instead a florist's assistant from Great Barrington, bearing a trailing purple orchid sent by friends of Marina's mother's in California, addressed to "Marina & Hugo, The Happy Couple"—but of course nobody did. Nor did anybody mention his mother. They were only significant in their absence: had they been there, nobody would have noticed, he the silent, rather forlorn youth, scoffing cake alone at a table and mooning quietly over the bride; and she, his mother, in Danielle's imagination, blousy, ruddy, slightly tiddly and by the end tearful, lace handkerchief aloft, burbling sentimentally about her niece, the ties of blood, all that she and Murray had shared growing up. No, Marina's perfect wedding had been too tasteful for them; they could never have come, the commoners at the feast. The falling out—the family feud—had been necessary, if only for that reason.

Nobody to say this to, either. Murray, the only possible ear, felt too strongly to laugh about it. Danielle, in David's rental car, missed laughing so hard she couldn't breathe, so hard she almost peed, wheezing, bent double, tears forced from the corners of her eyes. When they were in college, out to dinner at an Italian restaurant—it must have been someone's birthday—Julius, clean and controlled Julius, once laughed so hard he'd fallen off his seat, had crawled out of the restaurant on his hands and knees and rolled helplessly on the grubby sidewalk, still overcome. Or again, at a faculty dance performance with Marina, they'd been so possessed by the comedy of it that they'd snorted in their row like truffling hogs, repeatedly, uncontrollably, until finally they dashed from the auditorium, leaving the door to slam behind them, and fell to loud hilarity in the lobby. (That time, they'd been spotted by a professor who sought them out and reprimanded them, and asked them to write notes of apology to the dancers.) Was that all over forever, then? Was that type of laughter, in and of itself, immaturity? Something adults didn't do, especially not in couples. Something lost forever. How unutterably sad.

David left her at the door to the station and drove away with a wave, she'd recognized, more cheerful than any gesture she'd seen from him till then, so pleased was he to be rid of her, and she found herself with an hour and twenty minutes to kill in the barren, bland waiting room, in the company of a couple of vending machines (from which Danielle retrieved, after lengthy perusal, an ancient and faintly soggy granola bar in a green foil wrapper) and a harried mother of two, whose strapping infant and lurching toddler between them filled the space with such commotion—wailing, clattering, stomping, bawling—that it was impossible even to read the newspaper. Eventually, Danielle retreated to a bench along the platform in the shade to escape the racket, and marveled, newly glum, at her strange and unnecessary isolation. She might fall, here, in front of a train, and nobody would even know she'd been there—at Albany, for God's sake, alone on the Sunday of Labor Day weekend, completely unmoored, headed back to the bunglings—the lipo was a "go"—and the deafening quiet of her lonely life.

Murray, Murray, Murray. She took the cell phone out of her pocket, looked at it, put it back. She imagined him still asleep, Annabel's proprietary arm across his chest, the beautiful light falling on the foot of their bed, the house finally quiet in that secret, delectable way, as if they were returned at last to Eden, to a life without children, and could undress anywhere, romp naked on the grass, feed each other grapes and honeyed cakes in bed, like a late Roman emperor and his empress. In which scenario, Danielle became some unnecessary trifle, an exhausted amusement. This was one of two incompatible but equally certain visions that she held simultaneously in her mind. In the other—and how could it not be so?—having at last and belatedly discovered his soul mate, his Platonic other half, he pined for her, waking and sleeping, and when she so much as entered the room, or even the building, he knew it, and prickled to be near her, his inner voice speaking always already to hers and yearning telepathically to be heard. She wanted him to be wanting her, even now, in bed with Annabel, to be wanting to reach for his cell phone, to establish a connection: their connection.

And yet: maybe it didn't matter which vision was true because he *wouldn't*—surely that was the point: he wouldn't—pick up his cell phone. So the desire, whether a fact or a figment—and yet, its reality, its unknowable fact-ness, was of consuming importance to her—was not ultimately even relevant. How had she got herself into this situation? A hot breeze blew wrappers and grit across the platform, as if in disgust at Danielle's weakness. And what detoxifying remedy could return her to herself? Even the prospect of her apartment—of the Rothkos, like the bed, waiting, waiting—was poisoned, now. She would turn on the cell phone, would go directly from Penn Station to her office, and leave the rejoicing to everyone else. And damned though that Conehead might be—she hadn't liked him any better than she'd imagined she would—she hoped that he made Julius, funny old Julius, happy.

CHAPTER FIFTY-FOUR

An Evening on the Town

They had a good time, all in all, in Stockbridge. A quiet week-end away, into which the wedding intruded for only a few lively but aesthetic hours. David had been charming, had graciously conceded to putting up Danielle for the night, had gallantly driven her all the way to Albany in the morning. He refrained from making cutting remarks about Marina and Danielle—although he couldn't resist a few catty jibes about the vows, about Murray ("that crusty old dinosaur, with entitlement written all over him. I'm surprised he wasn't wearing madras plaid") and, with a certain frisson, about Ludovic Seeley, too—and even claimed to have enjoyed meeting them at last. Julius both believed him and didn't believe him, was at once pleased and disappointed. It seemed, indeed, that cohabitation, rather than a state of peace, was, for Julius at least, a state of constant, rather wearing, contradiction.

One of the things they did discuss that weekend, Julius and David, was the state of their union: they had a "talk about us." David brought it up, in the context of the wedding: what was marriage, after all, and how were they different from, say, Marina and Ludovic? They'd been together longer, already, and their relationship, he pointed out, was no less intense. If they could marry—maybe someday they'd be able to marry: after all, civil unions were legal in Vermont, and surely from there it was only a few short steps—would they want to, and what might it mean? Julius had said that even if they married, it would mean something different from a heterosexual wedding.

"Totally," David agreed. "But how so?"

"Well, I wouldn't wear a chiffon dress, for one thing. But it's like, I think, a gay mind-set is a more sophisticated approach to relationships." He'd said this as they lounged on the porch of the inn, watching a couple—wide-bottomed, beshorted, slow—remove cases from the trunk of their maroon Lexus, apparently while squabbling almost silently. "Like that: we wouldn't end up like *that*. In part because we know love, and we know desire, don't we."

David narrowed his eyes at the couple. "My God. I wouldn't ever wear those stripes," he said. "You're safe from that, at least."

"But I mean about relationships, we make them work because every gay couple precisely has to rewrite the rules. You don't get the rules handed down by society."

"No."

Julius paused. The couple shuffled past them into the inn, creaking the door for an unnecessarily long time. "So what are our rules, then?" he asked, looking back out to the street, its New England charm and its ice-cream eating tourists.

"How do you mean?"

"Mutual respect, tolerance, forgiveness . . ."

"Of course."

"And we know, like I said, not to confuse love and desire."

"Sure."

Julius looked at David, who was now flipping through a copy of *Vanity Fair*, left on the porch by an earlier guest. "Are you even listening?"

"Love and desire," David repeated, glancing up. "The great gay couples absolutely know the difference."

"And we?"

"Are a great gay couple."

There they had left it, turning instead to the profile of Mark Wahlberg, whom they'd recently seen in *Planet of the Apes*, just because they both found him attractive. Julius understood them to have exchanged a moment of powerful honesty, an acknowledgment of their needs, of the need for Lewis, or for Dale. It was thrilling, quietly thrilling, to be able to speak not wholly openly but with such clarity about something so fraught. He felt relieved, and assumed that David, too, felt this way.

When they got back to New York—back to the wearying job hunt, back to the Pitt Street hovel, about which David wouldn't stop complaining—it seemed crucial to keep hold of that conversation, of the memory of what made this union, for all its bickering (now there was a good deal of bickering) and all its sulking (of which there was also a good deal), strong and unique. Because Julius, unshakably, felt oppressed. He felt the weight of David and of David's need upon him. David, for example, now wanted but didn't want sex, seemed, rather, to want Julius to want it, but then not to reciprocate, as if initiating some unpleasant and faintly demeaning spiral, willing between them a theatrical misalignment from which there might be no simple retreat. Speaking to Danielle on the phone (and he found himself dialing Danielle's number more than once—it turned out, of course, that he still knew it by heart), Julius guiltily observed that without work and without money, David was not the blithe, fun-loving man he had once been. Querulous, he proved also black-tempered, even pessimistic.

One morning, after a night of abortive and awkward attempts at intimacy, in which David had all but rebuffed him, Julius had to bully his lover to get dressed. David lay sprawled on his belly, crucified on the futon naked, in what amounted to the middle of the room. Julius, wanting to get dressed and organized—he'd decided to take his laptop to a café to work, because he wanted to get the piece for Marina finished (okay, the differing ethoses of gay club generations was hardly Proust; but it would pay the bills) as quickly as possible—had to step around and over his boyfriend's protruding limbs at least half a dozen times. Finally, David snarled, "Leave me the fuck alone, okay?"

"I'm trying to leave you alone, although why you want to be left alone in this apartment you hate so much is beyond me."

David grunted.

"You could get up and come out for breakfast. We can sit on the terrace at the Time Café. Egg white omelet? Chai latte?"

"I said fuck off."

Julius put his hands on his hips. "If you don't sit up and look at me right now, I'll walk, you know. I'll walk."

And David sat, bleary, pale, his eyes webbed with misery and sleep.

"Now stand," Julius said.

David didn't move.

"You're coming to breakfast. Stand up."

"Fuck off," David said again, but he stood, and, without

washing, dressed, and, a mass of sweat and glower, followed Julius out the door. He didn't speak and he didn't come to breakfast; but instead brusquely detached himself and went off to lift weights. He maintained that the very shower in Pitt Street was infested with cockroaches and too filthy to use, and insisted upon washing at the gym. To which he retreated obsessively in the week after Labor Day, for three, sometimes four, hours in a day. As if he had appointments. As if he were CEO of the cross-trainer, a Nautilus Nero. By Friday afternoon, Julius snapped: "Do you think you're going to find a job there? Maybe you see yourself as a future personal trainer?" In the wake of which, remorseful, he then suggested supper at their restaurant.

"Paid for by you, I suppose, Lady Muck?" David said.

"I'm almost done with this thing for Marina, and I've got a column for the *Voice* to do, and probably a piece for *Slate,* too. I'm just waiting to hear. So yes, paid for by me, actually. We need a treat." It had been only a week since Stockbridge, but they did. *He* did. "And if you're a very good boy, I'll take you out for a drink afterward as well."

And if only they had come home directly from supper, everything would have been fine. Okay, not fine, but survivable. The restaurant—their restaurant, to which, until a month before, they'd gone each week—welcomed them with open arms: the funny, bow-legged maître d' scurried over to them with a grin on his toadlike face; and Inge, their waitress, the long, horsy girl from Berlin with the nose ring and the fabulous Marlene Dietrich voice, hissed at them gloriously, "Vere have you been, you guys? Drinks on ze house for you, yes? To say velcome back?"

David delicately implied that they'd been traveling for the month of August, to Europe, no less, which made Inge roll her eyes dramatically and hiss, "*Sso* nice. So very nice."

They ate salad—frisée with lardons—and they ate steak frites, which was what David always ordered; and they drank two scotches apiece and two bottles of expensive Barolo, and the restaurant, *intime* as it was, with the tables clustered together, buzzed and thrummed around them (no music, though: it was one of the reasons David was so fond of it, that there was no music, that and its mittel-Europa, mid-century aura), and by the time Julius signed on his credit card for the— to him—astronomical sum, they were both floating in good humor, even comedy, and Julius was thinking "This, this is why we're together, I knew it. For this."

Which was why he suggested the bar on First Avenue, a fairly sedate gay bar with granite tables and leather banquettes, rendered lurid only by its crimson lighting, so that everyone in it appeared bathed in blood, a host of extras from some Stephen King movie. And that wasn't a problem, that place was just fine, they ran into a friend of David's, Jan, a Nordic guy, a sometime model with a silly accent—at the time, rather blurry though things already were, Julius had thought they'd have a round of silly accents when they got home, a grand, pre-bed diversion to blot out their surroundings—and it was Jan, eventually, near one, who proposed the dive on Avenue C, rougher but, he said, more fun, too, than this bland if ever noisier spot. The dive was a sort of club, with a bouncer at the metal door and the thrill of going downstairs, as if into a bunker. It was hot and close and teeming with dancing men, some in states of near undress, perfect torsos and biceps like new fruit, along with plenty of others, less lovely, who kept their shirts on. Jan found them a table; he hailed another friend of his, a tiny man with a close-cropped black beard, a cross between a munchkin and a devil, who looked as though the Subterra had spawned him but whose voice emerged as high and fluting as a boy's. He sported a leather collar above his T-shirt, and Julius longed to tell him that it just looked silly: you're the size of someone's pet, he wanted to say, and planned to say to David afterward: don't insist upon it. They drank, and danced, and in the bathroom did some coke, in turns—it was either Jan's, or the little guy's, he couldn't be sure, and maybe they both had some, and in the end what did it matter as long as it was there? And the music was very loud, insistent, persistent, sexy in its way, a thrumming and thudding that reverberated through you, and at some point, he didn't know when, Julius thought that this was how his head would feel in the morning; and then, too, a little later, in a flash of clarity, like the clearing in a thicket into which the sun, immense and crystalline, suddenly permeated, he realized, looking across at David, sweaty in the blue gloom, that they were, as a couple, doomed. The thought flitted off as fast as it had come to him, something at once known and unknown, inadmissible, and only later would he remember thinking it, and wonder whether the thought had permitted, or caused, what came after.

He'd gone up to the bar to order another round of drinks when he saw the man, he never knew his name, a slender but muscled dark-eyed man, perhaps ten years older, his hair all but shaven, his lips as full and dark as if they'd been painted on. He looked Mediterranean, Greek maybe, or Italian, and when he smiled, slightly, Julius could see that one of his front teeth was crooked, and this, the protruding tip of his tooth, suddenly made him the most alluring vision possible. While he waited for the drinks, Julius glanced again, and then again, and each time was met with the smile, the flash of tooth, the dark eyes heavily lashed, like a Gypsy's or a pirate's.

From there to their tryst in the lavatory stall was a matter of perhaps a quarter of an hour: in memory, the indications, the unspoken assignation, conveyed through the throng and then with David, Jan, and the tiny Satan imperturbable around him, were difficult to recapture. It seemed somehow miraculous, to flirt so outrageously in plain sight and apparently unnoticed by the others, by David in particular; but the swill of drink, the music, the heat had perhaps numbed him—he, Julius—more than he realized; and when he excused himself to go pee, although unaware of it, he wasn't unmonitored.

Even afterward, he would know it to have been one of the most exciting sexual adventures of his life: the brazenness of it, the danger, the exoticism. His lover at the table on the other side of the wall, barely thirty feet away, the slightly dank and sordid bathroom—unwindowed, purple concrete, metal stalls like some hideous junior high school—made it better, not worse. It pressed the urgency of their meeting. They were quick about it, grasping, opening, panting, both of them slightly off their heads, the beautiful man surprisingly strong and moaning at the prospect of him, like a salivating animal, and Julius was so caught up in it that at first he didn't realize that David was in the room, in the stall, was dragging them both by their skin, viciously, out into the bathroom, their trousers flapping open, dicks out, and he was pummeling at Julius, and the other man scrabbled to get his clothes right again, and he had blood on his chin, from a split lip, it was running down his chin, David had cut him, had punched him, and was still roaring, bellowing like an elephant, and Julius was trying to get to the door and David wouldn't let go, he was clawing him and scratching his arms, his chest, then he'd grabbed—it was his hair, Julius's hair, and there was a searing pain, at once specific and across the whole side of his head, and a sound, a terrible sound, almost a crunching sound, and then wetness at his scalp, it was blood, was it, seeping, because David had pulled out a hank of his hair by the roots, and Julius put up his hand to try—to try to stanch the pain, if not the blood, if it was blood at his scalp—he couldn't tell if there was blood or just the sensation of it, and that was when he realized the walls were concrete and purple, eggplant purple, because David slammed him up against one and there was a pipe, a plumbing pipe against the small of his back, hurting him, bruising his kidneys, and the purple wall next to his eye, and his damaged head, its sticky hairless patch against the cold stone, and he realized the other man, the beautiful man, was gone, there was nobody else in the bathroom—how could that be?—and still the elephantine bellowing, like no human sound, but it was David, it was words—"You fucker! You fucker! You fucker!"—and still tearing at him and slamming him against the wall, the pain in his kidneys bursting to the fore, worse than his scalp, though maybe not, all of him in agony, suffering, and then David, like an animal, lunged, his mouth wide, and he bit. He bit Julius's cheek, and there was the sound of it, of the skin breaking, of the teeth in his flesh, it wasn't fast as you'd imagine it would be, it was oddly, horribly, painfully slow, appallingly slow, as if he were prey in the jungle, a condemned meal, destined to be eaten alive.

David pulled back, spat, breathed. "You fucker," he rasped again, and Julius saw his chance, saw it wasn't going to end, and as hard and fast as he could he kneed David in the balls and kicked at him as he fell and then staggered, bleeding, bleeding, crying, too, though he was hardly aware of it, snot and tears running down his face and into his mouth, staggering through the heat and the noise and the bodies and up the stairs, onto the street.

He made his way past the loiterers; he made his way out of the light; and like an insect, shuttled home in the shadows with his trembling fingers—wet, red, like the light in the bar so long ago—to his ruined cheek.

It wasn't over then, although he'd thought it would be. He looked at himself in the mirror, the gouged flesh still bleeding, his left eye black and swollen, the hairless patch at his temple suppurating, throbbing; and he barely recognized his face. Othello, he kept thinking: the rage had been there, as he'd always suspected, and here it was, on him and in him, he was lucky to be walking, lucky to be home, the whole world upside down, and bleeding. How, he wondered, could he go on from here? And as he stood, transfixed by his distorted image (how could this be he, Julius? How had things come to such a pass?), he heard a car pull up outside, saw the blue and red lights reflected against his wall, and was called to the door by an officer of the law. David, whose face gleamed pale with demented triumph, lurked in the background, taunting him.

"This young man claims you're in possession of his belongings—"

"I don't see—"

"Stand back, sir, please stand back and let us in."

"But I don't see—"

"Are there items belonging to this man in your apartment?"

"Of course there are—he's—he lives here."

"His claim, sir, is that he needs protection in order to remove the belongings safely, sir."

"That's ridiculous. I'm not—"

"He claims you assaulted him, sir."

"*I* assaulted *him*?"

"If you could step back, sir, I'm just going to stand here while this gentleman picks up his things, sir. He says he doesn't want to press charges but he's concerned for his safety, sir."

David was grinning.

"His safety? *His* safety?"

"We won't be long here, sir. Please keep calm."

And Julius stood with his back pressed to the open door and the fleshy cop's clanking chest not six feet away, his thick, freckled hand playing upon his holster, while David winnowed methodically among the piles of clothes and papers, tidily packed his bag, all the while smiling, utterly silent. It may have taken twenty minutes; it seemed forever, and the throbbing of Julius's head grew to a roar, a roar that sounded like David's earlier bellowing, the different sites of agony seeping and melding into one another, into one universal and intolerable roar. He thought he might be sick, but he wasn't; he waited and watched David's peculiar calm, and was certain, again, that there was triumph in that calm—the cat that ate the canary, the cream, the whole kit and kaboodle, the whole kitten kaboodle, maybe. Julius could see it. Where he didn't hurt, he tingled, the adrenaline impulse to flight, so that even though he stood unmoving—and the cop, except for his deep, inflating breaths that made his badges rise and fall, stood also unmoving—he felt as though everything, each last cell and particle, were in orbit.

At the end, when they left, David, still smiling, creepily, though not at Julius, and the cop without having cracked the bland cement of his tiny, tight features, Julius started to shiver, a febrile shimmy, and barely heard the policeman say "Good night, sir. Thank you for your cooperation, sir. I'd get to an emergency room, sir, if I was you, with that gash."

"He bit me," Julius whispered, but the cop didn't turn around, and nor did David, and as Julius watched the dark curls at his long nape disappear in the stairwell, he felt a hot wash of anger and sorrow and, still, of desire, and he knew that he would never see David Cohen again.

Back in the apartment, pale dawn fingered the room's paltry objects, the length of the wall, and far away Julius detected the sounds of the city, Saturday morning breaking. He washed, and dressed, gingerly, suffering, and set out to walk to the emergency room at St. Vincent's, a fair trek away, but the nearest one he knew.

CHAPTER FIFTY-FIVE

Married

Maybe it would feel different to be married after the hubbub of the launch, she told Danielle. But for right now, on the Sunday evening a week after the wedding, it just felt as though she were married not to a man but to *The Monitor;* or rather, that *he* was married to *The Monitor* and she was not married at all, because it was after nine p.m. and she had packed in hours ago—the issue in all its glory wouldn't be sent to the printer until Tuesday night and her part was done, for this first time at least, and the pieces for her section in the second issue edited and ready to go, and only Ludo still had tweaking and fussing and frankly obsessing to do, because the issue was finished, even for him, there was nothing to be done, it was Sunday night for God's sake and the final checks could be made on Monday, or even Tuesday, even till late Tuesday night if need be. This was just his mania, his control-freakishness; she'd known him all along for a perfectionist. She admired his high standards. She'd fallen in love with them, after all. But to be honest, he'd snapped harshly at her when she announced she was going to go home, even brutishly, when she suggested he could leave with her—his tone had been different, a new tone, exasperated, that she'd not heard before, or not heard directed at *her* before, that was for sure, and now she was wondering was *this* what it meant to be married?—and on the walk back to the apartment, she'd felt like crying, really, just weeping, because in any normal relationship they'd be on their honeymoon now, on a beach in Thailand, say, instead of spending every waking minute, day and night, in that stupid, canned-air office with its beige wall-to-wall and floor-to-ceiling windows and his horrible snippy prim secretary Lizbeth, who still managed to look at Marina as though she were an Ebola carrier, even though she was now frankly and legitimately Mrs. Seeley (though of course actually she was keeping her own name—nothing political but Thwaite was just a better name than Seeley, don't you think?).

"Oh, Danielle," she said, "is it going to be like this every damn Sunday? Have I made a terrible mistake, what have I done?"

And Danielle said of course not, that they'd known all along that this week would be bedlam, how could you blame him for wanting it all perfect, it was the moment, this Thursday, would be the moment he'd been working toward all year; and it wasn't just the magazine launch, it was his own American launch, you know, our chef is very famous in London. Which she then had to explain because Marina didn't remember the reference; but the point was that he could be Jesus Christ in Sydney, yet even in the era of the Global Village he was nothing in New York, not until he'd worked his miracles in Manhattan, which was as far as most New Yorkers ever cared to look.

"He's got to dazzle them this time, or he's missed his chance," she said. "You understand."

Marina sighed. "Of course I understand, in principle. And you know, Mom said to be sure not to idealize things, to be realistic. But a week, you know? It's only been a week."

"Just wait till you've got a copy in your hands, not a dummy issue but the real thing."

"Yeah. Can't wait." Marina turned on the television with the sound off. "What are you doing, anyway?" she asked, wishing almost at once that she hadn't. Poor Danielle couldn't expect anyone to come home.

"I'm waiting for Julius to come over."

"Julius? What's happened? David dumped him?"

"I think it's a bit more complicated than that. He called me this afternoon, and told me, more or less, what happened."

"Why didn't he call *me*?" They'd all three always been close, but she had found him, that first week of school, and she'd always thought of him as her friend first. All summer long he'd called her, not Danielle.

"You're a newlywed. He didn't want to interrupt your connubial bliss with his tale of woe."

"How woeful can it be?"

"Pretty woeful." Danielle repeated the story as Julius had told it to her, including the words of the resident at St. Vincent's emergency room, who'd warned him that even with her best efforts, the cheek would have an impressive scar. "If it were a dog mauling," she'd said, "the animal would have to be put down. Are you sure you don't want to press charges?"

"Don't you think he maybe should?" asked Marina. "You can't let some guy like that—I didn't like him at the wedding, did you?—you can't let a guy like that think he can get away with it. I mean, what if he does it again, to someone else? What's *wrong* with a guy like that?"

"I'll eat you up I love you so," Danielle said. "And Julius said 'no!'"

"It isn't funny."

"It's a little bit funny. But I know, it's mostly awful. It's surreal. The kind of thing you can't really believe has happened to someone you know. You can't believe he lived through that. I mean, it was early Saturday morning. Where were we, you know, while that was going on? At suppertime on Friday, it hadn't happened, and now he's scarred for life. It makes you think, doesn't it?"

"That's what it's like when somebody dies, I think," Marina said. "You know, unexpectedly. One minute they're there and the next they're not, and you don't have any way to really get your head around it. Surreal."

"Or it's real. If you know what I mean." Danielle, Marina thought, was being oddly flippant about the whole thing.

"When's he coming over?"

"In the next half hour or so. I've got a bottle of scotch here, and I figure we might tackle it together. He seemed pretty shaken up on the phone."

"Since when do you drink scotch?" Marina asked. And then: "Tell you what, why don't I come over, too? Ludo won't be here for ages. And when was the last time it was just the three of us?"

She thought she detected a second's hesitation at Danielle's end, and struggled not to succumb to pique when Danielle said, in a voice slightly too cheerful, "Of course. That's a great idea. Come on over."

"Unless the two of you were planning to gossip about the wedding all night?"

"Don't be ridiculous. Come right on over."

None of them could remember when last they had gathered, just the three of them. They climbed onto Danielle's immaculate bed (though not before carefully removing their shoes).

"You've got your good sheets on," Marina noticed. "Special occasion?"

"Consolation prize," said Danielle. "Those of us with no love life have to make going to bed a treat somehow."

"I'd trade my love life for these sheets any day," said Julius.

"It's pretty bad, isn't it? Is it hurting right now?"

"Seven stitches," he said. "They gave me codeine at the hospital yesterday, so I've been wafting through. Toward the end of a dose, it throbs, though."

"Go easy on the scotch."

"Oh, lighten up, girlfriend. I need a good buzz on, at this point."

"Will your hair grow back okay?" Danielle asked.

"Apparently. But not before I wander around town for a couple of months like some scabby Frankenstein with a hole in my head."

"I think it makes you look intriguing."

"Great. An intriguing temporary secretary. Just what everybody doesn't want."

"You're going to be temping?"

"I'm calling the agency tomorrow. It's pathetic, but I need

the cash. Even after he was fired, David was covering the rent. Mommy and Daddy, you know."

"Do you think he's gone out to Larchmont?"

"Scarsdale, actually. Totally different, my dears. What do I know?"

"Scarsdale? You're joking. *Scars*-dale? How can it be true?"

"He should go to prison, is where he should go. Who the hell does he think he is, acting like that?"

"Entitlement," said Danielle. "It's about a sense of entitlement. Don't you think?"

"So what *isn't*, exactly?" Julius said.

"How do you mean?"

"I mean that it seems as though entitlement, that mysterious gift, explains everything everyone does these days. And I'd like to know why I got skipped over in the entitlement stakes. Is it a Midwestern thing? Danny, sort me out."

"You felt entitled to have sex with that guy in the bathroom," Marina said.

"Entitled? I felt compelled. But precisely the knowledge that I wasn't entitled is what made it so sexy."

"We're all of us entitled," Danielle said. "Comparatively, I mean. We're so lucky we don't know we were born."

"Do we even know anyone who isn't?"

"You mean personally? That's pathetic. Of course we do."

After a minute, Danielle said, "Your cousin. Marina, your cousin. Bootie. He doesn't feel entitled. I think that's fair to say."

"And what's happened to him?"

"He's gone to Brooklyn, right? Poor guy."

"Shake Your Booty. That's right. He left a forwarding address in Fort Greene. But no phone number."

"I wonder how he'll manage?"

"I put him on to my temp agency," Julius said. "This is good scotch."

"It's the same kind as my father drinks; did you know that, Danny?"

"I didn't, no."

"There are no other kinds," said Julius.

"He was in love with you, M," Danielle said.

"Probably still is," said Julius.

"What am I supposed to do about it? As Ludo says, love should feed on mutuality, and when it doesn't, when it's one-sided, it's just narcissism. It's not my fault if he's in love with me. I didn't encourage him."

"Nobody said you did. But he's in a sort of sad situation now. Maybe you should call him."

"Julius just said he didn't leave a phone number. And I'm sorry, but I'm not trekking all the way out to Fort Greene just to see if he's eating right."

"No. But someone—"

"Then why don't you take it on, Danny? You could make it your project. You could even make a film about him: A Pilgrim's Progress, or An Autodidact in New York."

"Well, if nobody else will, maybe I should. But I'm the person in the room with the least connection to him. Julius, he lived in your apartment, after all."

"My encounters with him have only been—" Julius paused. "Unfortunate. I wonder if he put a hex on me, or on my place. You admit there's something creepy about him."

"I don't admit that at all," Danielle said. "Pathetic, yes. Creepy, no. For some reason both of you have it in for him. Think what it must feel like to be a kid—he's just a kid—stuck here with no connections, now, and no friends. Who do you think he talks to, in a day?"

"Why do you even care?"

"I don't know. He seems poignant to me. I feel like in some way I am him, or he is me. Or that could have been me. Does that sound ridiculous?"

"A little."

"Julius, he could've been you. It's different for Marina. But you or me?"

"Scarred for life I may be." Julius put his hand dramatically to his bandage. "But I was never fat."

"He isn't fat," said Danielle. "He's a little chubby." She turned to Marina. "Don't you ever wonder if your dad was a little bit like Bootie when he was young? I mean, that's where he's from, and—"

"To be honest, I don't think my dad was anything like that. And he tried to destroy my dad. He'd like to destroy him. Not that it matters to either of you, but it was a pretty big deal in the family."

"Of course it was."

"Oh, Danny, don't take that tone."

"What tone?"

"That patronizing, therapisty sort of tone. I hate it when you do that."

"Girls, girls. Let's keep the reunion sweet."

"Short and sweet. I'd better get going. Ludo said he'd call

when he was leaving the office, but he might forget, and I want to be there when he gets back."

"Sweet little wife, tending hearth and home?"

"Hardly. It's the only time I get to see him at the moment."

"It won't last," Danielle said. "It's just this week."

"Take care of your cheek, Jules. Who knew he'd be crazy?"

"Crazy? I don't know."

"Crazy," said Marina, firmly. "There's a point in anything, isn't there, when no matter how upset you are, you know you're doing the wrong thing. And you get a grip. You just get a grip. It's a choice, to give in to rage like that. It's crazy."

"Well," Danielle said, "you could say he got a grip of a different kind."

"That isn't funny."

"I think it's pretty funny," Julius said. "Even if it touches a sore spot."

CHAPTER FIFTY-SIX

Not Telling

After Marina had left, Julius lay spread-eagled on Danielle's bed and shut his eyes. "Why can't I live here?" he said. "It's so much nicer than Pitt Street."

"If you had a real job," she said, "you'd be able to afford it."

"So now that you've bullied Marina into the workforce, and married her off, too, you're going to start working on me, are you?" He sighed. "Who's working on you, I want to know?"

"What do you mean?"

"The sheets," he said, running his hands over the duvet. "Mmm. The scotch. I don't know, there's just something different about this place. It almost smells like cigarettes, though maybe that's just your neighbors."

"You haven't been here in a very long time."

"And there's something different about you." He blinked lazily at her, his black eye puffy and already yellowing. "Marina thought you were in love with her Ludovic; but I could tell at the wedding you don't like him." He paused. "You didn't like David much either, did you? Not that it matters."

"Mostly I thought he didn't want to be bothered."

"No. So if it's not Ludovic Seeley?"

"What makes you think there's anyone?"

"Please, Danielle Minkoff. How long have we known each other?"

Danielle wanted very much to tell him. He, of all people, would understand, would feel the joy and excitement of it. He might even, if he were exercising his intermittent empathetic gifts, see the other side, the madness of always waiting, always wanting, of having renounced composure and continence for a state of constant, insatiable hunger. The madness—the ineffable, horrible deliciousness—of the whole situation. But Julius was not discreet; and if she told him anything, she would eventually tell him who; and once she'd told him that, it would all be over. She knew he wouldn't be able to resist. But if only she could tell someone, that tomorrow, Monday, just for one night, he would stay; that she'd planned to procure flowers, and a bottle of extremely good wine, and had ordered a meal from a French *traiteur* that she would pick up in the afternoon; and she'd thought, even, of breakfast, was going to buy croissants and raspberries and cream and fresh-squeezed orange juice; and had already countless times imagined the perfect unfolding of their evening, their unbroken night, their waking together. To Julius, she said only, "In your dreams, there's someone. Or maybe I should say, in mine. Only in my dreams." And laughed, a little bitterly, because sometimes—like this past week, when she hadn't seen him once, had spoken to him, sure, every day, but had had hopes of a sighting several times raised and dashed—it felt as though this grand passion, this union which would, under other circumstances, have been so perfect, did exist only in her dreams.

CHAPTER FIFTY-SEVEN

A Speaking Engagement

In all the years, in all the adventures, he'd never quite done this. Never packed his bag and called the limo, taken it to the airport only to get into a cab and come back into town. He'd thought it all through, had the cell phone with him, would call her late, around eleven. He'd said he wasn't sure where they were putting him up—that happened often enough—and that there was bound to be a big dinner that went till midnight, so not to be surprised if he called from the restaurant. He'd even thought of a dinner—a dinner that had taken place in Chicago two years before—which he would more or less reconstruct for her if called upon to do so. The restaurant, its décor, the seating arrangements. It wasn't so hard. Thank God his memory for these things was good.

It felt strange. He wasn't, in some regard, a liar. An actor, yes; and a good one. Guilty, upon innumerable occasions, of sins of omission, a great believer that what you didn't know couldn't hurt you (a dictum of which he knew he ought to have been cured by his nephew's recent perfidy: there, better to have known: what might it have been had he first encountered Frederick Tubb's musings in print?), a smoother of waters whose techniques had been known to include a gentle reshaping of the facts. And to be fair, Annabel didn't ask. Her dignity, his, theirs, were premised upon trust, perhaps for each of them a slightly different thing (his definition of trust, on his wife's behalf, being that she could always know herself supremely loved, and always—ah, until now!—know that at day's end he came home faithfully to rest his head beside hers. Whereas he was aware, sometimes, that her unspoken understanding of trust might have been rather more strict than his own), but nevertheless, a mutual, a familial value, which left well enough alone. He didn't delve too deeply into her separate life, hadn't wanted to meet the famous DeVaughn, say (although he had, that once, in the summertime, without meaning to), or any of the other clients who drew so heavily and zealously upon his wife's angelic resources. He knew that this was justifying: there was no genuine comparison between her de facto secrets and his own. The point was to assuage this feeling, for which he had no purpose, which could only be named guilt.

He didn't feel it strongly in the limo to LaGuardia, a journey during which he was almost persuaded of his own lie. But in the cab, heading back—a particularly shockless and ill-smelling vehicle in which he was jounced, painfully and at speed, over every possible pothole—he suffered torment. It was, in that ride, not too late to redirect the driver, not too late to return to Central Park West, where Annabel would find him upon her evening return, and to tell her, relievingly, that it had all, at the last minute, been cancelled. But in spite of everything, he didn't really want to. More life, more: he wanted it, and juggling for dominance in his mind, along with visions of domestic safety, was the prospect of Danielle's fresh flesh, of her blushing cheek, across which stray dark tendrils were prone to meander, escaped from the great waving vine of her hair. He could picture the Rothkos, the view from the window, southward, at sunset, the glinting towers in a gilded sky—being in her apartment was like being aboard a ship, many stories above the earth. It always felt, when he was there, that one could so happily survive with so little, that all the trappings of his adult life were vain and unnecessary. To arrive at her building with his tidy overnight case, with a gaudy bunch of gerberas from the Korean at the corner, at two o'clock on a Monday afternoon, to find her smiling, slightly awkward, in her doorway when he stepped off the elevator, her head coyly bowed, her hair unruly, a mere girl, with the charm and embarrassment— that delicious embarrassment—of youth, was to be cast back, to be liberated unexpectedly into a younger, freer self, even as, miraculously, he could hold close his grander, statesmanlike persona, left to wait, perhaps, in the corridor like a macintosh on a hook, but never relinquished, always immediately retrievable. He reveled in the many-ness of it all, all the things he was, and was to her, Danielle—journalistic eminence, husband, father of her best friend, potential mentor, old and failing body—all these things torn away by their mutual desire, that left him a mere stripling in this time-traveling ship, attended but unmolested by the ghosts of his selves. So enticing, the state left him always eager to regain it: why couldn't he stay in this doll-sized studio, in this lovely young woman's arms, forever? But he wasn't naïve enough not to know how large a part of its allure stemmed precisely from its transience. He loved this, he loved her, and could not contemplate giving it up, only because he was always already giving it up, only to find it—still more delicious—anew the next time.

"I thought we could have our ride this afternoon," he said. "I booked it. For dusk."

"What ride?"

"The helicopter ride," he said. "Remember? To see it all from above. What do you say?"

"I hate flying."

"You don't think it's *dangerous*?"

"A helicopter? Seems pretty dangerous to me. All that keeps you up are a few swishing blades, like a ceiling fan."

"You'll remember it all your life."

"Oh, sure. Just as we plummet into the East River, I'll remember how much I was enjoying it."

"Let's have lunch," he said, "and you just think about it. You've got all afternoon to decide. I know you'll make the right choice."

"Staying on the ground is always the wisest choice."

"Really?" He raised an eyebrow. "I've always felt absolutely the other way. More. Higher. Faster."

In spite of her nerves—and they, too, charmed, and enabled him to hold her hand, almost a child's hand, smooth and faintly palpitating—they went. Ducking the rotors, they climbed into the buzzing glass bulb of the copter on its West Side landing tarmac, shortly after seven, and then, enveloped in the roar and the glory of it, ascended, lurching, directly upward, before swinging sideways, out and away. He tried to speak to her, to say "Rothko would have loved this. It might have saved him," but his voice was lost in the din, and she merely gaped at him in barely veiled terror, her eyes' whites wide, her hair in floating rebellion, as they rose toward the sky's brilliant striations, through the beginning of a late summer, intoxicated Rothko sunset, gold, pink, red, white, lavender, and palest blue, and over the glinting river, around the vast buildings upon which the shadow of night was beginning to fall, down, out in an arc to winking Lady Liberty and back around the island's tip, everywhere the lights just flickering on, innumerable fireflies in the waning day. The sun sank at the western horizon as they followed the East River northward, and she was holding tightly, still, to his hand, but the wide-eyed cast of her face was now of childlike wonder rather than fear, and when she turned and smiled at him, conspiratorially—they were co-conspirators, that's what they were—he was, even in the furthest ravaged brachts of his lungs, in the helicopter-throbbed tendons at his heels, in his very heart, suffused with some hitherto unexperienced delight.

Over supper—she'd ordered lamb chops, potatoes dauphinoises, and had herself sautéed the spinach—he grew for a time quiet. He'd forgotten, and then remembered, the sin of what he was doing.

"What are you thinking about?" she asked, her smile a trifle too bright.

"I was just wondering how my talk was going. The imaginary one, that I'm giving right now."

"You're going to call her later."

"I have to."

"What will you tell her?"

"Don't worry. I'll go down the hall. Or downstairs. It doesn't matter."

"But you're thinking about it."

He shrugged.

"You're not regretting?"

"Never regret, my dear. I never regret. It's so wasteful."

But the shadow settled on them, obliquely, and was shuffled off only when Danielle rose to put on music, a Spanish soprano singing Cantaloube, her pure, agonized strains floating, their minor harmonies wavering in the small room, as if to remind them both that beauty and loss were inseparably entwined.

CHAPTER FIFTY-EIGHT

The Morning After

In the morning, when they woke—late-ish, for both of them, both by habit and separately early risers—Danielle put the croissants in the oven, and went to take a shower. They would have, at least, the better part of the day: he wasn't due at LaGuardia for his limo home until three. She was planning their walk—could they walk safely in Lower Manhattan? Surely Marina and Ludo would be ensconced at the magazine without interruption; but Murray was known, could run into anyone who might then speak of the encounter to Annabel— when she heard him cry out. Her first thought, as she hastened to dry herself and rushed to rejoin him, was that he'd had a heart attack, that she'd have to call an ambulance, that everything would be exposed. But when she emerged, he stood at the window, in his boxer shorts, his grizzled chest bare to Lower Manhattan—she was going to make a joke about it, about a striptease, maybe, when she saw that he was pointing: "Look at that," he said. "They've got some colossal fire going. It must be a bomb or something, so high up."

She grabbed the remote and waved it at the television, and they lived the next hour and a half in stereo, watching through the window—their view spectacularly, hideously unimpeded—

and watching on the screen, as if they were simultaneously in Manhattan and anywhere on the planet, Columbus, even, and everything they saw seemed somehow more and less real on the television because what they saw with their own eyes they couldn't quite believe. Danielle thought, at one point in the blur of it, that it was like witches, who couldn't be pho-tographed—that had always been the belief, at any rate, in her childhood lore—by which you knew they were witches, and that by the same token what took place outside the window could have been credited as sorcery, some trick of the light, almost comical, so absurd, were it not for the fact that it was being filmed—the filming of it the assurance of its reality: the whole world was seeing this, and the Pentagon, too, and this was how you knew that it was really true. The sirens on the screen echoed, with a disconcerting lag, the sirens out the window. The cacophony on the television was more bearable, more reassuring, because it was contained in a little box; because unlike the sirens and yelling and the visceral rumbles outside, you could imagine, at least, that you could just turn it off. Better to have them both going, to indulge the illusion that they could, if they chose to, call a halt to the whole catas-trophe.

It took a long time for either of them to dress. They stood watching, all but naked, arrested. The croissants, untended, blackened at the edges and grew hard, but it didn't matter; they weren't hungry.

"I need to call her" was the first thing Murray said after a silence so long that they were both surprised by his voice.

"Of course you do," Danielle said.

"I can go outside if you like."

"What will you tell her? Will you tell her you're here?"

"I don't know."

He tried to ring from the corridor, but the circuits were all busy.

"You could try from my phone," she said. "That might work."

"I'd be— She'd have— The number comes up on the phone."

The television explained that flights all over the country had been grounded. That flights from Europe had turned back over the Atlantic. That nobody was going anywhere. Danielle thought Murray might cry.

"I'm in Chicago," he said, in his shirt and undershorts and dark socks, sitting on the edge of the bed, looking not at her but at the television screen. "Nobody's moving. I'm supposed to be in Chicago."

"You can stay with me," she said. "Until, you know, you can get home from Chicago."

"She's probably trying to call me there right now."

"She'd call your cell. You can't get through. Nobody can get through." She went over to the window, leaned up against the glass and peered down at the street. "There are tons of people out. The streets are—well. Maybe we should go outside."

"Why?"

"Because. I don't know. Because it seems crazy to stay cooped up in here."

"I need to go home."

"How do you mean?"

He was standing, now. He had put on his trousers, fastened his belt. It was a relief to her, Danielle realized: she, who thrilled to his vulnerabilities, did not want him vulnerable on this morning. She wanted him to put his shoes on.

"Annabel," he said.

"Yes, but you're in Chicago, remember?" Danielle knew what he was telling her, but it seemed too appalling to contemplate.

He sighed. "I might have to not be."

"You're going to tell her? You can't tell her." For a fleeting second, she thought she saw a new path, a path down which she and Murray could properly be together: he would tell Annabel, they would part, it would be natural and right. But as quickly, she knew it was absurd: he would tell her only because he wanted so much to go home to her. He had made his choice.

"I can walk uptown," he said. "It's only a few miles. It's probably the best way to get there." He combed his hair with his fingers, haphazardly. It was still messy. He was unshaven, his silver bristles gleaming slightly in the bright sun. "And don't ask me what I'm going to say because I couldn't tell you."

She bit her lip.

"Whatever I say, you won't come into it. A chance encounter at the airport. Something."

"You don't have to go."

They both looked out the window at the black smoke still hovering where the buildings had once been.

"I'm sorry," he said. "Are you going to be okay?" To which there was no possible answer. Incredulous, she almost laughed.

He kissed her before he left, a small, chaste, final kiss. His cheek was rough, hers damp, and she had the impression of feeling everything, of her skin being suddenly all sensation, almost unbearable. He said again that he was sorry, and he went. For a time, she stood at the window, her fingertips to the glass, looking down—she did not see him go, as if he'd vanished—but she watched and there were still dust-covered, bewildered people, some crying, drifting up the avenue, lots of them, like refugees from war, she thought, remembering the famous Vietnam photograph, the little naked girl fleeing the napalm, crying, her forearms oddly raised at her sides; and on television behind her they were talking about the planes, just imagine the size of them, it was all too big and too much to take in and she wanted, now, to turn it off, just to turn it all off—and then she kicked off her shoes and with her skirt rucked up, climbed back into her beautiful bed and pulled the duvet—such soft cotton, so very fine, Murray's special sheets, and they smelled of him—over her head, as she used to do as a child, and she thought she should cry, she thought that perhaps later she might cry; but just as a few minutes before she had felt, so intensely, now she was as if anesthetized, she felt nothing, nothing at all, you could have amputated a limb and it wouldn't have mattered. She had seen the second plane, like a gleaming arrow, and the burst of it, oddly beautiful against the blue, and the smoke, everywhere, and she had seen the people jumping, from afar, specks in the sky, and she knew that's what they were only from the TV, from the great reality check of the screen, and she had seen the buildings crumble to dust; she could smell them even inside, even with the windows sealed, the asbestos-smoke-gasoline fuel, slight airplane, slight bonfire reek of it, she had seen these things and had been left, forever, because in light of these things she did not matter, you had to make the right choice, you had to stay on the ground— but God, the sky last night had been gorgeous, the colors, the lights, the towers, and after she let go of her terror, the joy of it—you had to stay on the ground and there was no call to feel anything, there was nothing to feel because you weren't worth anything to anyone, you'd had your heart, or was it your guts, or both, taken out, you'd been eviscerated, that was the word, and the Spanish woman singing last night, she had known, she had known all along, and now there was nothing but sorrow and this was how it was going to be, now, always.

CHAPTER FIFTY-NINE

The Monitor

By noon on Tuesday, Ludo had taken the decision to cancel the launch party. He gathered everyone in the office who had come and stayed—which was a surprising number, considering—and he spoke eloquently about how everybody needed to be with their loved ones rather than in an office, it put things in perspective, and it was hard to know how things would unfold from here, but the important thing was for people to be sure that their families and friends were safe and if anyone wasn't, God forbid, *The Monitor* would be there to support them, and of course there'd be plenty of time to regroup and reassess, and it wasn't clear when they'd launch—in fact, the printer was unreachable and in Brooklyn, so they couldn't have gotten the issues printed anyway, that's just how things were—but not to worry, because they were a team, a strong one, and ready for adversity.

In the privacy of his office, he put his head in his hands at his desk and said to Marina, "We are completely fucked."

"Everything's fucked," was all she could say. The television was on in the corner, CNN with the volume down. They were playing again and again the same images that had been airing all morning, interspersed with anxious but eager talking heads. "So what now?"

Ludovic straightened in his chair. Only now she noticed how drawn he looked, his beautiful eyes ringed as if with soot, his skin of a yellowish pallor. She could see a blood vessel beating beneath the fine skin at his temple. He hadn't slept properly since before the wedding.

"Damned if I know," he said.

"You were great. You said all the right things. It feels as though the world has stopped."

"It has." He rearranged papers on his desk. The magazine cover of the issue that was to have been, with the title in black capitals and the logo—he'd helped design it—of an all-seeing eye, lay on top of the pile. Already, with its vermilion, orange, and yellow graphic, a sunburst, a remarkable photograph of a sunburst, the idea having been that they were exploding upon the scene, illuminating truths, and different, down to the images, from the rest; already it looked out of date and faintly forlorn, like some child's abandoned artwork.

"What should we do? Now, I mean? You and me?" She sat on the edge of the desk, reached to stroke his hair.

"I guess we should go in the streets. Walk downtown. See it."

"Because we're journalists?"

"Or because it's history. Because you can't just walk home and pretend it hasn't happened."

"Is it right, do you think, what everyone's saying—all those people, on TV—that nothing will be the same again?"

Ludovic didn't answer. He put on his jacket, fussing to keep his turned-up cuffs from bunching up to his biceps. Then he started sorting papers, stuffing some of them into his briefcase to take home. As if it were a normal day.

"Do you think we'll know anyone?"

He didn't answer.

"It's hard to believe we won't. People I went to college with, or their parents . . . I think that boy DeVaughn's mother works in the towers."

"Who?"

"DeVaughn. The boy my mother's always worried about. The fire starter, you know?"

"The fire starter?"

"Yes. His mom. A mailroom, she runs the mailroom in one of those sorts of companies."

"It may not be in the towers. Downtown Manhattan is surprisingly capacious."

"Up to fifty thousand people in those buildings, Ludo. We're bound to know someone."

Later, from their apartment, they walked over to Union Square, where vigils had started, candles flickering in clusters even before dark. People thronged and milled about, as if in aspic, as if their limbs could move no faster, many of them configured into new human forms by their embraces, like the walking wounded, two women supporting a third, dissolved, between them, a man holding a somber child precariously upon his hip, two clean-shaven young men clasping each other by the neck, their heads touching, like Siamese twins of sorrow. The posters, thick and thickening like some mad foliage, each with its photographs, its carefree snap at a wedding, a beach, a picnic, and its plea, shone white in the dusk, and people circulated, quietly, wet-faced, examining them. Marina, too,

crying as they walked, paused to read a clutch of details
("MISSING! MISSING! MISSING! Has a star-shaped tattoo
on her lower back. Wearing a gold crucifix and pendant earrings. Has three tear-shaped chicken pox scars on his left cheek.
Last seen wearing a white shirt and tie with elephants"), walked
on again.

"This is disgraceful," Ludo muttered, as they approached
a tree the trunk of which had already been almost wholly
papered. "This is necrophiliac pornography."

"What do you mean?"

"What are you thinking?" he burst out. "They're all dead.
Of course they're all dead. Okay, maybe fifteen, or twenty, or
even a hundred of these people may be dug out of that mess.
But what good does it do to pretend they'll all come home,
that they're all just wandering around Manhattan in a post-
traumatic daze? They're all fucking dead, Marina. Dead."

"Keep your voice down." She could see two women, a young
man, peering, shaking their heads.

"This is what we should have a cover piece about, this," he
went on, in an apparent seething fury. "About how in this
country everybody wants a happy ending. To the point of dishonesty, as if sticking up these posters can somehow undo, or
fix, or change what's just happened. Who's going to say to
them, 'Go home and face the facts! Your son, mother, niece, is
dead, dust, gone. There's nothing left'?"

"We don't know that."

"Don't we? Let's face the facts, here."

"I know you're upset, sweetie, but this isn't the place."

"But it's the fucking land of lies here, isn't it? So nobody's going to say that. And we're not going to say it, either, because we don't have a fucking magazine."

"We *will*. Don't be silly. We're all upset. It's been a hard day. It's been unreal. We need to go home now."

"You think we will because next week might be a good time to launch? Or next month? Or maybe next year? Come off it, don't kid yourself. The bubble's burst, now. It's over. We're fucked."

"We'll just have to wait and see."

"Do that if you want. I prefer to see and wait. And what I see is what happens, I promise you."

Marina led him away, he reluctant and slow, fidgeting in her embrace, she at once firm and affectionate with, she knew, an air of patience about her, and she could tell from the sympathetic glances around them that people thought he had been posting a flyer, that one of the smiling lost faces along the barrier belonged to him—a mother, maybe? A sister or brother? A wife?—and that he was trying, with only moderate but nevertheless laudable success, to release his grief to her care.

CHAPTER SIXTY

At Home

On that terrible day, she waited for him to call even though she knew pretty quickly—someone said so on the TV—that he couldn't. The lines were busy, the lines were crossed, the signal had been on top of the towers, something like that. She was in the school parking lot when she heard, gathering handouts from the trunk for her second period class. Joan came hurrying up and told her, and Bootie was the first thing she thought of. School was canceled, in Watertown, but even after the kids had all cleared out, she stayed in the teachers' lounge for a while and watched the television. It made her sweat, that footage, and once the towers had fallen they showed them falling over and over again, the same bits of film, in all of them the exquisite blue sky—it was sunny like that in Watertown, too, though it could have been a million miles away.

She kept wondering whether it was creepy or reassuring how normal the day felt, even though nobody knew where the president was (North Dakota?) and even the Veep was hiding somewhere—in a secure location, they said on the TV, and Joan, who was always pretty vocal about her views, said, "A secure location, my eye! Like a coffin—how's that for a secure location?" She repeated it several times, until Hal Speed, who taught junior physics, told her to knock it off because it was disrespectful in a time of crisis, no matter what her politics were. Joan asked Judy to lunch at the diner on the square, but by then she said she thought she should be at home, because Bootie would be trying to get through to her, and he'd know she was worried—of course, she wasn't naïve and she knew New York was a big place, but still, to be honest, it was kind of unnerving and she did just want to hear his voice and know that he was okay.

The house was very quiet, which was horrible—somehow, even the brightness of the sun falling through the window onto the kitchen table, so peaceful and calm, was horrible just then—and she debated with herself about turning on the TV and couldn't help it, really, because you needed to know, didn't you? She opened a can of chicken noodle and made a ham sandwich—with mayo and a couple of slices of cucumber, the way she liked it—but she found she couldn't really eat much, which wasn't really a surprise, because she was waiting. At about three the phone rang, and before she picked it up she felt relief, but it was just Sarah, calling from Alexandria Bay to say had Bootie called yet and was she okay? Did she want Sarah to come over, maybe, with the kids, because somehow a disaster like this just made you all want to be together, didn't it?

Why don't we wait and speak later, when I've spoken to him, she said, because who knew, but it couldn't be that long till the phones were working; and when they'd hung up she thought, Heck, I'll just try it, what have I got to lose, and rang the number she had for him, that sublet somewhere downtown, but surely it wasn't near the towers, he'd said the other side of the island, she was pretty sure. To her surprise, it rang through on the first try, but she got only a machine, the machine with that other boy's voice on it, of course, the friend of Marina's whose place it was, so that was no good. Maybe that was the first time she really felt scared, because she thought of him out on the street somewhere, instead of safely tucked away inside, but that was silly because of course probably everyone was outside down there, getting out to see one another and to make sure the rest of the world was still standing.

Because life had to go on, she forced herself into the car to go to her hair appointment at four. Dolly was cheerful about it all, in her weird, oblivious way, as she snipped at Judy's nape. A blur in her pink smock alongside Judy's left ear, she shook her head and said, "Awful, isn't it? Awful. It's those Arabs," she said, pronouncing it *Ay-rabs*. "My sister Lily, she's in Buffalo, she says they're all over everywhere up there, and they live just like they were back in Arabia. No English to speak of, the headgear, the whole lot. They'd kill every one of us if they could. It's scary, isn't it?"

"It sure is," Judy agreed, although she knew that Dolly's feelings about foreigners were very particular. Joan wouldn't have her hair cut by Dolly anymore on that account, even though she was probably Watertown's finest.

Judy was home by six, though, with her hair looking a little funny (they hadn't done the perm today. She'd put it off till next time. Somehow, she couldn't face it, was all) but surely better than it had, and proud of herself for keeping the appointment in spite of things, because what good did it do to worry about things you couldn't do anything about?

And it was just before seven that she called again, the number, and the fellow answered—Julius Clarke, she'd remember that name—and said that he didn't know a thing about Bootie (she thought it slightly strange that he called her boy Bootie, because Bootie didn't generally encourage that), that he'd moved to Brooklyn but that there was no telephone number as far as Julius knew. She remembered now, he'd said something about moving, but she'd somehow thought it wasn't for a while. He was working in a restaurant, too, just now, but she couldn't for the life of her remember what it was called. Mexican, maybe? Upscale and Mexican, fine dining, she thought he'd said. Certainly ethnic. She'd been surprised.

Julius said he didn't know about that. He'd given Bootie the number of a temp agency, but didn't know if he'd contacted them. Sure, he had the number; and he gave it. He was sorry not to be of more help, but they didn't really know each other much.

"Who does he know?" she asked, trying to sound brisk rather than plaintive.

"I'm so sorry, ma'am," he said—he was a polite young man: he said "ma'am." "But I don't have any idea."

She tried to calm down, after that. She was working herself up. Just because she could call New York didn't mean they could call out, did it, because sometimes things worked that way, didn't they? She did call the temp agency that Julius Clarke had given her, so as to know she'd done all she could, but all she got was a machine. And then she did call Sarah because she couldn't stand waiting all by herself, and Sarah said she'd come over, but tomorrow, after school, because the kids were about to have their baths and go to bed.

"Don't worry so much, Mom," she said, "because Bootie *will* call. At least you know he wasn't there, of all places, at that time in the morning. He can be a little selfish about stuff; I'm sure he isn't even thinking that you're worried. Can you imagine what it's like to be down there, I mean, like that movie, *Independence Day,* right? He's probably with other people, you know, friends, trying to feel okay about everything. I'm sure he'll call tomorrow, if he can't call today."

Which made her feel a little better. Sarah was right, after all: at least she knew he wouldn't have been there. The restaurant was somewhere else—hadn't he said Fifth Avenue? Wasn't that far away? At least not close—and besides, no busboy had to show up for work at that hour. But if he was with friends, who were they? She couldn't quite fathom how her boy's life had become such a mystery to her, when even a few weeks ago, it seemed, he'd been with Murray and she'd known—okay, only more or less, but still—what he was up to every day.

But he didn't call that night, and he didn't call in the morning, and when she came home from school, where all the class time was spent talking about the disaster, of course, he hadn't left any message. And as she said to Sarah when she came over, the terrible thing was just having to wait. Just waiting. Who could be good at that? When Bert was sick there'd been so much waiting, in hospitals and at home, and she'd hated it then, hated the powerlessness and the waste of it, but this felt worse, in a way, because she knew it was ridiculous to be worrying, but what else could she do? She couldn't bring herself to go out, really, not without having someone there to pick up the phone, so eventually she made her supermarket run (she needed milk, and bread, a few staples) while Sarah set up the playhouse in the backyard for the kids.

On Thursday, she broke down and called Murray. She wasn't

sure to whom it fell to be contrite, and so did her best to clear the air from the start.

"I know we've been on the outs, Murray," she said. "But you're my only brother and we need to get over it. My Bootie did a very stupid thing, and he's been regretting it every second since, but he's just a kid, and I still think you didn't need to be so hard on him."

"Judy. I was going to call you. This whole thing—"

"I know. A disaster like this, it makes you think. Families shouldn't argue. It's not right. And I need your help."

"Help?"

"I haven't heard from him, Murray. It's been two days and he hasn't called. It's probably silly of me—kids'll be kids, and Sarah says he's just not thinking, but it's the only thing on my mind."

"Oh dear."

"Can you find him for me? Murray, please?"

"Of course, Judes, but I don't know how."

"There isn't any phone number. That's the problem. That Julian boy, he's given me an address—I have the address. It's in a place called Fort Greene, apparently. Do you know where that is? In Brooklyn, somewhere?"

"I'm sure we can find it."

"Well, if one of you wouldn't mind—I know it's kind of awkward, given, you know, everything. But it's been forty-eight hours and I haven't had a word." She felt herself near tears.

"You don't really think that . . ."

"Of course not. Of course not. I mean, this Fort Greene, it's nowhere near, right?"

"Nowhere near."

"So it's not as though . . . but a mother worries, Murray. You know that. Ask Annabel."

"I know you do. Don't worry about it, Judy. I'm sure he's perfectly fine, but one of us will go check in on him. I'll tell you what: I'll get Marina to do it. They get on like a house on fire. Wouldn't that be good?"

"Whatever it takes, you know? Because I can come down there, too, if I need to."

"Don't be silly, Judes. That's the last thing anybody wants. People are turning up in droves, around here—on buses, trains, any way they can—to help dig this mess out. To look for survivors, you know."

"Tell me something, Murray: Can you smell it? What does it smell like, for God's sake?"

"We're too far away, up here. I'm going tomorrow. I'm writing something. But Marina's already been. I think it smells pretty strong, depending on the air. You know, the wind. Like burning dust, mostly, and some other stuff, fuel. And other stuff. You know. A lot of dust."

"But it's going to smell like death, isn't it? Soon, if it doesn't already? A great big grave like that. It's going to smell like death."

CHAPTER SIXTY-ONE

Fort Greene

When Marina and Julius went together out to the house in Fort Greene, they stood on the doorstep for two or three minutes after ringing the bell. Julius, whose eye was now rimmed with yellow and green, fiddled with the bandage on his cheek.

"Nobody's here," he said. "It's Friday lunchtime. Who would be home on a Friday at lunchtime? Shake Your Booty is probably at work. Temping, you know? I gave him the number."

Marina pursed her lips and pressed the bell again, for a long time. They could hear it ringing in the hallway.

"These are great houses," Julius said, peering through the etched glass of the door. "If I had a million, I'd buy this dump and do it up. Sooner or later, it's going to be worth a lot."

"I'm sure it already is," Marina said. "Didn't you see, one block down, it looks like they've all been done."

Julius continued to squint at the inner staircase. "I think we've roused someone," he said. "Looks like an ax murderer."

The man who came to the door had as much stubble on his fleshy jowls as he did on top of his head. His shoulders were like hams, round, dense, and tight against his grubby T-shirt. "What do you want?" He had an accent.

Marina, all charm, explained about Bootie, and how they were sure he was fine but just wanted to check.

"He's not here now."

"Are you sure?"

"I'm downstairs from him. You think the house is solid, but the heating vents are all open. The guy farts, I know it."

"So don't let us bother you more—you've heard him since Tuesday, right?"

The man scratched his stubbly neck, in a mimicry of thought. "I don't know," he said. "I didn't think about it. But I haven't heard him for a few days."

"Since the planes? Have you heard him since the planes hit?"

"I don't know."

They asked to see his room. "You know, if there's Wednesday's paper in the garbage, then we don't need to worry about him."

"Right." The man looked at them with half-hearted suspicion. As though he knew he should keep them from coming inside—on a matter of principle, perhaps, though he didn't look very principled—but couldn't quite be bothered.

"I'm his cousin," Marina repeated. "His mother—my aunt—is very worried."

"The door's locked," he said. "The door to his room."

"You don't have a set of master keys around somewhere?" Julius asked.

The man nodded, seemed almost sheepish, now, and motioned for them to come in. Marina was assailed, as she passed him, by his smell of garlic sweat.

The stairwell was shabby, and not very clean. Rubber matting was peeling off the steps, and a wealth of grit crackled beneath their shoes. The uneven stucco had been painted, long ago, with a shiny sky-blue paint, presumably for good cheer and ease of cleaning, but clearly nobody had taken a damp rag to the walls in years, and they were streaked and filthy. The corridors upstairs, windowless, were ill lit, and daylight seeped only beneath the rooms' locked doors. The man stopped on the second floor, told them to wait, and slipped into the room at the back in a furtive way so that they could not see inside it, shutting the door behind him. He reemerged with a fistful of keys on a cloth strap.

"I shouldn't do this," he said, with a shrug, as he led them up another flight. "People should be allowed their privacy."

The top floor was narrower, more cramped than the ones below, but a bathroom door stood open, at least. Marina noticed that someone had put a spider plant on the window ledge; the shower curtain, of fiesta stripes, had been chosen to match the bath mat. It was not too bad.

Bootie's room made them all draw breath. There was nothing in it to speak of: a pile of rumpled sheets beneath the window, an unplugged computer on the floor in the corner, next to some books, a few sorry postcards pinned randomly to the wall. There was a dirty mug, and a plate encrusted with what looked like tomato sauce. A half loaf of curling sliced bread in a plastic bag kept company with a few cans, atop which a spoon and can opener had been carefully set. Marina went to look out the window at the rooftops, then turned her back to it. Not only were there no newspapers, there was no wastepaper basket in which they could have been put.

"Maybe he went away?" Julius suggested, kicking vaguely at the sheets. "Those are mine," he said, and pointing to a towel hung over the handle of the cupboard door, "and that, too. Your cousin's a thief."

The big man stood in the middle of the room with his arms hanging awkwardly at his sides. They were short, as well as thick. "Okay," he said.

Marina opened the closet. Bootie's suitcases lay on the floor inside, vomiting their contents: underpants, unmatched socks, some crumpled shirts, the flailing legs of a pair of jeans.

"He hasn't gone," she said. "He just doesn't have anything." She shook her head. "I feel so bad."

"It's not your fault."

"I could've tried to persuade Dad to keep him on. I was too angry all around, I think."

"Are you done now?" The man shook the keys a couple of times. "He's not here."

"No." Marina agreed to the obvious. "But thank you."

Back on the doorstep she turned to Julius. "What next?"

"Maybe he's at work. Why don't we call the agency?"

"But what if he's not?"

"Then we'll figure out the next step. He's probably eating a sandwich at some deli at Midtown right now. Just because he's not here and his room is depressing—it doesn't mean anything."

"It just felt . . . I don't know. Forsaken. The room. It was awful."

"So he's been sleeping on the floor. There are worse fates."

"And if we can't find him? Do we call the police?"

"Calm down. You're getting way ahead of yourself." He put his arm around her shoulder, and they walked back down the street, which was still in the bright light, in a manner at once suburban and mournful. On their way to the subway, they passed a squat brick fire station draped in black crepe, outside which people had piled bunches of flowers, mostly yellow, and Marina let out a little moan.

"Julius," she said, "I told Ludovic, on the day, right after it happened, I told him 'We're bound to know someone.' I thought, you know, friends' fathers or someone we were at college with, or even, I thought of the mother of this kid my mom represents, and—"

"And she's fine, right?"

"No. That's the thing, she's not fine. She's missing. She was on the hundred and first floor, or something, and nobody's heard from her."

"Wow. How old is the kid?"

"It's a mess, God, that's a mess, because he's fourteen, and no dad in the picture, just this horrible stepfather who's the reason for all the trouble. My mom says it's like he's been shot, he walks around completely silent and can hardly breathe. He usually knits to stay calm—weird, I know—but my mom says he can't even do that, even though his fingers keep moving, like they have a life of their own. He says nothing, but the fingers are going all the time." She sighed. "So you know, she's still considered missing, but oh God, Julius, it's awful."

"It *is* awful," he agreed, pressing himself close to her, so that his collar tickled her ear. "It's completely horrific. But it doesn't have anything to do with Shake Your Booty. I promise you."

She sniffled a bit, daubed at her lip, her cheek, with a linty Kleenex from the pocket of her jeans. "Is my nose red?" she said. And then, "Do you realize, when I put this Kleenex in my pocket, the world was a completely different place?" And finally, in a different, smaller voice: "We've got to find him. You know that, don't you? We have got to find him."

When Julius called the agency, they wouldn't give him any information. "I'm really sorry, but it's against our policy," the woman said. "Even if you are registered with us. The inquiry has to be official. You know, through the police. Can you just get the police to do it?"

"What, along with five thousand other people?" he snapped. "You don't think they have enough to worry about already?"

"I'm sorry," she said again, with obvious regret. "I know it's a difficult time."

But then he went into their office, along with Marina, just before five, and the only woman there was not the receptionist but someone more senior, a small potato-nosed person in her fifties in a smart red suit. Julius recognized her.

"Everyone's gone," she said. "I think you'd better come back on Monday. We should have a full staff in then, finally. Some people have been out all week." She sighed.

"But it can't wait till Monday," Marina said. "I'm very sorry, but it can't."

The woman listened to their story, and nodded, and looked closely at Julius. "Sure," she said, "I've worked with you. I remember the name. It's an unusual first name. Fidelity, Fidelity, right? You're supposed to start next Thursday. Three months. You're always highly recommended." She paused. "That's a nasty cut you've got."

He shrugged, sorrowfully. She might think it was from the tragedy.

In the end, she agreed to look for them. And yes, Frederick Tubb had been placed right after Labor Day, starting the Tuesday, a two-week placement, a financial firm on Cedar Street. His hours were the usual, nine to five, five days. "There's a note in the file," she said. "And you know, now I remember Mary talking about him. He came in last Friday with his time sheet and he wanted to be paid right away. She said he was really desperate, and she felt so bad for him that she wrote him a check out of the petty cash account, which is completely against company policy. I could've let her go for that. But she was honest, at least, and we had a talk about it, and now I think she understands how important it is. He said he wouldn't be able to eat for the week, or pay his Metrocard. Nothing. A young kid, she said. Serious seeming."

"Oh dear," Marina said.

"Did the company, did someone call and say he hadn't shown up, or anything?"

"This week, you mean? I don't think they're even open. Do you know where Cedar Street is?"

"Not exactly."

She got up to show them on a map of Manhattan that was pinned to the wall near the reception desk. "It's only a few blocks away," she said. "I'm sure all their windows were blown out, toxic dust everywhere. No power, probably no water, even. Nobody's working there right now." As they were leaving she gave them a sad smile. "Good luck," she said. "We all need it, these days."

"Even if he was going to an office two blocks away, there's no reason for him to have been at Ground Zero," Julius said, as soon as they were in the elevator. "It isn't his subway stop. And what, the first tower was at, like, ten of nine, right? So that means unless he was weirdly early, he would only have been in the neighborhood once it had already happened. They were telling people to get out of there. He would've gotten out, walked uptown, or back to Brooklyn. Lots of people walked back to Brooklyn that day."

"So what, you think he was trampled by the mob on the Brooklyn Bridge?"

"You laugh, but he could be in the hospital with a broken leg or something. Easily."

"What am I going to tell my dad? What are we going to tell Aunt Judy?"

"It's not the end of the world, you know. He's going to turn up somewhere. That's how life is."

"It's how it was. I don't know how anything is, anymore."

"No," he said, touching his cheek. "Scarred for life, and we don't know how it will turn out."

CHAPTER SIXTY-TWO

Clarion Call

On Friday afternoon, Bootie had his first bath in days, in the plastic bathtub of his room in the Clarion half a mile from the Miami bus station. He ran it fairly cool, because it was hot out, and he was hot. The bathroom had no window, either, and seemed to hoard the heat. He'd been sticky for days, and filthy, because he had only what he'd been wearing on Tuesday morning, his striped dress shirt from Brooks Brothers, and his chinos, now blotted with ketchup and grease, and the same pair of black socks, so clammy and sweat-soaked they felt they'd never again be dry. On the bus, as his beard grew and his hair stuck limply to his head, he'd been aware that he stank, as if every hair on his body were coated in stink and were quietly emanating that odor, of him, out into the air, among the seats. In a funny way it had made him feel alive, more present than he'd felt in weeks, as though every other passenger would have to admit that Bootie Tubb *was*, because of his smell; and when an old man, a small, wiry black man with a felt hat on his head, had sat beside him for a time, out of necessity, and had wrinkled his shiny nose and put his fingers preventatively to his nostrils, Bootie had felt at the same time ashamed and proud.

He had never before been so conscious of making an impression.

He hadn't woken up that morning, of course, with any intention of going anywhere but the offices of Reading and Lockwood, where he'd already spent the better part of a week checking the sums of endless columns of figures using an addictive little adding machine that printed everything out on a roll of tape as he went along. His job, once he'd checked the sums, was to attach the appropriate segment of tape to the document at hand and return it to his boss, a leathered woman with wispy blond hair who smelled powerfully of perfume and cigarettes. It was not taxing work, but finicky and quickly dull, and the office—he'd never spent time in an office before, not like this—struck him as unhealthy, everyone breathing recirculated air high above the ground. The first few days, he was very prompt, but it became clear that his boss, Maureen, didn't care when he arrived, so long as by the end of the day he'd moved all the papers from the in-box to the out-box, with their tapes tidily appended. His fingers, though thick, grew nimble at the adding machine, and he was able to complete the work more quickly than she knew, which left him time. He read Musil during his lunch hour, hunched at his desk, with a bag of Doritos. He bought the largest size at the deli down the block, to save money, along with the two-liter size of Coke, and he kept these two items stowed beneath his feet. The Coke was always warm, then, and progressively flatter, so that eventually it became like some toxic juice, pressed, perhaps, from sugar-coated tires, or from some unnameable deadly plant in the Amazon. He read Musil, and he came late to the office, late because the subway he so loathed was marginally less crowded when the nine a.m. cut-off was past.

On that morning, he'd been very late. He'd had to get off two consecutive trains after only one stop because they were too tightly packed, and had set his heart pounding and closed his throat. It had taken great effort to get onto the third train, and even so, he'd been able to stand it only until they were across the water (he hated going under the water at all, felt he could feel the weight of it pushing down upon the tunnel, the car, himself), had been able to stand it only because he knew he absolutely had to, and had got off at Whitehall Street, sweating and panting as he rose to ground level, to walk, then, the rest of the way. It was a shame, he'd not been this late before, it was 9:10 already, but he'd be there by 9:25 or 9:30 at the latest, and Maureen would just have gone for her first cigarette break down on the street, so if she didn't actually spot him, then she'd never know how late he'd been.

Something was wrong, above ground. The air. The smoke. The sun, the bright sky, was eclipsed by smoke, an ocean of black smoke, high up but still all-enveloping. People were shouting and pointing, and he turned and could see, above all the other buildings, the tips of the towers, and flames, and he could smell it. He couldn't get his breath because he'd been wheezing anyway; but this, what was this? He couldn't make sense of it. The end of the world. A sign from God.

He asked a man in a suit, with expensive black shoes, not unlike his own dress shoes left at home, but of better leather, and shinier—he found himself looking mostly at the shoes—and the man told him about the planes, not one but two, and the second one, well, people right here had seen it—hadn't

Bootie heard it? He'd been underground? Well. A better place to be, the man said, because this is like Armageddon. There were people trapped up there, he said, who couldn't get down. People surely dying from the smoke. And another man came up to them, his tie loosened, his eyes wild, a man in his fifties with a tidy white tonsure, and said, "They're jumping. I've heard that they're jumping."

And the first man said, "Who wouldn't. My God, my God. Wouldn't you?"

That was when Bootie started walking. He had Musil in a plastic bag, his fingers slick upon the handles, and he had fog, or dust, or something on his glasses, but he loosened his tie and undid the top button and he walked, uptown.

He felt a pull to go over and look at the buildings from up close; but they frightened him, so much death frightened him, more powerfully than it lured him, and the smoke frightened him most of all. Not to be able to breathe. He stuck to Nassau Street, and then Lafayette. There were many people in the streets, the whole way, and eventually he kept his head down, his eyes upon his own feet, his white-coated shoes, one foot in front of the other. People milled all in the same direction, like film extras crammed in the streets, brushing up against one another but not frantically so, oddly like a massive cortege, like a slow river, in which individuals, like boulders, stopped and stood for a time and let the water, the other walkers, break quietly around them. He didn't want to know. He was at Canal when the first tower fell. As everyone shouted and gasped, he stopped, turned, looked: the smoke and the dust took over the world. He looked away, down at the ground.

Because he wasn't with anyone, didn't speak to anyone, but

watched alone from behind his eyes, it felt as though this might not actually be happening, as though this were some waking dream from which, if he only tried hard enough, he could escape. In the throng, he felt absolutely alone, more so than he had before. He felt no connection to the faces, the voices, that came to him as if from far away. He was a man in an unknown country, he thought, and sometimes the cries sounded not like words but just like noise, the sound and the fury of it. A tale told to an idiot. Head down, he pushed through the standing crowds, the river around him frozen while he, perversely, walked on.

In the pocket of his pants, he had all his money, the remaining cash from the check the kind woman at the agency had illicitly given him. As he made his way northward, beneath the clear and bright sky, in a stunned semblance of normality—the farther he got, the more the streets had a holiday feel, subdued but rather extraordinary, as if a beloved king's death had just been announced and the citizens, albeit mournful, were baffled by their liberation from routine—he was assailed by thoughts. As if the roar in his head were subsiding for the first time in weeks, a switch flicked in his brain, he couldn't keep them from coming. He'd been immersed in some madness to think Marina could ever love him, would ever love him. She'd made her choice, the poxy kangaroo, and the issue was settled: her kindnesses had never been significant, that is to say, they had never *signified.* From the first trip downtown—she'd asked him along, doubtless to appease her mother's notions of politesse—to the *Monitor* commission—pushed, in fact, by the mysteriously kindly Danielle, whose moral turpitude somehow muddied a very good soul—there had been no Marina in her actions.

Because Marina—anyone could see it—was always all about her father. Even when she turned against him, or purported to. As were they all, around him, the women without exception but the men no less so. Even Ludovic Seeley was always, unwittingly, in his thrall. And surely this was where the man's greatness lay. How could Bootie have failed to understand? Because, of course, it guaranteed, it predetermined his own failure; and there had been too much at stake for him in that. Until now: this, the end of the world as he knew it, had known it, changed everything. The Tower of Babel tumbling. An end to false idols. And Murray, whose greatness lay not in his words or his actions but simply in his capacity to convince people of that greatness, starting, naturally, with himself, Murray who was emperor in this place of pretense, a land that stretched from Oswego to the heart of Manhattan and beyond—surely even Murray, above all Murray, would be toppled by this.

But Bootie didn't want to be crushed by the falling idol any more than he had wanted to be felled by the volcanic debris downtown. His instincts for survival were much stronger, thank God, than his voyeuristic impulses. He could witness it all from anywhere.

From anywhere: where once he had feared that this immense city would set him adrift, a spinning atom in the ether, and where once he had seen in this the ultimate terror of insignificance, he now, and suddenly, and so clearly, saw that his fate had led him here. His fate had taken him off two trains this morning, had raised him to the surface at Whitehall Street, had shown him the spinning atoms, unraveling, the end of life, all of them people tethered by love, and habit, and work, and meaning, tied into a meaning suddenly exploded, because contrary to all he had imagined, being tied, being *known,* did not keep you safe. Quite the opposite: this, surely, was the meaning of Emerson, which he had so willfully and for so long misunderstood: great geniuses have the shortest biographies. Even their cousins know nothing about them. He had never been known rightly—how could he be, in the carapace of his ill-fitting names—but had thought that this imperfect knowledge was to be worked upon, bettered. But of course: mutability, precisely the capacity to spin like an atom, untethered, this thrill of absolute unknownness was not something to be feared. It was the point of it all. To be absolutely unrelated. Without context. To be truly and in every way self-reliant. At last.

This, now, then, was his mutability canto. He thought this as he turned westward at Fortieth Street. He had been given— his fate—the precious opportunity to *be* again, not to be as he had been. Because as far as anyone knew, he *wasn't.* It had been true for ten days, of course, but he hadn't realized it, as an animal loosed from his cage, not having known freedom, doesn't at first run. He hadn't understood until now. He had overheard, as he walked, in spite of himself. They said maybe tens of thousands. People in the towers, on the planes, but some, too, in the crowds, in the streets down below and nearby, where he ought to have been, had destiny not stayed him. But for anyone who went looking (would the beautiful Marina go looking, perhaps? Or only his disconsolate mother?), it would be as if he had been there, in the lee of the towers, vanished, pulverized, the loathed Bootie Tubb meeting his unspeakable fate.

*

Port Authority was closed, when he arrived, with no announced plans to reopen. The crowds were dense outside, as people arriving, trying to get home to New Jersey or upstate, encountered those already disappointed. Bootie, detached from the worry—he had no home to go to; he had nowhere to be; he had, after all, in some strange way just ceased to exist—watched serenely. One woman near him, lank-haired, swarthy, her peacock blue suit wilted, her sneakers, beneath her stockings, a neon white, opened her mouth like a pelican and started to cry.

Another woman, older, stout, grayed, who reminded Bootie of his mother, put her arm around the weeper's shoulder. "It's all right," she cooed. "There, there. Don't worry. We're all in the same boat. But your kids are safe and you're safe and that's what counts. We'll all get there in time."

In the end, he spent Tuesday night in Central Park. He wasn't alone. It hadn't felt frightening (he remembered again his mother's dire warnings of years before: a body under every bridge), but rather like a storybook adventure, or like something out of the sci-fi novels he read at thirteen, only tamer. He had with him a corned beef on rye, after all, and a large bottle of Coke, and a mini-pack of Oreos to help keep his spirits up; and in spite of the situation, the man at the deli had remembered to put in a dill pickle, which, as Bootie chewed it noisily at dusk beneath a tree at the edge of Sheep's Meadow, surely implied that this strange new world was, at least to a degree, contiguous with the old. Not, then, a fully postapocalyptic scenario. He was cold in the night—he had only his blazer and no blankets at all: he hadn't expected to be much out of doors that day—and slept fitfully. Although it was expensive, he treated himself to a diner omelet the next morning, and to eight refills of coffee, staying huddled in his blue booth, reading Musil, slowly, sleepily, until the last vestigial shudders had ceased and he no longer felt the chill. By then it was lunchtime, and he ordered soup. The television in the diner was on the whole time, and confused with his imaginary impressions of Vienna and plans for the Kaiser's party were grainy images of a man named Mohammed Atta and a young associate—handsome, happy-looking—at an ATM, just the night before last. Only on Monday night, they'd still been planning, and it had all been in their heads, then, and not yet unleashed upon the world. It was an awesome, a fearful thought: you could make something inside your head, as huge and devastating as this, and spill it out into reality, make it really happen. You could—for evil, but if for evil, then why not for good, too?—change the world. How petty Uncle Murray appeared, next to this; how petty their family squabbles; how petty the life he, Bootie, had been leading.

The second night he'd spent at Port Authority, because there was word, there, that it would soon reopen. He didn't sleep—aside from a couple of hours dozing on his haunches, but still, and vitally, given the police, appearing patiently to read his book—knowing that once on the bus he would have all his time. An older man in a windbreaker, an athlete gone to seed in middle age—still sandy-haired but too ruddy, and thick, thick in his fingers, his neck, his broad chest—twice offered Bootie a smoke, and Bootie wondered, the second time, whether the man had forgotten or whether he was, however discreetly, propositioning.

"Good book?" the man asked, the second time, but Bootie

kept his eyes on the page as he nodded, and did not look up again for a long while.

He'd chosen Miami because when the station opened at five, it was the farthest and earliest one could go; and it was, in the bargain, a warm destination for his aching body. He paid in cash, picked up three doughnuts (two honey-glazed and one powdered, filled with strawberry jam) and some more Cokes and found himself a seat as soon as they were allowed to board. The bus pulled out at seven, setting off on its twenty-nine-hour journey, again to a different, and surely better, country.

But that hour, Friday afternoon, in the Clarion's plastic bathtub, felt truly like his new beginning. A baptism. He'd decided to take a new name, to shed the agonies of the old. Ulrich was to hand, of course, from the Musil: not so far from Frederick, but pleasingly irreducible in comparison. As for a surname, he'd never cared for Tubb: Who would, or could? It was tempting to take Thwaite: he felt entitled to it, felt he could make of it what it ought to be. But then again, it was not new enough. New: there was a name. Ulrich New. What did he know? How to be New.

He rose from the grimed water and scrubbed himself dry with the paltry Clarion towels. It took three of them fully to do the job; but what luxury, to have three towels. What luxury, to have a room with a bed—so big—a television, running water. He had carpet underfoot, bristly, but still. It was the nicest room he'd had in months. He would find a job, he would keep learning, he would bide his time and rise from the ashes, like the phoenix, more powerful than before. Would they— would *she*—recognize him then? She might, in time, be ready to see him, to know him as he was. Or rather, as he would then be. Because Ulrich knew he was at the beginning of a long road—a long, hot road, he could tell in spite of the Clarion air-conditioning window unit—but at last it would be—without relations, unstuck—the right road. A road to the top of a mountain, as yet unnamed: power, or discovery, or truth, or all three. His own road.

He stood unabashedly naked at the window in the Miami afternoon sun, the towels on the floor behind him, and, to the whining soundtrack of the a/c, watched a battered blue Taurus pull into the parking lot, watched two black boys his own age get out, walk to the glass front door. They were in his mind like the falling towers, his own personal cinema. It was all about control. Ulrich would fashion the reality inside his head and then, when the time was right, would give birth to it, would make them all at last understand, would take them by surprise.

He would cast no shadow, in this new incarnation; but that was fine, just fine. He would be his own idol, the one he had never yet found. He would be all right.

NOVEMBER

CHAPTER SIXTY-THREE

Burying the Dead (1)

Judy organized the memorial service for the week before Thanksgiving because, as she told Joan, she badly needed some closure on this. And because she didn't want to ruin Thanksgiving, and beyond that, Christmas, for Sarah's kids, not any more than they would be ruined anyway. Everything was ruined forever, but you weren't actually allowed to say that. She'd been to New York City, she'd been to that place, she'd thought it might help; but the vast hole just seemed like an extrusion of her own grief. She'd met other relatives, but mostly they seemed different to her, hard to talk to, in part maybe because they could claim that dreadful place, they knew why their husbands and daughters and brothers had been there: theirs no fleeting, horrible fluke, but a sense of bleak entitlement. She hadn't met them, but felt kinship with the families of missing tourists, or of foreigners on whirlwind business trips: How could chance, fate, God, have been so maliciously aligned against *my* blood? Why mine? As for Murray and his lot, how could she not blame them, that callous, callow girl and her own monstrous brother, she wouldn't speak ill of him out loud, but he'd always been that way, an ego the size of a house, their mother had made him that way, from the beginning, fed him

on kisses and cream, her firstborn, heart's love, sickening
garbage if she let herself remember it, like some fatted calf, only
he'd sent his nephew in his stead to the slaughter. Murray's
vanity had killed her Bootie, there were no two ways about it;
and it wasn't clear to her in her heart whether she would ever
be able to forgive him: his whole life, and now hers, too. He
had taken *her* heart's love, her most precious.

She'd taken the epitaph for Bootie's stone from a much older
grave, at the other end of the grounds, and didn't mind repeating it because it was so true: "Here is not a life, but a piece of
childhood thrown away." He'd had everything ahead, and his
uncle to surpass. He'd had a future.

But she wasn't like her brother, one selfishly to turn her back
in her trouble, to pretend they weren't related. You couldn't
escape that, no matter how you tried. So when he'd asked if
they could come, she'd said yes, because they could come
unforgiven: they were, aside from Sarah and Tom and the children, all the family she had left now.

And it would be a fitting good-bye to Watertown. She was
finishing up the year at the school, because she wasn't a quit-
ter, never had been (she'd taken only one term off when Bert
was at the very end, and afterward had heard terrible things
about the substitute, a boy just out of college who stuttered and
couldn't keep order), but she'd already decided, with Sarah, she
couldn't stay in the house, would put it up for sale come spring,
because how many ghosts could a person live with, even if she
loved them more than anything?

His shoes! How many times since that day had she held
those abandoned dress shoes, one in each hand, to her breast?
She couldn't polish them, though they needed it, because that

would mean covering the surfaces his hands had touched. She played with the laces, spoke to them—it was crazy, but what else did she have of him? And that was what they would bury, all there was, because the rubble had, as yet, returned no trace. Some shoes, a stone: a piece of childhood thrown away. She'd gone to the desolate room in Brooklyn, not with Murray but with Annabel, who had been gentle, careful, her soft, high voice alternately a balm and an irritant, and she'd wept to see to what Bootie had been reduced: sleeping on the floor, in a tangle of borrowed sheets, probably not eating, or barely, his few belongings a meager and inadequate testament to his short life.

They had repacked his cases, put the books and cards in a paper grocery bag, and had stowed the computer in a carton, wrapped in the sheets and towel. At first she'd thought simply to give it away, because Annabel, given her work, would know a deserving young person; but then it occurred to her that he might have left something on it that would tell her, would reveal to her, who he had been becoming, in this strange and lonely journey upon which he had fatefully, fatally embarked months before. Having kept it, though, she still hadn't found the courage to turn it on, had left it packed in its box on the floor of his Watertown bedroom. Annabel and Murray had invited her to stay with them on that trip, but she had declined, gone instead to a motel on the far west side, a place where she didn't feel very comfortable walking around outside. Still, it had been the better choice; and she wasn't going to have them stay in her house, either, when they came. She'd booked them rooms at the Hampton Inn across town. It was just like Bert's funeral: the same season, for one; and the three of them coming, Annabel, Murray, Marina. The new husband was off overseas—England, was it?—which did seem a bit odd, just now, but who was she to say? Then again, it was like Bert, in so many ways. Bootie had been a boy then, but a rock for her, so calm and strong. He'd been what made her get up in the morning, the reason she bothered to wash her face. She didn't have that from anyone, now. If she wasn't careful, she'd lose sight of the point of it all, would forget, not just why but how to live. She'd been so sure of it, once.

CHAPTER SIXTY-FOUR

Burying the Dead (2)

Marina was dreading going to Watertown. The whole thing was so unbelievable, so darkly absurd—Beckettian, she'd said to Julius—and Watertown, such a dump, seemed the crowning surreality. But maybe that was fitting: that they should witness the laying to rest of her strange, troubled, unlucky cousin ("It was just dumb luck. Dumb *bad* luck," Ludo had said several times, to try to assuage her guilt. "If you won the lottery, would you look around for someone to blame for it?") in that strange, unlucky place. She remembered the graveyard from her uncle's death: weirdly close to downtown, with a fast-food joint— KFC, was it?—right next door. A blustery, forlorn field of stones—her father had shown her her grandparents' graves— and a big, cold sky. Of course, Bootie wouldn't really be there. They'd be burying some idea of him, because that was all that was left. It was for Aunt Judy's sake. When Marina's father had asked her to go and she'd demurred, only slightly, about the horridness of it, he'd said, tight-lipped, "You do it for your aunt Judy"; but then, that was guilt talking. She knew he was per- meated by it, because so was she. But she'd never really known her aunt, and couldn't imagine how to speak to her about this. When she'd seen her in New York, a few weeks ago, Judy had seemed smaller, her clothes loose, her round head bobbing on a crepey neck, and she'd looked at once old and much younger than Marina remembered, as if something, some essential part, had been removed. Which, of course, it had.

Marina was angry at Ludo for being in London, and not by her side on the way to Watertown, but knew he had no choice. He was interviewing for a job on a paper over there; he'd had to go. Not only was it a matter of income—her parents could help, for a while—but of his career, of course. He'd said so only days after the events: "They won't want foreigners here now. Time to call in my UK connections. I can't lose momentum, here, you understand?"

"And what about me?" she'd asked.

"What about you?" he'd said. "What momentum have you got to lose? You're still your father's daughter, aren't you?"

She hadn't known how to take this. What it seemed he was saying was too hideous—rendered him too hideous—to contemplate. But she decided that he was speaking from some baffled, pain-filled place, and so forgave him, even consoled him. She loved him, didn't she?

And it was very possible, in not so long, that she'd have no choice, either, that they'd have to settle on the other side of the Atlantic. She couldn't begin to think about that: she knew she didn't want to go. She couldn't leave Manhattan, especially now. But *The Monitor,* as Ludo had predicted, was not to be, not now at least. According to Merton, all the hundreds of thousands already spent were better written off: nobody wanted such a thing in this new world, a frivolous, satirical thing. Ludo said Merton had made it sound like a fashion magazine he was dismissing, instead of an organ for radical cultural commentary. But even Ludo, master debater, hadn't been able to persuade him to change his mind, so that was an end to it. So much for taking New York by storm. So much for revolution. The revolution belonged to other people now, far away from them, and it was real.

Marina knew how disappointed Ludo was, and how angry: he'd traveled all the way from Australia for this, had labored day and night for months to create from (almost) nothing this magazine that would, he knew, have made his global reputation once and for all. He had considered many scenarios along the way, including the adverse, but none as bad as this. Nobody could have foreseen this. He didn't talk about it to anyone but Marina, and to her only sparingly—because they both knew that Bootie's death made a free discussion somehow impossible, immoral—but his misery seeped into his face, his voice. He sniped at her, told her her clothes looked bad, carped about her father—for whom the nation's tragedy had brought a resurgence of celebrity, as Murray Thwaite opined in the press, on television, on what Ludo called the "blasted" radio—and even about her friends.

Her friends: Ludo didn't like Danielle anymore, if he ever really had, perhaps because she had taken it the hardest of all of them, and he felt she had least cause. In the days after 9/11, Marina and Julius had literally had to pry her out of her bed: they'd all spoken, of course, on the Tuesday night, checking in; but when first they'd actually stopped by to see her, on Wednesday afternoon, she had clearly not been outside since it happened, her hair and clothes disheveled, her eyes gummy and small. The three of them stood at her picture window and gaped at the hole in the skyline, at the clear air, and Danielle wanted at once to get back into bed. Maybe, Marina had said to Ludo, maybe seeing it all unfold so clearly was more traumatic, even at some distance away; but Ludo thought the problem was pure self-indulgence. Since then, Danielle had been peculiar, elusive, had gone into therapy, was on antidepressants, now, doubtless like half of the city; but more than that, Marina felt that she had lost her, that the Danielle she had always known had been vacuumed out, and only a flat, monosyllabic shell remained. Danielle never called Marina, these days, and when Marina rang, their conversations were strained and curtailed. Marina had stuck her neck out—she'd thought it would be good for both of them—and asked Danielle if she would accompany Marina to Bootie's memorial. After all, Danielle had always been solicitous of him, had seemed to see through his unnerving loner persona to some wounded, striving soul, had tried to help him, or at least had urged Marina to. But Danielle had curled her lip in what amounted to a sneer, and said, "I don't think I'd belong there, do you? It's not a party, it's a wake." And as Marina opened her mouth to speak, she'd gone on, "Anyway, I don't think I'll be here."

"Where are you going?"

"I don't know. Away. I think I need to go away."

Marina was flummoxed by the whole exchange, by its coldness, somehow. Far more acutely than the loss of Bootie, which struck her only intermittently and often as an idea rather than a yawning maw—she couldn't quite believe he wasn't still out there, in Brooklyn somewhere, just not speaking to them all— she felt she had lost her best friend. You couldn't feel the same kind of grief about someone you barely knew, Ludo had pointed out about Bootie, even if he was a blood relation. You felt guilty: that was different, visceral, miserable but not personal, somehow. As for Danielle, you just had to hope that with the drugs, or after the drugs, she would come back to herself. Though why or how anything should ever be as it had been before was anybody's guess.

Julius was the same, at least. Or rather, Julius had come back. More or less. It gave Marina hope. He seemed in all aspects more sober for his Conehead interlude—more cynical, if that were possible. And he still didn't know what he was doing, wasting his talents on trivia, like the piece on nightclubs that he'd resold to *Interview*. The welt on his cheek, still fairly fresh, gave him a rakish aspect that amused him when it didn't depress him. He said it clearly made him more alluring—men commented on it, as if it were a beauty mark—but on off days he confessed that he couldn't quite believe he would look this way always, would carry David's mark on him, a brand.

"Think about it," he said over coffee at the beginning of November. "You don't think of yourself as scarred. You forget. And you think you can just keep being your same self. But everyone sees you, and they see a changed person, and the ones who know the story see you as changed in a very particular way, which isn't so nice. And then they remind you, over and over again, and then, I think, eventually you get changed, from the outside in, you have to absorb it, somehow."

"It's like my book, a bit," Marina had said. "Change the clothes, you change the person. Seems silly, but it's true."

"M," Julius had retorted with some exasperation, "a scar on your face is *not* like a new T-shirt or a pair of cowboy boots. It isn't optional."

"No, I didn't mean it that way," she'd said, but could tell he was still annoyed.

He'd agreed to come with her to Watertown, bless him. Because he felt guilty, too: that same afternoon, in Starbucks, he'd told her about the Lewis incident, about calling Bootie fat.

"You were high, you were drunk. It wasn't good, but you've got to forgive yourself," she said.

"He ended up in that flophouse because I turfed him out of Pitt Street, you remember."

"Darling," Marina said, "Pitt Street is a flophouse."

"Thanks."

"It is. Our goal for next year will be to get you into a proper apartment."

"And get me a proper job, too?"

"I'm unemployed myself, remember."

"With a book coming out, thank you very much."

"Well, but . . ."

"It will change everything. It's huge."

"Or will slip into the bookstores and out of them just as fast. And it won't change anything."

Julius raised an eyebrow.

"I'm not being precious, you know. It's entirely plausible. Happens all the time. If you get a bad review in the *Times,* that's the end."

"It's a long way off—what, September next year? Couldn't you just be excited about it?"

"Sometimes I wonder about you, Julius. Morally, I mean. Hello? Where have you been? Right now it seems like it'd be a miracle for us even to make it to next September."

"Oh, come on."

"I'm serious. If Ludo gets a job in England, then who knows where I'll be, or what I'll be, by then. And if we stay in Manhattan, there could be another thing, a dirty bomb, whatever, and bam."

"You're not going to live like that, with that mentality. Because I won't hang out with you anymore. I mean, at that point, go live in Michigan, with my parents."

"Or in Watertown, New York?"

At which point they had exchanged glances and fallen briefly silent.

"Do you think," Julius said, "that he's somehow a better person than we are because he's dead?"

"Because of how he died, you mean?"

"Because he was miserable, and now he's dead. Whereas we—well, in the great scheme of things, let's face it, we've always been fucking lucky, and have just kept right on."

"I know Danielle thinks he was a better person."

"Did she say so?"

"From how she talks about him. 'Gravitas,' 'ambition,' 'integrity.' You know."

"She's idealizing adolescence. That's *so* her. You know, torn between Big Ideas and a party. She's always been that way."

"Haven't we all?"

"No, no." Julius laughed. "We just want to be at the Party of Big Ideas. Ideally, to throw it. We see there's no contradiction."

"Only the insufferable suffer for art. That's what Ludo says. 'It's so déclassé.' "

They laughed, a little awkwardly.

"Does he really believe that?"

"He doesn't believe in suffering, no."

"Like suffering is a choice?"

"Whatever." Marina had stood, put their cups in the garbage, and they had gone back out into the cold.

CHAPTER SIXTY-FIVE

Burying the Dead (3)

The day of the memorial service, Friday, November 17, was clear and brisk. Murray woke early, despite the gloom of the motel room, washed and dressed without disturbing Annabel, and went outside for a walk. The vista, from the Hampton Inn just off the highway, was not encouraging: it could have been anywhere. The tarmac already had its leached winter aspect, the salt-white rime at its edges, drifts of garbage sodden along the curb. The huge neon signs of the chains provided the only color: the golden arches, the jangling bell, the colonel's cheerful grin. Even in the early morning, the wind-swish of the highway traffic blanketed the air, like background music. Murray was the only pedestrian in sight.

They had flown to Syracuse the evening before, with Marina and her friend, and had driven the hour north in the dark. He'd called Judy when they arrived, but hadn't gone over to see her: she'd been with Sarah and Tom, who were putting their children to bed, and she hadn't invited him. They had taken supper, an inedible excrescence, at a restaurant across the parking lot, in a booth beneath a faux Tiffany lamp, served by a spotty high school girl with an eerily keen smile and an imposingly cleft chin. Julius had been very bright about it all: "This is like being back home, for me," he said. "I always think you have to respect these restaurants, in their way. I mean, what was here before Bennigan's and Applebee's? Probably nothing."

"Not much," Murray said, remembering the rare steakhouse outings of his childhood, the thrill of shrimp cocktail or canteloupe on ice.

"So that's got to be good, right? They don't pretend to be anything they're not."

"I traveled a long way to escape this," Murray said. "And you did, too, I bet."

"So did Frederick," said Annabel, and they were all quiet for a moment.

"Who's coming tomorrow?" Marina asked.

"I don't know." Murray sighed. He knew nothing about his sister's life, which only now and momentarily seemed egregious.

In the morning, walking along the side of the road among the gas stations, fast-food places, and a couple of other motels (TAY HER ! RO MS FROM ON Y $39.9 !), a rough scrub of gravel and dead weeds beneath his feet, Murray tried to imagine that Bootie's memory might peaceably belong here, but could not. He remembered the boy at his dinner table, in his office, trying so hard, and yet so ill-equipped for that existence. A matter of confidence, no doubt. He might have learned, in time, if he'd been tough enough. Which—Murray felt entitled to think this because the boy's story was over; no possible turns or new beginnings—he had not been. Murray's nose reddened, in the wind, and he could feel his ears, burned knobs on either side of his head. Toughness was about doing what needed to be done. No regrets, no waste, no giving in. The boy had given in,

THE EMPEROR'S CHILDREN   551

too many times. Who knew what went on in his head, but whatever it was, it had killed him. Murray had thought a good deal about this: the boy had been working blocks away. He'd not been at the office before the towers were hit—his supervisor, Maureen, had said so. Which meant that for him to be crushed, he had to have gone closer, on purpose, drawn to the horror; he had to have been watching it at the epicenter itself, had to have gone, and stood, and stayed. Which was, in such a boy, its own perversity. He felt some grudging admiration, but that was a separate matter. Nobody had thought the towers would fall, of course, but even so, so many bystanders— most—had survived. Murray would not feel responsible for something he had had nothing to do with. At any moment, the boy could have turned and walked away. The firemen and police would have tried to make him. Instead, he had delivered himself to the fires. It was positively Greek.

You could control what you did, if you wanted to. You had, like an actuary, constantly to be calculating the odds. Was it efficient? Was it productive? Did the benefits outweigh the risks? So many people didn't bother—a kind of stupidity, Murray felt, a lack of vision, or purpose. Anyone who said that they just woke up and found themselves in the place they'd always wanted to be was lying; and anyone who believed such a person was a fool. It was all a matter of will.

He'd walked home, on the eleventh, and had taken a shower and gone to his study and waited, aware that in his actuarial efforts he had miscalculated. His desire to be with Annabel was ultimately never in question: she was his life. He'd managed to reach Marina on the telephone, late in the afternoon, and had not mentioned Chicago to her. She didn't even seem to remember about it. Annabel had finally come home near eight, drawn and pale, with the boy, DeVaughn, in tow. She'd spent the day with him, it transpired; his mother was missing, his mother had set off from Harlem for work in the North Tower at 6:45 that morning. Unlike some others, she hadn't called her family, hadn't spoken even to her husband after that. Which had encouraged them to hope—maybe she'd been held up somewhere, out on an errand, even in the mall in the basement, buying a bagel, maybe she would emerge, unexpectedly, from the subway, with her weary smile, her long dark green raincoat a little dusty, but otherwise unharmed. Annabel had helped DeVaughn make posters, with a picture of his mother at her last birthday party, in a sparkly gold and black sweater, her close-cropped Afro glistening in the light, the girlish sprinkling of freckles across her cheeks showing. In the photo, she was smiling broadly, her teeth glinting, and because DeVaughn had taken the picture, her crinkling eyes showed love, and concern, and hope, too. Or that's what Annabel felt, and told Murray, through tears, in bed that night. She'd helped DeVaughn make the posters (D.O.B. Dec. 12, 1968; Distinguishing Marks: freckles, burn scar on her right wrist, etc.), and then had helped him post them downtown, or as near as possible, which was why they were so late getting in. They'd called the hospitals, but couldn't get through. The plan for the morning was to go back downtown to try to find her.

"I didn't expect you, lovey," she said to Murray, in his arms. He held her for a long moment, aware of the boy lurking behind, looking at the floor, the wall, anywhere but at them, his hands moving like birds in the shadows. "How did you get here?"

"It's a long story," he'd said. "I'll tell you later." And then he, with uncommon effort, had made them all scrambled eggs on toast and slices of tomato, and they had sat in surreal and agonizing silence, the three of them, in the dining room, the large boy with his face set in barely restrained panic, and Annabel staring largely at the wall, as if there were nothing left of them but their husks.

In bed, he'd tried to say something; but Annabel had hushed him. "I'm just glad you're here. It means everything that you're here, now. Hold me close. Don't talk."

And in the morning, he'd started again to explain, when DeVaughn was still sleeping in the room that had been Bootie's, and she said, "No. You chose to come home. That's all I need to know."

"But I've never, you should know, never—"

"It doesn't matter. Maybe someday, okay? But not now. Now, what matters is that you're here. Yesterday morning, I actually sort of prayed. I complained, anyway, to the God that doesn't exist. Why isn't he at home, I said, because in such a time, he should be home. I was angry. And then you were home. So. Like a miracle. Think of poor DeVaughn. He's been praying, so far for nothing."

"Which is why one shouldn't believe in God," Murray said. "Because there is no answer to the problem of theodicy."

"She may be in the hospital as we speak."

"She may."

And then DeVaughn had wandered into the kitchen, wearing the same clothes as the day before, and his sneakers, and his jacket. He had his hands in his pockets. He nodded at Murray, mumbled, "Morning, sir."

"Murray, please. Call me Murray."

"We'd better go." Annabel had clapped muffin crumbs from her hands, over the sink. "We've got a long day ahead of us. You need to eat. Take a muffin. Lowfat bran, with raisins. There might be nuts in it—you're not allergic to nuts?" She held the muffin out, and after a moment DeVaughn took a hand from his pocket with which to accept it. He looked at it as if it were a space rock, and then dropped his hand, with its muffin, to his side.

"We'll see you later, lovey," she said to Murray. "Or I will. Aurora might come today—it depends, I guess, on the subway. But I'll come back when I can. I love you." She had kissed him full on the mouth, a proprietorial kiss, and he had known that in this way she was saying what she wanted to say.

After they'd gone, he'd waited a short while and had dialed Danielle's number. He got the machine, and left her a message, apologizing for his hasty departure, and asking her to call to let him know she was okay. He left a different version of the same upon her cell phone; but heard nothing, and as the hours passed, he began to worry about her. He rang again, and again, although the third time he left no message. In the days that followed, he was eaten by her silence, more invasively than he might have been by any words; and although, by the time her message came—on his cell, a week later: "Please could you leave me alone"—he was not surprised, neither was he liberated. He found himself, unhealthily, obsessed. Still more than when they had been lovers, he thought about her, heard her laughter, turned, thinking to have seen her, in the street. He sat at his desk, supposedly penning articles on the events—and indeed, he did write numerous articles, suddenly called upon

to provide moral or ethical guidance, to offer a path for confused and frightened liberals through the mad alarums and
self-flagellations of those hideous, tumultuous weeks—while
actually staring at the wall, repeating her name over and over
inside his head. It was as if she stood directly in front of him,
not just blocking his vision but making it impossible for him
to see her whole. He couldn't accept that he would not see her
at all; couldn't believe that when he had so much, of such
importance, to think upon, she could, in her sirenical unim-
portance, so fully occupy his mind. But after she left her
message, he didn't call her. He was tough. He gleaned from
conversation with Marina that Danielle had fallen into a
depression, that she was badly off, and this almost prompted
him to capitulate; but he had his pride, too, and while he wrote
her e-mails daily, he did not send them, kept them instead
stored in his "send later" file.

And all the while he was waiting for Annabel to ask about
the night of the tenth. Sometimes it seemed that this was his
punishment, to be continually wondering what she thought, or
knew, or imagined. Their most ordinary exchanges were, he
felt, permeated by her silence, her imposition of silence, on the
issue; but he could detect no wrath, no resentment. She did not
snap at him, or look askance, or berate him. She remained her
own self, if anything more indulgent, though abstracted. It
made him want to tell her everything, the whole truth, and in
moments, late at night, a scotch by his side, he could imagine
her calm acceptance of him, of his story, her loving embrace,
her absolution. But on this, too, he remained firm, knowing
this harmonious vision could only be fantasy. He gave away
nothing.

And she, for her part, remained preoccupied. The days and weeks made clear that DeVaughn's mother could not appear, that she had been where she was supposed to be, on the 101st floor of the North Tower, among those most unfortunate whom he and Danielle had witnessed, choosing between one hell and another, like the enactment of some Byzantine icon. Eventually, perhaps, a ring would be identified, or a sliver of bone; or perhaps nothing. And the boy, Annabel said, was sapped of all fight, blank and docile now, though whether this was in preparation for a new and more terrifying onslaught of rage was not clear. A cousin had been found, in White Plains, who might take him, take the shards of his life and self and begin again, if such were possible. The stepfather had already retreated, removed, with DeVaughn's mother's disappearance, from the scene. Murray watched Annabel cry over this boy, this lost soul, and cry, too, over Bootie.

Because it was largely Annabel who took on that burden, too, of helping Judy negotiate the hospitals and registers, of retrieving his belongings, of visiting with Judy the smoking maw downtown into which her only son had vanished. Murray was called upon by his public. He had much writing, and speaking, to do. He formulated a reasoned middle ground that, while not stretching so far as those who claimed America deserved it, nevertheless gently reminded his suffering compatriots of the persistent agonies of the West Bank, or of the ever-growing population of disenfranchised Muslim youth around the globe. He argued in favor of understanding rather than blind hostility, commended policies emphatically not of appeasement but of productive realignment, a reordering of America's foreign policy priorities that might affect the balance of anti-American sentiment in the world, while providing the United States, at the same time, with potential Middle East and Asian partners. He wasn't opposed to the invasion of Afghanistan, but qualified about its methods. He held firm on civil liberties, on human rights, on international sovereignty. He did so not merely in print and on the radio, on panels on CNN, but also, early on, in a prolonged television interview, late-night, in which he found himself, surreptitious scotch on the rocks tucked close beside him, momentarily flummoxed by his interlocutor, a heavily made up, aging blonde, who marveled in a Southern accent of closed "O"s and sharp punctuations, "What I'd like to know, Murray—and forgive me for getting personal, here—is how you manage to stay so intellectual, so detached about it all, when this tragedy, I believe, robbed you of your nephew? Am I right in saying these evil people killed your only sister's only son?" He had blinked, aware of blinking, reminded, in the instant, of Bootie's tic of blinking, and had cleared his throat, then bowed his silver head—a gesture that could be construed as respect, or resignation, or dismay at the interviewer's crass intrusion—and said, "Some things are family matters. It's an indescribable loss. And ours is just one of thousands." After that, people wrote about it. Other journalists expressed astonishment that this tragedy hadn't turned him hawk, did not have him baying for blood, and saw therein, no matter their political stripe, a mark of the man's immovable integrity; and Murray couldn't help but be aware of the irony that Bootie's death had granted him greater nobility, an importance—he knew it to be false—as a man of justice, unswayed by the arrows of misfortune. But perhaps, had he been able to see it, Bootie would at last have been proud of his uncle.

And as for the book: it waited. He'd thought, before the events, that he might abandon it; but now he saw that this had been merely a small man's fear. He had been afraid, when it appeared now, so clearly, and without vanity, that even if his words were not genius, they were still more truthful, and thoughtful, than those of most of the men and women who surrounded him. They were good enough; and he was called to write them. Who knew, perhaps he would dedicate the book to his nephew. He was taking notes, through the weeks, in the knowledge that the tragedy would completely reshape his endeavor: how to live was a different question, now. More urgent. Less answerable. He would begin again, and would write, he knew, a better book because of it.

Back at the motel, he found his family—Annabel, Marina: they were his family, everything—at breakfast with Julius. Julius, peculiar-looking always, but now positively bizarre, with the bald patch at his hairline, from which new tufting sprouted, and the raw mangle of his cheek, a pirate's scar on his boyish face. In this strangeness, he had gelled his hair like a porcupine, but Murray refrained from comment because he thought that at thirty, for all they might seem it, Marina's friends could no longer be treated as children. (He thought, and then banished the thought, of the pale flat of Danielle's belly, of the way her hipbones jutted when she was lying down.) All of them were subdued, gray like the day, with its high, moving clouds.

"Are we ready?" he asked.

Annabel took Marina's hand across the fake-wood table, and Murray noticed that his daughter had been crying. Her violet eyes were red-rimmed and puffy, her makeup a little streaked. He suddenly remembered her small, three, perhaps, upon his knee, the warm wriggle of her, her black hair clinging in silken strands at his chin, the high-pitched infectious laughter: so simple a happiness. Bootie had brought such joy to Judy, before he grew plump, and sullen, and angry with the world for all it had not given him. It was, Murray finally felt, truly an indescribable loss; and his own eyes filled, at last and for once, with tears.

But he banished those, too. It did not do to feel too much. He was called to higher things than feeling; and if he broke his vigil and allowed it, he might lose himself altogether. Judy had not asked him to speak at the service—he knew it was because she blamed him; how could he not know? Looking at Marina, he realized that he would, in her stead, have done the same—but he was prepared to, if need be. He had written a few words on an index card that he carried in his pocket: "Bert's funeral. Bootie's ambition. The article. Integrity." If he spoke, here of all places he would tell the whole truth. Not that anyone would care to hear it, except Bootie himself, who could not be present. He wanted to tell the story of their division, of how he had felt himself betrayed and, in weakness, had in turn betrayed the boy. He couldn't undo it, wouldn't, in the telling, sentimentally claim responsibility for Bootie's death (the boy had chosen his own path: Murray was clear on this), but he wanted it known. The truth was all anyone had to hold on to.

The church—St. Paul's, downtown, the church of his childhood, so gratefully fled, its waxy pews and mote-filled air, its smell of damp unchanged in all these years—was much fuller than he had expected. It stood not far off the broad main square, with its stretch of balding turf and decrepit benches, its marble memorial pillar, all grand and abandoned on a scale that

ensured the town's bleakness: impossible not to feel, downtown, all the hope that Watertown had lost. The church,
though, persisted, surprisingly full on this day. Not just the kids
from the high school, Bootie's old classmates, and some from
the current batch, all of them in their ill-fitting Sunday best,
some with parents in tow; not just the teachers, Judy's faded
cohorts, and their families; but unexpected faces from his lost
past, Judy's friend Susan, the redhead, all the way from
Kingston, Ontario, and others from Judy's girlhood circle—
Margaret, and Eleanor, once a beauty but now haggard, even
craggy, with a wattled neck, and odd little Rose, even smaller
in age, with her tiny husband, Vito, who owned the liquor store
on the eastern edge of town, inherited from his father, Vito
Senior. Vito had been in the same class as Murray, Napoleon-
sized, loud-mouthed then, frequently truant, but now he was
bald and mournful, his dark Italian eyes pouched and oddly
wise. Murray saw a young woman wheel in a chair-bound
ancient whom he did not at first recognize as Mrs. Robinson,
his mother's great friend, mother of six, two lost in Vietnam,
now surely well into her nineties, her scalp gleaming through
her sparse, flossy hair and her ears, stuffed with hearing aids,
enormous. He saw, too, the acquaintances of his youth who
must have remained Judy's acquaintances, greeted all these
years in the supermarket or at the post office: Lester Holmes
and Betty, Ed Bailey and his daughter, it looked like; and Jack
Jackson, once almost albino-blond, with whom Murray, as a
very young boy, used to catch frogs in the stream near his
house.

Judy stood at the door to the church, all dignity in her
widow's weeds, and greeted everyone by name, as if she were

consoling them. "Thank you for coming. Thank you for coming," she repeated in a whisper, to each. Tom was with the kids outside, letting them run around till the last minute, but Sarah stood alongside her mother, her arms dangling, a hankie in her fist, her black dress like a sack and her face a blur of grief. Murray did not stand with them; he wasn't invited to. He gave his sister, his niece, each a hug, saw Judy's lips tighten slightly, like a pulled string, then shepherded Annabel, Marina, the unlikely Julius (what was that boy doing here? How did he come to be of the party?) to a pew at the front on the right. Once they were settled, it was tempting to turn and watch the rest arriving; but he resisted that temptation, too. This was not a peewee hockey game or school play. It was a memorial service.

Reverend Mansfield, known to some (though not to Murray) as Billy, had baptized Frederick, had confirmed him. As he said—and there seemed to be tears in his eyes; certainly his voice broke—he never expected to bury him. Murray, with, in his knees, the St. Vitus dance occasioned by all religious observance, couldn't help but think that this was a mistake: Bootie wasn't being buried. Merely artifacts, to lie in his place. An eponymous, but not actual, Bootie burial.

Judy spoke next, about the gift of life and a gift for living, with which she claimed—not quite honestly, Murray felt—her son had been blessed. She spoke about his promise, and ambition, about how he had seemed, recently, rather to have lost his way. "But losing your way is part of growing up," she said— she who, with the exception of college at Binghamton, had lived no farther than Syracuse in all her life, and that for three years in her early twenties; who had so cleaved to the known path that she acknowledged no other—"and you don't expect to pay for it with your life." Her bitterness manifest, she tried to refine her thoughts: "God has to have had some purpose," she said, to which there was a tiny murmur of assent among the congregation. "But I haven't yet figured out what it is. I know that my Bootie was upright, loving, strong, and destined for great things." She stood back from the microphone and recomposed herself. "And I want to try to make sure that his spirit lives on in the world."

Murray could detect heads nodding around him, congregants in full agreement. But what did she mean? What could it mean to keep his spirit alive? His spirit had been unformed, an embryo, a bean. It made no sense.

Sarah spoke—reminiscence, largely—and a girl from the school, who had been at Oswego with him, named Ellen something. A schoolteacher friend—was it Joan?—and then the vicar, his hands raised, palms flat, in that type of ecclesiastical gesture that so repelled Murray. It was all he could do to stay in his seat, while silly Billy Mansfield in his long white sheet fussed over the coffin and led some prayers. Marina and Annabel were still; Julius picked his fingernails. Murray was desperate for a cigarette. He hadn't spoken; Judy didn't want him to speak. All very sad, of course, but the bottom line was that she was afraid of the truth, and of life itself, as she had ever been: even now, when the very worst had happened—what could be worse than the theft of your child?—she was still afraid, full of it, and full of regret.

This must not be. Not for him. He'd done his duty, and as soon as this was over, they would go. He'd hoped to speak the truth here, but nobody wanted it, she least of all, she wanted him to lie and say it was his fault, so she'd have someone to blame, so she could understand it. He hadn't expected his whole past still to be there in this way, intact, like a box unopened for forty-five years, some parts crumbling, of course (Mrs. Robinson's ears! Vito's bald pate!), but everything there, a time capsule, the same smells, the same wan light, the same choking sensation in the back of his throat, the same dance in his knee, the instinct for escape so strong it was a taste, a bitter taste. This was what Bootie had felt, too, Murray knew it, suddenly truly could feel it, the need to flee this hideous safety; they had been the same, somehow. And Murray had tried to help, and failed; and for a moment felt he was both of them, that they were one soul, and that what was being buried was Watertown itself, that strange, unrelieved realm of impossibility. So that they might turn again to the wider world: in the face of death, more life, always, more.

Very few went to the graveyard, perhaps because that was the etiquette, but perhaps because it was a sham. But they went. Standing there, after more prayers, after they lowered the coffin into its cold, dank hole, after flowers and dirt were symbolically thrown (but what was the symbolism, exactly?), Murray hugged his sister tightly, kissed her moist cheek, and looked into her eyes as much as to say he was sorry, not in a guilty way but in the pure way of understanding, genuinely understanding, the depth of her grief, and then he stood aside to watch Annabel, gently whispering, clasping Judy's formidable arm, the right thing always, thank God for Annabel (though there was no God). And then Marina, in what seemed to him an extraordinary outburst, dissolved in Judy's embrace, a gush of tears and "I'm so sorry"s as if she herself had plunged a dagger.

It was, to him, unseemly, but he had the distinct impression that Judy, with Marina's hair in her face, with her own tears and nose running, with her gloved hands tightly on Marina's shaking back—he had the distinct impression that Judy was pleased, somehow fortified, by this.

While this tiny drama played, Murray noted, the newly ghoulish Julius had turned his back and wandered among the tombstones, his hands clasped behind his back, bending to read the inscriptions and then strolling quietly on. Like a tourist, he was: like a tourist visiting death. Julius's scarred face was frightening, and his hair looked ridiculous, with its glistening quills; but his long navy cloth coat was rather fine, and at least from behind, gave him an official aspect. Perhaps, then, a representative: sent to the funeral *in lieu*. *In lieu* of Ludovic, obviously; but of something more, too. They were all representatives, and tourists, from another world. They could be known simply by their coats.

CHAPTER SIXTY-SIX

Burying the Dead (4)

You didn't know, until it happened to you, what it would be like. That you would find yourself in your same apartment, where you'd lived a long time with everything just so, and that it would look to you like a place you knew only in a nightmare. That the Rothkos would seem to be bleeding off the walls, that the light—so much light—would cut you, that you would find your limbs too heavy to lift, food dry as dust, too dry to eat, that you would be so cold, as cold as if you were dead. And you couldn't call him, even though he kept calling you, as if he were taunting you, from the other side of a great river—the Styx, was it? He'd left for the land of the living, left you to watch everything burning and crumbling, you could still smell it, all these weeks later, in your sheets and your sofa and no matter how many times you'd washed it, in your hair, too. And you couldn't answer the phone, not just to him but to anyone, and you couldn't read, and you tried for a bit but you couldn't go to work, either. Because what nobody knew or could ever know, of course, was that you'd found your other half, your Platonic completion, and then your self—he'd been her *self,* although she still didn't understand how quickly this had happened, and how completely—was wrenched apart, leaving a

great suppurating wound, a jagged gape of flesh, that nobody
could see and that you couldn't ever talk about. And the world,
in spite of the bigger disasters, or perhaps because of them, sto-
ically kept on, you could see the bustling citizens from the
window, and when you were out in the street (only when you
had to be), they jostled and butted against you as if not just
your wound but you were invisible, as if it would be better all
around if you just weren't there. With which, if anyone had
asked, you would heartily have agreed. It was ridiculous. And
somehow, after days, or even weeks, of this, and everything
hurting so much all the time, and not being able to bear it—
who could bear such a thing?—you found yourself at three
o'clock in the morning, though you couldn't have said what day
it was, standing on the now-graying white bathmat, in a torn
T-shirt and your oldest sweats, cold, because your feet were
bare, your sad little toes wriggling like grubs in the rug—it was
almost funny; everything was almost funny, but the trouble was
that nothing actually was funny anymore—and on the sink
before you was a tooth glass full almost to the brim of scotch
(*his* scotch, of course, but he didn't need it anymore, or
wouldn't come back to claim it, and the fact that you still didn't
like the taste of it was, by this second glass, immaterial).

She had spent already some time—it was blurry, time—
ogling her reflection, wincing at it, examining her pores, the
stray hairs of her eyebrows, the lone unplucked whisker
beneath her chin. She had bothered to pluck it, too, as if it mattered. She had held her cheek tight to see that it was, as he had
once said, like porcelain, not yet wizened or mottled. It was a
fine cheek. A fine but useless cheek. How many times had she
stood and stared, since childhood, thinking thereby to know

herself better, or hoping to find herself suddenly changed, suddenly more beautiful; and how disappointing, even now, to find the same face, meaning and thinking the same things as always, only now without anyone to say or mean them to, a sign with no referent, a mask. She had in front of her on the sink ledge also a small saucer, bereft of its cup (given her by her grandmother, a Spode cup with peonies on it, and long ago shattered), in which she was accumulating pills: sleeping pills, pain pills, her stored medications of several years in addition to more recent ones, pills from bottles and pills popped out of foil blisters, a little pyramid of pills gathered almost unthinkingly, as one part of her mind prepared to take them and another part marveled, in a detached, almost amused way (the same part, perhaps, that saw her toes like grubs), at the triteness of it all, at her absurdity, at the sucker she had allowed herself to be. That part, the detached part, watched the tears welling up in her bloodshot eyes (what ghastly light in this bathroom—she would have to change it, so she could look less ugly), and scoffed, and thought how clearly like a parody of madness this was. Did that make it a parody? Were some, upon their suicides, wholly in the moment? In which case, what did it say of her that she could not still this voice, couldn't not be watching? And if she couldn't not watch, then could she actually watch herself do this, could she actually put a pill in her mouth—try it, just one—and swallow it? It seemed she could, though not without a rictus of displeasure; it was still the taste of the scotch, like something intended for cleaning furniture. Could she do it a dozen times? Could she do it the thirty-seven times for all the pills in her saucer? No, she didn't imagine she could. She looked again at her toes, wriggling balefully, swallowed another pill—just a Tylenol 3, this one, saved from her wisdom teeth three years ago; she could tell because it was a great horse pill, scraped her throat going down—and with it, a huge, gagging gulp of the scotch, and looked at her face and thought how silly it all was, and if anyone could see her, they'd mock her mercilessly, for being fool enough to get into this situation, and having got into it, for behaving this way. If she herself knew she was a fool, then there was no excuse. She drank some more, looked again. Her left eye was too close to her nose. It always had been. She couldn't fix it. It was her mother's eye, Randy Minkoff's eye, with its incipient dark circles, ticking slightly at her through her single-malt haze.

Her mother. Randy Minkoff. Easily mockable, too, but always bright and brave, and she had surely been through this and more. You couldn't tell her about it, and you couldn't guarantee that she would have the sense not to ask—in fact, she would ask, for sure. But could be deflected. And most important, would come. Would come now and take care of you and take you away, and probably drive you crazy, she always drove you crazy, but given that you were driving yourself crazy anyway, that might be no bad thing. She might surprise you. She was surprising even when she was predictable, Randy Minkoff—and she'd been wanting to come and get you, had been wanting you to breathe better air, she'd said, apparently unaware (but who would've told her?) that you could hardly breathe at all, that you were barely alive. First she'd worried about the anthrax—it could come on the morning paper, even a few lethal spores—and then she worried about the air. She didn't think they were telling the truth about its safety—they probably weren't, but what could you do, and you weren't down in the heart of it so it wasn't so bad—and she wanted to save you. Even though she'd never really thought you could be near those towers, she'd not managed to speak to you for two days afterward and had lived the whole thing, drama queen that she was, as though you'd vanished and been resurrected, miraculously, from the ashes, said a lot about how this taught a person what love was—tell that to Frederick Tubb's mother, poor devastated creature—and she really wanted to help.

So. So Danielle took another gulp of the Lagavulin for good measure, and carried it with her out of the bathroom to feel safe, and sat on the edge of her bed looking out at the forlorn but already familiar skyline—what had been the shape of it before? The shape of anything? But this was melodrama: her tiresome face, her too-close eye, hadn't changed at all—and Danielle Minkoff called her mother.

"Mom," she said, in a small voice that also seemed to her like a mockery and the truth at the same time, just like those minutes in the bathroom. "Mom," she said, "I know it's late but I need you to come."

And Randy Minkoff didn't ask, she just said, "I knew it, baby. I knew things weren't right," and Danielle was struck by her mother's saying "baby," it seemed so camp, somehow; how could her mother be so camp? Julius would have loved it. And then she was saying, "I'll be right there, my little girl. I'll be right there." And she called back ten minutes later to say there was a plane at seven, and in preparation, Danielle put her fingers down her throat, which was disgusting, and the scotch burned on the way up, and the horse pill came almost intact, but the other pill, whatever it had been, the little one, didn't come; and then she felt very tired and had to go to sleep—it was such a bleak, blank day, dawning—and when she woke up it was her mother calling from the taxi on her new cell phone to say she'd be there in twenty minutes. Which was time enough to flush the pills and wash the glass, and even though she felt like hell—like death warmed over, they'd say back in Columbus—to put on some clothes and even wash that tedious face without looking at it.

And three days later they were on South Beach. Through a friend, Randy called in a favor and got a place in an apartment hotel on the strip, a post-9/11 cancellation, all very swanky— an orange juicer and a bowl of oranges in the kitchen when they arrived, and transparent muslin draped in tropical allusion over the high posts in the bedroom—and their flat was above a restaurant that cranked Bob Marley from eight a.m., the whole experience blinding, turquoise and surreal, and it was as if Danielle were newborn, naked, everything up till now erased. They lay, bare and oiled, on plush hotel towels on the white sand, watched the heavy-bellied midget cruise boats cross the horizon, the undaunted tourists (fewer, perhaps, than other years, but no negligible number) frolic around them, so many tattooed backs and ankles, so many flailing limbs, and Randy, beneath the wide brim of her sunhat, asked, "Will you go back?"

"Go back?"

"You don't have to," she said. "I don't see how you can go on living there."

"Because?"

"Because it's not safe, and you know it. This is just the beginning."

"Beginning?"

"Just the beginning. For New York, especially. All those policemen, the soldiers they sent in—they still couldn't stop someone really determined. A dirty bomb, that's what they call it, that's what people are talking about."

"What people?"

"Oh, snap out of it, Danny. This isn't a joke. Look, it's almost torn you apart already. You can—you could come down here, you could live with me for a while."

"Here?" Danielle gestured at the sand, the water.

"Not on the beach. Of course not. Please. You could come to me. Stay with me."

"I can't live with you, Mom." Danielle squinted at her mother. "Don't look that way. I know you'd take care of me. But I'm thirty years old."

"So?"

"So, I have a job."

"You can have it somewhere else. You can have a different job."

"I like my job." As she said this, she thought it was true.

"Okay, then why not go to Australia, make that show now? It's a good time to go to Australia. I could come with you, make sure you're okay."

"They don't want that show. Nicky killed it, months ago."

Randy made an exasperated click in her throat. "You make me want a cigarette," she said. "After all these years."

"So have one."

"Don't you get it?"

"Get what?"

"You called me. Because you needed me."

Danielle watched two girls—teenagers, probably—shimmy

by in high-heeled mules, slipping in the sand, bravely perse-vering. They wore thong bikinis, and jewels in their navels, and one of them had glued false eyelashes around her doll blue eyes. Both were made up—foundation, eyeliner, big wet lips. The girl with the eyelashes had a tattoo of a small sailing ship on her somewhat dimply butt. She was laughing and slipping as they passed in front of Danielle, a harsh, staggered laugh.

"Are you listening to me?"

"Sorry."

"I'm just telling you what I think. I'm still your mother."

"Of course I'm going back." This, too, was true. She had a film about liposuction to make. It seemed, in some lights, triv-ial, but it wasn't really. By the time it was finished, people would be tired of greater tragedies, and would be ready to watch it again. Mostly, people's tragedies were small. She'd be doing the right thing.

Randy stood up and brushed off the sand. "I'm going in," she said. "I don't know what all this is for, if you won't listen to me."

"I'm grateful, Mom. Really."

Randy bent and kissed the top of Danielle's head, the News Café baseball cap picked up upon arrival. Danielle wondered about how much her mother suspected—not who, but that there was something, someone, a private sorrow—because Randy hadn't asked anything about it. Then again, she prob-ably thought it was about Marina's marrying Ludovic Seeley. Or about Frederick Tubb. Bootie.

Danielle watched her mother pick her way down to the shore, brace herself against the water. Small and sturdy, she stood in the shallows, her elbows bent, hands out in front of her, as if warding off the gentle surf. Her straps cut into her freckled shoulders; her breasts, iron-clad, could not move, her stomach pouching rebelliously beneath their corsetry. She'd kept the hat on, her glasses. She wouldn't, Danielle knew, go much farther before coming back, her legs sparkling with drops, her manner deliberately invigorated. Randy waved; Danielle waved back, a small salute, then lay back again and closed her eyes. She wanted so much to tell someone about it all, about him, about everything leading up to that day and the day itself. She wanted to tell her mother, have her mother take care of her, put her arms around her, kiss it better, the way in childhood kissing really worked. How could Randy be her mother and not know about this, this most momentous change, the gaping crater in her self? She imagined, for a few minutes, the words she might use, the conversation they might have; but couldn't, even in her mind, make it proceed the way she wanted it to. And so knew she would never have it aloud. It wasn't a conversation for her real life. Maybe none of it—lying here, near naked, on the hot sand, this seemed just possible—had been real at all. Here she was, erased, reborn, with her brave mother, albeit blindly, watching over her, with the chance of a new beginning, a new forgetting; and that was all she had now. The sunlight was dark pink through her eyelids, and she followed the little transparent creatures—what were they?—as they swam back and forth across her field of vision. She used to do this as a child, lie in the sun at the pool, at the country club in Columbus, feeling the water evaporate from her skin and watching the play on the insides of her eyelids. It was restful. It made everything else seem far away. She thought that maybe Randy was right; she thought that maybe she shouldn't go back. But she knew that she would, because she didn't want to go anywhere else, or have anywhere else to go. She knew that her life—her future—was there.

Later, near dusk, Danielle and Randy went for a walk. They wore flippy, bright skirts, sandals, as if celebrating something. They turned inland, away from the shorefront parade, the muscles and stomachs and golden, golden skin. The restaurant beneath their apartment was blaring Frank Sinatra when they left, and a lone waiter on the terrace nodded at them as they passed, his arms crossed over his chest. He didn't look as though he expected many customers: the restaurant was loud, but unpopular.

Behind the beach, the neighborhood felt quickly uneven, like a pioneer town in which the sidewalks run out into prairie. The avenue one block in was crowded, each store lit and open to the street, fancy clothes places and cafés and kitsch. The second avenue was dotted with little hotels, newly renovated, and restaurants, quieter ones, but down to the right they could see the fluorescent light pooling outside a seedy market and fish-fry in the middle of a row of disused storefronts. The block beyond, as far as they went, was residential, spookily quiet in the failing light. None of the houses seemed to have people in them, and only an occasional dull wattage burned behind the curtains, the sort of little light you put on to keep burglars at bay.

"Shall we head back?" Randy suggested. "Maybe get a drink in one of those places?"

"Why not?"

The makings of their supper—salad and fruit salad, for Randy's perpetual diet—were laid out on their kitchen counter next to the orange juicer. They would, Randy joked, dine with Sinatra.

But first, Randy chose the place for a cocktail, the garden restaurant of one of the little hotels, overhung with palm fronds, dotted with fairy lights. A balmy breeze rustled the foliage, caused the candle on their woven metal table to flicker.

"It's nice here, darling, isn't it?" Randy said. "It just feels special."

"Sure. It's a real treat. Thank you, Mom."

"I'm glad we have this time. My baby." She sipped her bright, fruity drink. "We haven't had this in years."

"No."

"Your father would be jealous. Will be."

"Don't gloat."

"I'm not gloating. But I can't help it if I'm grateful." She paused. "You could always go back to Columbus if you preferred. I'd understand that."

"I'm going to go home, Mom. As soon as I'm ready. Let's not talk about it anymore."

They were quiet. It was, Danielle felt, an amicable silence. A small lizard scuttled across the paving stones, and a man, several tables away, whooped with laughter.

Danielle turned to look at him. He was fat, with a fair nimbus of cherubic curls. His belly looked as though it might escape the confines of his plaid shirt, a short-sleeved garment from which his stubby arms protruded like stockings full of sand. He had a long upper lip, and was very red in the face, though it was hard to tell whether this was from sun, or drink, or emotion. Maybe he was German, she thought. It would fit her idea of them.

Something behind him caught her eye. A gesture. A particular, fisty way of pushing glasses up the nose. A particular arc of the arm. He was standing in the gloom by the doorway to the lobby, in a uniform, black and faintly zen, with a mandarin collar. No curls, his head almost shaven, and thinner; but it had to be.

She looked back at her mother, who was smiling slightly to herself, sipping again from her drink. "Mom," she said. "I'll be right back, okay?"

But he was gone, when she reached the stairs. She went inside, past the large, softly burbling mouthwash-colored aquarium and its garish purple fish, to the concierge desk. Another uniformed man puttered quietly at the reception. He was older, Latin, handsome.

"Excuse me," she began. "I think I just saw a friend of mine. Maybe he works here? Frederick? Frederick Tubb?"

The man stopped puttering, eyed her wearily.

"I just saw him. In uniform. Young guy, glasses? Frederick?"

"I don't know, miss. Frederick? I don't think we have any Frederick."

"Bootie, maybe? Sometimes people call him Bootie."

The man snickered softly. "No, miss. Not at this hotel."

Danielle rested her hands flat on the countertop, at chest height. The black stone was cool. "So maybe he has a different name," she said. "But I just saw him."

The man was just shaking his head when Bootie Tubb—it had to be—crossed the lobby bearing a sweating metal pitcher full of water. He had his head down, and both hands on the pitcher, as if it took all his concentration not to spill it.

"Bootie?"

He didn't break stride, perhaps faltered a tad; it was hard to say.

"Bootie Tubb?"

If anything, he walked more quickly.

She followed him back outside, waited on the top step until he had finished pouring water for the fat man's table. She wanted to see his eyes. When he approached, she said again, barely above a whisper, "Bootie Tubb. What are you doing here?"

"It's Ulrich," he said, still holding the jug. He didn't look at her.

"Everyone thinks you're dead."

He said nothing.

"Your poor mother. It's devastating. I think Marina's at your memorial service almost right now."

He shifted, then. He almost looked at her. But didn't. "She's okay?"

"It's a relative term. What the hell are you doing?"

He turned at last. His eyes, behind their thick glasses, were immense and a little watery. "Just leave me alone, please."

"But your family—everyone—how could you?"

"How could I what?"

"Let them think you're dead?"

He looked into the pitcher, as though something vital floated there. "I'm just," he sniffed, "surviving. I'm doing what I've got to do to survive. You wouldn't get it."

"Try me."

"No. Frederick doesn't exist; and for me, for Ulrich, you don't exist. I don't have to explain anything."

"Actually, I think you do."

He was angry now, she could tell. He almost spat at her. "I needed to go. I would be dead, otherwise. I needed—I haven't done anything wrong. If I would've killed myself otherwise, then I'd be dead, really dead. Maybe that would be better. Then would you be satisfied?"

"No," she said. She wanted to say she understood that, at least, but he wouldn't look at her. She reached out and touched his arm, but he flinched, retreated, and the water sloshed in its pitcher, jangling the ice cubes.

"I'm not the same person," he said. "My name is Ulrich." He stood up straighter, spoke more firmly. "I'm sorry for the confusion. And sorry about your friend."

"Me, too," she said. She felt it as another gash, another invisible wound. How many would it take to finish things off? Which would be the mortal blow? *Sauve qui peut,* she thought. "Do you think I don't know?" she said. "What it's like? Murray—I loved him, too. Just as much as you. Maybe more."

"I know." He shrugged, faintly. "But he isn't who you thought he was, is he?"

"I don't even know that. I'm not sure I know who I think *I* am."

Bootie—Ulrich—looked at her for a minute. He held on to the water jug. His face bore no discernible expression. "So it happens to us all," he said. "Marina would tell us we just need a change of clothes." He indicated his own zen suit.

"Maybe so."

"I'm going now," he said. "I've got work to do." He paused.

"Good to have met you," he said, as if they'd never met before, and as if he really meant it. "And good luck."

"What was that?" Randy asked, back at the table, well into her pretty drink, goose bumps rising on her arms from the cooling breeze.

"Just someone I thought I knew." Danielle shook her head.

"It's funny that way, this place. I could've sworn Lauren Hutton walked by while you were gone. Right outside on the sidewalk. That's who I mean, isn't it—the one with the big gap in her teeth? Probably not much younger than me?"

"Yeah." Danielle watched Bootie out of the corner of her eye, as he moved between the tables. There were more customers now, ordering food, and it was noisier, a parroting chatter among the greenery. Bootie—Frederick—Ulrich—did not raise his eyes to her even once. Still slightly awkward, physically, and a little chubby, he was nevertheless much changed, almost handsome in his mandarin-collar jacket, with his tightly cropped hair. She thought that somebody might love him, in time. Her, too, for that matter. She thought of his mother, and of her terrible, ineffable grief; she reached across and took her own mother's hand.

It was a small hand, so like her own, but bonier, veinier, drier. The stones of her mother's big fake rings dug into Danielle's palm as she clasped Randy's hand tightly, and it hurt, but Danielle didn't mind.

CHAPTER SIXTY-SEVEN

Take Them by Surprise

After he left her, he had two sentences in his head all that night: at work, in his room, in the street. They were always in his head now, but tonight more insistently, because he wished he'd said them aloud to her. She might have understood, then. Maybe she understood anyway, though probably not. She, of all people. The one most like him. What did it matter? Would she say something? It wasn't all over: he would just move on, now. If she said something, who would believe her? What had he done that was wrong?

When he got back to his room, he started to pack his few things into the navy nylon rucksack he'd bought just in case. He thought of taking a bath, one last time in the plastic tub of which he'd grown fond; but there wasn't time. He left the Musil, volume one, behind on the nightstand, for someone else to discover, silently said good-bye to its baffled, blurred face. He ran his hands lightly, like a healer, along the top of the television, the dresser, the paisley synthetic bedspread. Lastly, the window ledge: it was after midnight, and the parking lot was quiet, the vista, with its lone fizzing streetlamp, as still as a painting. Outside, on the macadam, he breathed deeply, aware of his warped black shadow, born of the artificial light, behind him. He would remember the smell of the air, here, and the way the breeze played significantly on his skin. He would carry its message with him, along with all the others.

This time, he was ready. This person in motion was who he was becoming: it was something, too: a man, someday, with qualities. Ulrich New. Great geniuses have the shortest biographies, he told himself; and take them by surprise. Yes. He would.

picador.com

blog
videos
interviews
extracts